CHAINBREAKER

Also by Tara Sim

Timekeeper

CHAINBREAKER

BOOK TWO OF THE TIMEKEEPER TRILOGY

TARA SIM

Sky Pony Press
New York

Sky Pony Press books may be purchased in bulk at special discounts for sales promotion, corporate gifts, fund-raising, or educational purposes. Special editions can also be created to specifications. For details, contact the Special Sales Department, Sky Pony Press 307 West 36th Street, 11th Floor, New York, NY 10018 or info@skyhorsepublishing.com.

Visit our website at skyponypress.com
https://eachstaraworld.wordpress.com

10 9 8 7 6 5 4 3 2 1

Library of Congress Cataloging-in-Publication Data available on file

Print ISBN: 978-1-5107-0619-4
eBook ISBN 978-1-5107-0623-1

Cover design by Sammy Yuen

Printed in the United States of America

Interior design by Joshua Barnaby

To those who resist.

And to Mom and Dad, for all the adventures.

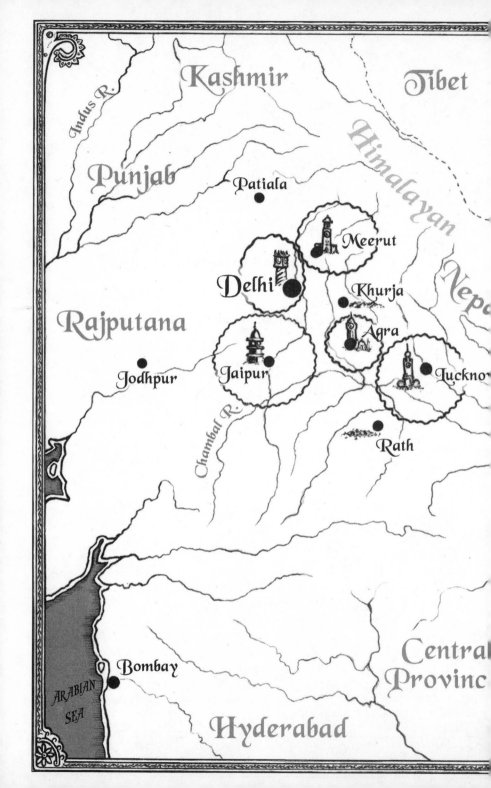

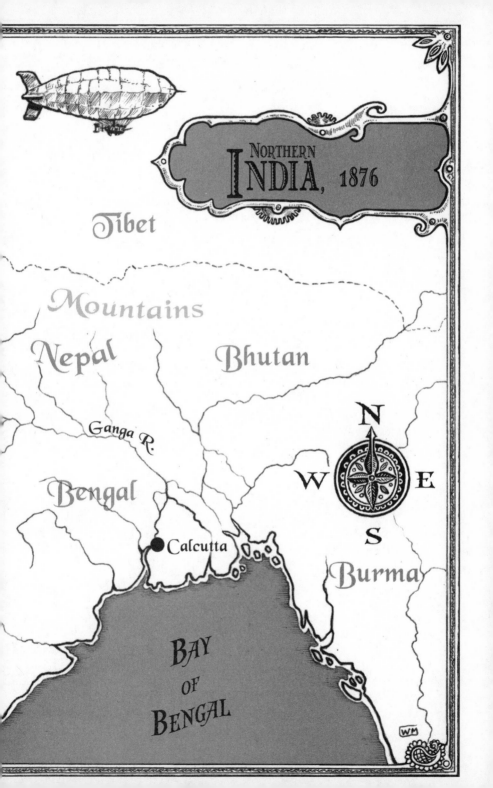

She pushed back her veil
And revealed what has been revealed to many
But that few have seen,
Beauty that can mask the unseen
As in a dream,
When what we see is
Not always as it might seem.
She is of the East, divine or beast,
Of the day and of the night,
Moving through time without measure
In darkness and in light;
She is the way to destitution
And to bounteous treasure.
Come hither and join with me
And I will join with you,
Her many looks convey;
For to love them all is to love them as one,
To love them as one is to love them all.
She is my India

— Ralph Steven Sim

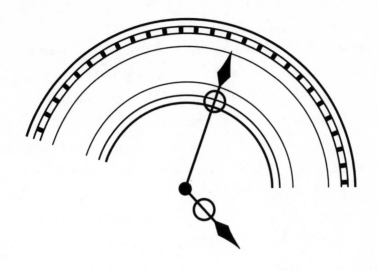

London, September 1876

The clock counted every painful second with ticks as thunderous and regular as a heartbeat. It was half past two, the hands slowly climbing their way up to three o'clock. Ten minutes hadn't yet passed, but already Daphne felt as if she had been sitting here all day.

It didn't help that the chair beneath her was uncomfortably hard. The plain, whitewashed room contained better, padded seats than the wooden one her mother had been slumped in when she arrived, but Daphne didn't want to drag over another and draw attention, lest it upset her mother.

St. Agnes's Home for Women was a quiet place, where residents woke at seven in the morning and went to bed at seven in the evening. After they performed chores and underwent

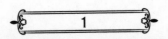

treatment in the afternoon, they gathered in the parlor for tea and socialization. Over and over, the cycle reset every night to begin again at dawn, like the old Greek tale of a mechanical eagle pecking out the fire-stealer's liver.

The radio crackled and Daphne started; she'd forgotten it was on. The box beside them was a clunky, wooden-framed device that had grown popular in the last few months, a new marvel of telegraphy. Her mother liked to turn it on after luncheon, according to the nurses. The knobs were large and stained with greasy fingerprints.

"—it is, of course, quite an honor, and I'm sure I speak for everyone when I say that England is quite proud of Her Majesty. Only fitting she should officially be named Queen-Empress of India this year. She's done a marvel there already, even after the events of the Mutiny—"

The male voice coming through the speakers was tinny and high-pitched. Daphne wished she could turn the dial down, but her mother raptly watched the radio, as though the words would form an image if she stared hard enough.

Daphne realized that her mother's fair hair was beginning to pale, her thin hands knobby and dry. A hawk-sharp face had grown even sharper in this place, her nose and chin more prominent, her eyes more sunken. Still, she had managed to hold onto a bit of beauty about her mouth and cheekbones, relics of a time when men's eyes would linger as she passed them on the street, even when she tugged her young daughter behind her.

Those other eyes had meant nothing; Daphne's father's had

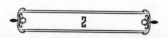

been the only ones that had mattered. Until they'd closed forever, and her mother's had grown vacant.

"—so let's all congratulate Her Majesty on a job well done!"

Daphne leaned forward. "Mother," she said softly, "don't you want to speak with me?"

Her mother sighed, gaunt shoulders rising with the breath. "What is there to talk about?"

Me. My job. How the hospital staff is treating you. If they medicated you last night to make you sleep.

"We can discuss the news." Daphne gestured to the radio. "What do you make of it?"

"Make of what?"

"Her Majesty being named Queen-Empress." The subject of India had always been a delicate one between them, yet Daphne still scrounged up a thimbleful of hope that this, at least, would spur her mother into conversation.

Her mother's shoulders lifted again, this time in a shrug.

Daphne leaned back, defeated. A year ago, she would have prattled on just to fill the empty space. Now she didn't bother. She could no more conjure hope than she could conjure birds from thin air. She'd learned too soon how painful it was to have disappointment constantly sinking its barbs into her. How they liked to twist and rip her open, filling her with holes.

A girl full of holes had no room for hope.

Daphne tried to visit St. Agnes's at least once a week, but she wondered if her mother would even notice if she stopped coming. Guilt choked her at the thought, and she looked down at the

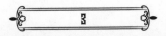

weak sunshine that touched the edges of her boots. The distant roar of a busy London rumbled through an open window under the radio's chatter. Daphne found it strangely soothing. She was unquestionably a child of London, bred from metal and steam and ash. All better caretakers than the woman before her.

Her whole life, her family had suffered echoes of the scandal caused when her English mother had married a man born to an English officer and an Indian woman. The struggle certainly had not improved after her father had passed. Listless days and frantic days and *kill me* days and *I hate you* days. Days when Daphne had been glad to be an apprentice clock mechanic, busy earning her own money, and days when she'd been reluctant to leave her mother alone to play with knives and hollow herself with hunger.

Doctors had advised committing her mother to the asylum many times, but it wasn't until she had nicked Daphne with one of her treasured knives that she'd finally condemned them both: her mother to this place, herself to loneliness.

Daphne looked around the room. A nurse shuffled to each woman, handing out little pills. A weary-looking woman with frizzing hair stuck her hand out for the proffered tablet, then knocked it back like it was a tumbler of whiskey.

"Dreams," her mother muttered. Daphne wondered if she had misheard. Then, again: "Dreams."

"Dreams? Of what?"

Her mother lifted a hand and let it fall back heavily into her lap. "I have them."

The nurse stopped beside them and offered a pill. Obediently, without even looking down, her mother accepted it and swallowed.

Daphne waited for the nurse to leave before she repeated, "Dreams of what?"

"My parents. My old stuffed rabbit. A silk fan my uncle brought back from China. James."

Daphne winced at her father's name. "Do you . . . miss these things?" Her mother nodded. "I'm sorry. I wish I could give them to you."

"So do I," she whispered.

They slipped into silence again, but it was a different kind; not the silence of deep water, but the silence of a lazy Sunday. Daphne almost felt pleased. It had been weeks since her mother had spoken so many words.

The radio warbled, and her mother instinctively leaned forward to adjust the knobs. When the channel returned clearly, the high-voiced announcer was still at it:

"—tell them to try Bill's Brake Solution, the only solution to all your automotive troubles. Now we—oh." The radio was unnaturally quiet for twenty loud ticks of the clock. "It seems we have incoming news from the jewel colony itself."

Daphne grew very still.

The announcer cleared his throat. "Early this morning, a protest broke out in the heart of the city of Rath, where their clock tower stands. In the midst of the commotion, there was a loud report, and a mechanism within the tower was blown to pieces."

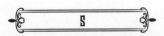

Daphne couldn't tear her eyes away from the radio. Neither could anyone else in the room.

"Although the rioters were subdued, the cause of the explosion remains unknown. After consulting the local clock mechanics, it's been confirmed that the tower . . . has fallen."

Hushed whispers and gasps from the other women. Daphne's vision tunneled. Suddenly, she was back at that moment of perfect horror in Dover, frozen as the world went white and time shuddered to a stop.

Her body rang with an echo of that terror. As nausea clenched her belly, she swore she could smell blood.

"Soldiers helped the injured out of the rubble, but a search through the debris yielded no bodies. The central frame of the clockwork has not yet been located."

Muttering issued from the radio, the announcer conferring with someone just beyond the microphone. "At this time, there is no clear connection between the riot and the tower falling. The strangest part the soldiers have reported"—the announcer's voice faded—"is that Rath has not Stopped. There is no barrier.

"So far, time continues to move forward."

Daphne released a sharp breath, then inhaled another. The announcer must be mistaken. The news was coming all the way from India. Along the way, some piece of the report must have been misinterpreted.

It wasn't possible for a city to run without its tower.

"Unfortunately, we know nothing further regarding this

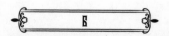

6

incident, but we hope to have more information soon." There was a lengthy pause. "And now, the season's cricket rankings."

The room gradually stirred back to life. Voices rose in speculation, some entranced by the report, some startled, some skeptical. Her mother continued to watch the radio.

Daphne thought of the clicking sounds she'd heard just before the Dover clockwork had exploded. Of the little girl who had flickered before her eyes. Daphne rubbed her neck where a small scar lingered. There was a larger, more jagged scar on her shoulder where a gear had cut her, and it ached.

Music drifted from the radio. Or at least, Daphne thought it was coming from the radio until she realized her mother was singing.

"Hickory dickory dock, the mouse ran up the clock." Her voice was raspy and thin; she had not sung in years. "The clock struck one, the mouse ran down . . ."

Daphne gaped at her mother as she sang, gripping the wooden armrests of her chair.

"The clock struck one, the clock fell down . . ."

Daphne stood, uttering a quick goodbye before she hurried from the room. Her mother didn't even look up.

The once comforting roar of London became overwhelming as soon as Daphne stepped outside, swallowed by sticky heat and smoke and the ripe odor of bodies. She was jostled this way and that, following the current like a clueless fish.

When she found her motorbike, she threw a leg over its metal bulk but didn't start it up. Instead, she sat waiting for her blood to

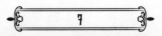

settle and her pulse to grow quiet, staring at the macadam road beneath her as her shoulder throbbed.

The clock struck one, the clock fell down . . .

It was happening again.

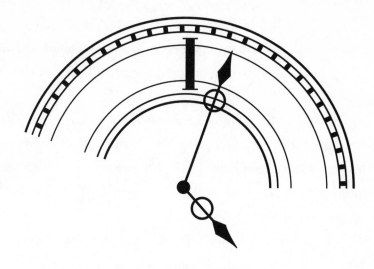

T he view of Enfield from the top of Colton Tower was always
lovely. Seeing it from this angle, however, was another matter entirely.

Danny Hart held on for dear life to the ladder propped
against the tower wall. The ladder wasn't flimsy; it was an industrial metal contraption firmly suctioned to the ground below. Or
so the maintenance crew had assured him, multiple times and
with mounting impatience.

Yet the fact that he was perched nearly fifty meters above the
ground, with nothing more than a thin rope attaching his belt to
the aforementioned ladder, could not be overlooked. It was like
being on the scaffolding, but worse. Much worse.

"Sod this," he muttered to himself. He tightened his grip on
the brush as he slowly reached for the tower wall and carefully—
very carefully—started scrubbing. A breeze ruffled Danny's dark

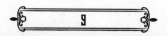

hair, cooling the sweat on his forehead. He scrubbed as hard as he was willing, removing dirt and grime and the old film of rainwater.

Members of the maintenance crew were similarly engaged with the other tower walls, having already rinsed away the patina of dust that had collected during the hot summer days. The head maintenance worker had brilliantly suggested that they do a "deep cleanse" while they were at it.

"We'll be done a lot sooner if you'd help us," one of the crew had suggested as he'd jostled Danny's shoulder. "C'mon, lad, up for a little adventure?"

"In no way, shape, or form is this an adventure," Danny mumbled as he continued scrubbing, his arm already growing tired. "Don't treat me like a child."

Under different circumstances, the maintenance crew wouldn't have been nearly as familiar with a clock mechanic, but Danny had been living in Enfield for about eight months now. Not to mention he'd saved the town from being permanently Stopped the previous year. Did they make him mayor and award him a medal of valor? No. Did they insist he never pay for his own drinks at the pub? Yes, and God willing that wouldn't end anytime soon.

The breeze returned, carrying a wave of pollen with it. Danny suppressed a sneeze, but of course that only made the urge stronger. Unable to hold it in, the sneeze exploded out of him, and one of his feet slipped on the rung. Yelping, he scrabbled to grab hold of the ladder as his stomach lurched.

A hand caught his wrist. Looking up, Danny's breath hitched at the sight of Colton grinning down at him, hanging off the roof in a manner that would have sent any normal person tumbling to the ground.

"Having fun?" Colton asked, amber eyes crinkling.

Danny exhaled a small laugh. The quickening of his pulse wasn't only due to his near fall. "Not in the least."

Colton reached for the brush. "Let me do it."

Danny held the brush out of reach. "Oh, no. This is my job, not yours."

Colton's blond hair stirred in the wind. He lifted one pale eyebrow at Danny. "It'll take you ages this way."

"Hope you don't mind if I grow a beard, then."

"Or: I find a better way and spare us both that image." Colton crawled forward, dangling off the lip of the roof with one hand, and grabbed the rag that hung from Danny's back pocket.

"You're going to make my heart stop one of these days," Danny said as Colton returned to the roof.

"I hope not." Colton leaned forward again, but not to perform circus tricks. This time, he planted a gentle kiss on Danny's mouth. Danny enjoyed it for two seconds, then broke away to quickly scan the ground.

"You can't do that out here. Someone might see."

Colton ignored him and began to scrub at his tower. "Less talking and more working, Mr. Hart."

"When did you become so bossy?" Danny attacked the wall again, a tiny smile wavering on his lips. He longed to be as

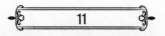

carefree as Colton, but his concern was well-founded. Colton, after all, was not a normal boy.

He was a clock spirit.

Danny glanced up at him as they worked: a boy seemingly his own age, gilt-touched and bronze-skinned. A boy wrapped in the golden threads of time, the heart of an elaborate and terrifying tapestry. Without Colton's influence over Enfield's time, without the very tower they cleaned, the town would Stop altogether, just as it had months before.

Danny had been able to fix it then, but at a cost. When his father's old friend Matthias had stolen the central cog from Colton's tower, Enfield had risked the same fate as the town of Maldon, where time had been frozen for three whole years. But Danny had managed to get the cog back, and Maldon's clock spirit had returned to her tower, freeing both towns from time's punishing grasp.

If there was anything Danny had learned from the experience, it was that there was a barrier between *want* and *need*. Matthias had put his love of Maldon's clock spirit before all else, and now he faced a life of imprisonment. His longing had turned him down a darker path, one on which Danny never wanted to find himself.

But Danny was just as guilty, mistaking that diamond-hard barrier between *want* and *need* for glass, something he could easily shatter to make the two indistinguishable. The difference between him and Matthias—the thing that made him a hypocrite—was that no one knew. No one who would report him, anyway.

Now that Danny lived in Enfield, he was free to spend time in the tower with Colton, but he still had to be cautious. As it often tended to do, his mind drifted back to the letter he'd received eight months before, and the subtle weight of the threat it carried.

We'll be watching.

"That's cheating, Hart!"

One of the maintenance crew stood at the foot of the ladder, hands on his hips.

"What is?" Danny asked.

"Getting help!"

"He needed it," Colton called down, making Danny flush with indignation.

The man laughed. "I can believe that. Carry on."

"I am a very prestigious clock mechanic in London," Danny reminded them both.

"I know, Danny." But Colton couldn't hide his puckish smile.

A slow, grueling hour of work followed, and Danny was sore and sunburned by the end of it. Colton followed his progress down, leaving his perch on the roof to hang from the ladder rungs instead. The wind rippled his loose white shirt, and Danny could see hints of his back whenever he looked up.

"Back to join the humble ground-dwellers?" the lead maintenance worker joked as Danny's foot met sweet, solid earth.

"Hopefully for good," Danny replied. "Are the others finished?"

"Half an hour ago." Danny groaned, and the man laughed again. "You're handy with the clock, and that's what matters." The man nodded to Colton, who was now standing beside Danny. "Good work, son."

Colton waited for the man to walk away before he asked Danny, "Why does he call me son when I'm not his son?"

"It's just an expression. It means he likes you. They all do."

The Enfield folk had taken a great interest in their clock spirit once they'd learned he was more than a myth. There had been such a steady stream of visitors that first month that Danny had irritably asked Mayor Aldridge to make a rule: no one could enter the tower without Danny's say-so.

Besides, what if someone accidentally walked into the tower while he and Colton were . . . not cleaning?

"Your face is getting red," Colton observed.

"Well, your hair is a mess."

"So's yours."

Just as Danny reached up to fix Colton's fringe, he noticed a young woman jogging their way. Danny quickly dropped his hand. The young woman's skirt swished in agitation as she stopped before them.

"Sorry . . . Danny . . . but . . . telephone."

"Hold on, catch your breath."

She nodded and fanned her face with one hand. Jane, the mayor's assistant, tended to handle her duties with an intensity that often made Danny worry after her health.

"Hello, Jane." Colton smiled.

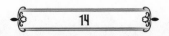

She returned it with a faint blush. "Hello, Colton. Your tower looks lovely."

"Thank you. I helped clean it."

"What about the telephone?" Danny cut in before they got lost in pleasantries.

"The hub telephone rang for you. It's not the London office, though—I checked. The caller is waiting now."

Telephones were expensive and worked poorly in smaller towns like Enfield, which was why they had just the communal one located at the mayor's office. His parents didn't make it a habit to call him, as he frequently visited them in London. Cassie would only call in an emergency, and Brandon knew to ring him at his parents' house.

"I'd best see what it is," Danny said to Colton. "Go enjoy your clean tower."

Colton wanted to say something; Danny could see it in his eyes. But he only nodded and watched as Danny followed after Jane.

In the mayor's office, Danny closed the door to the telephone room. Picking up the receiver, he leaned toward the mouthpiece.

"Hullo?"

"Danny? It's Daphne."

He swallowed a curse. He hadn't spoken to Daphne Richards in months, and for good reason.

"Oh. Hello, Miss Ri—Daphne."

"Your father gave me the number. I hope you don't mind."

"I don't mind." He shifted on the bench, nervously tapping

his fingers on the tabletop. "I don't mean to be rude, but *why* are you calling?"

They weren't exactly chums, but neither were they enemies—not anymore. After the mayhem of last year, when Matthias had tricked Daphne into stealing Colton's central cog, things had been awkward at best.

The line went silent. Danny started counting in his head, and when he reached seven, she spoke: "I need to talk to you. In person. Have you heard the news?"

"What news?"

"You haven't, then. Come to London. Meet me at the Winchester."

"Daphne, I have things to do."

"It's important." Then, softer: "Please."

Danny pinched the bridge of his nose. "Fine. Give me two hours." He hung up.

"You're leaving?" Colton demanded when Danny stopped by the tower afterward. The spirit sat on the steps beside the clock face. "I thought you weren't going to London for a few more days."

"I'll be back tomorrow morning. Why, is something the matter?"

Colton shook his head. The mirth of that morning was gone, as if his levity was a thing meant for open air and couldn't survive once his feet touched ground. "No. I just don't like seeing you go."

Danny wanted to tell Colton he'd rather stay, too. Instead, he held out his hand. Colton didn't hesitate to take it. That familiar spark flared between their skin, the acknowledgment of time. It grew stronger with every resonant tick of the clock, traveling deep into Danny's chest and stilling the doubt he felt there.

"I'll be back soon," Danny said. "Wait for me."

"I always do."

As soon as Danny stepped into the Winchester, he scanned the late afternoon crowd for Daphne. Instead, he was surprised to see another familiar face.

"Brandon?"

The apprentice lifted his mug. "Danny."

Danny slid into the sticky seat beside his former apprentice. Brandon was a tall black boy a couple years Danny's junior, but well on his way to becoming a mechanic. Danny often wondered if Brandon would soon inherit the title of "youngest clock mechanic on record."

"She summoned you, too?" Danny asked.

Brandon ran a hand over his close-cropped hair. "I reckon I know why."

"Mind informing me, then?"

But at that moment, the orchestrator of their strange conference appeared, looking just as dour as the last time Danny had seen her. Daphne was tall and sturdily built, with long blond hair and sharp blue eyes. She wore trousers with a dark jacket and a blue kerchief tied at her throat. But the most curious thing about her appearance— other than the fact she was part Indian, yet had inherited her mother's fair complexion—was the diamond-shaped tattoo beside her left eye. After all this time, Danny still had no clue what it stood for.

"Thank you for coming," she said as she sat across from them, placing her motorbike helmet on the table.

Danny would normally have replied with a curt yet effective "Why am I here?" Instead, he said, "How are you, Daphne?"

She gave him a look, as if suspicious of his newfound manners. "Fine, I suppose." They endured a long, torturous pause. Brandon quietly drank his beer. "And you?"

"All right."

"As riveting as this small talk is," Brandon drawled, "perhaps we should get on with it?"

"Yes. Of course. Brandon, you've heard the news about Rath, haven't you?" The boy nodded. "Danny, your infuriatingly blank face tells me you haven't."

"All the time you spend whinging about what I don't know is time you could be telling me what it is."

Daphne took a deep breath. "A clock tower fell. In India."

A beat passed. Two. Under the table, Danny's hand curled into a fist.

"Fell?" he repeated, relieved that his voice came out steady. "Why? How?"

"They believe it was the result of explosives. It's nothing more than a pile of rubble now. As for the why of it . . . no one knows."

Explosives.

The air was close and humid around him, and Danny made a valiant effort not to touch the scar on his chin. Tried not to think of the shuddering mess of time when the mechanism he'd been repairing had exploded in his face. Tried not to think of another young mechanic who had lost his life in a similar accident, his chest impaled by a flying gear.

But the thoughts were like skipping stones across a pond. Even the briefest touch sent ripples across his mind, until he was devoured with dread.

Daphne had survived a targeted tower, too. He noticed her hands shaking on the tabletop.

"Danny," she whispered, "do you think—?"

"No." He shook his head. "It couldn't be Matthias. How could he plan a tower bombing all the way in India from his cell?"

"Who knows what he was plotting before he was captured?"

"Matthias's place was searched. According to his notes, he had no plans to leave England. I mean, of all places—*India?*"

Brandon cleared his throat. "You know they're going to question him."

"Yes, and he'll know nothing. What then?" Danny didn't know why he was being so protective of the man. Matthias had engineered the tower bombings that had caused the Mechanics

Union so much grief the previous year. He'd nearly killed Colton and trapped Danny's father in Maldon forever. Danny owed him nothing.

But what Daphne and Brandon were suggesting sounded absurd.

"Then the investigators will turn to someone else who knows an awful lot about tower bombings," Daphne said. "You."

Danny leaned back in his seat. "They wouldn't—"

"Suspect you? No. But they'll want your opinion. That's why I asked you here, to tell you to watch for their call. Because they will call you, Danny. They might even ask you to investigate."

In the summer months, pubs could become broiling in the crush of sweating bodies. Even so, a chill swept through him.

"In India?"

"Perhaps."

As Danny mulled this over, Brandon spoke up. "Why did you ask me here, then? Am I to go as well?"

"I'm not going anywhere," Danny argued, but Daphne ignored him.

"In case I'm reassigned to Enfield in Danny's absence, you'll likely be my apprentice. I can help you prepare for your next assessment."

"Cheers."

Danny stood, chair legs shrieking across the floor. A few curious patrons looked over. "I'm not going anywhere! This is all speculation. I don't know why the tower fell, but if it did, what do they expect *me* to do if the city's Stopped?"

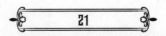

The other two stiffened, sharing a look Danny couldn't decipher.

"Danny," Daphne said, her tone a little gentler than before, "Rath isn't Stopped."

He glanced at Brandon, who studied the tabletop. "What?"

"Time is moving. The tower is gone, and time is moving."

Slowly, Danny sat back down.

"That's . . . not possible."

"That's what everyone else says. And yet, there it is all the same."

"The clock—"

"Was ruined."

Danny was having trouble breathing, strangled as he was by useless questions. How does one face the impossible? There was no rational explanation for this, nothing to prepare him for the difficult and daunting task of *belief*.

Magic, he thought, conjuring the image of Colton wreathed in golden threads, *is not rational*.

Finally, he found his voice again. "Even . . . Even if Rath isn't Stopped, the Lead wouldn't send me. My place is Enfield. He relocated me to get me out of his hair."

"No offense, mate," Brandon said, "but I don't think anyone could ever get you out of their hair."

Daphne shifted in her seat. "I wanted to warn you. Just in case."

"There's no point. I don't want to go to India."

"This isn't about what you want," Daphne said, eyes narrowed.

"I can't leave Enfield."

"Try telling that to the Lead when he calls. Because he *will*

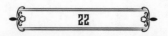

call." She stood, grabbed her helmet, and left without so much as
a goodbye for either of them.

He barely made it one foot in the door before his mother started
fretting.

"Look how thin you are! What are those Enfield people feeding you? Are you sure you're taking care of yourself?"

"*Mum.*"

"Well, we hardly see you," she complained, straightening his
collar as he stood frowning in the entryway.

"I was here last week!"

"Leave the boy alone, Leila." Christopher ducked out of the
kitchen into the hall. Like Danny, he had long limbs, green eyes,
and unruly hair. "Can't you see he's tired?"

"I am, actually," Danny said. "I had to clean the tower this
morning." The soreness in his limbs was a muzzy weight that
would only grow worse by tomorrow.

"Come into the kitchen, then. Supper's nearly on."

He asked if it would be all right to invite Cassie, which of
course it was. Cassie often complained her mother couldn't cook
worth a fig.

She showed up within five minutes, still wearing her work
coveralls and a streak of oil in her auburn hair. She was just as
obsessed with auto mechanisms as Danny was with clockwork.

"You're a savior, Dan."

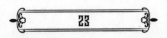

"I figured you'd want an excuse to leave the house."

Cassie groaned. "You try living with two sisters and two brothers and not lose your blooming mind. Mum and Dad have no idea that I'm planning to find a place of my own soon." Danny caught the look on his mother's face that screamed, *What, without a husband?*

Surrounded by light and the smell of sizzling sausage and the voices of those he loved, Danny couldn't help but be amazed. If someone had told him a year ago that he would be here now, eating a meal with both his parents, he would have scoffed. Such a notion had been impossible, once.

A testament to just how difficult belief truly was.

Christopher told Cassie a joke that made her laugh so hard she nearly choked. As Leila admonished her husband, Danny studied his father's face. He was still in his early forties, near the same age he'd been three years before, when he'd left to fix the tower in Maldon. Leila had aged ahead of him—it showed in the worry lines around her eyes and the threads of white in her hair.

Despite those years apart, they were just as devoted, just as capable of exchanging wordless conversations. Even when his mother needed her quiet healing days, when she was too wan and withdrawn to handle the world around her, Christopher need only put a hand on her shoulder. Danny had once thought he would never be capable of such a bond.

And then he'd met Colton.

Danny reached into his pocket and touched the small cog Colton had given him, a castoff from his clockwork that had been

replaced long before. When Danny touched it, he felt sunshine on metal, heard the hum of gears and the soft chime of Colton's laugh. He sensed a world within and apart from himself, reserved only for the two of them.

His mother knew about Colton. Though it was dangerous, she'd come to accept—with a fair amount of resignation—that her son could not choose whom he loved.

But his father still didn't know. Christopher had been the one to tell the Lead about Matthias and Evaline. If he ever caught on that Danny's relationship with Colton was anything other than professional . . .

"Danny, eat up," his mother scolded. "Your food's gone cold."

After supper, Danny and Cassie lounged in the sitting room at the back of the narrow house. Well, Cassie lounged; Danny perused the cramped bookshelves. He'd already taken a few books to Enfield, including the green leather-bound collection of fairy tales and the book of Greek myths Colton so loved.

Cassie was sprawled on the worn couch behind him, and hummed curiously when he told her about Daphne's warning.

"She seems fairly sure of herself," Cassie remarked.

"I dunno, Cass. What if they *do* want me to go?"

"Would you say yes?"

Danny paused, crouched before the bottom shelf. Despite telling Daphne he didn't want to go, he was searching for any book that mentioned India. "I'm not sure. I don't want to leave Enfield."

"You mean you don't want to leave Colton."

"It's the same thing." He worried out a slim book packed in tightly among the others and added it to his pile. "We've only just managed to find something that feels halfway ordinary. If I leave . . ."

Danny wasn't only concerned about Enfield and the clock tower. He worried that if he was gone too long, Colton would forget him, or that his feelings for Danny would somehow fade with time. Danny had no idea how the heart of a clock spirit functioned, other than mechanically.

"Take it a step at a time," Cassie said, running a hand through his hair. "The Union will likely send others first. No need to fret just yet."

"That's true."

"Now that's out of the way," Cassie said coyly, "tell me about you and Colton."

Danny glanced at the door, but his parents were still talking in the kitchen. "Would you stop asking about that?" he hissed. "I can't—do *that* with a clock spirit." He paused. "I don't think."

He started to wonder about Matthias and Evaline, then waved away the image with a sound of disgust. He did *not* want to think about that.

Cassie ignored his outburst. "Well, what's the rest of it like?"

He returned to a memory of just the other day, when he and Colton had been in the clock room. Somehow, they'd ended up on the floor—nice and clean, thanks to Danny's efforts—and Colton had wrapped a hand around his hip. That little movement in itself wasn't much, but Danny had shuddered all the same, keenly aware of that hand as they kissed. Colton's fingertips had reached up ever so slightly, between the buttons of his shirt, burning his skin.

"You're redder than a baboon's bum," Cassie said cheerfully. Danny grabbed the nearest pillow and whacked her with it. She yelped and grabbed her own, and then it was an all-out war. For a blessed moment, clock towers were the last thing on Danny's mind.

Sitting on the edge of his bed, Danny held a wad of crumpled paper in his hand. The creases were soft, the paper having been unfurled and refolded many times. He was about to flatten it out when there was a knock at the door.

"Danny? It's me."

He shoved the paper in his pocket. "Come in."

His father eased the door open, wearing his *I want to talk to you* smile. "All right, Ticker?"

He hadn't heard his father use that name in years. Hearing it now, he wanted to cringe—or cry.

"All right, Dad. How are you?"

Christopher settled beside him, dipping the mattress even more. "Well, let's see. I have a brilliant job, a beautiful wife, and an incredible son. How did I ever get so lucky?"

Shame bloomed hot and deep in Danny's chest. His father wouldn't say such a thing if he knew the truth.

"I am troubled by the news, though," his father went on.

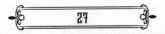

"Do you mean the tower in Rath?"

Christopher's expression darkened. "I was wondering if you'd heard. It's been flying around the office since yesterday. The Lead's thinking of sending a few mechanics out to investigate."

Danny's heart beat a little harder. "Do you know who?"

"A couple of the senior mechanics, I'd imagine."

Danny's shoulders sagged a bit in relief, but there was a strange quiver deep inside him that faintly resembled disappointment.

"It's bad enough the tower fell," Christopher said, "but the fact that time is still *moving*? What on earth could make that happen?"

Danny shrugged. "I couldn't say."

Christopher nervously scratched his knee. "You don't think . . . Matthias . . . ?"

So that was why his father was here. "No. I really don't think he'd be able to."

Christopher nodded. "I don't think so, either. But, then again, I didn't think he'd be capable of what he did." He sighed. "It's over now, at any rate. Just goes to show you can never truly know someone. Still, I miss him."

"I know. I miss him, too."

They shared a quiet moment together until Christopher stood. "Good night, Ticker. I'll see you in the morning."

"'Night, Dad."

When the door closed, he drew the wad of paper from his pocket again. Slowly, he flattened it against his thigh to reveal the familiar message scrawled in heavy black ink:

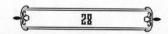

Do not think this is finished.
You know something.
We'll be watching.

He stared at the words until they blended together, serpentine tracks leading to some unfathomable distance.

You know something.

No, this was not Matthias's work. This was something well beyond the machinations of a middle-aged, washed-up clock mechanic. Something Danny wanted no part of.

That night, he dreamt of crumbling towers and cogs slicing through the air. They ripped open his body, and Colton watched as he bled.

T hose books are new."

Danny looked up from the pages he was turning. "Hmm?"

They were sitting against a wall as the sun slanted through the opal glass of the clock face, dust motes dancing in the golden beam. No matter how hard Danny worked to get this place completely dust-free, the grime always came back with a vengeance.

Colton pointed at the books in Danny's bag, the ones he had brought from home. He'd spent all morning reading them in his cottage behind the clock tower, the one Mayor Aldridge had loaned him when he'd been relocated to Enfield. It was small but neat, with white walls, a shingled roof, and planters under the windows. And, of course, it was close to Colton.

It was odd living where Colton could peek in on him at any given moment, though. The clock spirit had preternatural senses, allowing him to see and hear everything that went on in his town.

"You don't watch me, do you?" Danny had once asked him.

"Of course I do."

Danny had choked back a flustered cough. "Even when I'm ... ?"

"Oh, I don't watch you *all* the time. Everyone deserves their privacy."

Privacy was a rather loose term when Colton was involved. Danny was sure he'd seen his fair share of intriguing things throughout the years, given his tendency to let curiosity get the better of him.

"Danny."

He blinked. Colton had pulled one of the books from his bag to read its title, but he put it back and came to sit beside Danny again, not bothering to conceal the worry in his eyes.

"Is something wrong?" the spirit asked. "You're distracted today."

Danny had been wondering how to broach the subject since he left London, so he took a deep breath and explained about the tower in Rath, and how the city in India was not Stopped. Colton listened quietly until Danny was finished.

"The tower isn't working, and time's still moving?"

"Yes."

Colton wore a puzzled frown. "I don't know much about how the towers work, but this sounds strange, even to me."

"Me, too." Danny hesitated. "They may question me. Or send me to India to inspect the site. At least, that's what Daphne thinks," he quickly added when Colton's eyes widened. "Because of, you know, all the things I went through."

"*We* went through."

Danny couldn't help a smile. "Yes, sorry. All the things we went through."

Colton put a hand on Danny's knee, slowly tracing the curve of bone with his fingers. Suddenly, the only thing that mattered were those delicate fingertips mapping the impression of his kneecap. "How long would you be gone?"

"That's just it—I don't even know if I'm going. Daphne could be completely wrong."

Again, that little quiver of disappointment. He tried to keep it out of his expression.

Colton leaned against him, rubbing his leg absently. Danny pressed his lips against the top of Colton's head, inhaling the familiar scents of fresh oil and coppery metal and the sweet, balmy air of time passing. For all his strange qualities, Colton's blond hair was soft as fox fur.

"You were supposed to read me a story," Colton said quietly.

"Right. Sorry." Danny searched through the book of Greek myths open on his lap. He'd taught Colton how to read, but the spirit still liked it when Danny read aloud to him.

"Have I read about the Titans?" Colton shook his head against Danny's shoulder. "Then let's start with Prometheus."

He told Colton about the Titan Prometheus who had created mankind out of clay, giving life to his creations so they could populate the earth. But when it seemed that the humans might die out, Prometheus was driven to steal the gift of heavenly fire.

"He granted this stolen fire to humanity, allowing his creations to live on, progress, and form what would eventually become modern civilization. But Zeus wasn't too pleased about that, and bound Prometheus to a rock as punishment. Every day, a mechanical eagle would come and devour his liver right out of his body. In the night Prometheus's liver grew back, and when dawn broke, that blasted eagle came to start the process all over again."

"Does it say *blasted* in the book?"

"My own little touch." Danny touched the drawing on the page, which depicted bearded Prometheus suffering on his rock. His wrists were fettered, drawn to the rock with heavy chains. The eagle's wings were a patchwork of gears. "I loved this story when I was younger, but I'm not so sure I like it anymore."

"It's sad," Colton murmured.

"I think it's a bit stupid, defying someone like Zeus."

Colton sat upright and tilted his head to one side. "He willingly sacrificed himself to help others. One soul over thousands. That doesn't sound stupid to me."

There were moments, like this one, when Danny saw the fathomless age in Colton's eyes. It unnerved him, and it bewitched him. He wanted to learn every secret of the universe through his gaze, to lose himself in some distant, golden galaxy, restless and ancient.

"I suppose that's true," Danny admitted, a tad breathless.

Colton looked down at the book. "I feel as though I've heard this story before. It seems familiar."

"I've likely already read it, then. Sorry. Thought I'd picked something different this time."

"That's all right." The spirit shifted so that he was leaning forward on his hands, putting his face an inch away from Danny's. He stayed there a moment, watching Danny's expression as if searching for an answer to a question he wouldn't voice. Danny flushed under the scrutiny until he met those gleaming amber eyes across the tiny gulf between their bodies. The sunlight against Colton's skin was another sort of kiss, hugging his body and showing off the miracle of him.

It felt like it had always been this way, just the two of them and this light.

Colton closed the gap, kissing him firmly on the mouth. Danny's stomach leapt as time shivered around them. He could feel every tick of the clock as if it had replaced the heart in his chest, the steady rhythm that kept them alive. If there was a way to kiss Colton forever, he wished he knew how to find it.

Eventually Colton pulled away, but he kept a hand on Danny's cheek. His thumb gently traced the scar on his chin. "Do you think you'll have to go?"

"I don't know," Danny whispered. "But if I do, I want to be prepared."

Colton nodded to the other books. "What do they say, then? Tell me about India."

Danny dragged out a book and opened it to a random page. He'd read this one the previous night and been surprised by how little he actually knew. He'd had no idea how complex everything was in India, least of all the religions: Hinduism, Sikhism, Islam,

Jainism, and plenty more aside from those. And then there were all the different castes. It made his head spin.

"I read about the Mughals who came to India in the sixteenth century," Danny said, automatically searching the book for pictures, since Colton liked those best. He found one of a mustachioed emperor sitting upon a gilded dais amid columns and brocaded pillows. "The Mughals were invaders, and there was quite a bit of fighting done in their name. But they unified different societies and taught them how to rule themselves. They created new trade routes and standardized currency."

Danny thumbed through the book until the dates grew closer to present day. "I suppose Britain wanted to do the same. They rather made a mess of it, though. There was a big fuss about the East India Company."

Danny turned to a drawing of uniformed British soldiers on the plains of India, armed with bayonets. "There was a row in 1857, just before I was born. People here call it the Mutiny. Indian soldiers attacked the Company to try to claim their freedom, but they lost. After that, rule was passed from the Company to the Queen. I heard they're going to announce her as Empress of India at New Year's."

He flipped through pages of bloodshed with a grimace. What England had done to India seemed truly unfair, like someone breaking into your house to suddenly declare it belonged to them. But then his eyes caught a particular word, one he knew very well.

Colton was about to turn the page when Danny grabbed his hand. "Wait! They mention Enfield."

"They do? Where?"

Danny stabbed a finger at the middle of the page. They leaned in at the same time and knocked heads. Danny barely noticed.

"'The Enfield rifles were produced at the Royal Small Arms Factory in Enfield, England,'" Danny read quickly, "'and shipped to the soldiers in India. They were the newest model, and easily the best at the time, but had one major design flaw: their cartridges.

"'The sepoys'—those are Indian soldiers," he explained to Colton, "'were asked to bite off the paper cartridges of the Enfield rifles, but the cartridges were greased with animal fat. The Hindus and Muslims refused to handle the rifles, as the use of beef and pork fat was against each group's respective religious observances. This disagreement has been credited as the final straw that triggered the onset of the rebellion.'"

Stunned, Danny leaned back against the wall. "I didn't know rifles were manufactured here," he said. "You knew, didn't you?"

"Was I supposed to tell you?"

Danny shook his head. "No. I just . . . didn't know. No one talks about it."

It was a strange coincidence, the only tenuous connection between his world and India. It seemed almost sinister in design.

Colton's hand returned to his knee, a solid weight. "You could ask to take a look. Maybe you'll learn something."

Though the prospect of being near so many guns was unappealing, Colton's curiosity infected him. "I think I will."

The factory was a long, red building in the marshy reaches of Enfield Lock, a small island of sorts that sat on the River Lee. Water wheels disturbed the river's surface as they slowly turned, powering the machinery inside. Danny eyed the building's reflection in the water, lips pressed together.

He wasn't quite sure why he had agreed to do this. It wasn't as if he would learn anything more than how a gun was assembled. Still, the tenuous connection between Enfield and India had shaken him, and he couldn't help but want to see it with his own eyes.

Colton, at his side, looked around with genuine interest. Danny had tried to keep him in his tower, but more and more Colton wanted to venture out and explore. When he did, he usually grew weak, the faint golden glow around him fading. Sometimes, Danny even had to carry him back to the tower.

"We shouldn't stay long," Danny warned Jane as she led them to the factory gates. She had volunteered to show them around, much to Danny's surprise; he had expected more hemming and hawing.

She smiled over her shoulder at them. "The quick tour, then. Let's start here." She stopped, gesturing to the large building where ribbons of smoke rose from chimneys. "As you can see, the factory is perfectly situated, drawing power from the river while

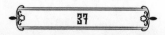

allowing barges traveling downriver to transport the finished goods to London."

"Wonderful," Danny muttered under his breath, thinking of all those deadly guns floating innocuously down the Lee.

They passed through the gate. Danny could smell the smoke now, the acrid flavor of saltpeter crouched on the back of his tongue.

Colton was too busy taking in their guide to notice. "You look nice today, Jane," Colton said with a winning smile, eyeing her small lilac hat, which matched the shade of her bodice exactly.

She half-turned with a pleased flush. "Thank you, Colton."

Danny glanced sidelong at Colton, who raised his eyebrows as if to ask *what?* Danny knew he had no business growling at him about it; not just because Colton couldn't distinguish flirtation from being nice, but because of that unfortunate run-in with an Enfield boy named Harland several months before.

The inside of the factory was even hotter than the muggy summer air outside. Light from the overhead windows illuminated machinery that pumped and whirred and hissed. Conveyor belts lined with parts rolled through the building, and a large gearwork tableau churned on the opposite wall, generating power.

In spite of himself, Danny was awed. Factories like this were common enough in London, but he had never been inside one, and was immensely thankful for that. Many of his nursery school classmates had found backbreaking—and sometimes deadly—work in the factories that kept England at the forefront of industrial innovation.

Jane led them through a metal jungle, raising her voice to be heard over the clanging and whirring of the machines. "These mass production lines run on steam. The gearwork over there filters the electricity from the water and steam, providing different areas of the factory with different types of power."

Workers stood at attention along the assembly lines, quickly putting their parts together before the product moved along to its next destination. Danny watched and listened, but his stomach twisted. It would have been one thing if the factory built autos, or automatons, or any other type of machinery. But they built weapons, things specifically designed to harm others. *Kill* others.

"Jane," he said as they continued forward, "is it true that these rifles are why the Indians rebelled?" Jane would have been a child when it happened.

She faltered, but quickly regained her composure. "Unfortunately, yes. The Company didn't respect the natives, and the Mutiny was the result. Understandably, we no longer use animal fat to grease the cartridges."

Danny kept an eye on Colton as they continued down an aisle. The spirit was quiet, soaking in another opportunity learn about the human world. Even so, his shoulders had begun to droop.

"Here," Danny murmured, taking the small cog out of his pocket and pressing it against Colton's palm. "This should help."

Colton's lips twitched. "Thank you, Danny."

"You can go back if—"

"I'm all right." There was a certain stubbornness in his expression that Danny knew better than to question.

"Over here," Jane said, gesturing to another station. "This is where the rifles are given a final examination before they're polished and prepared for shipment."

Danny looked at the workers. One of them, a young man with dark hair, turned to pick up the next rifle. When he saw Danny, they both started.

"Danny!" Harland exclaimed, not sure whether to be happy or embarrassed. "What are you doing here?"

Danny glanced at Jane. "Taking a tour. I was curious about the factory."

"Oh. I see."

Any interaction with Harland tended to be uncomfortable since that strange kiss they'd shared. Danny looked at Colton to gauge his reaction and was not disappointed; his eyes were sharp as gilded knives.

If Jane sensed any tension in the air, she went on regardless. "Maybe you can explain what your role is at this end of the factory, Mr. Thomas?"

Harland did just that, his explanation peppered with *uhs* and *ers* as he pointed out the rifle's features, including the engraving on the barrel—B3005—a serial number that indicated something about the design. Danny wasn't paying much attention, too distracted by Colton's less-than-thrilled expression. Colton didn't hate any residents of Enfield so far as Danny knew, but he felt hate's milder cousin, dislike, radiating from the spirit beside him.

When they finally said goodbye and headed for the exit, Colton slumped against Danny.

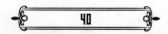

"That's it—we're going back to your tower," Danny decided. "Jane, thank you for showing us the factory. I think I understand it a little better now." By which he meant not at all.

"You're very welcome."

Danny and Colton walked toward the village green in silence. The closer they got to the tower, the more Danny sensed the clock running strangely. A glance up confirmed his suspicions: the hands slowed for five seconds, sped up, then slowed again. He could feel the shift in the way the time fibers around him quivered. Fear tapped a finger against his chest and he urged Colton along at an even faster clip.

Once inside, Colton leaned against the wall to steady himself and released a small sound of relief. The clock began to run smoothly again, and the distressed time fibers settled around them, smooth and interlocking.

Colton turned the small cog over in his fingers, then returned it to Danny. "I'm sorry," he said before Danny could break the silence. "I know I shouldn't behave like that around him. I can't help it."

Danny took Colton's hand. He'd desperately wanted to hold it in the factory, but there had been too many people.

"It's just . . ." Colton's eyes were narrowed in pain. "I can't help but feel you should be with him, not me."

This again. "And I've already told you: I don't want him. I want you."

"But look at what happens." Colton gestured up toward the clock. "I'm—"

"A clock spirit, yes. After all I've gone through to be here with you now, you really think that's going to stop me?"

Colton ran a hand up and down Danny's chest, trailing over the V of his waistcoat. "I feel like, sometimes, what we want and what's right are two separate things. Do you ever feel that way?"

Danny took Colton's face in his hands, thumbs brushing against his jaw. "No. Things are fine the way they are. We're doing what's right for us, and that's enough."

Or so he kept telling himself. Maybe this was how Prometheus would have felt, had he not been punished for his crime—this lingering guilt, this slow-burning sense that something would become undone.

They stayed quiet a moment, listening to the ticks and tocks of the clock above their heads. Danny suspected that it really did match the tempo of his heartbeat, pumping beneath Colton's hand. A heart of metal and a heart of flesh. Water and lightning, separated by different currents, like the power generated in the factory. Together, they formed some idea of unity.

Danny wondered, sometimes, if that was enough.

The call came the next day. Danny had just eaten breakfast when he was summoned to the mayor's office. He hoped to hear his mother or father on the other end of the line, but the knot twisting in his stomach tightened when he was greeted by the Lead Mechanic's voice.

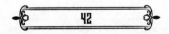

"Daniel, I need you to come to London today."

Danny swallowed hard. "Yes, sir. I can be there in a couple of hours."

Daphne had been right.

He headed straight for Colton Tower. Colton didn't look surprised; he must have been watching Danny in the telephone booth. Danny wasn't sure he would ever get used to that ability.

"The Lead probably wants to ask me about my experience with exploding towers," Danny said. "I'm sure it won't take too long."

"Will you spend the night?"

"I might. But I'll be back tomorrow."

Since Colton still seemed on edge, Danny gave him a lingering kiss. The spirit wrapped his arms around him, one hand protectively caressing the back of Danny's neck. He shivered and couldn't help gasping slightly against Colton's mouth. Colton's lips curved up in a smile, his own private way of making sure Danny would return.

The drive to London was filled with conflicting emotions: anxiety over what the Lead wanted from him, anticipation of being involved in something momentous, and residual excitement from Colton's kiss. By the time he pulled up to the Mechanics Affairs building opposite Parliament, the knot in his stomach had retied itself tighter than before.

Danny glanced at Big Ben, the gleaming, golden clock tower that presided over London. Time in the city was thriving, the fibers strong and powerful. He tried to imagine the tower exploding and London's time unaffected by the loss. It was too eerie to contemplate, so he hurried inside and up the stairs.

The secretary showed him in. The Lead Mechanic's office was spacious, done up in sophisticated, dark colors, though a large window behind the desk let in enough sunshine to give it warmth. At first all he saw was the Lead himself, a stocky man with a receding hairline and a face that could change from stern to amiable in a blink. At the moment, he simply looked tired.

Danny paused when he saw the other figure in the office, standing behind one of the chairs. Daphne turned her head and gave him an "I told you so" look.

"Both of you, please sit." The Lead leaned back as they followed the order. "You may be wondering why I called you here this morning. Given the last time I summoned you here, I'm sure you can hazard a guess."

Danny and Daphne shared a look. They'd sat before this desk after the Dover tower attack, when Daphne had been injured. The room had been charged with anger and accusation then. Now, Danny actually felt some sort of alliance with her.

"Another clock tower fell," Daphne deduced.

The Lead nodded once. "In Khurja. It's a small Indian town north of Agra."

"And it's not Stopped?" Danny guessed. Another nod.

"The tower is destroyed, and time is—" The Lead broke off coughing, as if the word refused to leave his throat. "Time is . . . stable."

The words hung heavily in the air. Nothing like this had happened in the entire history of the clock towers. Since the god of time, Aetas, had died hundreds of years ago, time could not progress without them. Or so the story went.

"But, sir," Danny said, "what about Maldon? And Enfield? And the other Stopped towns around the world? Those towers malfunctioned, and time was effected. Why wouldn't India's clock towers operate the same way?"

"Explosives were found at the sites of the towers," the Lead said, "but I doubt that's the whole of it. The clocks aren't simply falling and restoring time. Something else, or someone else, is making it happen." The man hesitated, glancing at Danny. "Matthias has been questioned. He didn't know anything. We, of course, can't entirely rule out his involvement, but I don't believe this is his work. His style and that of the current bombers seem quite different."

"But why India?" Daphne asked, a small furrow forming between her eyebrows.

"That, we do not know. I've asked you both here not to engage in conjecture, but to get answers. You are two well-qualified mechanics who have directly witnessed attacks on towers. Never mind your . . . past conduct," he ended in a near mumble.

"What about Tom and George?" Danny asked. The two senior mechanics had survived the destruction of the new

Maldon clock tower last year. The third mechanic on that assignment, Lucas Wakefield, had not been so lucky.

"I've already asked them, and they chose not to participate. They're about to retire, and I don't blame them. The new Maldon tower put too much strain on them."

Danny stared at the Lead's desk. His breaths came faster, waiting for what would surely come next.

"So," the Lead continued, picking up two files, "I am extending the offer to the pair of you."

Daphne accepted one of the folders. Taking the other one, Danny opened it to a picture of military barracks surrounded by palm trees and scrub, a large white building in the distance.

"Agra?" Daphne asked, looking up.

"Yes. There's a cantonment where you can stay while you investigate Khurja. I already have a couple mechanics in Rath, and there are others in the south. Still, I would like you to go."

Daphne paled. She had predicted the Lead sending Danny to India, all right; but he suspected she hadn't considered the Lead would ask her to go with him. After her involvement in Matthias's plans and taking Colton's central cog, she'd had to earn back the Lead's trust. It seemed she was finally back in his good graces.

Danny wondered, too, if her reaction had anything to do with her father.

"You have every right to turn the assignment down, of course," the Lead said gently. "There is some risk involved, what with the recent reports of riots. I wouldn't expect the investigation to be easy—"

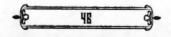

"Yes," Daphne blurted, her pallor deepening to a flush. "Yes, I want to go."

The Lead smiled wearily. "I'm glad to hear it. You'll find all the details for the trip in that file." He turned to Danny, who sat as if turned to one of Westminster Abbey's gargoyles. "And you, Daniel?"

Danny felt their eager eyes on him. His heart beat hard, and his chest was sore. This was a once-in-a-lifetime assignment, and he knew it.

He thought about the atlas he sometimes showed Colton, the flat depiction of the places he wanted to go, but probably never would. He thought of Colton trapped in his tower, unable to travel the world he longed to see. He thought of that morning's kiss, his north star guiding him home.

And then he thought of the Enfield clock malfunctioning. Because of him. Because of what he made Colton feel.

I'm sorry, Colton.

"Yes," he whispered, the decision settling heavily across his shoulders. "I'll go."

The others released their breaths.

"Very well," the Lead said. "You'll depart on Monday."

His parents sat staring at the papers on the kitchen table like they would rear up and attack at any moment. Danny had slid the file containing information about his trip across the wooden surface to them: Agra, lifestyle at the cantonment where he'd be staying, some words in an Indian language he'd butchered the pronunciations of. When he had finished, they'd entered this uneasy silence.

Danny fiddled with the small cog in his pocket. His father's eyebrows were drawn together, but he wasn't angry; Danny could tell because the small vein on his forehead was still. His mother's lips, however, were pursed more tightly than usual.

"I already told the Lead I would go," Danny said. "I'm not changing my mind."

"But *India*?" Leila said, finally roused from her stupor. "Good

Lord, who knows what you'll find there! Highway robbers and snakes and cholera—"

"Pretty sure we have all those here," Danny mumbled.

"He's eighteen," Christopher reminded her. "He can decide for himself."

"But it's absurd! The Lead Mechanic shouldn't be putting his problems on the shoulders of a boy."

"He's not a boy," Christopher argued. "He's already a young man, and making a fine name for himself as a clock mechanic. At this rate, he has a good chance of being named Lead one day."

Danny had forgotten how much he missed his father's praise. Christopher saw his grateful expression and winked.

"It'll only be a few weeks," Danny assured his mother. "And there are a lot of soldiers in Agra. I'll be safe."

Leila opened her mouth at the same time the telephone rang in the hall. Seeing that his wife would not budge, Christopher rose to answer it. "Don't harry our son until I get back."

But as soon as they heard his "Hello?" from the other room, that's exactly what she did. "Danny, this is ridiculous. I know this opportunity seems new and romantic, but you've just been through something harrowing."

"That was months ago, Mum."

"You still have nightmares."

He winced. He'd forgotten that when he slept in his room upstairs, it was easy for his parents to hear him wake up screaming. Leila hadn't mentioned it in the past. That she acknowledged it now was proof she was still trying to mend the cracks that had formed between them.

Last year, he would have traded anything for her concern. Now he wanted to be as far from it as possible.

"I can take care of myself," he said to the tabletop.

"But it's so very far away, and what if something happens? What if—" Her voice caught, and Danny had to look away. She had already faced unbearable loss when Christopher had been trapped in Maldon. He couldn't blame her for fearing that she might go through it all again.

"I couldn't bear it," Leila whispered. "I couldn't, Danny."

"Mum," he said, his voice softer, "I promise I'll be all right." He reached for her hand, and she seized it both of her own, clinging to it like she would drown if she didn't keep hold. "There'll be all sorts of people looking after us, and it won't take long."

Leila was quiet a moment. The low murmur of Christopher on the telephone drifted into the kitchen.

"What'll happen to him if you're gone?" she finally asked.

"Dad's the one who says I should go."

"I mean Colton."

Danny frowned. "He'll stay in his tower, of course. He'll be fine."

"But what will happen to him if something happens to *you*?"

Danny hadn't given the scenario much thought, but he supposed his mother had a right to ask. When Matthias had been exiled from Maldon, the tower's spirit had dismantled her clock,

Stopping the town. Danny had once made Colton promise never to do the same.

"I really don't think Colton would do what Evaline did."

"How can you be so sure?"

"I just am." He stood, frustrated. "I wish you'd stop being so suspicious of every little thing. If Colton promised he wouldn't hurt himself or Enfield, then he won't."

Leila rose, color staining her cheeks. "I'm trying to be practical. I'm sure Matthias never expected Evaline to act as she did."

"Evaline isn't Colton! How can you stand there and accuse him of things he hasn't even done? Why are you being this way?"

"Because you're in love with a bloody clock spirit!"

The air suddenly shifted, and mother and son stood staring at each other, accusation turning to apprehension. They turned slowly to the kitchen door, where Christopher stood. He looked between them, confused.

"What?" When there was no answer, he stepped into the kitchen. "What did you say?"

"Christopher . . ." Leila glanced at Danny, eyes wide. "What you heard . . ."

"You said he's in love with a clock spirit. Danny?" Christopher looked to him, but Danny couldn't meet his eyes. "Is this true?"

Danny remained silent. He didn't know what he could possibly say to erase his mother's blurted words, painted on the kitchen walls for anyone to read. He began to shake, one hand clutching his stomach. A foundation had formed at the base of his lungs over the last few months, a steadying mixture of routine and contentment as he built his life in Enfield, as he learned at last to breathe. Now that foundation began to crumble, and he struggled for air.

"It's that boy spirit," Christopher murmured to himself. "The one in Enfield."

"Christopher, wait," Leila said. "You have to know the whole story before—"

"What were you thinking?" he demanded, the vein on his forehead jumping. "You know full well that kind of relationship is forbidden. And after what happened with Matthias!"

"Dad, please don't report me." Danny cringed at the sound of his own voice, helpless and young.

Christopher clenched and unclenched his hands as he considered the situation. "If you weren't my son, I most certainly would. But I want you to have a promising career. To not end up like *he* did. You'll leave Enfield when you return from India."

Leila clasped her hands together, tight enough for her knuckles to turn white. "Christopher, please just listen. Danny would never—"

"I'm not worried about him. But you can't predict what clock spirits will do. They're not human, and they don't think like we do."

Danny still couldn't get a full breath. Christopher noticed and tried to calm himself. "Danny, please tell me you understand. It's not right."

"You just said he's a young man who could make his own

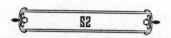

choices," Leila reminded him, the hypocrisy of her words lost on her.

"This is different. Danny, tell me you understand. You know why you must leave Enfield."

Danny couldn't get a breath.

"Danny. Ticker, please."

Couldn't—

"Daniel!"

Danny grabbed the file with all its loose papers and ran for the door. His parents shouted after him, but they might as well have been calling from the top of some distant mountain. He hurried to his auto, slammed the door, and started the engine with shaking hands.

"Shit, shit, shit," he kept whispering as the auto jerked into motion and he sped down the street. *"Shit."*

He hadn't wanted the truth to come out this way. He'd wanted his father to meet Colton, to like him, see that his friendship with Danny was beneficial. Then Danny would have explained everything. But now his father would never see them as anything but another possible Maldon.

Wouldn't see Danny as anything but another possible Matthias.

Danny pulled the auto over and rubbed a sleeve over his eyes, shoulders shaking under the weight of his suppressed sobs. He took a minute to gather himself, choking over his own breaths, tangled in the thorny vines of panic and guilt.

When he was calmer, he slipped out of the driver's seat

and walked toward a house with a green door, picked up a few pebbles, and tossed them at the window on the second story. He'd done this so many times before that he hardly ever missed. After a couple of taps, Cassie's face peered out. She waved and disappeared.

He leaned against his new auto as Cassie trotted out to meet him. Her smile faded when she got a good look at his face.

"What's happened?"

Danny told her everything. About Colton, India, his father. By the time he finished, his voice was low and flat, as though all his emotions had leaked out of him like air from a tire.

Cassie had raised a hand to her throat, but now she reached out to touch his arm. "Dan, I'm so sorry."

"I couldn't even stay to pack my things. Most of my stuff's in Enfield anyway, but"— he cleared his throat—"I couldn't stay."

Cassie's blue eyes were fixed on one of his waistcoat buttons. "You're really going to India, then?"

"I'll be safe. People travel from England to India and back all the time."

"I know." She bit her lower lip, and Danny knew he owed her this moment. She'd never used to worry so much, but ever since her older brother, William, got into a fatal auto accident, her world had been tinted a little darker and a little more dangerous.

"There will be soldiers," Danny added.

"Oh. Well, that's good, at least." Still, her next breath was strained. "You'll have to tell me all about it when you come home," she said, thumping a fist against his chest.

He thought again of that mysterious letter, lying crumpled in the drawer in his bedroom. *We'll be watching.*

"Cassie, just in case something happens—"

"*No,*" she snapped. "Don't you dare talk to me like that! You *will* come back."

"Cassie, listen." He took her wrist. "Just in case, you have to make sure Colton will be all right. Check on him for me. Make sure he's safe. And if anything happens to me, or if I come back and they exile me from Enfield . . . Please promise you'll talk to him." Colton liked Cassie. He would listen to her.

She grimaced, and he shook her arm.

"*Cassie.*"

"Yes, all right. I'll do what I can."

"Thank you."

They stood together another minute, Danny listening to the autos passing up and down the street, the nearby whistle of a bird on a telephone wire. London seemed too familiar to leave. When he returned from India, he wondered if it would be the same: the autos coming and going, the birds singing. He wondered if his father would change his mind.

"I should be go—"

Cassie threw her arms around his neck, choking off his words. "Can't I at least see you off, when you go?"

"Yes. I'll be back in London on Monday."

She kissed his cheek. "Drive safely."

As he started up the auto, she leaned in through the open window. "I'll talk to your dad when you're gone. If it'll help."

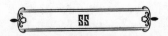

"I don't think it will."

"I can always use this," she said, pulling a wrench from her pocket.

To his amazement, a weak laugh escaped him. "Cass . . ." There was no way to tell her how much she meant to him. That she was the only person who could coax that laugh out of him when his world was on the brink of collapse. "Thank you."

She backed away and he drove down the street, toward Enfield.

"You have to close your eyes," Danny insisted.

Colton rolled them instead. "I already know what it is."

"If you keep mouthing off, I won't give it to you."

Colton shut his eyes at once, and Danny grinned. It felt odd to smile after his father's anger the previous day. But after telling Colton about the assignment and the argument, some of the weight had lifted, mostly because Colton's reaction to the whole situation had been so simple.

"I may be similar to Evaline, but I'm not her. I won't hurt myself while you're gone."

"I know you won't, but my father—"

"Should come here."

"What?"

"Here, to my tower. I'd like to speak with him."

The idea seemed absurd at first, but his father *would* be more

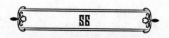

likely to understand if he spoke to Colton. Strangely, the conversation had made him feel better. Perhaps he'd been overreacting to something that had an easy solution.

Still, he had no idea what he would find when he returned from India.

Now, standing in the clock room, Danny watched Colton waiting, his blond eyelashes quivering impatiently against his cheeks. Danny's chest tightened with the urge to say so many things—things that went beyond language, things that felt the way the shape of Colton's name felt. But every other word remained cramped and messy inside his head.

He took Colton's hand and placed the object on his palm. Colton's eyes shot open and widened in delight. It was a photograph of Danny from the shoulders up, taken with a camera box Danny had borrowed from a friend of his mother's. In the photo, Danny was looking at the camera, barely smiling. His hair had actually been somewhat tame that day.

"I hope you like it, because that's the best one of the lot," Danny said. Cassie had wanted to take more, but Danny had been exhausted after an hour of posing.

"I love it. Although I wish you were truly smiling. You look so nice when you smile and it shows in your eyes."

Danny blushed. "It was the best I could do."

Colton examined the photo for a while, then put it carefully in his pocket. "What about the one you took of me?"

"It didn't come out," Danny sighed. "I didn't expect it would.

It was all blurry and out of focus." He took his sketchbook and a pencil from his bag. "Since the photograph didn't work, I'd like to draw you. If . . . If that's all right."

Colton, always fond of watching Danny sketch, nodded eagerly.

Danny directed Colton to sit on a box near the clock face—Danny had cleared most of them from the room, but had left a few to use as seats—and positioned him just so. Thankfully, clock spirits could sit still for a long time, so Danny didn't have to bark at him about moving around. The clock tower bells rang four o'clock as he sketched. He tossed away the first attempt and focused more on the second, but it was difficult to concentrate when those amber eyes were taking in Danny just as thoroughly as he was taking in Colton.

Danny carefully penciled in the tiny nuances of Colton's face, the way his hair fell in a clockwise whorl, the small shadow of his nose against his cheek. Colton's gaze never strayed from his own. Danny tried to capture those eyes, innocent and old and warm, but couldn't quite manage it. He struggled to find the source behind what made those eyes so special.

It's the way he looks at me, he realized. Like nothing the world had to offer could compare to what sat before him in that moment.

Each tiny stroke with his pencil was a plea. *Don't forget me. Don't change the way you look at me. Please be here when I return.*

When he was finished, he showed the sketch to Colton. The clock spirit examined his own face and smiled softly.

"Is that really what I look like?"

"Yes." *In my eyes.*

They sat in the fading sunlight. Danny leaned beside Colton's box, putting his head on the spirit's thigh; he smelled of sunshine and winter mornings. Colton threaded his fingers through Danny's hair.

"I'll miss you."

Neither was sure who said it first.

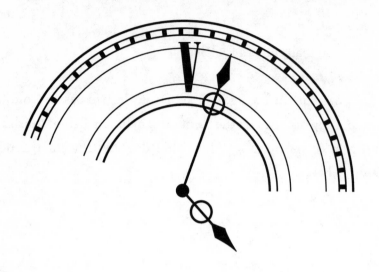

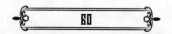anny couldn't sleep. He lay awake in bed, staring into the depths of his humble Enfield cottage, wondering if it would still be his in a few weeks' time.

Sighing loudly, he turned onto his back. The curtains were drawn across the window near his bed, but moonlight shone through the crescent window above, splashing across his sheets. Most nights, the moonlight crept up the bed, caressing his face briefly before it hid beyond the window. It seemed almost purifying.

He didn't want to think about tomorrow, or the day after. He wanted to stay right where he was and force the moon to stay still, to refrain from pulling the night onwards. But on the nightstand his timepiece ticked away the seconds, reminding him that the night would eventually end and time would go on as usual.

There had been a moment—just one moment—when

Danny had been able to manipulate time beyond the normal limits of the clock tower. Reaching out, he picked up the small cog that rested beside his timepiece and ran a thumb over its surface, thinking about how his blood had connected him to Enfield, when he had shifted time with just a thought.

In India, time was moving forward even when towers were destroyed. Who was to say someone wasn't controlling it the same way he'd controlled Enfield's?

A small knock made him jump. Danny threw off the covers and hurried to the door.

Colton stood on the threshold with a sheepish smile.

"What are you doing here?" Danny demanded.

"Sorry. I wanted to see you."

Danny leaned out the doorway, looking both ways, then ushered Colton inside before he was seen. "Is something wrong?" Colton usually didn't knock, taking great joy in waltzing into the cottage whenever Danny least expected it.

"No, nothing's wrong."

"You saw I couldn't sleep," Danny guessed.

Colton shrugged. The spirit, like Cassie, tended to worry about him. Danny recalled the fever he had run back in February. He'd been too sick to leave his bed, so Colton had fed him broth and watched over him as he slept. It had almost felt normal.

"I just wanted to see you," Colton insisted. "To stay with you." When Danny hesitated, studying him for the signs of weakening he'd shown in the factory, Colton added, "Please?"

The thought of having Colton beside him was more

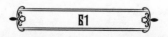

comforting than having only the moon for company, so Danny passed him the small cog to put in his pocket for strength.

"I still have to sleep, though," Danny said as he crawled back under the covers. "You'll be terribly bored."

"I won't be." Colton joined him under the blankets, settling into the space Danny left unoccupied.

Danny shifted so they were face to face. "Did you mean it? About speaking to my father?" Colton nodded. "I don't know if it will help, but you can try. Dad's not unreasonable. I think he's just scared."

"He was trapped in Maldon. It makes sense."

Danny breathed, in and out, a slow and steady pattern that Colton couldn't imitate. As if reading his thoughts, Colton placed his fingers against Danny's neck, feeling for his pulse.

"I wish I could be like you. Things would be so much easier."

"Stop talking about it, Colton." *It's too painful.*

Colton idly traced the vein down Danny's neck until Danny shivered. "But it's true. Your father likely wouldn't have a problem if I wasn't . . . this. I could offer you so much more."

"You're fine just the way you are."

He couldn't tell Colton that he secretly wished for the same thing: for them both to be the same, equal in all things. That he wanted what Colton could never give him. That life didn't have to be made up of secrets and compromise.

Slowly, Colton scooted closer. Danny could see the faint glow of his skin, the amber gleam of his eyes. The moonlight inched up the bed, contesting its silver shine against Colton's gold.

The spirit leaned in and kissed him. His lips were soft and parted easily. Danny closed his eyes and returned the pressure, matching the slow, thoughtful rhythm of his mouth as Colton's thumb swept over his throat.

The air around them warped slightly, and Danny could almost sense it gliding over his body. The timepiece still ticked on his bedside table. The moon still journeyed through the sky. But in this bed, time was momentarily forgotten.

Colton reached under the covers and slid a hand up Danny's nightshirt, over his bare ribs. Danny's breath hitched.

"I can't give you much," Colton said, "but I can give you something."

Colton gently turned him onto his back. The touches on Danny's chest and sides seared into his skin. They made something deep within him tremble, the first signs of an earthquake traveling from core to surface. It didn't feel like his body—it was as though Colton were touching someone else entirely.

When Colton's fingers reached his stomach, he finally found his voice. "You don't have to." His words barely stirred the air between them.

"I want to." Colton looked at Danny through his lashes, and they were spangled with moonlight. There was a tenderness in him that broke Danny's heart a million times over. It was in the way Colton caressed his cheek, the slope of his neck. It was in the way he leaned down and kissed Danny on the mouth, slow and gentle, like testing new waters.

"Can I?" Colton asked against his mouth.

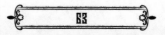

Danny shaped the word *yes*.

Colton's lips trailed down his neck. He found his pulse, life under his lips, and then there were *teeth*. Danny gasped, and Colton let out a small laugh, lower than usual, as he traced his name on Danny's hip.

Danny was burning. It scared him; he had never felt this way before, this punch-drunk sensation of affection and longing, allowing his body to speak for him. Allowing Colton to read that body to his own interpretation. Even the slight weight of him lying on top of Danny was too much, too close, too everything. He was going to turn the bed to ashes.

His bones ached with the force of his want, this intangible thing now being measured in sighs and kisses and whispers. He ran his hands over Colton's shoulders, pressed his palm to the still chamber where Colton's heartbeat would have been. But Danny's heart beat so hard he could feel it for the both of them, monstrous with desire.

Everything was raging and desperate and splintering. The cracks started straight from the middle of his chest, where Colton's tongue tasted his skin, to the insides of his thighs, where Colton made patterns with feathery fingertips. He opened his eyes but couldn't see. Only feel. Only breathe. Only hear his blood echo on Colton's lips.

His chest pulled like a magnet, toward this brilliant golden boy who was everything.

And those eyes, looking at him that way, devouring him like *he* was the shining one, like *he* was the one full of light. But it was

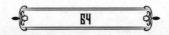

Danny who was blinded. He pulled Colton closer and buried a hand in his hair, putting his lips to his temple, his jaw, anywhere he could reach. He tried to reach under his shirt, for the waistband of his trousers, but Colton gently caught his hand and pressed it to the bed.

He nearly didn't catch the way time contracted around them. Almost effortlessly Danny cast out his own power, reining Colton's in, recognizing the moment when Enfield's time got snarled in Colton's emotions.

But together they made a shield against the night, a barrier of golden threads where time was theirs to control. Each small contact scattered him across the sky, as distant and bright as stars. Every second Colton took from him was a second he gave back. Each gasp was like being reborn. Building and stretching, as thin as glass.

"Danny," Colton whispered in his ear.

He shattered.

Danny woke in the middle of the night to find Colton watching him. Half-embarrassed, Danny smiled shyly.

"You don't have to stay if you feel tired."

"I feel fine," Colton said. Danny smoothed away the spirit's fair hair. "What about you?"

"Good. Thirsty."

Colton rose before he could get up, so Danny fell back onto

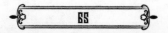

the pillow. Fully dressed, Colton padded to the kitchen and returned with a glass of water. Danny sat up and let the covers slip off his bare shoulders. Strangely, he wasn't embarrassed anymore. He savored the weight of Colton's hands and lips on his body, the welt of burn marks without the pain.

"Come here a moment," Danny said. Colton put the water on the nightstand and stood before where Danny knelt on the bed. He held Colton by the hips, looking up at him with curiosity.

"You really can't feel anything?"

Colton shook his head. "I can feel your touch, but not like you do. It's not the same."

"But…" He thought of what they'd just done, and that intense moment in the clock room, when time had skewed so sharply.

"It's more emotions than touch," Colton explained. "I'm not sure how it works. I just can't . . . do certain things. The things your body does."

"Oh."

Danny's thumbs brushed up under Colton's shirt. A silent question passed between them, and Colton nodded. Danny carefully removed the shirt to reveal Colton's belly, flat and flawless and smooth to the touch. Danny couldn't even feel any small, downy hairs on his skin. "You have a navel," he said, surprised.

Colton looked down. "Is that what it's called?"

Danny circled the spot with a fingertip. He leaned in and kissed it.

"Are you *sure* you can't feel anything?"

Colton smiled sadly. He framed Danny's face with his hands, then trailed one down to his chest.

"I feel this." He pressed his palm over Danny's beating heart. "That's all I need."

Danny rested his head against Colton's chest and wrapped his arms around his waist. There was a strange urgency to this moment, as if he held a memory, something made out of prisms of light. He didn't want to separate himself from this thing that grew sharp and irresistible every time they were close. Every time he held him in his arms, or counted every shade of gold within his eyes, he felt it grow and spread and tangle deeper. It bled him with every tiny kiss Colton pressed to his jaw and every laugh he managed to draw from within him. He chimed like a bell, infectious and unfading.

The moon was already gone. Tomorrow beckoned, and beyond was a land too far away and too unfamiliar to fully imagine.

"Wait for me," Danny whispered, holding Colton tighter.

"I always do."

Danny stared at the fading wood of the front door for several minutes, silently willing his hand to reach for the knob. He was still caught up in memories of the night before, the weight and promise of Colton's touch. It turned the world around him fuzzy and inconsequential.

When he finally opened the door, he found his mother reading the paper at the kitchen table. She leapt to her feet.

"Thank goodness!" She hurried over to hug him, the top of her head resting just underneath his chin.

Danny was out of practice with hugging his mother, but as he uncertainly returned the embrace, it helped his mood somewhat. It was like embracing a thought instead of a woman, the kind of nostalgia that brings both a smile and a sigh.

She stepped back to wipe her eyes. "We were afraid you wouldn't come back. Your father was upset for scaring you off. For all he insists you're grown now, he still has trouble remembering you aren't fourteen anymore. We tried to call you."

Jane had told him his mother had rung twice, but Danny had claimed he was too busy. "Sorry, Mum. I just needed some time." He looked around the room. "Where is he?"

"He was called to the office for something minor. He should be back soon."

They had tea and discussed the India trip. Leila was still flustered—"And on such short notice, the nerve of it"—but she seemed more willing to let him have his way so long as he wasn't cross with her. There had been too much tension between them in the past to risk opening up a new rift.

She helped him pack upstairs. He was only taking one trunk, and as he latched it closed, they heard the front door open and shared a look.

"I'll tell him you're here," Leila said, standing.

She went downstairs while Danny sat on the trunk, hands clasped between his knees. Just as he was unused to being on good terms with his mother, he was unused to being on poor ones with his father. The reversal made his mind that much foggier.

Christopher didn't waste time, nudging the door open a moment later. He let out an almost pained breath when he saw the trunk.

"Hard to believe you'll be gone."

"Not for long," Danny reminded him. It was the same thing he'd said to Colton that morning before giving him one final kiss goodbye.

Christopher sat on the edge of Danny's bed and mirrored his pose, perhaps unintentionally. "I'm sorry for how I acted."

"I don't blame you."

"But it was wrong." He started to jostle his leg up and down. "I almost didn't think you'd bother coming to say goodbye."

"Of course I would." Danny and his father had argued before Christopher had left for Maldon, and Danny had carried the guilt of his words like a sharp-edged stone for three years. If he went to India and something happened to him, or to his father, he would regret this argument just as much.

"Danny, I only want what's best for you. I hope you know that."

"Dad—"

"It might be exciting to love a spirit—I was your age once, and loved to do the things I shouldn't—but you're so young,

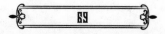

and he's . . . well, not human. You'll grow old, and he won't. It just won't work. More than that, it's dangerous. Every day could potentially jeopardize Enfield."

Danny thought back to the day they'd visited the factory, and the way the clock had run slow then fast. He hung his head to hide the wetness in his eyes.

"I've seen what this spirit's been doing to you," Christopher went on. "You keep putting Enfield—*him*—before yourself. Before anything else. That's not right, Danny."

Danny couldn't even argue. Given a choice between what he wanted and what was right, he would choose Colton every time.

"I know that," he said softly. "I know."

"Then why are you letting this continue?"

Danny tried to swallow and almost couldn't manage. "Because I lo—I—" Danny angrily rubbed his cheeks with a quick motion of his wrist. "I can't control what I feel."

They sat in silence as clouds rolled across the sun, briefly sheltering them from its glare.

Christopher moved off the bed and knelt before him. "I'm sorry, Danny. I don't want to see you get hurt." He rubbed Danny's head, mussing up his hair. "You don't have to make a decision now. We can discuss it when you come back. Let's have a nice dinner as a family, and your mum and I will see you off tomorrow morning. I'm sorry."

Danny shook his head. "I'm sorry, too." *Sorry I can't change the way I feel.*

That night he dreamed of fire rolling across a barren desert. It consumed the ground, traveling toward a looming palace of white and gold. Between the fire and the palace stood a tower.

He watched helplessly as tongues of flame licked up the sides of the tower. A golden figure was trapped inside, pounding on the glass of the clock face, screaming for help. Danny screamed back. He tried to get up, but he was chained to the earth.

The tower burned.

The airship sat brooding in the middle of the tarmac where the auto had dropped him off. It made a horrific noise—a continuous, roaring breath, like a dragon stuck in a never-ending yawn—that traveled directly into his stomach, which had hardened into a ball of dread.

Danny saw other ships and dirigibles across the busy hub of the aviators' playground, simply marked DOCKING AREA 3. Sunlight glinted off the airship's metallic wings, which slanted across its great, hulking body, over the steam turbines and the generators. Twin propellers peeked out on either side, almost as tall as his parents' house.

It was a monstrosity.

"It's beautiful," Daphne said. They had come together from the Mechanics Affairs building.

"Beautiful?"

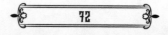

"You don't think so?"

"Aesthetically, I like the dirigibles better, but I hate all airships." Perhaps it had to do with his familiarity of the open gearwork of clock towers, but he preferred seeing how a machine ran over trusting that it would. "How's that thing even supposed to stay in the air?"

"The engine, for one thing. And see the wings? See how they're sloped? It'll deflect the air downward, creating a lifting force that helps the ship stay up."

"You like these things, do you?"

"Very much." She glanced at the auto that was pulling up behind them and grabbed the handle of her trunk. "I'll see you inside."

Doesn't she have anyone to see her off? he wondered as his own farewell committee—his parents and Cassie—climbed out of the auto. They could have said their goodbyes at the house, but Cassie and his father had wanted to see the airship take off.

Cassie threw her arms around him. He stumbled and held her close, pretending not to hear the choked sound his mother made. *Ladies shouldn't embrace men they aren't married or related to*, she would probably complain during the auto ride home.

"I'll miss you, Dan. Will you write?"

"If I have the time." She pinched his arm. "*Ow!* Yes, I'll bloody write."

When she stepped back, her eyes didn't match her smile. Danny tried—and failed—to remember the last time they'd been apart so long.

She chucked him lightly under the chin. "I'll keep an eye on everyone," she promised.

"I know you will. Thanks, Cass."

His mother was next, already in tears. She made him promise to be safe, and to look out for snakes, and eat only British food, and to boil his water before he drank it.

"Mum, for the love of God . . ."

"Just say you'll be careful. And don't take the Lord's name in vain."

"I will. And I won't."

Then it was his father's turn. Christopher shifted from foot to foot, giving Danny a weary smile, and put a hand on his son's shoulder. "Make sure you pay attention, and take plenty of notes. I want to hear everything when you get back." Danny nodded, and something like an unspoken truce settled between them. His father drew him into a hug. "I love you, Ticker. If anyone can find out what's behind these attacks, it's you."

Danny fought to swallow. "Thanks, Dad."

And then he was pulling away from them, floating off like a balloon until its string went taut. As he walked toward the roaring airship, that string tightened, then tugged itself free. He was about to drift into the sky and land in an entirely new world.

He paused on the gangplank to turn toward Enfield. Taking the small cog from his pocket, he pressed it to his lips.

Daphne was waiting by the door, where a crewmember took his luggage.

"Our cabins are this way," she said.

As they moved along a hallway, Danny realized the airship didn't look nearly as big on the inside. Maybe it was all the machinery clogging up the place. There had to be someplace for the cargo and engines, as well as cabins for the crew and the other passengers. Those passengers were mostly soldiers, by the look of the olive green uniforms he spotted down a metallic hallway.

Daphne stopped at a door with a round porthole. Below it was a small, handwritten sign that read Mr Daniel Hart. The door to the left was marked Miss Daphne Richards.

"Aren't you going to settle in?" Danny asked when she turned to leave.

"Think I'll have a look around, first."

Danny was more than happy for a moment alone. He had a sneaking suspicion he might toss up his breakfast when the airship took off, and it would help his pride immensely if Daphne weren't around to witness it.

Inside, he discovered his cabin was similar to a train carriage, with two green, plush benches situated on either side. His trunk had been hoisted onto a wire rack above. He'd barely stepped through the doorway when a man sporting curling sideburns and a finely trimmed mustache called out to him.

"You must be Mr. Hart, the mechanic. I'm Captain Eckhart, and I'll be flying the *Notus* today."

The man gripped his hand and Danny noticed a set of wings tattooed on the captain's wrist, the symbol of Caelum, Gaian god of the sky; it matched the symbol drawn on the airship's hull. Danny listened politely as the man rambled on about the *Notus*, silently begging him to leave.

When the captain finally departed, Danny closed the door and sat by the round window, staring out at the tarmac. His parents and Cassie were probably still out there, but he couldn't see them from this angle. He turned the small cog around in his fingers, pressing channels into his skin with its spokes. If he concentrated, he could sense Enfield: the smell of cut grass and the warmth of sunshine on brick.

The door opened a minute later and a flushed Daphne barged in, nearly slamming the door behind her.

"You've got your own cabin, you know," he said.

"Those soldiers keep gawking at me. I'm staying in here." She settled across from him, folding her arms over her chest as she sank low into the seat. Her blond braid fell forward when she ducked her head toward the window.

"I'm sure they don't mean any harm," Danny tried, but his words were met with a snort.

He shared what the captain had told him—everything he could remember, anyway—and they sat in silence until the engines revved. Danny gripped his knees, only slightly comforted by the hard ridge of the cog against his palm.

Daphne sat upright. "Here we go."

The engines vibrated around them like the muscles of an animal before it took off running. With a heaving push and the hiss of released gas, the contraption lifted itself from the ground and steadily climbed into the open air.

Danny didn't see the dwindling shapes of his parents and Cassie below. He was too busy keeping his eyes shut tight and whispering curses whenever the airship rattled or made an unfamiliar sound.

"Danny, you have to see this!"

Reluctantly, he peered out the window and gasped. London looked like a neighborhood of dollhouses.

Unable to look for long without his stomach revolting, Danny spread out on the bench and put his cap over his eyes. If he tried to block everything out, maybe he would be able to survive the next ten hours.

He only lasted ten minutes before he asked, "Can you see India yet?"

Daphne laughed. He had never heard her laugh before. It was strangely attractive, low and full-bodied. "Not yet."

Maybe distracting himself would work better. "Did you already say goodbye to your family?"

He heard Daphne shift. "I said goodbye to her yesterday."

Danny lifted his cap to look at her, but Daphne was still staring out the window. All he could see now was a mantle of gray as they passed through clouds.

"Who?"

"My mother."

Danny's fingers twitched when he remembered that she was

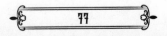

in an asylum. Shame curled low in his stomach as he recalled what had driven Daphne to steal Colton's central cog.

"You've no one else?"

She shook her head. "Just an aunt on my mother's side, but she's in Austria. They were never close, and I haven't seen her since my father passed."

"I'm sorry."

Daphne shrugged.

Danny studied her profile in the gray light. Sitting up, he ran a hand over his hair. "May I ask you something?"

"You may. Not certain if I'll answer, though."

He tapped the corner of his eye. "Why do you have that tattoo?"

She finally turned to look at him. Her pale gaze was unnerving, but Danny didn't look away. "It's nothing special." She touched the diamond-shaped mark. "Just a reminder."

Danny crossed his legs, wondering how to respond, but the airship bumped over a pocket of wind and he groaned. He spent the next several minutes with his eyes closed, teeth clenched, trying to imagine himself back in Colton's tower. But that only brought a different kind of pain.

The door opened and closed. He couldn't blame Daphne for risking perverse soldiers to get away from him, so he was surprised when she returned with a glass of something vaguely yellow.

"It's ginger water. It'll help your stomach."

"Oh. Thank you." Taking small sips, he felt like a child in the

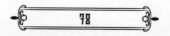

care of a no-nonsense governess. Feeling slightly better now that the turbulence had passed, he asked, "Do you have any theories about the fallen towers?"

"Just ones that don't make sense. Why? Do you?"

"Not really." He glanced at the cog, then slipped it back in his pocket. Daphne noticed but said nothing. "Only something exceptionally powerful would be able to keep time running without a tower. After all, that's why the new Maldon tower didn't work. There was no spirit to make it run."

Daphne frowned. "I've always wondered about that. Why are the spirits even necessary? I know the towers need guardians, but how did the spirits come to be in the first place? What makes them so powerful that they can influence time?"

"You know there's scads of books on that. We had to take Time Theory for four bloody years."

"I know. But no one's found answers." Daphne tapped a finger against her knee. This close, Danny realized that she smelled like bergamot. "Do you believe in the Gaian gods?"

"Er. Not really. But I never believed in clock spirits, either, and then I met Colton."

"Some people think the god of time is a fabrication. Something to justify using the towers."

Danny shrugged. He'd heard it all before. The creator of time, Chronos, had given Aetas the power to control it. Aetas was supposed to keep track of time while Chronos oversaw the world, but when Aetas shared the power with humans, Chronos killed him.

"The point being?" Danny asked.

"They say time shattered when Aetas died, and clock towers and their spirits were left to take over the responsibility. If something truly powerful is making time continue despite the fallen Indian towers . . . it could have to do with the gods themselves."

Danny gave her an incredulous smile. "Do you really believe that?"

"It's just a theory," Daphne mumbled.

"I suppose."

They retreated into their private thoughts, Danny watching the liquid in his glass ripple.

"Not to disprove your theory," he said a moment later, "but it's humans destroying the towers, not vengeful deities. What could give humans the power to restore time?"

"I don't know." Her eyes trailed back to the pocket where he kept the cog. "What could give humans the power to stop it?"

The tower was quiet. Well, not entirely; it could never be truly quiet. Ticks reverberated through the floorboards, the pendulum swung in lazy arcs through the air like the beating of a bird's wings, and gears slowly turned with a low and methodical hum. The orchestra of time.

Colton sat at the window of the clock room, gazing out at Enfield. The sun was shining in full force, drenching the streets, the roofs, and the people passing by.

It had been one day since Danny left.

Colton didn't get bored easily. He loved to watch people, and now, thanks to Danny, he could even go outside and talk to them. But today he only sat and stared. His eyes followed a couple walking down the street, but he didn't listen in, or draw closer to look.

The way his senses worked was vastly different from the way

Danny's did, as Colton had found out after laughing at a conversation between two brothers.

"What's so funny?" Danny had asked.

"Didn't you hear the joke?"

Danny had peered down at them. Colton loved the way the sunlight had brightened his face, turning his green eyes two shades lighter. "How can I when I'm all the way up here?" He'd glanced suspiciously at Colton. "How far can you hear, exactly?"

"In Enfield? Everywhere."

"And . . . your vision works the same way, I take it?"

"A girl is playing with a red ball a few streets down. You can go check, if you like."

"No, I believe you." Danny had grown pale. "Damn, that's unnerving."

Colton wasn't sure why it was unnerving. It gave him something to pass the time, of which he had an eternity.

But today he didn't use his senses at all. He didn't do anything, except sit and stare in the direction of London.

He hadn't been this prone to moodiness before he met Danny. Now his thoughts, once so fluid and immaterial, were rapid and thorny. He couldn't stop the onslaught of emotions that compromised his mind. They were all so sharp, so painful, so maddening that he wondered—as he often did lately—if humans felt this, too.

Danny thought his clock spirit senses were frightening. But feeling what a human felt was terrifying.

Colton drew the photograph from his pocket. This strange,

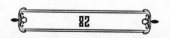

thick paper had somehow captured Danny's image, but it wasn't the Danny he knew. It wasn't vivid, alive, with bright eyes that changed in sunlight and a smile like slow-thawing spring. How could this image be so like his Danny, and yet so different?

Still, he would take it over no Danny at all.

"Where are you now?" he asked it.

Colton leaned against the window and pressed the image to the pane, as if Danny could somehow see through the paper and into Enfield, the place where he belonged. The place he was needed.

Something tugged at his consciousness, and he turned and made an aggravated sound. The hands of the clock were rotating faster. Time had sensed his desire to speed up, and had done precisely that.

"Stop," he commanded. The hands slowed, waited until they made up the difference, and then resumed at their normal speed.

He knew he was being ridiculous. He couldn't mope the whole time Danny was gone, like Chessie the dog did when Thom went to work at the factory. Colton sometimes looked in on that poor dog, whining and watching the door, and wished he could do something to help. But seeing Thom return every night was its own reward. He, like Chessie, just had to be patient.

Colton sat on the floor and dragged over one of the books he'd taken from Danny's cottage, the one full of Greek myths. He'd decided he wouldn't read any new ones before Danny got back, so he browsed the ones they had already shared: Perseus, Troy, the labyrinth.

He flipped to the back, to the list of the Titans. Hyperion, Atlas, Rhea . . . Prometheus.

"I know I've heard this story before," he said, before looking up and realizing he was speaking to himself. He'd never been guilty of that human habit before. It made him irrationally angry—yet another new peculiarity.

Colton's memory was excellent, and he knew almost all these tales by heart, and even where he and Danny had been sitting while they read them. Yet there was no memory of reading this one.

Something rumbled in the distance, similar to the sound of an oncoming summer storm. Colton ignored it as he read and reread the story. In the illustration, the eagle flew in from the corner, coming to devour Prometheus's liver while the Titan was chained to his rock. Over and over again, an unending cycle, and all because—

The tower trembled.

Startled, Colton vanished from his spot on the floor and reappeared at the window. Townspeople had begun to wander outside, disturbed by the noise. The sky was still bright and clear. No storm?

Then a cloud blocked out the sun, casting Enfield in darkness.

Colton looked up and his eyes widened. Not a cloud.

An airship.

He winked out and appeared on the roof, staring as the aircraft drifted above his tower like it was the eagle about to peck out his liver, if he had one to give. It glided in a smooth

circle above the town, trailing a ring of smoke, until something detached from the ship. A piece of metal?

No. Something else.

Something bad.

Colton winked himself back inside the tower just as the object smacked the building's side. It went off like a thousand peals of thunder, rocking the tower so hard that Colton fell. He screamed at the pain that lanced up his side.

He'd seen Danny hurt. He'd seen humans bleed. Colton did not bleed, but he felt the pain coiled deep inside him, sparking along on the surface, everywhere. The tower groaned, or maybe that was him. The windows were smashed, jagged remnants of glass scattered across the floor.

Time pulsed and writhed. He winced with each jab, hours slipping out of the loop even as they tried desperately to keep pressing forward. Colton grabbed at them, but it was too late. One second—four—negative ten

s
  e
    c
      o
     n
    d
  s

Colton struggled to his knees and swayed. Holding his side, he rushed for the stairs, almost stopping to retrieve Danny's books. He used one of Danny's favorite swears—"Shit on a toast

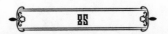

point"—for being foolish and kept moving. When he reached the stairs he lost his footing, falling down each step until he crumpled at the landing. He tried to disappear, but found he was too weak. Groaning, he crawled down the next flight. He had to get to the clockwork.

The tower began to crack, then crumble. Metal heaved and moaned. The structure would start falling soon. There was only one way he could prevent it.

Colton grabbed his central cog and steeled himself. Closing his eyes tight, he pulled it away from the rest of the cogs and gears with a grunt of pain.

Time rippled and stiffened. All at once, a wave of gray nothingness washed over Enfield, and the injured time ceased pounding away on his body.

In fact, it ceased altogether.

The tower was quiet. Now, the sound of time was completely gone.

He held his chest, the ache there now a twin misery to the one in his side, sickly and poisonous. The tower stood frozen, its tumbling stones awkwardly defying gravity until the central cog, the heart of the clock, was replaced.

But he couldn't replace it now. There was no telling what would happen to Enfield if the tower fell.

If *he* fell.

Using the last of his strength, he stood and hugged the cog to his chest as he tripped down the stairs. He could barely feel the wood beneath his feet.

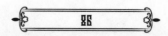

Colton heard the crowd before he staggered outside—screaming, shouting, crying. He looked where they pointed. Against the gray dome, the clock tower was dull and lifeless. The face was ruined, Roman numerals scattered at the base of the tower. The structure could hardly even be called a tower, halfway to crashing to earth. The right side was exposed, metal and brick blasted away to reveal the broken pendulum within.

Colton stood unobserved for a moment. When Jane saw him, her mouth fell open.

"Colton!"

That quickly drew everyone's attention. Soon they were shouting for answers, lunging forward like a wave. Colton shrank back, hiding behind his cog, a feeble shield against their fear.

"Everyone, stop this! Stop!" Mayor Aldridge broke through their circle and came to Colton's side. "Yes, we've just been attacked. I don't know by whom, or why. No one does—especially not this boy, who's our only link to time. Let's focus on taking care of him until a mechanic comes."

"But no one can get inside!" a voice called out.

"Danny can," Harland said above the mutterings. "He did last time, didn't he?"

Only because he had me, Colton thought.

The mayor sighed. "Perhaps. For now, Colton, please come with me."

Colton wanted to follow. But there was so much pain. Taking a step, his legs gave out, and he, like his tower, began to fall.

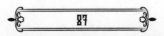

Colton's awareness gradually returned. Danny called it waking up, but Colton knew he hadn't been sleeping. He'd shut down, his gears ground to a halt, in order to preserve what little strength remained.

Someone had carried him to a chair in the mayor's office. He looked slowly to one side, where his central cog was propped against him.

It wasn't nearly powerful enough, but it would keep him functioning for now. Colton reached down to touch it, then froze.

He could see through his hand.

"Why am I so faint?" he whispered.

"We don't know, but I admit it's rather alarming."

He turned and saw Aldridge walk into the room. Then the mayor disappeared. He walked in again. Disappeared again. Walked in again. Colton blinked. This was what happened in a Stopped town: time distorted one's actions. People got caught in loops.

"Danny told me he was going abroad, but do you know for how long?" Aldridge asked when he finally managed to stay put.

"He said it might take a few weeks."

It would feel like no time at all to a Stopped Enfield, but the mayor still looked worried. Someone had bombed the tower—*his* tower—for a reason. There was no telling what could happen outside the town during those few weeks.

"How was Danny able to leave before?" Aldridge asked.

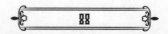

"He had me. Spirits can go through the barrier."

"Then anyone can go through, so long as they're touching you?"

Colton shook his head. "They have to be a clock mechanic, too. Connected to time."

"Blast." Aldridge started wringing his hands. Then he disappeared again. When he walked through the door as if for the first time, Colton patiently repeated his side of the conversation.

"Blast." Aldridge started wringing his hands. "Is there any chance you could go?"

"Me? Go to London?"

"You've been before."

"I was very weak, though." Then he remembered all the clockwork pieces in his tower. If he took a few of them, not just his central cog, maybe he would have enough strength.

"If you go to London and bring back a mechanic, we can get this sorted before Danny returns."

Colton tried to imagine Danny's reaction upon seeing the ruined tower. His voice would climb higher as he sputtered, "I leave for five sodding minutes and your tower gets *attacked*?"

For some reason, this made Colton smile. He picked up his cog and cradled it to his chest. It was disturbingly visible through his faded arms. Before, when something happened to his tower, there was a physical mirror on his body. This transparency seemed to be the reaction to the amount of damage his tower had sustained.

"Something is very wrong here," Aldridge went on. "I've

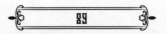

heard of those cities in India, where the towers fell but time didn't Stop. So then why are *we* Stopped?" He looked at Colton, as if he might have answers. "Will you be able to reach London? Will you bring back a mechanic?"

Colton nodded. "I'll try." And he knew just the mechanic for the job.

Colton stood in Danny's cottage staring at the books arranged on the shelf. There were a few gaps, but only one he could fill. He had climbed his tower to retrieve the book of Greek myths, which had been precariously perched on a broken beam. He'd dusted it off, but there had been, thankfully, no real damage to the book.

Colton slid the volume back into place, ran a ghostly finger over the spine, and would have sighed if he could. He looked around. The bed hadn't been made; Danny never made his bed. Colton walked over and slowly pulled the sheets straight, wanting so badly to hide beneath them and wait for Danny to return. His body still hurt, but now another ache joined in, something elusive and indescribable.

He picked up one of Danny's satchels, which now contained his central cog and a few smaller ones he'd detached from the clockwork. Their absence wouldn't make a difference now. Together, the cogs made Colton stronger, more opaque. They even dulled the pain a little. His appearance was still a problem, though.

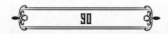

He grabbed Danny's overcoat and put it on. Danny's spare boots fit him well. Finishing the disguise with one of Danny's flat caps, he hoped it would be enough to prevent others from giving him a second look.

Outside, Enfield citizens milled about. There was nothing else for them to do. What felt like a minute was only the illusion of time passing. The minute would repeat, conversations would repeat, thoughts would repeat. Over and over and over, Prometheus bound in chains.

The mayor and Jane escorted Colton to the barrier. He recalled that terrible moment the year before when Enfield had Stopped for the first time. The panic in Danny's eyes, their frantic drive to London.

Now, he would have to walk.

"Are you certain none of us can pass through with you?" Aldridge asked.

"I'm fairly certain. And I don't think we should risk trying." Horrible visions of them getting trapped in some otherwordly time dimension made him grimace.

Jane eyed the barrier distrustfully. "You'll be careful, won't you?"

"Of course." He didn't miss their pinched eyes and mouths. "I'll return. I promise."

They stood back as he passed a hand through the barrier. It slid through easily, the grayness shimmering and distorting around his fingers, as though the wall recognized him. And why shouldn't it? Colton looked over his shoulder at the town he knew so intimately, taking one last look at the sad, crooked figure of his tower. Gathering himself, he stepped through the barrier.

It flowed over him, tendrils of stale seconds and stolen moments and breaths he couldn't breathe. A sea of gray, of blurred life streaked with the faintest hints of gold.

On the other side, the sun returned, and so did time; he recognized the sensation of Big Ben's power. He gazed around the field, the forest in the distance, the nearby river. The road that stretched toward London.

He was alone, armed with nothing but a few cogs and a picture of a human boy. Colton drew the picture from his pocket and addressed it sadly: "I guess I'll have to do it on my own this time. I wish you were here with me."

He couldn't waste these precious seconds on regrets, so he put the picture away and set off to find the only person who could help him now.

anny woke to a gentle shake. Daphne stood over him, illuminated by the overhead lantern she had turned on when the sky grew dim.

"Figured you might want to eat before the mess closes," Daphne said. "We're only a couple hours away."

Danny sat up and hid a yawn behind his hand. "Brilliant. I'm starving." During his nap, his stomach had grown used to the altitude and the airship's movement, and he realized he hadn't eaten since his hurried breakfast several hours earlier. "Have you been in here all this time?" He wasn't overly fond of the thought of Daphne watching him sleep.

"I went out and found the observation deck. I even spoke to the captain for a while about what class of airship the *Notus* is."

Daphne knew the way to the mess, as she had gone for some tea earlier. Danny stood to follow her, but hesitated in the

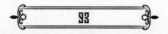

doorway. He went back inside, climbed onto one of the benches, and unlocked his trunk.

He took out the cog and brushed his thumb over it, then frowned. Usually, it radiated a tranquil sort of energy, only faint enough to feel if he touched it directly. Now it felt like any other piece of metal.

Probably the distance. Reluctantly, he slipped it into his trunk. The idea of being around soldiers spooked him, and he didn't want to risk anyone finding it.

As they walked, Danny caught Daphne glancing at him a few times. "You said his name," she said eventually. "In your sleep."

Heat rose to his face. He'd been thinking about Colton just before drifting off, wanting so badly to recreate the peace of the night he'd fallen asleep beside him—his arms wrapped around Colton's body, Colton's mouth pressed softly to his forehead, bidding him to sleep.

The next few weeks were going to be difficult.

Tables and benches were bolted to the floor of the mess. The hallway outside was cool, but the interior was warmed by the stoves in the back, the air scented with onions. The kitchen was divided from the seating area by a wall with a large window, through which passengers could pick up food.

Some of the soldiers and crewmembers had had the same idea as Daphne and were getting one last meal before landing. Danny saw that the soldiers were indeed eyeing her with undisguised interest. Normally, he wouldn't want anyone to assume there was any kind of relationship between Daphne and himself, but if that's what it took to keep their roving eyes away, he'd take up the role like a martyr. St. Daniel, patron saint of keeping soldiers away from girls who didn't want their attention.

"What are you doing?" Daphne demanded when Danny sidled closer.

"Getting those idiots' eyes off of you."

"Don't you dare put your arm through mine, Danny Hart. I can handle myself."

"But you said—"

"Never mind what I said. They'll be gone soon enough." She gave him a sideways glance. "Besides, what would your darling spirit say?"

Danny remembered the last time Colton had gotten jealous and shuddered.

There were two options for dinner: bubble and squeak, and a steak and ale pie. They both chose the latter. After they received their food, still steaming from the oven, they found seats in the far back corner, Daphne with her back to the soldiers. The men were now engrossed in a loud card game.

Danny blew on his first bite, though the hot gravy nipped his tongue anyway. Daphne ate slower, picking around the crust before taking her first real bite.

"Are you nervous?" Danny asked. He kept wondering what this was like for her, being part Indian.

"A little. I feel . . . far removed, I suppose. Growing up, I could only rely on what my father told me."

When she said nothing more, he changed the subject. "What

are we supposed to be looking for, anyway? Do they expect us to find the ones responsible for the bombings?"

"I think that's their job." With her fork, she pointed at the soldiers, one of whom cried out in delight as he revealed a suit of cards in his favor. "What about you? Are you nervous?"

"Somewhat. I just hope I don't do anything offensive."

"I think the British are past the point of offense," Daphne said dryly.

They discussed what Danny had read and what sorts of food they would likely eat. Danny told Daphne what he'd learned about the rebellion that took place twenty years before and, after some deliberation, even told her about the Enfield rifles. She stopped eating to listen, her eyebrows lowered in thought.

"What a strange coincidence."

"In any case, rule under the East India Company was one thing, but the British Raj is different. We'll have to be careful."

Daphne was quiet, taking small sips of water from a glass stained with fingerprints. Danny finished his pie, even though the carrots weren't completely cooked through. He was still hungry and debating going up for more when Daphne broke the silence. "Here's another theory. What if the Indians are destroying their own clock towers?"

"Why would they?"

"If they're angry—if they want to give the British a good slap in the face—messing about with their own clock towers would do the trick. There was a riot in Rath the same time the tower fell, and a smaller uprising in Khurja. They could have easily been distractions."

"But how would they keep time running?"

She shrugged. "It's just something to keep in mind, in case another tower falls while we're there."

They sat contemplating this new theory, slightly more probable than the first, though just as confusing. Daphne ran a finger around the rim of her glass and mumbled something under her breath. Danny strained to hear her.

"Hickory dickory dock, the mouse ran up the clock . . ."

Danny joined in. "The clock struck one, the mouse ran down."

They were both drawing breath for the last line when the airship gave a sudden, painful jerk. Danny's chest banged into the edge of the table and their cutlery crashed to the floor.

"The bleeding hell was that?" yelled a soldier from across the room. Some of the men had been thrown to the floor.

Danny rubbed his chest and swore. Daphne looked around. "That didn't feel like turbulence," she said as the soldiers and kitchen staff ran from the mess. "C'mon, Danny. Something's up."

She sounded frightened, and it doused Danny like a bucket of ice water. When he'd worried about something happening to the airship earlier, he had been in such a state of panic he'd barely been able to think. Now he felt oddly detached, like he was still in his cabin dreaming.

The speakers in the hall crackled, and the sound of Captain Eckhart's voice came through: "Everyone, please stay calm.

There appears to be another airship on the same course as us. It banged up against us—probably an accident. I'm signaling the pilot now."

But on the word *now*, another *bang* sent those in the hallway hurtling into the wall. Captain Eckhart grunted in annoyance. Crewmembers shouted for everyone to please return to their cabins, but it was rather hard when the hull kept shuddering, forcing them to stagger like toddlers attempting to walk for the first time.

"Gunners, to your stations! Everyone, to the emergency landing crafts on wings C and D!"

There were loud, booming noises just outside the airship, striking repeatedly like thunder. Attendants ushered people to the emergency aircrafts. Another hit sent Daphne lurching, and Danny caught her.

"Our things!" he yelled into her ear.

"Leave them!"

But he couldn't. He had left the small cog in his trunk.

He took off. Daphne yelled after him, and an attendant tried to stop him, but Danny took advantage of another rumble to sprint by.

He didn't know why he was risking life and limb for a piece of metal. But just as he couldn't control his dreams, he couldn't control his actions, and only one thought blazed across his mind: *I can't lose my only connection to him.*

As he rounded the corner, an explosion blew him off his feet. He landed hard on his shoulder with a loud *pop*. Groaning, Danny tried to get to his knees, but when he rolled over he gasped.

The explosion had ripped a hole in the *Notus*'s hull, taking out the cabin next to Danny's. All that remained was a jagged window into the Indian evening, a soupy mix of blue, gray, and red. The wind stung his skin and tugged him toward the hole.

He scrambled to find something to grab onto, but the force of the wind dragged his body across the floor, and he shot outside with a scream. Even as he was falling, he searched for something, anything, until his fingers closed around a loose cable that had been rent free in the explosion. Danny dangled from the airship over a dark, barren stretch of ground, miles and miles from his feet.

He let out a dry sob. His shoulder ached, but he clung onto the cable for dear life, the wind whipping his clothes and hair.

He was going to die because he was an idiot who wanted to save a cog.

And if he died, then Colton . . .

The dull throb of gunfire split the air. The *Notus* shuddered each time it was hit, steadily losing altitude. He could barely feel his hands. His fingers slipped and he gripped the cable even tighter.

From the corner of his eye, he saw something move. A bulky figure was climbing down the side of the airship. The more he stared, the more Danny realized it was a person swaddled in a thick jacket. Hope flared hot and bright in his bruised chest. Someone from the crew, maybe, who knew he'd come this way.

The person climbed down a metallic rope that had been affixed somewhere on top of the *Notus*. When the person reached the hole, he swung inside without being sucked out through the hull; the ship must have repressurized.

It was then that Danny noticed his supposed rescuer wore dark goggles and a kerchief around the lower half of his face, and a gun strapped to his waist. As Danny watched, the person detached a length of canvas rope from his belt.

Danny could only hang there as the figure approached, his dark jacket flapping in the wind, the rope coil he held in one fist dancing like the head of a cobra.

At the end of the rope was a noose.

Danny scanned his surroundings for a way to escape, but the only way was down. The man knelt above Danny, ready to either lasso or hang him with it.

"Stop!" Danny yelled, kicking his feet ineffectively through the open air. "Don't do this!"

To his surprise, the figure tossed the rope to him.

"Grab onto it," the man ordered.

Danny clutched tighter to the cable. His fingers were past numbness.

"Grab hold of the rope!"

"Who are you?" Danny demanded. "Are you with the *Notus*?"

The man, losing patience, unstrapped his gun and pointed it at Danny's face.

"Grab the rope!"

Danny couldn't move. He hung there like a worm on a hook and stared at the dark lenses of his soon-to-be-killer's goggles.

Before the man could pull the trigger, something collided

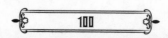

with his head and he tumbled to one side. Daphne stood in his place, a length of pipe clutched tightly in her hands. She panted as the wind made a wild mess of her long hair.

"He has a gun!" Danny yelled.

She saw where it had fallen and kicked it out of the hole. It plummeted to the Indian plain below.

The man quickly leapt to his feet, but before he could round on Daphne, she smacked him again with the pipe and he lost his footing, following his gun out into the approaching night.

"Shit!" Danny watched the man fall. He was going to die.

But then the man threw something. A disc shot up into the clouds, trailing another metallic rope behind it. The man swung from the rope as he was pulled upward by an unseen force. He looked over at Danny, then flew out of sight.

Daphne dropped the pipe and reached for his hand. The rope had slithered out, so Danny had to pull himself up the cable before he could grab onto Daphne's forearm. She steadied herself against the hull and heaved, face red, teeth bared.

Danny crawled back into the airship and scrambled to one side, away from the hole. He leaned against the wall, gasping hoarsely. Daphne's own breaths were high and wheezing.

She looked out of the hole, and he followed her gaze. Another airship, larger than the *Notus*, with a high bridge at the front and a long, bulky body, rose up into the air. That was all Danny had time to notice; the ship was little more than a dark mass as evening fell in earnest, an ominous cloud climbing back into the sky. The other clouds swallowed it into their company.

When Danny and Daphne could move again, they hurried from the corridor toward the emergency aircrafts. Attendants shoved them into a small carrier ship with some of the soldiers, then latched the doors behind them.

Danny sat in a cold metal seat as he was strapped in. He couldn't lift his arms.

An announcement was made. The engine started. They took off.

Something touched his thigh. It took all his effort to look down and see Daphne's hand resting there.

"Danny," she whispered. "Are you all right?"

I'm alive, he wanted to say, but no sound came out.

"What happened? Who was that?"

He couldn't even shake his head. Daphne said that maybe he was in shock, but it was all right now. They'd be on the ground within minutes. He wanted her to be quiet; for everything to be as still and silent as he was.

As if his body heard the plea, he closed his eyes and passed out.

As the plane landed, he roused himself. Daphne hovered at his side, and an attendant came to take Danny's pulse. She gave Danny two small, white pills.

Daphne eyed them distastefully. "Isn't there anything else?"

"They'll calm him."

Danny was forced to swallow the pills, which scratched his throat on the way down. Others were getting out of the plane, grimly murmuring among themselves. A soldier said they were an hour's drive from the military base. Another said help was coming.

Danny sat under the supervision of Daphne and the attendant. When they heard shouts coming from outside, he forced himself to stand. His legs were wobbly, but he had to see what was happening.

The *Notus* fell toward earth, but the captain had deployed an emergency balloon to inflate over the airship. It wasn't enough to keep the ship in the air, but the balloon allowed it to drift slowly to the ground. A few smaller ships flew toward it from the direction of what Danny assumed was the nearby military base. They looked like birds of prey waiting for the mammoth to die.

"I suppose we'll be able to recover our things after all," Daphne said. Her hair was a mess, and there was a scratch on her cheek. Danny's shoulder and chest still hurt, and his hands were rubbed raw.

When she felt his gaze, she looked away from the *Notus* and met his eyes. He swallowed. The pills felt trapped at the bottom of his throat.

"Thank you," he croaked.

Her lips thinned and she turned back to the falling airship. "You're welcome. It's your own fault, though. Who's daft enough to run for their things when they're told to evacuate a crashing airship?"

"Me." For some reason she laughed that clear, throaty laugh of hers. His lips trembled.

"Who was that man, anyway?" she asked again. "Why was he about to shoot you?"

"I don't know."

"He wasn't Indian, was he?"

"No." The skin Danny had seen between goggles and kerchief was white. "He spoke like us. English."

They watched as the *Notus* skidded along the ground. Great clouds of dust rose up in a desert storm as steam billowed into the air with a hiss. The balloon deflated, blanketing the airship as if it were a funerary shroud.

Danny felt woozy and detached; the pills were already starting to work. "I wish I could have seen his face when you hit him with that pipe."

"Me, too." Daphne laughed again, quietly, and this time he joined her. Then he laughed again, louder. She did, too. They couldn't stop. Danny had to put a hand over his mouth when the other survivors turned to glare at them. The attendant hurried back to offer Daphne the same pills she'd given Danny.

They sat in the dirt and laughed, hysterical, grateful, tired, alive.

Military autos from the base came to retrieve the soldiers and crew. Danny and Daphne climbed into the back of one, the night veiling their blank, weary faces. Daphne had refused to take the pills, instead slipping them in her pocket. But she was now just as quiet and calm as Danny.

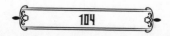

They jostled in their seats as the auto rumbled over bumps and pits. Danny closed his eyes and reached for his pocket before remembering that the cog wasn't there. What would Colton have done if Danny had died today, on the first leg of his journey? He recalled his mother's concern, the insinuation that Colton could not control his emotions. His father's claim that he always put Colton's welfare before his own.

And it was true. The first thought blazing across his mind hadn't been pain or death—it had been what that pain would do to Colton.

But I didn't die, he told himself firmly. *Not today.*

The image of the strange man swam behind his closed eyelids. Had he been trying to save Danny, or hurt him? Had he been singled out or chosen only because his idiotic actions had put him in harm's way?

He may have dozed off, for when he next opened his eyes, the plain outside had changed from an arid yellow to a grass-stained green. Trees were scattered on either side of the dirt road, swaying gently with the breeze. The auto rattled on toward the cantonment. Beyond that, Danny saw the dark forms of city buildings like slumbering giants.

The British private driving the auto pulled up inside the perimeter of the cantonment, past the stone wall. Squat buildings lined the road, many windows still lit. Soldiers, British and Indian alike, meandered outside under the pale moon.

"Took a hell of a time, but here you are," the private said. "Welcome to Agra."

The last time Colton had gone to London, he'd been mostly unaware of his surroundings. He was therefore completely unprepared for what awaited him.

Upon entering the city proper, he was greeted with the smell of ash and sweat. And the *noise*. He first mistook the crowd for a roaring beast lying in wait for him, but it was only people jostling up and down the street, yelling, mumbling, hawking. More people than he'd ever seen before, a frightening, teeming swarm poised to discover who he really was at any second.

Colton ducked into a foul-smelling alleyway, clutching the front of Danny's overcoat. He waited for the throng of people to disperse, thinking maybe they were all going somewhere together.

No such luck. The crowd was unending.

He slowly made his way through the twists and turns of the streets. There was so much to take in—the autos, the machines, the smoke, the shops. Behind windows, automatons worked as clerks. Outside, vendors called out that newspapers were only one shilling. A little boy chased a dog down the street, his mother calling after him. A constable directed traffic at an intersection. Pigeons congregated in messy areas, flew into the air when someone walked by, then settled back about their business.

Colton kept his head down and his hands deep in his pockets. That's what Jane had instructed him to do. She'd been quite clear on what he was *not* to do: talk to anyone; stop for any reason; buy anything except a hansom cab ride (they had given him money just in case, but he didn't know how to use it); or get distracted from his goal.

But London was so *huge*. He kept stopping to stare, whether it was watching a chimney sweep on a rooftop or a street performer juggling. If he caught someone looking at him oddly, he ducked his head and moved along.

Most confusing of all, however, was that Colton could no longer use the senses he'd always relied on. In Enfield he could see and hear everything, but here he felt disconnected, isolated. Was this how humans normally felt? It must be terribly lonely.

It took him a while to realize that street names were written on signs above his head. After that, it was much easier to figure out where he was. At one point, he found himself in a place called Piccadilly Circus, but it looked nothing at all like a circus; at least, not the sort he'd heard of. It was merely an intersection between large buildings with a statue of a winged man in the middle. If this was London's idea of a circus, it was a boring one.

He had to stop several times to sit on a bench, or on the curb, or somewhere out of the way. He was weak, but his strength gradually improved as he drew closer to Big Ben. London's time wrapped around his body and hugged him, familiar and calming. It might have been Big Ben himself, welcoming him. Colton longed to pay London's clock spirit a visit.

No. No distractions.

Mayor Aldridge had given him Danny's London address, and he was at the point of collapse by the time he tottered through Lambeth and reached Danny's street. He remembered this place also. The snow had been falling in soft, quiet flakes, the street darkened by night. Danny had leaned over him, worried and pale.

Colton hesitated outside the gate. He had met Danny's mother before, and though odd, she'd been pleasant enough. His father was another matter entirely.

Maybe I should go to the mechanics' office. It was right across from Big Ben.

But he had promised to seek out Christopher Hart first. There was no telling what the Lead Mechanic would want to do with him.

Colton opened the gate and approached the front door. From what Danny had told him, the Harts worked during the day and were home by evening. Above, the sky was red with dusk.

Colton knocked. He strained to hear movement inside the house, annoyed that his senses were so dulled.

He was about to turn and make his way to Big Ben after all when the latch scraped inside. The door opened, and a tall, long-limbed man stood on the threshold. He had green eyes and dark hair, with feathery black eyebrows. Colton briefly wondered if this was what Danny would look like in several years' time. Not quite, he decided. Danny's face was sharper, more like his mother's.

But it was enough to make him pause.

"Hullo? Can I help you?" the man asked. Even their voices were similar.

"I…uh…" How was he going to do this? "Are you Christopher Hart?"

"I am." He took in Colton's bag. "If you're selling something, we aren't interested, thanks."

"Oh, no, nothing like that. It's—It's about your son. Sort of."

Christopher blanched, and Colton winced. He'd said the wrong thing already.

"Danny? Is he hurt? What happened?"

"That's not what I meant!" Colton raised his hands, and realized his mistake too late. Christopher stared at his see-through palms, glowing faintly in the dusk shadows.

For a long moment, neither man nor spirit said a word. Then Christopher moved so he was no longer blocking the doorway.

"Come inside," he whispered. He looked up and down the

street as Colton hurried through the door, then closed and locked it behind him.

He whirled on Colton. "What's the meaning of this?"

Colton took off his cap and held it between his hands. Christopher's eyes darted around his face.

"Has there been news about Enfield?" Colton asked.

"Not that I've heard. Why?" Judging from his tone, he'd already guessed.

"It's Stopped."

Christopher's paleness was overtaken by an angry flush. All at once, Colton understood his second blunder.

"I didn't do it on purpose! That is, I didn't *want* to Stop Enfield. We were attacked. My tower was hit. It was going to fall and Stop time anyway, so I had to detach my central cog." He touched Danny's bag. "We didn't know what to do. The mayor told me to get help. I was the only one who could leave."

Christopher swayed. Wordlessly, he walked past Colton into a room that looked to be a kitchen. Colton cautiously followed. He'd only seen Danny's bedroom on his last visit, and now he took in his surroundings: faded green walls, a telephone in the hall, portraits painted in muted colors.

Danny's father poured himself some form of alcohol and knocked it back in one gulp. Exhaling loudly, he turned back to face Colton. "You're the spirit of Enfield. The one my son . . . You and he . . ."

If Colton were human, he would have blushed. "Yes."

"He's not here. He's gone to India."

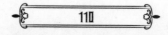

"I know. That's why I'm here, talking to you. I thought maybe you could come back to Enfield with me."

Christopher rubbed his face. "This is too much."

Maybe coming here had been a mistake after all. Colton felt that sense of disconnection again. More than that, he felt ashamed, and wasn't sure why. The emotion was new, and it unsettled him. He didn't like it at all.

"Where's Mrs. Hart?" he asked in a small voice. Maybe she would understand.

"Work," Christopher mumbled. "She'll be here soon enough." He swallowed hard. "I can't focus right now. I have to think. I'm sorry, but I have to think."

Colton nodded, though he didn't understand. Christopher walked past him, then stopped. It made Colton very uncomfortable, standing so close to Danny's father.

"That's his coat, isn't it?"

Again, Colton nodded, trying to shrink inside its shelter. It smelled of Danny, and that was the only thing that had kept him going today. Christopher swayed again, then left the kitchen.

Colton sat on one of the chairs to wait. He wanted to take off Danny's coat, but at the same time, he wasn't eager to shed its comfort. Hugging the satchel bag to his chest, he closed his eyes.

If he were human, he would have cried. He wondered if doing that ever made humans feel better.

Leila screamed when she found a clock spirit in her kitchen half an hour later.

Christopher hurried downstairs as she stood there gasping, one bony hand pressed to her chest.

"Oh my God," she sputtered. "Colton! What on *earth*—?"

"I'm sorry," he said. "I didn't mean to scare you."

"Leila, are you all right?"

"Yes, I—I'm fine. Just a shock. What's going on?"

"It's not about Danny," Colton said at once, not wanting to repeat the same mistake he'd made with Christopher.

"Oh . . . good." She still sounded confused. Christopher took her bag and led her to the table before he began to fix some tea. Leila just stared at Colton, who tried not to fidget under her gaze.

"Enfield is Stopped," Christopher said from the stove. "His tower was attacked."

"Attacked?" Her head whipped around. "By whom?"

Christopher glanced at Colton. "Do you know?"

"No. I saw an airship above Enfield, and it dropped something onto my tower." He touched his side. The ache had dulled the farther he'd walked from Enfield, but it was still there, lingering. "The tower would have fallen, but I Stopped the town before it did."

"Oh, you poor thing." Leila touched Colton's shoulder. Finding it tangible enough, she gave him a hug. Colton, startled, returned it. It was different from the hugs Danny gave him; those were comfortable, close, sacred. This was something else, something foreign yet reassuring.

Christopher seemed more relaxed when he handed Leila her tea. "Are you sure you didn't see a name on the airship?"

"Not that I recall. And I would know. Danny taught me to read."

Christopher's eyebrows rose, and Leila hid a shaky smile behind her teacup. Colton wondered why humans had such complex reactions to the things he said.

"Well, news will probably get out tomorrow, or soon after." Christopher sighed. "And Danny's in India, on a much bigger assignment. They wouldn't send him all the way back."

"You don't think so?" Leila asked, sounding hopeful at the prospect.

"The Lead will find someone else. Probably me." Christopher drummed his fingers against the tabletop. "The office is closed now. Maybe we should wait until morning."

"For what?" Colton asked.

"I'm going to bring you to the Lead. Whomever he assigns can go with you to Enfield and help repair your tower. The authorities need to be alerted as well."

Leila glanced nervously at the kitchen clock. "Can it wait until morning?"

"It'll have to. A few hours won't change anything. Not like that airship can do any more damage, if Enfield's already Stopped."

"But what about the other towns?" Colton asked. "Or London?"

"London's had a sky watch ever since the Seven Years' War." At Colton's blank look, Christopher explained, "That's when

France tried to attack the clock tower from above. Soldiers will be on the lookout for strange airships."

Leila got up to cook dinner, but since Colton did not eat, he asked if there was somewhere he could go and rest. He would need all his strength for the following day. Mainly, he just wanted to be by himself, and the thought of his tower broken and crumbling made the ache in his side grow worse.

"You can use Danny's bedroom upstairs," Leila offered. "Will you need anything during the night?"

"I have everything I need right here." He lifted Danny's bag, and the cogs inside rattled. "But thank you."

He was on his way out of the kitchen when Christopher cleared his throat. Colton turned back, wary. But the man didn't look angry. He looked . . . sheepish.

"I'm sorry for snapping at you earlier, Colton. You gave me a scare. I know this is quite the mess right now, but I promise I'll help in any way I can." Leila, blinking back tears, put her hand on top of her husband's.

"That's all right. I know I frightened you. I'm sorry." He glanced at Leila, who gave him an encouraging nod. "Thank you, Mr. Hart."

Danny's father waved the words away. "Call me Christopher."

Colton sat on Danny's bed. He remembered this place, too. He had been weak without his central cog to help him, drifting in

and out of consciousness. Now, with his cogs and Big Ben nearby, Colton felt five times as strong—but it still wasn't enough. He bitterly examined his translucent hands.

The house was quiet. He could hear the occasional clink of plates from downstairs, and the distant rumbling of autos, but that was all.

Weary, he spread out on the bed and put his head on the pillow. It smelled so much like Danny that Colton let out a painful groan. Clock spirits did not breathe, but they could sense smells if they were close enough, in the same way their ears could hear. He hugged the pillow closer, burying his face in the fabric.

Time normally passed so quickly for him, but now it trudged torturously on. A few months ago, a little girl in Enfield had been trying to cross the muddy road after a solid week of rain. The mud had sucked so hard onto the soles of her boots that one had popped off as she staggered forward without it. Colton was that boot. Time forced him to stand still.

Colton hugged the pillow tighter and wondered what would happen if he left London. Left England. Followed Danny.

He thought of Leila at the kitchen table, putting her hand on Christopher's. A new shade of hurt slipped into the spectrum of his newfound emotions. Colton might not feel what a normal boy could, but he could still feel Danny's hand, warm and strong in his own. He could still feel Danny's lips against his own. He knew what it was to miss those things, and the loss was deep and cutting, the weight of absence heavier than anything he'd ever held.

By midnight, the house was dark and silent. Colton was wracked with pain.

He sat up and put a hand to his side. Reaching down with the other, he took his central cog from Danny's bag and pressed it to his body. It had little effect.

Still so many hours to go.

Around two o'clock, he crept out of Danny's room. He toured the house on silent feet, barely disturbing the air. He ran his fingers over the spines of the books downstairs, and picked up different kitchen utensils, wondering what they were for.

Back upstairs, he turned on the lamp in Danny's room and looked through his things; he had to distract himself somehow. In the drawers Colton found old drawings and lecture notes in Danny's slanted, blotchy handwriting. Danny liked to give his *g*'s and *y*'s long stems.

There were letters in the drawers, some yellowed with age. A few were from an uncle in Scotland. One was dated ten years ago, from a grandmother. Danny had never spoken about his relatives before. Were they dead? Colton decided he would find a sensitive way of asking later.

He found drawings of Cassie, of clocks, of classmates—mostly boys—and then found small sketches of himself. Colton standing by the window, Colton sitting on a box, Colton and Danny on the scaffolding above the clock face. The smile that spread across his face felt like an unexpected gift.

A wad of paper had been stuffed into the bottom drawer. He

pulled it out and smoothed it flat. He read the message written there, but it was not in Danny's hand.

Do not think this is finished.
You know something.
We'll be watching.

Colton froze, his smile dissolving. This did not sound normal. This sounded like . . . a threat.

He looked around, but for what, he wasn't sure. The words were sinister enough that he half-expected someone to materialize from the shadows and make a grab for him.

Someone had sent this to Danny.

Someone had attacked Enfield—where Danny lived.

Danny was in trouble.

Colton hesitated outside Danny's parents' bedroom door. He had one hand raised to knock, the other still clutching the note. It was six in the morning, and he didn't know when they normally woke. Danny often didn't roll out of bed until eight. Sometimes, he even slept until noon.

He lowered his hand. As soon as he had read the note, his first thought was that Danny needed help. Then, that his parents ought to know about it. But in the ensuing hours he'd waited for a polite time to wake them, his mind had been busy thinking of the different outcomes.

If he told Danny's father, the man would likely leave Colton with another mechanic who might bring him back to Enfield. He'd be trapped in his tower again, unable to get news.

Christopher was already wary of him. He would insist Colton go back while he tried to protect his son from this new threat.

If he *didn't* tell Christopher . . .

Colton retreated to Danny's room and decided to think some more. This was a conflict of what humans called *morals*. Colton knew the basics: killing was bad; adultery was bad; hurting someone was bad. But keeping information away from concerned parents?

By the time he heard Leila and Christopher go downstairs, he knew what he had to do.

He cautiously descended the stairs and peeked into the kitchen. They were drinking tea, and waved him inside. The atmosphere was much lighter than it had been before, but there was still an awkward twinge when he walked in.

"Did you have a good night?" Leila asked. Colton nodded. "I would offer you breakfast, but . . ."

"Thank you, anyway."

Christopher looked Colton up and down, scrutinizing his outfit. "I think it would be best if you changed into some of Danny's things. You're of a size, so they should fit. We want you to blend in as much as possible on the way to the office."

Colton hesitated, touching the note in his trouser pocket. But after a moment, all he said was, "I'll look for some."

He decided he wouldn't make a very good human.

Upstairs, he silently asked Danny's forgiveness as he rifled through his clothes. He picked out black trousers, a white shirt, and a black waistcoat. When he asked if these were decent enough, Christopher said they would do the trick.

"There's a washroom down the hall. You can use the mirror."

On the stairs, Colton saw Christopher kiss his wife goodbye before she left for work. His mind was in guilty knots as he heard their quiet murmuring until the front door closed.

Colton undressed in front of the body-length mirror in the washroom. He examined his reflection curiously, tilting his head to one side. Devoid of clothes, he looked like any other boy. He touched his arms, his chest, his lower stomach, his thighs.

He touched his navel, thinking of Danny's surprise when he'd seen it. He had touched Danny's navel, too; an inverted little hole that made Danny jerk when he'd kissed it. Colton did not jerk when he touched his own. Strange.

Another strange thing: his right side was red and ropy, like a scar that was still tender. He realized it mirrored the damage to his tower.

He couldn't do anything about it.

Dressing slowly, he began to piece together a new Colton. Christopher was right: the clothes fit him well. When he was finished, he stared at this confusing hybrid of Danny and Colton and couldn't make heads or tails of it. He brushed his hair, feeling weak.

Coming out of the washroom, he bumped right into Christopher.

"Well, look at you."

"I did. In the mirror."

Christopher smiled. "It means you look nice. The style suits you."

"Oh. Thank you." Guilt flared inside him, and Colton touched the pocket where he'd hidden the note. In his other pocket was the picture of Danny.

I'll tell him soon. I promise.

The journey to the office was even better than his walk yesterday. For one thing, they were in an auto, which meant he could stare out the window all he wanted without risking distraction or attention. Christopher said he normally took an omnibus, but with Danny gone, the auto was his to use.

"It's only been a day, but I miss him like hell," Christopher said, almost to himself.

Colton sat back in his seat. "I miss him, too." Christopher glanced at him, but neither said a word until they pulled up beside a large, gray building.

Time pulled at him, called his name. It danced across his skin like lightning, and in its threads was woven the essence of London, garlands of stone and smoke and steam. He got out of the auto and looked for Big Ben. The tower stood across the street, tall, proud, and golden. Colton waved, once again marveling at the strength it emanated.

Christopher led him through broad doors into a wide marble atrium. Colton gawked at the columns and the large chandelier above, dripping crystal amid intricate carvings on the ceiling. There was nothing near this grand in Enfield.

"Colton," Christopher called, already halfway up the stairs. Colton unwillingly followed, leaving the beautiful atrium behind.

They walked up the flight of curving stairs, passing people left and right. Colton kept his head down, but couldn't help peeking up every so often. So many mechanics in one place. He wondered if he would recognize any of them.

As it turned out, he did. A tall boy walked out of a hallway and noticed Christopher. Brandon's dark eyes went from him to Colton, perhaps expecting to see Danny. When Colton raised his head, Brandon's eyes widened and he opened his mouth, but Colton put a finger to his lips.

Later.

When they reached the Lead Mechanic's office, Colton was all nerves again. Christopher spoke to a woman sitting across the hall from the Lead's door.

"I'm sorry, but he's busy," the woman kept saying.

"This is urgent."

"Do you want to make an appointment?"

"*No,* I need to see him right bloody now!"

"Sir—"

"Just tell him Christopher Hart is here. Please."

The woman, frowning, walked to the Lead's door and cracked it open. "Sir, Christopher Hart is here to see you. I told him you're busy, but—" She paused. "Yes, sir. You can see him," she told Christopher with a disapproving sniff.

On the other side of the door, Colton finally saw the man Danny spoke of so often. The man who would cast Danny out of Enfield if he learned about their relationship. He was squat with a round belly and a broad, care-lined face. It looked as if he had taken hair from the top of his head and pasted it above his upper lip.

The Lead set aside a stack of papers, his eyes pinched. "Christopher. How am I not surprised you'd be the first to come?"

"You already know?"

"Just heard an hour ago. We're trying to keep it from the public for as long as we can, but it's only a matter of time." He flinched at his poor joke. "Of course, your son would have been the first one we called, but the lad's likely in Agra by now. I was going to ring you instead." The Lead paused. "But I'm a bit baffled as to how *you* know about Enfield."

Christopher had the same look Danny got when he was trying to figure out how to explain something, a slight channel between his eyebrows as he pressed his lips together. In the end, he must have decided that no words were necessary, and gestured to Colton instead.

The Lead had barely spared him a glance when they'd walked in, but now he had the man's full attention. Colton took off his cap and held it between his hands.

"Hello, sir," Colton said. "My name is Colton. Danny Hart is my mechanic."

The Lead blinked. He looked at the satchel filled with cogs, then back up at Colton.

"Good Lord," he said at last, the color draining from his face.

Christopher told Colton to sit down and tell the Lead about the attack, and then, when the spirit was finished, he explained their options. By the time they were done, the Lead looked positively bloodless.

"We need others to help rebuild the Enfield tower, when it

falls," Christopher said. "Because as soon as Colton starts time again, it *will* fall, and Enfield will Stop again. If we can get the building crew inside the town while it's falling, we can attempt to get Enfield to some level of functionality in the interim."

The Lead was shaking his head. "I'm not sure if that will work."

"We have to try."

"Christopher, listen. If we do restore Colton back to Enfield and time resumes, what if there's another attack? No other towns have been affected. Just Enfield."

"What do you propose we do, then?"

The Lead studied Colton. "We'll first have to find out who attacked Enfield, and why. Once we apprehend those responsible, Enfield should be safe to start again. *If* we can start it. But when the tower falls . . ."

They continued their speculation, but it was all circles, round and round until Colton felt his only choice was to block them out. He started paying attention again when he heard his name.

"Christopher, I want you to put Colton up while we investigate," the Lead said. "No one must know the spirit is here. We can't keep him at the office with so many mechanics about. Someone might catch on."

"But, sir, he's weak and getting weaker. He can't be away from Enfield for long."

The Lead eyed Colton again. "I'd like you to work with the clockwork smiths. You showed some prowess in that field when you were an apprentice. I'll talk to them, let them know the situation, and we can put our heads together to find some contraption to help the boy—er, spirit. Something to make him stronger for now."

Christopher didn't seem to like this plan, but to Colton, it sounded perfect. He needed more time to think about what he would do next.

"One thing after another," the Lead mumbled. "I hope Daniel's having a better time of it in India, away from all this commotion."

The note burned in Colton's pocket.

Danny wasn't able to get a good look at the cantonment that first night, as it was dark and he was medicated. He only remembered speaking to a man with a mustache, Daphne leading him somewhere, and lying down on a bed. This caused minor confusion come morning, and not a small amount of panic.

His boots had been pulled off for him, but his shirt and trousers were dirty and rumpled. For one heart-pounding moment he worried he had lost the timepiece his father had given him as a present years ago—maybe it had fallen while he dangled from the *Notus*—but was relieved to find it on a spindly table by his bedside. The bed frame was made of hard, twisted rope and covered with only a thin pallet, but the pillow was enormous, decorated with tassels and a yellow-threaded brocade along the edges. There was an imprint of it on his cheek.

Danny's mouth was paper dry. A tin pitcher sat on a wooden

set of drawers, along with a matching cup. He woozily poured some water and downed it all, then eagerly guzzled a second cupful. The water was warm, but he didn't mind.

In fact, the entire room was warm. He took off his waistcoat and wandered toward the window. He had to blink a few times and remind himself where he was.

The window faced the central road running through the cantonment. A few soldiers were out in the bright morning sun, huddled under the shade of a hut's thatch-roofed awning as they smoked and played cards. A green parrot preened its feathers in a hole under the awning before taking flight. In the distance, tall palms stood well above the heads of the shorter neem trees, their fronds looking like the many legs of some outlandish insect.

Instead of tents, the cantonment was comprised of long buildings and bungalows. Dirt roads had been laid by hundreds of pairs of feet in broad, yellow avenues, where tufts of grass still stubbornly grew along the edges. Autos trundled down the dusty roads, carrying supplies, soldiers, and visitors from the city.

It wasn't at all what Danny had expected. Though he had never been in a military barracks before, he had assumed it would look much like a camp from Alexander the Great's army. But this was a far cry from Macedonia.

England had become a distant dream.

A knock sounded at the door and Daphne peeked inside. Her long hair was tied in a braid that slipped over her shoulder.

"Good, you're up. We have a meeting with the major soon."

"Major?"

"Major Dryden. From the notes?"

Danny picked through his muddled brain and realized, yes, he had read that name in the file. Major Dryden was currently in charge of the soldiers stationed at the Agra cantonment, and would be supervising them during their stay.

"You'll need to change," she noted, taking in his wrinkled shirt.

"Into what, may I ask?"

Daphne pointed at the corner behind him, where his trunk had magically appeared.

"How—?"

"Some of the soldiers fetched our things from the airship."

Danny shivered at the word *airship*. "The captain and the others . . . Did everyone get off safely?"

She nodded. "There's going to be an inquiry. At least, that's what I gathered from all the yelling I overheard last night. The officers are livid an unregistered airship got by them. They have no clue who attacked the *Notus*."

Danny pressed his lips into a tight line as he kneeled and unlatched his trunk. Right on top of his clothes and shaving gear was the folded-up parchment that held Colton's likeness. He caressed the edge of the paper, then dug around until the edge of the little cog scraped his fingers. Breathing a sigh of relief, he drew it out.

"Why did that man want to shoot you?" Daphne wondered aloud. Danny looked over his shoulder at her. Today, she was dressed in tan trousers and a sleeveless blue bodice. A couple beads of sweat showed on her high, smooth forehead. "You didn't do anything to him. Did you?"

"Except for falling out the hole he blasted into our airship, no."

"Maybe he knew you were a clock mechanic. Maybe he wanted to prevent us from reaching Agra and finding out what's going on here."

Danny grimaced and dug out fresh clothes. "Perhaps. Any chance of food?"

"Change first, then I'll show you where to go. I haven't eaten yet either."

"You didn't have to wait for me."

Daphne shrugged. "I wasn't hungry."

She stepped outside while he dressed. He tucked his shirt in, then caught a glimpse of himself in the mirror. There were deep circles under his eyes, and his hair was beyond fixing without a proper bath. He tried his best to flatten it by dipping his fingers into the pitcher and dragging them through his hair, but stubborn dark locks popped up anyway. He sighed and left with his timepiece in hand.

Outside, the heat descended heavily onto his shoulders and the top of his head. There was an oil or cream the soldiers used to ward off sunburn. He would need to get ahold of some if he didn't want to end up red as a lobster by noon. Just as pronounced as the heat was the smell, an unexpected mix of woodsmoke, damp humidity, and something both musky and floral.

Wooden benches lined the mess hall, but there were a few

open areas with burgundy rugs on the floor and nothing else. Large wooden slats hung from the ceiling, attached to ropes. Their existence baffled him. Some sort of decoration?

Two Indian men were making porridge and heating round, flat bread over an iron stove. They wore red cloth around their heads, and were dressed in simple tunics and loose trousers. Danny had seen a few Indians in London, but there had been something vaguely Europeanized about them. These men were as British as a flamingo.

In this country, Danny realized, he was in the minority. These people would outnumber him a hundred thousand to one.

They probably didn't speak any English. Danny was trying to remember how to say *two* in Urdu, the hybrid language of the Indian army, when Daphne did it for him. The servants ladled out two bowls of porridge, two cups of steaming tea, and two rolled-up pieces of bread for each of them.

"Shukria," Daphne said, and they nodded politely. As she and Danny meandered toward a table, she asked, "Didn't you practice?"

"I only had a few days," he mumbled. "I'm horrible with languages. Remind me to speak French when you're feeling down, I'll have you in stitches."

"You know the basics, don't you?"

She forced him to practice as they ate. The porridge was filling, though it had a nutty spice that he couldn't name. Danny found the flatbread even stranger. They were called chapatis, and were apparently very popular in northern Indian cuisine. Danny preferred thicker bread. With honey. Or cheese.

My kingdom for a piece of toast with jam.

The tea, however, was the strangest thing of all. It was a milky, spicy concoction that landed wrong on his palate.

"What on earth is this?" he sputtered.

"Chai," Daphne informed him. "They have British stock, too, but I'm told that chai is the staple here. Some of the officers have taken to it as well."

It was no English breakfast, but it would have to do.

A private poked his head into the mess, spotting them at once. Danny and Daphne, without uniforms, couldn't help but stand out. "Are you the mechanics? Major Dryden is ready to see you."

Danny knocked back the rest of the chai—spices or no, tea was tea—and followed Daphne back into the glaring sunshine.

"Beggin' your pardon, but your airship caused quite a stir yesterday," the private said. He was young and stocky with a growth of blond stubble on his jaw. The Indian sun had long since toasted his skin to a healthy tan.

"It was . . . definitely a stir," Daphne said when Danny didn't offer comment.

"Good thing they found a clear place for the ship to crash. Would be a shame to have the local farms destroyed."

He showed them to a building with a slanted roof and windows with wooden shutters. They thanked him and walked inside, where a long table sat in the middle of the receiving room surrounded by chairs. Three men stood at the head of it, speaking in low tones. One caught sight of them and cleared his throat.

"Mr. Hart and Miss Richards, welcome. Please sit. May we offer you anything? Tea? Water? Nuts?"

"No, thank you," Daphne said. "We've only just had breakfast."

"Excellent. Sit, sit." The man gestured to the table and they settled into seats beside each other. The two other officers sat opposite them, while the man in charge took his place at the head of the table. He was the one Danny had seen the previous night—tall, broad-shouldered, with a waxed brown mustache and slicked-back hair. Major Dryden, then. The officers all wore the olive green uniform Danny had seen on the soldiers aboard the *Notus*, but their medals and decorations varied according to their rank.

"No doubt you're exhausted after that affair with the airship," Dryden said. "Nasty business. We have people investigating as we speak. However, that's secondary to the real issue at hand."

"The bombings," Daphne said.

"Exactly so. We have some of our own mechanics looking into it, but Indian mechanics are, ah . . ." He smoothed his mustache with thick fingers. "Shall we say it's a different organization?"

Danny resisted the urge to look at Daphne, but he could feel her stiffen at his side. The public didn't know much about clock mechanics in other countries, though he'd heard the Americans had a union system similar to England's. Daphne had been part of a committee to promote foreign exchanges, allowing mechanics and apprentices to travel to places like China to gain more experience. She had been eager to launch the exchange program for India, but that was before the bombings around London happened last year.

"We do depend on quite a few of the Indian mechanics, though," a blond officer interjected.

"Ah, where are my manners? Mr. Hart, Miss Richards, this is Lieutenant Crosby and Captain Harris." The two officers inclined their heads. Crosby was dark-haired, his skin deeply tanned, while Harris was fair and freckled.

"We actually have a few clock mechanics living in the city," Harris added.

"Yes," Dryden said, "so you'll have some help. It's a different world here, you know. You'll need a guide."

Crosby frowned. "Especially for mechanics so young. How old are the two of you, anyway?"

"Eighteen," said Danny, followed by Daphne's "Nineteen."

Crosby snorted. "Children! What's the Lead Mechanic doing, sending children to India along with crashing airships and mutineers?"

"That's enough, Lieutenant," Dryden said, but not angrily. They must have had this argument before.

"They're not children at all." Captain Harris awarded them a smile. He looked to be in his late twenties, and his eyes were a warm, earthy brown. "I've heard about you, Mr. Hart. You helped bag that terrorist last year. The one bombing the towers around London."

Danny reacted several ways at once: startled that this man

knew of him; flattered by the praise; embarrassed by the same; and despondent at hearing Matthias referred to as a terrorist. Though, in fairness, he supposed that's what he was.

"I don't care how many terrorists he's bagged," Crosby barked. "London's one thing, but India's quite another. Major, you don't plan to send them up to Delhi, do you?"

Dryden harrumphed. "No, of course not." He turned to Danny and Daphne. "We believe that the Delhi clock tower may be in danger during Her Majesty's coronation."

"When she's named Queen-Empress of India, you mean?" Daphne asked. "At New Year's?"

"It may be the perfect distraction to attack the Delhi tower. We hope to prevent this from happening, so it's imperative the clock mechanics figure out what's going on before then." The major fanned his face and glanced toward the back of the room. "It's too hot in here. Punkah wallah!"

An Indian servant Danny had not seen until now moved to the far wall, where a rope was hanging. When the man pulled on the rope, a wooden slat like the ones Danny had seen in the mess began to flap on the ceiling. It stirred the air and sent down a much needed breeze. Daphne somberly watched the servant as he worked.

"Much better. Now, on to business. The most recent attack occurred in Khurja, to the north. I believe you two should see the wreckage. It might offer some clues."

The door opened behind them, and the major rose from his

seat. "As I said, you'll have another mechanic as a guide. Here he is now."

Danny and Daphne turned in their chairs, but were startled when *he* turned out to be *she*. The Indian girl was short yet shapely under a long, green tunic with slits on either side and a V-neck collar. Her trousers were baggy but cinched at her ankles, her black hair tied into a braid that hung halfway down her back.

"Ah, where is Kamir?" Dryden asked her.

"He's unable to come," the girl replied, her English inflected with an Indian accent. She roamed dark eyes over the two British mechanics. "He's sick in bed. I am filling in for him."

Crosby coughed into his fist. "I don't think—"

Dryden waved him off. "Very well. Everyone, this is Miss Meena Kapoor. Miss Kapoor, may I introduce Daniel Hart and Daphne Richards? They flew in from London last night and are very eager to see Khurja."

"I'll take them today, if they wish." She waited for a response, and they both tripped over the words.

"Oh, that's—"

"If it's not a bother—"

"All right."

Meena raised a sleek eyebrow. Danny could tell she was enjoying this. The officers looked uncomfortable, with the exception of Harris, who was simply amused.

"I'll make arrangements," Meena said over her shoulder, turning to leave.

When she was gone, Crosby scoffed. "Sir, shouldn't we find someone else? Remember that there have been riots. Kamir was qualified to go with them, and he's experienced."

"Miss Kapoor is also experienced," Dryden said.

"She's just a girl!"

"That's enough, Lieutenant." The Major turned to Danny and Daphne. "Are you two comfortable with the arrangements?"

They stole a look at each other, then nodded.

"Then that settles it. Miss Kapoor will take you to Khurja. Please make any necessary notes and report back to me this evening."

W hat's a punkah wallah?" Danny asked once they'd left the building.

"I'm not sure."

"You mean the great Daphne Richards doesn't know something? I'm shocked."

Before Daphne could retort, a familiar voice said, "It means rope puller."

Meena stood off to the side, a small smile on her face. She was shorter than both of them by nearly a foot.

"Oh." Danny scratched the back of his neck, which, despite the punkah wallah, was tickling with sweat. Danny again felt an alarming ignorance in this place. This was a land he had only read about in the safety of his home. There was so much he didn't know.

Looking closer, Danny noticed a small red dot in the very center of Meena's forehead. Danny knew about this, at least; he had read about it in one of his books, in a section on the Hindu religion. Some Indian women wore these vermilion marks to show that they were married, or simply for religious purpose. Something about opening chakras.

"I've arranged for my brother to take us to Khurja," Meena continued, leading them away.

"Is your brother a soldier?" Daphne asked.

"He is not a sepoy, but often takes commissions from the army."

Danny could see more of the city when they left the low stone enclosure of the cantonment. The Taj Mahal presided over Agra, resplendent in the late morning sun. Meena followed his gaze.

"I will show you the city, if you like. Later."

"We would appreciate that very much," Daphne said.

Meena looked her up and down. "There are not many women around here. The wives of the soldiers don't dress as you do."

"I didn't bring any dresses or skirts, if that's what you mean."

"All the same to me." Meena slyly glanced at Danny. "But this one might not like you attracting so much attention."

Danny coughed. "We're not *together*."

"I'm not exactly his type," Daphne drawled. The underlying meaning was transparent to Danny, but seemed lost on Meena, who hummed in surprise.

"So sorry. I just assumed."

For some reason, Danny felt a wave of loneliness wash over

him. He wished he had brought along Colton's picture. Even if he couldn't look at it in public, having it in his pocket would have given some comfort.

When he saw what waited for them down the road, Danny skidded to a halt. "No," he said. "No, no, no."

"What's the matter?" Meena asked.

Daphne looked at the small, gray aircraft sitting on a crude tarmac. "Danny's not good with heights, I'm afraid. Especially after the incident yesterday."

"It's the fastest way to Khurja. Driving would take more time, and the major wants us back by sundown." Meena studied Danny, curiosity and exasperation dancing in her eyes. "It will be a short trip, Daniel Hart."

"Danny," he mumbled.

"Then, Danny, come and meet my brother. He will show you what a good pilot he is."

Danny didn't have any qualms about her brother's abilities. It was the possibility of falling from a very great height that he took issue with.

The aircraft was larger than a single-pilot plane, but smaller than the carrier they had used to escape the *Notus*. There were two seats in the cockpit and four seats behind, fitted along the sides, plus a little room for cargo. The wings were pointed up at the ends, with propellers positioned underneath. Danny looked for the familiar symbol of Caelum and caught no sight of it. Instead, along the side of the hull, Devanagari letters had been painted in red:

चांदी बाज़

A young Indian man stood leaning against the plane, grinning as they approached. He was about Daphne's height, half an inch taller than Danny. His black hair had been combed neatly to his ears, and his dark, full eyebrows rose slightly over clever brown eyes. He was dressed in a tan jumpsuit with mud-splattered boots and aviator goggles hanging around his neck.

He greeted his sister in Hindi. She replied with something that was much longer than *hello*. He nodded in response, but gave no hint of whatever Meena was gossiping to him about.

"This is Akash, my brother," Meena said. "As I said, he is not a soldier, but uses his plane for small missions."

"My own plane, too. Not a gift from the army." Akash patted the hull fondly. His words were clear and low, with a slight burr on his *d*'s and *r*'s.

"Akash, this is Daniel—I'm sorry, Danny—Hart, and Daphne Richards."

"Aha. I read those names on the luggage I found on the airship." Akash stuck out his hand, a startlingly British gesture. Danny was the first to shake the boy's hand, yet with Daphne, Akash raised the backs of her fingers to his lips. She turned bright scarlet.

"What are you doing?" she demanded.

"You are a lady. I cannot shake a lady's hand, Miss Richards."

"Please just call me Daphne." She tugged her hand back and seemed to not know what to do with it.

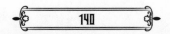

Meena, struggling not to smile, lightly kicked her brother's shin. "Get in and fly us to Khurja."

"Er, wait." Danny held up his hands. "Are you sure I can't take an auto? Because, really, it would be no bother."

"Don't worry, Mr. Hart." Akash gestured to the red lettering above his head. "The *Silver Hawk* has never failed me. We'll be there in an hour, and it will be a smooth ride."

"It'll be fine, Danny," Daphne whispered. But he heard a small tremor in her voice. The memory of the *Notus* had left her nervous, too.

Danny took a deep breath and nodded.

Meena clapped her hands once. "No more dawdling! Chalo."

Akash snapped to attention. "Haan!" He climbed the ladder, and Meena followed behind, advising the others to mind their heads.

Once in the aircraft, Akash shut the door and jumped into the pilot's seat. "Strap yourselves in, please. No standing until I say it's safe."

Danny's hands shook too badly to buckle his harness, so Daphne had to do the fastening for him. Embarrassed, he sat back and closed his eyes. The engine roared to life and the propellers whirred, rattling the metal hull all around them. The plane took off with a sudden lurch that turned Danny's stomach into a fitful balloon. He tried to hide a moan under the noise.

"Is he all right?" Meena asked from the seat across from him.

Daphne wormed her fingers into Danny's sweaty grip. "It's all right, Danny. Imagine yourself somewhere else. Think of Enfield."

As the *Silver Hawk* leveled out, that's exactly what he did. He imagined himself in Colton Tower, running his fingers through Colton's soft hair. His breathing calmed, but he still kept his eyes shut.

Daphne held his hand the entire way. He should have been surprised by the gesture, but he wasn't. He focused on the illusion of Enfield until the plane came to a jerky landing an hour later.

"Khurja," Akash announced.

They climbed out of the plane—Danny very slowly—and took a moment to stretch. The foliage was wild and jungle-like here, thick with peepal trees, the grass still clinging to dew around the landing circle. Insects droned among the ferns and Danny had to wave away a few curious flies.

Meena had told them during the flight that Khurja was a small city situated in a swampy land south of Delhi. Danny smelled the malodorous gasses of the swamps nearby and coughed into his sleeve. Inside the city, the odor faded a little, replaced by a musky scent that slapped his senses awake.

A rickshaw rattled by, the driver staring at them as he passed. But Danny and Daphne found their attention wandering from detail to detail: the water buffalo relaxing in the middle of the street, or the brown monkeys that raced across rooftops where patties made from what smelled like cow dung had been stacked to later use as fuel.

"Wow," Daphne said. Wonder sparked in her eyes, but Danny caught a hint of the same trepidation that rode his shoulders.

Meena and Akash led them past short buildings and huts,

toward a widespread bazaar. Wooden stalls with canvas tarps had been erected where merchants sold dates, nuts, cloths, and jewelry. Boxes brimmed with brightly colored powders and spices, a sunset spectrum of yellows and oranges and reds. Danny inhaled the spices in the air as they passed by and stifled a sneeze.

The group didn't go without notice. Men and women gawked at the two British mechanics. Wide-eyed children scampered up to them and held out their hands, begging in their native language. Danny and Daphne walked close together, arms brushing. All these people watching them was the definition of unnerving. Danny couldn't imagine being an Indian in London. It must feel exactly like this: exposing and oddly terrifying.

"They hate us," Daphne whispered.

"They don't even know us."

"Doesn't matter. We're British." There was a bitter edge to her words, as if she wished she could claim otherwise.

Away from the bazaar, they wandered down narrower streets, many of them crooked. The buildings grew taller, but less sturdy. Trash littered the ground and grubby urchins scuttled down alleyways. They walked by an old man in a lean-to who was naked save for a tattered loincloth, his ribs pressed sharply against his skin, his white beard grown nearly to his chest. Daphne had to avert her eyes.

The books hadn't described this India.

When they walked through another bazaar, Danny asked how far away the clock tower was.

"Not far," Meena said, glancing over her shoulder. "Why? Do you want to stop and catch your breath?"

"Pick out a nice pot?" Akash joked, nodding to the admittedly large number of stalls selling ceramics. "Khurja's known for its pottery, you know. The potters' families were run out of Delhi and they settled here. You won't find anything like that in Britain."

"Maybe later," Daphne said.

Meena and Akash shared a look, then continued on their way. Danny heard them mumble something in Hindi. Frustrated that he couldn't understand, he kept his eyes trained forward until they reached a couple of guards.

Meena spoke to them, handing over a message from Major Dryden. While she was occupied, Akash explained to Danny and Daphne, "There was a small riot shortly before the explosion, otherwise you wouldn't see guards here."

"I heard there was a riot just before the bombing in Rath, too," Daphne said. "Do you know what sparked it?"

Akash, hands in his pockets, shrugged. "A protest? Shortage of water? Someone spat in someone's dal? It's hard to say."

The guards gave clearance to approach the wreckage site, and Meena nodded the others over. When Danny laid eyes on it, he curled his hands into fists. Daphne covered her mouth in shock.

The clock tower had stood in a circular area, several feet away from any homes or buildings. All that was left was a large mound of brick, clay, limestone, and wood. A tremor spread across Danny's chest, the frayed edges of a memory teasing his mind—ash and metal and blood. He focused on breathing, in and out, as if that could expel the panic from his lungs.

When the worst of it had passed, Danny realized he could feel something in the circular clearing, a humming in the air. He waved a hand through it, concentrating. The air felt . . . sharper. Crisp.

Time was here. Second by second, slipping from this moment to the next, never-ending. The hairs on his arms stood on end.

"My God," Daphne murmured. She approached the wreckage, carefully lifting the end of a broken beam. "No one has cleared this yet?"

Meena shook her head. "Everyone is afraid to. Even the ghadi wallahs."

"The what?"

"Clock mechanics, as the British say."

Daphne carefully replaced the piece of wood. "Why are they afraid to move the debris?"

"We don't know if time will Stop. When the tower fell, a great feeling passed over Khurja, and time resumed as if nothing happened. If the pieces of the tower remain here, maybe time will go on as usual. If removed . . . we don't know."

Danny kneeled before the mound and touched a loose piece of brick. Nothing happened. He felt no connection, no spark, nothing. But the air remained sharp and sensitive on his skin. He took out his timepiece and saw that everything was normal. Carefully, he reached for the time fibers around him and received another nasty shock.

Time threads were supposed to be a tapestry, weaving in and out of each other in precise, predictable patterns.

Here, they were twisted up like twine. Disorderly. Complex.

Danny looked around and found an even bigger piece of brick. Hefting it, he bore down on the smaller piece so hard it broke. Meena gasped and Daphne winced. When time didn't jump or shudder, they sighed.

"I have no idea what to make of it. What about the cogs and gears?" Danny asked Meena.

"They're in the pile. A few may have been stolen by now."

He didn't want to think about the implications of that. "No one's seen anything strange, have they?"

"Like what?"

Danny met Daphne's gaze, a single thought passing between them: What had happened to the spirit of the tower?

"Like pieces moving on their own, or—"

Meena said something in rapid-fire Hindi. "I should think not!"

"And no one was *in* the tower when it fell?"

"No, not that anyone recalls."

Danny studied the ruins, his chest tightening. Whatever spirit had resided here in the Khurja tower was likely dead. He tried to swallow past the tightness in his throat and failed.

"And no one saw anything strange around the tower when it fell?" Daphne asked.

"There was one thing, but it's silly. Right after it fell, the ghadi wallahs who came to inspect the damage saw that the clearing around the tower was wet." She traced the circle with a finger through the air. "They said it was like someone had poured water around the tower before destroying it."

"Did anyone report the same thing about Rath?" Danny asked.

"Yes, I believe so."

Danny studied the outer ring of the tower. Sunlight stung the back of his neck as he bent to inspect the ground, but there was nothing more to see. Just pebbles, dirt, and frighteningly large ants.

Still, there was something he couldn't quite place. That sharp feeling, but intensified. It wasn't the jagged sensation of time malfunctioning, but a sweeter ache, like the experience of savoring something you've craved for longer than you can remember. The gasp of satisfaction after a drink of water in the desert.

"You feel it, too," he said when Daphne moved toward him.

"What is it? I've never felt such a thing."

"Neither have I. Whatever it is, it's fading."

"If it fades, do you think time will Stop?"

Danny thought about it, then shook his head. "No. Time is stable here. More stable than it would be with a clock tower." He bit his thumb. He couldn't stop thinking about the spirit of the tower, and where they had gone.

The mechanics jotted down notes and theories in the journal Daphne had brought, then sat in the shade as Meena and Akash bought a lunch consisting of buttered flatbread, spiced lamb, and thick buffalo milk.

"Do you have any theories?" Daphne asked Meena as they walked back through the bazaars.

The girl fiddled with her long braid. "There are people saying it's the work of the gods. Our gods," she clarified. "That maybe Lord Vishnu has decided to free us of one oppression, at least." She shot them a nervous look. "Their words, not mine."

Danny remembered how he'd searched for Caelum's symbol on Akash's plane, but couldn't find it. "Do you have stories of the Gaian gods here?" When Meena and Akash gave him confused looks, he told them the story of the elemental gods: Terra, Caelum, Oceana, Aetas, and their creator, Chronos.

"You mean the vasus," Meena said.

"The . . . I'm sorry, the what?"

"The ashta vasus, attendant deities of Indra. Hindu gods of the elements. We have eight, but it sounds as if the British only have five. Let's see . . . Prithvi for earth, Varuna for water, Vāyu for air, Agni for fire." She counted them off on her fingers. "But here, we consider Agni more than fire. Fire is something we need to live, and what else do we need to live? Time."

"So here, Aetas is also Agni," Daphne said.

"Yes. Some believe he is the one causing mischief, but I am not so sure."

"Seems like everyone has a different theory," Danny said. "It's going to be difficult, whittling it down to one."

"Do you think any other cities are in danger?" Daphne asked Meena.

"Yes," she said gravely. "Or else why stop at two?"

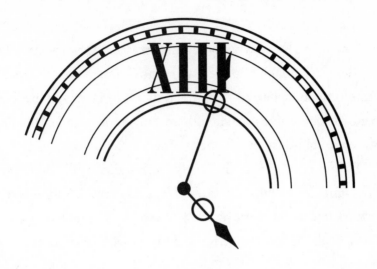

Much to the alarm of its pilot, Danny nearly threw up in the *Silver Hawk* on their way back to Agra to discuss their findings with Major Dryden. The major seemed disappointed, but they all agreed that this would be a difficult problem to solve. The other mechanics weren't having any luck either.

Every morning for the next week, Danny and Daphne woke with the reveille and traded theories until their brains stalled. Meena sometimes joined them, contributing her own ideas. It was the work of humans, a god, a reincarnated fish. They usually parted in worse spirits than when they met.

At the end of the week, the rain came. It fell intensely for hours then tapered away, only to return later in full force. While Danny was glad for the dip in temperature, he couldn't leave his bungalow without being soaked within seconds. Just looking out the window made him feel wet.

The palms swayed as the monsoon swept through Agra for another week, making soldiers and sepoys dash across the roads. Some actually appeared to enjoy it, much to Danny's bewilderment. He sometimes watched them run about outside, laughing as they roughhoused with one another.

Danny noticed that the British and Indian soldiers did not mix company voluntarily. In fact, when he and Daphne spoke with Meena or ate with her and Akash in the mess, they drew stares. Still, the more time he spent time with the two of them, the more Danny grew to like Meena's dry humor and Akash's stories about growing up in India.

One day the siblings came to his door. They held well-loved cricket bats and wore identical smiles.

"What's all this?" Danny asked.

"Come with us and you'll see."

They recruited Daphne from her hut before setting off for the field behind the cantonment where the men usually gathered to play field hockey. The grass was dark and moist, the ground swollen from this morning's rain. Dark gray clouds above promised more.

"Let's see how good an Englishman and Englishwoman are at cricket," Akash said.

"What?" Danny and Daphne asked at the same time.

"We've had no one to play with in a long time," Meena explained. "You know how, don't you?"

Danny recalled nursery school outings to the cricket field,

where the other boys had poked Danny with their bats and hit him with the cricket ball on purpose. "I know how," he muttered.

"We won't believe you until we see with our own eyes." Akash tossed Daphne the ball, and she caught it without fumbling.

"Erm," Danny said, looking upward, "not to put a damper on your enthusiasm, but isn't it going to rain soon?"

"Do the British melt when they get wet?" Meena asked. Akash sniggered.

Daphne arched an eyebrow and nodded at Danny. "All right, we'll play. What have we to lose?"

Her expression conveyed what Danny was already thinking: that this was the perfect opportunity to get to know their new guides better. If they were going to figure out what was happening to the Indian towers, they'd need to work as a team.

Much to Danny's surprise, Daphne turned out to be a solid thrower, but Akash was quite the batter. Meena wasn't as proficient as her brother, but Danny was a much sloppier bowler than Daphne, so he accidentally allowed Meena her fifth inning before he was able to get her out.

As Daphne took to bat, it finally began to rain. Danny watched as she cracked the wood against the ball and scored two—four— seven innings. When Akash got her out, she noticed Danny's expression. "Used to play with the neighbor boy all the time," she said.

"I am impressed, Miss Richards," Akash said, warming up his arm for throwing. "Now let's see if Mr. Hart can compare."

If his nursery school days were anything to go by, Danny would be out in the first inning. Still, he thumped the bat against the soles of his boots as the rain fell harder, flattening his hair and soaking through his shirt. Akash shook his head to clear his own waterlogged hair from his face.

Akash took his position, and Danny readied the bat. The ball flew out of Akash's hand—

Whack. Danny smacked it far into the field and rushed to the other side, grinning victoriously. But just as he was about to score, he lost his footing, slipped, and fell face-first in the mud.

He rose, sputtering and cursing, to the sound of laughter. He shook his hands, dislodging bits of muddy grass. The rain did little to cool his burning cheeks.

Daphne recovered first and made to help him up. "Sorry, Danny. But you ought to see your face."

Danny took her hand—and tugged. She yelped and fell into the mud beside him, splattering him all over again.

"Daniel Hart!" But he was laughing too hard to hear, and she couldn't help a rueful laugh of her own. They tried to get up and slipped again. When Akash and Meena came to help, a conspiratorial look passed between Danny and Daphne. They each grabbed a hand and pulled the siblings down with them.

"Foul!" Akash yelled as he crashed into the mud. "The British are sore losers!"

"At least we don't melt," Danny said, and threw a lump of mud at Meena. She squealed and hurled one back.

They played in the field like children until Lieutenant Crosby yelled at them to get to the baths immediately before they took ill. "What do you think this is, a school yard? Remember your stations!"

They hung their heads and made for the baths, but quick glances around revealed that they all wore the same small smile.

"Danny," Meena asked one night as they were playing bridge, "may we ask how you came by your scar?"

Danny looked up. Meena had tilted her head forward slightly, and Akash was watching over his cards.

"It's not really a secret," he said. "I was in a clock tower when it . . . um, exploded. The gears . . ." He mimed something flying through the air, and Daphne shuddered.

Meena looked aghast. "The tower fell?"

"No, only the clockwork was harmed. Well, and my chin." He touched the hard, white line. "I managed to reattach everything, though, and get time started again."

It was easier to talk about the accident now, a year later and half a world away, but Danny couldn't stop the dread that crept up his spine, or the pulse of heat in his stomach. He still remembered how vibrant a red his blood had been, a flash of crimson against a world gone black and white. The flicker of time all around him like a struggling heartbeat. Suddenly, he could feel his own heartbeat in the palms of his hands, twin rhythms of panic.

"Why did the clockwork explode?" Akash asked.

Danny didn't understand him at first, too wrapped up in the memory. He shook his head to clear it and tried not to look at Daphne, who was suddenly fascinated by her bridge hand. "A man was targeting towers, and I happened to be in one at the wrong time."

"Was this the terrorist I heard rumor of?" Meena asked. "The one in London?"

Again with that word. "Yes."

"Why did he do it? Wasn't he a clock mechanic, too?"

Is, Danny wanted to correct them. "He lost sight of what was right," he said to his cards. "He was so preoccupied with what he wanted that he didn't think of anyone else."

A short silence passed. Then Akash murmured, "I wonder if he could be working with the bombers here."

Why did everyone have to jump to that conclusion? Yes, Matthias was a terrorist, but all of that was behind them. Now others were trailing in his footsteps, and doing a much better job of it.

The question, of course, was why.

"Well, I happen to like it—the scar," Akash said. "It adds a bit of mystery. Daring."

Daphne snorted, and that was the end of that.

The only person in the cantonment who didn't seem confused by the new friendship between the four of them was Captain Harris.

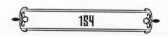

He actually passed time with the Indians beyond his requisite handing out of orders, and spoke their language with the ease of one who was born there. He had been stationed in India for five years already, and said he didn't miss England very often.

"Victoria's going to be named Empress in a couple months," Harris said one night as they drank hot milk before bed. "Everyone's excited about it, even the Indians. Well, the rajas are, anyway. The princes love any excuse to dress up and parade about."

Meena rolled her eyes in agreement.

"Are you going to the ceremony?" Danny asked. "We heard there might be an attack on the Delhi tower."

"There'll be a guard around the tower for certain, but I won't be part of it. And the Queen won't actually be there, of course."

"Who *will* be there?"

"The viceroy will be attending as Victoria's representative."

Akash's eyes narrowed. "Viceroy Lytton?"

"That's him. Not a popular fellow, I'll admit."

"Why would he be?" Akash made a dismissive gesture with his hand. "He is incompetent, a fool. He prefers poetry and gold over the running of this country. No wonder they call this the Black Raj."

The atmosphere at the table suddenly grew tense, the silence that fell after Akash's words taut and accusing. Danny exchanged a worried glance with Daphne.

But Harris deftly changed the subject. "We're all serving Queen and country, in the end. It's a decent living. They even pay me more for acting as a translator. Did you know this country has twenty-three languages? I only know Hindi and Urdu, but maybe I'll make my way to the rest one day."

"Too bad they don't pay for being a sharpshooter," Meena joked. Harris looked down at the table with a pleased smile.

"Are you good with a gun, Captain?" Daphne asked.

"He's the best," Akash said. "I've seen him at the range behind the cantonment. You should show them, Captain."

Danny wondered how to politely decline the demonstration, but he liked Harris, so he mumbled something about being eager to see it.

Indian vendors frequented the cantonment, including one who walked around with live animals dangling from a bamboo stick he perched across his shoulder. He sold his wares to the soldiers who had greyhounds that needed exercising, or those who were in need of live targets for shooting practice. Danny worried that Harris would use one of these creatures to show off his skills. A couple of days later, when he saw the stationary target situated at the far end of the range, he breathed a sigh of relief.

Akash was out running an errand, but the other three ambled toward the range. Danny longed to go back to his notes—he was working out a complex theory about the rain's effect on the clock towers—but Daphne's interest and Meena's wariness made him stay put. He hated to admit it, but he was a bit curious, too.

The rains held off in the mid-afternoon hours as Harris cleaned and prepared his rifle. It looked new, and dangerously close to the models Danny had seen being made in the Enfield factory.

A sepoy stood at Harris's side, holding the captain's rifle

equipment. His dark eyes were keen as he studied the three of them. Danny noticed the man's own rifle was an older, clunkier model than Harris's. Danny had read that ever since the rebellion, the Indian soldiers weren't allowed to have the newest guns.

"Partha," Harris said, addressing the sepoy, "would you mind moving the target farther away?"

Partha adjusted the wooden stand. A crude canvas target was stretched across it, painted with five scattered red dots.

"Good, thank you." Harris waited for the sepoy to return and gave him a handsome smile. Cocking the rifle, he brought it up to his shoulder. He took a deep, steadying breath, then fired five shots one right after the other.

The three mechanics jumped at the report. Partha brought the target back and Danny's breath caught. Every point had a bullet neatly blown through it.

It was one thing, Danny thought, to see the rifles being assembled in the factory back at Enfield. It was quite another to see them in action.

To see their full, deadly potential.

"Well done, Captain," Daphne said. Even Meena looked impressed.

Harris ruffled his hair, then smoothed it back down again. "Thank you."

The group heard a scoff behind them. Lieutenant Crosby had been watching the exercise as well, arms crossed over his chest.

"If you want a real demonstration, use a moving target," Crosby said.

"Would you care to give us your own demonstration, sir?" Harris asked. Partha, who had been cleaning and loading the rifle, shifted so that he stood a little closer to Harris, eyeing the lieutenant with thinly veiled dislike.

Crosby snapped his fingers at the animal vendor close by. The Indian man hopped forward and presented his struggling wares for Crosby's perusal. The lieutenant chose a particularly frazzled hare, which dangled by its foot.

"Gun," he ordered Harris. The captain handed over his rifle without complaint, but Danny caught the gleam of indignation in his eyes.

Crosby primed the gun, then nodded to the Indian vendor. He released the hare, who streaked across the field in a blur of gray.

A clear shot rang out, and this time everybody jumped. Everyone except Harris, who looked on coolly. Crosby handed back his rifle, the barrel faintly smoking.

"There you are," the lieutenant said. They all looked at the small form of the hare's body, now lying motionless. Daphne frowned and Meena turned completely away. Danny continued to watch the silent battle between Harris and Crosby until the latter turned and strolled away, hands in his pockets.

The monsoon let up a few days later, though the sky was still churning with gray clouds when Meena offered to finally make good on her promise to show them the city.

"We need a break from all this thinking," she said. "Also, there will be fewer people after the rains."

Danny was fairly certain she took this precaution because of the stares they had drawn in Khurja. Thinking back to how exposed he'd felt, he silently thanked her.

They asked for an auto to take into the city, as it was much too far to walk and—mercifully, in Danny's opinion—too short a journey to take Akash's plane. Danny stared out the window as the plain dissolved into buildings, from women walking with baskets and children on their hips to men carrying wood and goats in their arms.

Outside the safety of the cantonment, however, Danny felt his shoulders grow tense. He couldn't help but wonder about the man on the *Notus*, whom they still hadn't identified. Was he was still out there, plotting another attack?

More questions that couldn't be answered.

The Taj Mahal presided over a garden divided into four quadrants with a cross-shaped pond intersecting them, which Meena called a charbagh. Danny looked at the vast building, awed and struggling to comprehend how human beings could create something so vast and beautiful.

"Shah Jahan was a Mughal emperor who was married to a Persian princess," Meena said. "They were deeply in love and had many children. But the princess died in childbirth. Before she passed, she ordered the emperor to build a monument symbolizing their love. Shah Jahan carried so much grief that he ordered this tomb be built in honor of his beloved wife." She released a wistful little sigh. "The graves of the emperor and his wife are underground, but inside the Taj is the decorative tomb."

"Wait, this is a *tomb*?" Danny interrupted. "I thought it was a palace."

Akash laughed. "Too small for a palace, but too large for a tomb, in my opinion."

"No tomb would be big enough to contain the emperor's grief," Meena said, a slight edge in her voice. "Show some respect for the dead."

Properly chastised, they followed her to the central building.

A latticework fence around the tombs was covered with gold and gems that formed twisting vines and flowers. The tombs themselves, however, were plain. Meena explained that it was Muslim tradition not to decorate graves more than necessary.

Danny wished he could show this to Colton. That there was a way to shrink it down, put it in his pocket, and share it as he had shared so many curios with him. The only way to bring the world to Enfield.

Although the Taj was Muslim in design, there were marble Om inlays carved onto the walls. Danny touched one and thought of the emperor's despair. The maddening, aching loss that had driven him to fill a tomb with jewels and light and air. And grief. He could feel it here, almost as he could feel time passing in Khurja. Something sharp and powerful. Constant. But unlike the fulfilling sensation at Khurja, this was an ache—the sensation of something ripped away, missing.

He thought of the tower debris and how he hadn't seen

or sensed a spirit. Cruelly, his mind supplied him an image of Colton's tower as nothing but a pile of rubble, with no sign of Colton anywhere.

Danny wandered outside and stood at the railing, facing the Yamuna River, which curved behind the Taj. Women dyed and washed clothes in the water, letting the current carry away streaks of red and yellow.

Footsteps came up behind him. "Are you all right?" Daphne asked.

"Just thinking."

She hesitated before asking her next question, but Danny knew it was coming all the same. "Do you miss him?"

"Enough to build a second Taj."

"We'll be back in England soon, I hope. If we ever find a solution to all this." He heard the rustle of her clothes, then felt a tap on his shoulder. He turned and saw that she had taken out the two little pills the attendant from the *Notus* had given her.

"Do you need them?" she asked.

"No. Why do you still have those?"

"It seemed a waste to throw them away if someone else could benefit."

"You won't take them?"

"I don't trust pills. I've watched my mother swallow too many to be comfortable with the notion."

He scuffed his boot lightly against the marble floor. "I'm sorry."

"No matter." She tucked the pills away in her pocket. "One

day, I'll get her out of there." When Danny gave her a sympathetic look, she shrugged. "Don't bother pitying me, Danny. Your situation was far worse than mine."

He'd secretly longed to hear those words all throughout his father's absence. Now, they offended him. "Of course it wasn't. How do you reckon that?"

"At least my father is dead and I know he can't come back. You had to live without knowing one way or the other. I couldn't have borne it." She paused, then shook her head. "No, all that hope would have killed me."

Danny stared at the river again, at the women stretching their wet, dyed sheets out to dry on the rocks. "Speaking of your father . . . I noticed you haven't told them. About you."

Daphne tensed. "Why would I?"

The reason seemed obvious to him, but then again, Daphne didn't tend to say anything about it in England. It made sense that she wouldn't say anything in India. Still, he watched her out of the corner of his eye, taking in the longing on her face as she watched the women working below.

"Are you two all right?" Akash had sidled up to them. Meena was still busy fawning over the inner dome.

"We're fine," Daphne said. "Thank you. You and Meena have been so kind to us."

Akash smiled and scratched the back of his head. That wide, goofy smile was one Danny recognized; Colton usually grinned like that before he said something absurd, like *Your eyes are so green* or *I like watching your lips when you talk*. Danny had noticed

Akash's little glances, the excuses to hand Daphne something so that their fingers would touch.

"You're very welcome. I believe Meena wanted to show you the mosque as well."

He led Daphne toward said mosque. Danny was about to follow when he heard a metallic sound. He glanced at the marble railing and jerked back. A fat, black spider was perched there.

Though something didn't seem right about it. The spider was too precise. The eyes glowed faintly.

Mechanical spider.

"The bleeding hell is that?" he asked out loud. The others were too far away to hear. He considered calling them over, but before he could, the mechanical spider scuttled back under the railing, out of sight.

Hours later, Danny was still thinking about the spider as they rattled back to the cantonment. He knew the British had brought machines to India, but the creature seemed too advanced even for London.

As soon as they climbed out of the auto, Lieutenant Crosby descended on them. "Major Dryden wants to see you three immediately."

You three meaning the clock mechanics. Akash shrugged and loped toward the mess, leaving the mechanics to follow Crosby.

When they walked into the meeting room, Dryden nearly

pounced on them in his excitement. "We received a cable not too long ago from the north *and* the south. Intel has been hard at work."

"Regarding what, sir?" asked Daphne.

"We received word of suspicious activity around the clock towers in both Meerut and Lucknow. You've been sniffing at the tracks so far. Now it's time to dart for the fox."

There were many books in Danny's house, and it took Colton nearly an hour of deliberation until he picked one at random. The pages rustled pleasantly as Colton turned them for several long minutes, enamored with the sound they made, before going back to actually read the words on those pages.

He had been with the Harts for two weeks. Though his presence had initially sparked tension, Danny's parents had grown accustomed to him. Colton, however, still felt wildly out of place, a thistle in a field of poppies.

It didn't help that Christopher, though pleasant, put him on edge. He could practically read the man's thoughts, from his puzzlement about Colton's relationship with Danny to his worry over Enfield's tower.

Colton stared down at the words without reading them. He

didn't even know what book he was holding. His mind was still in Enfield, focused on another story.

On Prometheus, the Titan who stole fire for the humans. Zeus, angry, wanting the humans to die off, chaining Prometheus to that rock, leaving him to suffer until . . .

Until what? There was an ending to the story, but he must not have heard it. Even when he had read the myth in his tower, his eyes had skimmed over the conclusion, as if it were of no importance. He'd been too focused on the first part, trying to jog his memory.

Colton didn't forget the events that had happened over the past several years, yet too much time had slid by for him to remember the beginning. It seemed ironic now that all he had was the first part of a story with no conclusion.

He closed his eyes and imagined it. Bearded Prometheus, Zeus hefting a lightning bolt in one hand, the bloodstained rock.

Something flickered across his mind and he jerked in pain. Moaning slightly, he rubbed his side where the red, twisted scar lay. It hurt on and off, pulling him north. His tower wanted him to return.

But he couldn't. Not yet.

There was still no new information about the attack. Scouts had gone as far as the continent to search for answers, but without a proper description of the airship—Colton had only seen its underside—there was little chance of finding it.

There was news, however, about Danny, though it was nothing substantial. They'd received a message—Christopher called it a cable—that Danny had reached Agra. Since then, Colton had waited every day for another cable, but none was forthcoming.

The mechanics would say if Danny was in trouble, he kept telling himself. *They wouldn't keep that from his parents.*

And yet, here he was, hiding evidence in his pocket.

Colton started guiltily when the front door opened. Christopher made a beeline toward him, clutching a bulky bag.

"'Lo, Colton. I've got the new model here."

Colton set the book aside. His central cog rested next to him on the tattered couch, and it brightened slightly as Christopher entered the back room.

Whenever Christopher explained what he and the smiths were working on, Colton struggled to follow. From what he could gather, they wanted to use the same method of making clockwork pieces to make a cog holder for him. The metal of the harness, acting as a conductor of Colton's power, would strengthen the power of the cog. So far the first two attempts had failed, and Colton remained translucent.

Christopher took the holder out of the bag. It was sleeker than the previous model, made of a bronze metal that crisscrossed at the back and leather straps attached to the front. The sides were curved so that Colton's cog could fit snugly inside, rather than rattle around as it had in the first square-shaped holder.

"Give this a try," Christopher said. Colton's central cog slid into the holder with a satisfying *click*. "Feel anything?"

"Sort of." Colton could sense that the metal holder had attached itself to the power stored within his cog. That power stretched and pulled, a thin strand of time that ran perpendicular to the time of London. If he focused hard enough, he could feel Enfield in that strand—the smell of grass, the glint of the river, the tolling of the church bells.

He slipped the holder on so that the straps hung over his shoulders. Christopher waited for a reaction, staring at Colton's chest; rather, *through* Colton's chest. When nothing happened, his shoulders sagged in disappointment.

"This won't work. It'll have to be altered."

Colton removed his cog before he handed back the holder. "It's not your fault. It must be difficult, making something that's never been made before."

"I just wish it worked."

"It's nearly there. I felt a little stronger this time."

Christopher pursed his lips, just as Leila did when she didn't know what to say. Colton had noticed that Danny's parents sometimes mirrored each other in their gestures and voices. It was both strange and sweet, and it made Colton wonder if he and Danny would ever become the same way, so ingrained in each other that they almost started to become one.

I'm acting more human now than I ever did before Danny. I suppose that's a start.

Christopher looked at the couch, where Colton had left his book. "The *Iliad*?"

Colton hadn't even realized that was the book he'd chosen. "It's a little harder to read than I thought it would be. I liked the story better when Danny explained it."

"He's always been a smart boy. Top of his class, quick to learn." Christopher's expression turned wistful. "I suppose I can't call him a boy anymore, can I?"

Colton knew this was personal ground, so he trod carefully. "Why not?"

"The last I saw of him, before I went to Maldon, he was still so young. Only fourteen, still an apprentice." With one hand, Christopher mimed something growing taller. "Then, in the blink of an eye, he's a young man and already a mechanic. I wasn't even here to help him with his assessments. He had to do it all on his own." He paused, then said in a voice soft and ragged with loss, "I missed three years of his life."

Christopher dragged his gaze from the carpet to Colton. His eyes harbored accusation, as if already blaming him for a disaster that hadn't yet unfolded. As if Colton would someday prevent Danny from coming home.

I'm going to do the opposite, he thought fiercely, touching the note in his pocket.

"I should take this back." Christopher sighed, stuffing the holder back into his bag. "We'll try again."

"Mr. . . . I mean, Christopher? I'm sorry about what Evaline did to you. Your family didn't deserve it. But . . . Danny loves you. He always talks about you, and he tried so hard to find a way to free you when you were trapped. I think, in some way, you did help him. He's determined and hardworking because of you. He has a long future ahead of him, and I won't do anything to ruin that. I promise."

Christopher looked momentarily taken aback, but managed a faint smile. "Thank you, Colton. I appreciate hearing that." He shouldered the bag. "I'll return in the evening."

Colton watched him head back into the gray afternoon light. He stared out the window a moment, thinking, then drew the note from his pocket and read it again.

He walked into the hall, ignoring the panicked tug from his central cog. His side gave off a dull pang, but he ignored that as well. He stopped before the hideously green telephone sitting on the wooden table in the hall, wondering how on earth to use it.

Colton cocked his head to one side. Humans made technology look so simple. A less-formidable object sat beside the telephone: a little book filled with addresses and numbers. He opened it and flipped through the entries, delighting in the crisper, higher sound these pages made as he searched for a specific name.

At first, he couldn't find it. He knew her only by Cassie. But when he went through the pages again, he found an entry that was close: Cassandra Lovett.

Picking up the cylindrical part attached to a wire, Colton hesitated. There was a round wheel in the middle of the clunky base. Christopher, when making calls, stuck his finger in it and turned the dial to the corresponding numbers.

Colton put the cylindrical part to his ear and heard absolutely nothing, a void of sound. The sensation was eerie, so he tried to move the dial with his finger. Since Cassandra Lovett's number began with a two, he turned the wheel to two. Or at least, he thought he did. He tried the other numbers next.

The soundlessness was broken by a startling ring. Even more jarring was the voice that suddenly issued from the other end. It was male and spoke in a garbled language that Colton didn't understand.

"Er, hello? Is this Cassandra Lovett?"

The voice kept shouting at him, so Colton quickly hung up. After a moment to collect himself, he attempted the number again, this time being even more cautious about what numbers he turned to.

The telephone rang and rang. Finally, someone responded.

"Hello?"

Colton stood straighter. He knew that voice. "Cassie?"

"Hellooo? Anyone there?"

Why couldn't she hear him? He looked cluelessly about until he recalled what Mrs. Hart had done while making a call the day before.

He lifted the clunky part off the table to speak into the mouthpiece. "Cassie?" he tried again.

"Yes, who's calling?"

"It's Colton. From Enfield?" He wondered if she knew anyone else named Colton. "I'm in London, at Danny's parents' house. I wanted to speak with you."

The line went silent. Colton worried for a moment that he had accidentally called the wrong Cassie, but then he heard her snap, "Stay right there!" followed by a loud *click*.

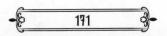

He put the telephone back down and closed the address book. *So much for that idea.* He was wondering if he should try to call Brandon when the front door shuddered under someone's pounding fist.

"Please open the door!"

Colton hurried to undo the lock, then pulled the door open just enough to peer out. Cassie stood there, red-faced and out of breath. Her auburn hair was frizzing out of its braid.

"It *is* you!" She pushed him into the house and shut the door behind them. "What are you doing here? Do Danny's parents know?"

"Yes, I've been here about two weeks."

"*Two weeks?* But doesn't that mean Enfield—?"

"Is Stopped," he confirmed. "The mechanics are trying to keep quiet about it."

He led her to the back room. His cog stopped pulling at him as he sank back onto the sofa and placed it on his lap. Cassie eyed the cog suspiciously from her seat in an armchair, one leg tucked beneath her. That's how she sat in his tower, too.

"I can't believe Danny isn't here for this," she said.

"I didn't come to London for Danny. I came because someone attacked my tower."

He told her the whole story about Enfield and how Christopher was working with the smiths to make him a holder that would keep him strong while the mechanics investigated.

"Blazes, that's rough," she murmured. Her freckles stood out against her pale face. "And poor Dan doesn't even know."

"We can't distract him from his assignment." That's what the Lead had said, anyway.

"But who in their right minds would attack Enfield? Why Enfield, and not London?"

Colton bit his lower lip. Cassie was trustworthy. She was honest and kind and loved Danny tremendously. Colton had seen that in the afternoons when the three of them sat talking in his tower. It had irked him at first, mostly because he saw how much Danny loved her in return. The friends mirrored each other, from a certain wave of their hands to a particular way of saying "right," that reminded him of how Danny's parents mirrored each other.

It had given him an ache like the one currently throbbing in his side. Danny and Cassie's connection was not a romantic love—he knew the difference from watching so many couples in Enfield—but it was easy and uncomplicated, demanding nothing, yet giving everything if asked.

That's how Colton knew he should tell Cassie about the message.

Taking the note from his pocket, he stood and handed it to her.

She skimmed the words at first, then read it two more times before looking up at him with a frown. "What is this?"

"Someone gave that note to Danny, and he didn't tell anyone."

"You . . ." She read the note again. "You think someone is after Danny?"

"That's what it seems like." Colton gestured to the crumpled paper. "Towers start falling in India. Danny is sent to India. Someone attacks Enfield."

Cassie's mouth dropped open. "You're not serious!"

Colton didn't know how to respond. "I think so?"

"But why? That doesn't make any sense."

"I don't know. All I know is . . . I *feel* as if he's in danger. That he needs help."

Cassie chewed her thumbnail as she read the note one more time. "Have you told his parents about this?"

"No."

"Why not?"

"I can't. They're already worried enough."

"You have to tell them. If Danny really is in trouble, someone has to go and help, or at least warn him. If you won't tell them, I will."

"No! Please don't."

"I'm just as worried about him as you are."

He opened and closed his mouth. Jealousy simmered within him, but he pushed it down.

Cassie leaned forward in her seat. "I know you're entitled to your worry. But so am I, and so are Danny's parents. We all love him."

Colton ran a thumb over the edge of his cog, tracing one of the spokes. "I know. I'm sorry. I'll . . . I'll tell them, all right? I just need to find the right words to explain."

Cassie handed the note back to him, her eyebrows furrowed. "I had a bad feeling when he left. My bad feelings are never

wrong. I had one right before my brother got into his accident."
She took a shuddering breath. "But why would anyone want to
hurt Danny?"

Colton had no answer. He could have spent hours turning
page after page of unanswered questions, listening to their
whispers.

That night, Christopher came home with plans for a new holder
model and explained it over dinner. They invited Colton to sit
with them at every meal, even though he never ate a thing.

"What if the holder included the smaller cogs I brought with
me?" he suggested.

"That might make it bulkier. Unless . . ." Christopher drew a
few sketches in the pad he'd brought to the table.

Leila clucked her tongue. "Chris, put that away."

"Maybe if we make little pockets—"

"*Chris.*"

"Yes, all right." He shoved the pad to one side. Leila gave a
little nod of approval as she sipped her plum cordial. "I didn't
even think about using the other cogs. Maybe it'll help."

"Hopefully." Colton glanced around the kitchen, trying not
to look awkward or guilty as he thought of his conversation with
Cassie. He'd promised to tell the Harts, and yet, as he sat there,
he couldn't bring himself to do it.

Tomorrow, he decided.

Colton was already in Danny's room when Christopher and Leila retired to bed. Through the wall, he heard Christopher's low murmur and the higher timbre of Leila's reply. Christopher gave a brief answer, and then they were silent.

Colton turned off the lamp and stretched out on Danny's bed. It was impossible for him to sleep, but the exertion of being away from Enfield and the pain sometimes made him black out for a few hours. This had happened a few nights before, when he had woken in Danny's bed with both Leila and Christopher hovering worriedly over him.

"We have to get this holder right," Christopher had said then. "The longer you stay here, the more danger you're in."

Colton's side throbbed, and he winced. He lifted his shirt and rubbed a hand over the ropy scar that traveled from underarm to hip. He had noticed several other little scars across his body, but this injury was by far the worst.

The more he thought of the scar, the sharper the pain became, and he couldn't stay conscious a moment longer. He slipped into a twilight world where he wasn't aware of senses or the space around him. Just time, ticking on without him, leaving him in the current like an abandoned child.

A river. It gurgled past him, heading south, taking fish and cargo with it. He raced upstream to the dock where men were pulling the cargo onto a small barge.

He ran into one of the men, who stumbled back with a curse. But when the man saw his face, a yellow-stained grin showed from within his dark beard.

"Yes, boy? What is it this time?"

"I get to go! I asked them if I could, and they asked if I was ready, and I said yes, and they said I could finally go!"

"Ah, did they, now?" The man knelt to be at eye level. "I believe this is cause for celebration. Why don't you run along and tell your mother? I'll bring a surprise for supper."

The river faded away, but the sound of water didn't. It lapped and chuckled, growing from trickling eddies to the distant roar of waves. The ocean stretched before him, gray and dark and fathomless. It was both terrifying and lovely. Seagulls wheeled over the heads of boys and girls standing on the beach, all different heights and ages.

"Who wants to go first?" asked a thin, middle-aged man. Hands shot into the air. "How about you, Castor?"

A dark-haired youth, tall for his age, stepped forward with a nervous smile. His brown eyes kept flitting toward the sea.

"Go on, lad. Show the others."

Castor walked into the foaming tide.

He sat on a barrel behind a noisy tavern, kicking the heels of his feet against the wooden seat he'd made for himself, listening to the hollow thuds. The boy, Castor, sat on another barrel.

"Am . . . Am I right?" Castor asked. His hands were clasped in his lap. He looked as nervous as he had that day at sea.

"Yes, I think so."

Castor's hands tightened. "So . . ."

"So."

Castor smiled. Laughter echoed from the alley behind the tavern.

Something was wrong. It felt strange, the air too thick, too sharp. It hurt. He sat at the base of the wall and held his head. The earth was spinning.

"It's gone off. It's all off."

"We have to do something."

"There's nothing—!"

"Look," whispered Castor.

The boy held out a timepiece. The hands spun faster and faster, the sky dark and light and dark again, the hands reversing, *where's the ticking?*, I think I've said this before, time stopped.

It Stopped.

Colton woke with a small cry, gripping at the bed as if he'd be thrown from it otherwise. The room around him was very, very still. He lay there in silence, wide eyes staring at a whorl in the

ceiling as a cold sensation traveled along his body. Judging by the thin, gray light coming through the window, it was dawn.

"A dream?" he murmured to the ceiling. But the ceiling couldn't answer.

He sat up groggily and reached for the small clock on Danny's desk, staring hard at its face. Time was flowing at its normal pace. The air around him was calm. London was safe.

Then what had that feeling been?

He sat back and studied his central cog, which was propped against the desk. Had he imagined it?

There was a knock at the door. Colton rose to answer it.

Christopher stood there, his expression shifting to a frown at the sight of him. "Is something the matter?"

"No, everything's fine. What do you need?"

"I was wondering if I could take your small cogs for measurements. I like the idea of including them in the holder."

Colton handed over the three small cogs he'd taken from his tower. Christopher thanked him, then eyed him warily. "Are you sure you're all right?"

"Yes, I'm fine."

As soon as Christopher and Leila were gone for the day, Colton slunk downstairs and spread out on the couch. He stared at his picture of Danny and wished he could tell him what he'd just experienced. And then he wished that Danny could tell him if he was safe.

He heard a small click at the window. Curious, he crossed the room, twitched back the drapes, and looked out.

There was nothing there. Then he heard it again: a click and a faint whirring sound. Movement caught the corner of his eye, and he turned his head to find a fat spider perched outside on the windowsill.

Colton made a face and let the drapes fall. He had greater matters to worry about than overlarge insects.

Christopher came bounding into the kitchen a few days later while Leila was attempting to teach Colton how to cook. Colton couldn't taste anything, of course, but that didn't stop him from being fascinated by the whole process. That, and Leila had noticed he was bored.

"Christopher, slow down!" Leila scolded when her husband nearly ran into the table.

"I think we've got it! Colton, try it on. The other cogs are already inside."

Colton eagerly grabbed his central cog from the table as Christopher unveiled the latest model. It was sleek and round, the bronze metalwork spiderwebbing over the front to support thin metal pockets containing the smaller cogs.

When Colton slipped the central cog into the holder, he could already feel it working. A warm and familiar power seeped into his body, as if he carried sunlight for bones. The straps settled over his shoulders, and his four cogs nestled snugly against his back, humming faintly.

Leila gasped. "I can see you! I mean, better than I could before."

He looked at his hands. They seemed flesh and blood, just as they'd appeared in his tower. Even the pain in his side had lessened.

"Your suggestion to use the smaller cogs was just the thing we needed," Christopher said with pride. "Do you feel better?"

"Much better, thank you."

"He looks better, too," Leila added. "Not as tired."

In fact, Colton felt energized and restless. Christopher must have noticed, for he said that Colton could try it out tomorrow.

"I can go outside?" he asked, hopeful.

"Yes, but with me, of course. Let's take a trip to the office tomorrow morning. There's a leather cover here, too, so people don't get suspicious."

Colton was too excited to drift out of consciousness that night. And it was just as well, because he didn't want any more of those strange visions. Time buzzed around his body, feeding off of London's like a plant absorbing water.

But his excitement withered the next morning when Christopher got off the telephone and said they couldn't go out today.

"I just got a call from a friend across town. His auto's died on him and he needs a lift. It'll take me a few hours. I'm sorry."

Colton tried to mask his disappointment. "That's all right."

"I've told the Lead about our success, though. He's ecstatic. Still frustrated there's no information about the airship, but at least we've bought ourselves more time."

Colton watched him slip on a jacket and head out the door. The auto started up, and the rumble of the engine dwindled away until all that was left was familiar silence.

An empty house had a particular sound, Colton had come to realize: a sigh made without lungs, the silent crawl of time passing with no one to measure it in beats of words and breaths. No one to speak to or listen to or watch. A loneliness that was cutting.

He couldn't stay here.

He dressed in Danny's clothes, put the leather cover over the cog holder, and crammed a cap onto his head. The Harts had given him an extra key, just in case, and he used it to lock the door behind himself. Putting on the holder, he made for Big Ben.

He wasn't afraid of getting lost. He remembered the route he and Christopher had taken to get to the Mechanics Affairs building, but more than that, he felt Big Ben drawing him closer, pointing him in the right direction. That presence was hard to ignore, especially now that he had the holder to magnify his own power.

The clock tower stood tall and beautiful, sheathed in gold. Colton had only seen it at nighttime, so the burnished glow it gave off during the day was a marvel to behold.

Colton walked toward it, crossing the street with a small

crowd. People looked at him and away, unconcerned. They saw only another human, and the notion made him grin from ear to ear. He loved blending in, becoming one of them.

It wasn't until he approached the tower that he realized he didn't know how to get inside. Last time, Danny had shown his mechanic's badge and the guards had let them through. Colton walked around to the front of the tower, where a few people had gathered before a tall black iron fence. Above them hung a sign that read TOUR STARTS ON THE HOUR, EVERY HOUR.

Colton moved forward with the group and was stopped by a guard.

"You here for the tour?"

Colton pushed down his sudden panic. "Yes?"

"One and five, please."

The panic promptly returned. What did that mean? Had Danny ever used that phrase before?

He glanced at the numerals of Big Ben's western clock face. "One and . . . five?"

The guard grunted. "One shilling, five pence for the tour."

"Oh! Money. Right." Much to his relief, he still carried the coins that Mayor Aldridge had given him for emergencies. With a silent promise to pay him back, he handed the guard all the money in his pocket.

The guard scowled at him. He picked through the coins until he had his one and five and shoved the rest back at Colton.

"Go on, get in line."

Colton hurried away, worried the man might ask him more

difficult questions. He didn't mingle with the tourists, who kept to themselves anyway. Instead, he made a game of noticing their different features until a different guard let them through the tower entrance.

As soon as he was in the tower, time acknowledged him like an embrace. Colton smiled and looked up, knowing Big Ben was watching. But the spirit couldn't show himself in front of all these people. Colton would have to find a way to sneak off.

The guide led them up the stairs, droning on about different details of the tower, but Colton didn't care much about building materials and architecture. When they passed a landing, he spied a door marked MAINTENANCE PERSONNEL ONLY. He crept toward it while the others were distracted, hiding himself within the dark closet. Pressing his ear against the door, he listened to the sound of many feet climbing the next set of stairs, the guide's voice fading away like the auto engine had that morning.

Colton crept back onto the landing and found Big Ben standing there, beaming at him.

"Never imagined I'd see you again, lad. Why's it taken you so long to come say hello?"

Big Ben was certainly big. His shoulders were broad, his frame tall, his chest thick. Like Colton, he had golden features, from his yellow-amber eyes to the short blond beard around his jaw. The sleeves of his shirt were rolled up to his elbows, revealing a black tattoo with Latin inscription that had been carved onto the tower. Danny had not yet taught Colton how to read Latin, so he had no clue what it meant.

"I'm sorry," Colton said. "It's been difficult to move around. This is the first opportunity I've had to leave the house."

"This sounds like a long story. Come along."

Colton followed him up into the rafters, far away from the prying eyes of tourists and mechanics on duty. The pair sat above the four main bells, one of them the namesake of the London spirit before him.

"Why do they have *tours* in you?" Colton asked.

"The mechanics need to get extra funding somehow. Besides, I've heard I'm quite impressive." He waited for Colton to finish laughing before he said, "Go on then, tell me what's happened."

So Colton explained everything: the towers falling in India, Danny leaving, and the threatening note. Big Ben sat with his head slightly cocked to one side, his expression at once intrigued and alarmed.

"And the mechanic who Stopped your town last time isn't behind it?"

"Danny said Matthias went to prison, and he's still there. He didn't know anything about the attack."

Big Ben stroked his beard while he thought. Colton looked down at the large bells, wondering if he could fit inside them.

Finally, the great spirit shook his head. "I don't know how you ought to proceed, to be honest."

"Neither do I. It's too complicated for me to understand. But until the mechanics find a way to keep Enfield safe, I have to stay in London."

"Probably for the best. It would be a shame to get everything up and running only to be attacked again. Strange to think your mechanic doesn't know anything about this, though."

"The Lead says he shouldn't have any distractions."

"But you said he may be in danger."

"Maybe. I don't know. He'll have soldiers with him, at least." Colton swung his legs back and forth, remembering the sound of heels striking a barrel. "I wanted to ask you something. Do you ever have . . . visions? Or lose consciousness and think of strange things?"

Big Ben gave Colton an odd look. "Not that I can recall. Have you?"

Colton told him about the visions, about the boy named Castor, the sea, and how it felt as if he'd experienced the life of another person through his eyes.

Big Ben leaned back. "I've never seen anything like that before. Sounds interesting, though."

"It wasn't interesting. It was confusing, and then it was frightening." Colton put a hand against his chest. "I felt this horrible fear, rising up like it would burst out of me and destroy everything."

"Well, now that you have this new holder, you won't lose consciousness again."

"I hope that's the case."

Below them, the bells began to chime. The sound vibrated through the rafters as they tolled twelve times. Colton had left the house at half past nine.

"I should head back. Christopher will be worried if he finds me missing."

"Hold on a moment." Big Ben winked out of sight. Colton waited patiently for him to return, which he did within seconds. "I want you to have this."

He handed Colton a small cog of burnished bronze. Colton took it and felt a little spark as the metal touched his fingertips.

"Don't you need it?"

"It's a spare. I keep a few lying around, just in case. You should see how frustrated the mechanics get when they can't find them."

"Why are you giving it to me?"

The spirit winked. "Just in case."

They said goodbye as the tour was about to pass below. Colton couldn't disappear and reappear here as he would in his own tower, since he didn't control the time boundaries. But he could climb down easily enough, and he waited until the group had passed him before slipping into the back.

Outside, Colton hurried past the dour guard and waited to cross the street. He furtively glanced at Big Ben's cog in his hand, then looked up at the clock tower. Big Ben sat on the roof, waving down at him. Colton waved back before the spirit disappeared.

As he passed the Mechanics Affairs office, he kept his head down, hoping none of the mechanics nearby could feel his presence.

He thought he'd succeeded when a hand pushed against his chest, stopping him in his tracks. His head shot up, but relief instantly flooded him at the sight of Brandon Summers.

"I knew it wasn't a hallucination," the boy said. "Come here."

Brandon led him around the corner. Leaning a shoulder

against the stone wall, Brandon crossed his arms and gave Colton a level stare. "Enfield's Stopped." Even though it didn't sound like a question, Colton nodded. "Can you tell me how?"

"We're out in the open."

"Say it soft, then."

Colton lowered his voice and described the events of the last few weeks.

"And Danny is in bloody India," Brandon mumbled.

"Yes."

"What's the plan?"

It was too much to explain out in the middle of the street, so Colton asked if they could meet later. "Maybe you can help with the investigation, since you know Enfield so well."

"Just tell me when and where."

They agreed to meet at the Harts' house in two days, when both of Danny's parents would be out; Colton had memorized their schedules. He and Brandon parted ways.

It was a long walk to the house, and he worried the entire way that Christopher would already be there, panicked and enraged. But when he approached the front gate, he saw no auto at the curb. He was in the clear.

Pleased with himself for having an outing with no major complications, Colton opened the front door and froze. There was a letter on the floor under the mail slot.

His name was on it.

Colton knelt to inspect the envelope. Since nothing seemed out of the ordinary, he broke open the seal. The letter inside was just a simple message, scrawled in the same handwriting as the note in his pocket:

He is in danger.
Come to India.
Tell no one.

There was something else inside the envelope. Pulling it out with shaking hands, Colton found a black-and-white photograph like the one he had of Danny.

This one was of Danny, too, but his back was to the camera. He stood by a pile of rubble in the middle of a circular clearing beside Daphne Richards and two others. The photograph was taken from the viewpoint of someone looking down on them through a window on a high floor.

In the corner of the photograph, a gun was pointed at the back of Danny's head.

Christopher and Colton went to the office the next morning to show the Lead how the holder worked. The man was impressed, and promised that Christopher and the smiths would be generously compensated for their work and discretion.

"That's not necessary, sir. I'm just glad to do my part."

"Nonsense, your family does outstanding work and I want to see that rewarded. Well now, Colton, are you feeling better?"

Colton looked up from where he'd been glaring at the carpet. "What? Oh, yes. I feel almost as strong as I would in my tower."

"Brilliant." The Lead still sounded a little hesitant speaking directly to a spirit, but the fact that Colton now looked like a human boy eased some of the awkwardness. "We're still investigating, but we'll get to the bottom of this soon. There's been shadowy activity in India as well, and I'm sure Daniel and the others are hard at work."

Colton sensed something furtive about the way the man said it. Apparently, Colton wasn't the only one keeping upsetting news from the Harts.

After that, Colton's day was torture. He couldn't stop reading the note or staring at the photograph. It was of poor quality, the image grainy, but it was clearly Danny. There was no mistaking him.

The next day Colton anxiously waited for his meeting with Brandon. He'd called Cassie over as well. She arrived first, and Colton led her to the back room.

"I wish I knew how to make you tea," he said. She laughed and touched his arm affectionately.

"That's all right. You look much better than you did before. Well, more solid, I should say. Have you told them?"

He shook his head. "Not yet."

"Colton—"

"Just wait until Brandon gets here. Then I'll explain."

The apprentice arrived ten minutes later, surprised to see Cassie. Colton introduced them, since he didn't think the two had ever met.

"He's mentioned you," Brandon said, taking a seat in the armchair where Cassie had sat last time. Colton settled on the couch, wearing the cog holder on his back. He had become used to its weight already. "The auto mechanic."

"That's me. Nice to finally meet you."

"I assume you're here for the same reason I am." Brandon gave Colton a pointed look.

"I'll have to start from the beginning," Colton warned.

"Maybe I'll go make that tea, then," Cassie said.

She came back with a small tray just as Colton finished up. Brandon thanked Cassie for the cup she held out to him, taking a few sips as he considered Colton's words.

"Don't you think someone should tell Danny?" he said at last. "About Enfield and all that? I mean, if he kept that note from everyone, he already knows something's up. He'll want to know."

"The India assignment is important, and they trusted Danny with it," Colton argued. "I don't want him hurrying back here for my sake. And there's . . . something else."

Colton hesitated. The note had warned him not to tell anyone. He went to close the drapes, then laid the note and photograph facedown on the table. "I'm going to leave the room for a minute," he said. "Don't touch these." He mimed flipping the letter and photo over, nodding his head. Brandon was reaching for them as Colton left the room.

He heard Cassie's gasp and Brandon's muttered curse. Giving them exactly a minute, he walked back into the room. The letter and photo were as he'd left them. Cassie was white as a freshly laundered sheet, and Brandon's eyebrows were furrowed.

"I have to go to him," Colton whispered. "They'll kill him if I don't."

"Bloody idiot, can't you see this is a trap?" Brandon whispered back. "These people know something about you. About Danny. If they get you where they want you—"

"I don't care. I'm not risking Danny's life to save my own. I promised his father that I would never put Danny in danger."

Cassie twisted her hands in her lap and looked at him pleadingly. "Colton, let's just tell someone. Please. There has to be another way."

But he shook his head. "I will *not* risk his life. They want me to go to India." He touched the small cog Big Ben had given him, secure in his pocket. "So I'll go."

"What about Enfield?" Brandon demanded.

"They'll be safer this way. Time will start again when I come back, and then we can fix my tower."

"If you come back at all! The Lead should know—"

"No!" Colton banged his fist against the wall and the entire frame shook. Brandon and Cassie jumped. "You two are the only ones I can trust right now. If you tell the Lead, or anyone else, they'll do something to Danny. I can't have that happen."

"But how would you even get to India?" Cassie demanded.

Brandon opened his mouth, then immediately closed it. Colton stared at him, and Brandon stared back, eyes shifting in indecision. Finally, he exhaled a long breath.

"I know a way," Brandon admitted. "My older brother's a copilot on a transporter airship. He's taking some cargo and soldiers to India at the end of the week. I can ask him if he'll smuggle you on."

Colton brightened at once. "Would you really? Do you promise?"

Brandon glanced at the photograph. He scratched his jaw and sighed. "Yes, I promise. Have to keep Danny alive, right? Since he's so awful at doing it himself."

Colton turned to Cassie. She blinked hard and met Colton's gaze, fighting back tears. But as Colton watched, her expression slowly hardened into determination. "Brandon, if you tell me the flight details, I can drive Colton to your brother's airship."

Colton listened as they worked it out between them, wondering if this was another of his strange visions. He was going to India. He was going to save Danny. He was going to keep his promise to Christopher Hart.

Although Colton could read, he hadn't had much experience in writing. He figured it would be a lot like reading, but in reverse: he would already know the words before they were put on paper.

He sat in Danny's room for two nights in a row, anxious about what he was going to say and how the Harts would react upon finding the note. Colton didn't want to give himself away. There was no telling if Christopher would follow him to India, or tell the Lead.

The words came out shaky but legible. His handwriting wasn't as confident as Danny's, but at least he wrote it himself, and he hadn't needed to ask Cassie to do it for him. He wanted this message to come from him—his apology, his reasoning, everything.

Just before dawn, he finished the note and sat back, rereading it several times to make sure it was what he wanted.

Christofer and ~~Layla~~ Leila,

Please do not be upset with me. There is something I have to do befor I return to Enfield. I will be back when I can. ~~Pleese~~ Please tell no one.

I promised that I would do nothing to ~~luv damm~~ damage my town or Danny. I will keep that promise. If you trust Danny, please trust me.

Colton

It didn't feel nearly enough. He knew he should mention that Danny was in danger, but he couldn't get anyone else involved.

Feeling oddly heavy, Colton put on Danny's clothes and the leather-covered cog holder. Big Ben's cog still rested in his pocket. He wondered if the spirit had somehow known that Colton would be traveling and would need this extra strength.

He still had money, but discovered more of it squirreled away in one of Danny's drawers. With a promise to repay Danny somehow, Colton added it to his traveling bag. He chose a spare shirt and trousers, just in case something happened to the ones he wore. He also packed the notes and both photographs of Danny.

Colton hesitated on the landing, looking at the Harts'

bedroom door. The letter sat on Danny's desk, waiting to be found. They deserved better. But it was all he could give them for now.

Cassie waited for him outside, the sky dim and gray in the early clutches of the morning. She gave him a sad look when he got into her auto, and they took off down the quiet London lane.

They were mostly silent, though Cassie asked questions every now and then. "Do you have money? Do you need more? What about a map?" By the time they reached the docking station, Cassie held the steering wheel in a white-knuckled grip.

"I don't think this is a good idea," she said when she'd parked. Colton could see the large airship being loaded several yards away. "I'm getting one of my bad feelings. There has to be another way."

He took her freckled hand in his. "Cassie, thank you for everything you've done. If Christopher and Leila ask you questions, pretend you don't know anything. I don't want you to get in trouble."

She drew in a deep breath that shook as she released it. She squeezed his hand gently. "Danny is lucky to have you."

"He's also lucky to have friends like you and Brandon." He looked back at the airship and found two people walking toward them. They got out of the car to meet them.

"Colton, this is David, my brother." Brandon gestured to the tall young man beside him. They looked similar, though David had a wider mouth and forehead. He was dressed in a blue uniform with aviator goggles hanging around his neck.

"Crikey, s'true then," David mumbled, looking Colton up and down.

"He's going to smuggle you into the cargo hold when the crew leave, before the passengers come on."

"I've never smuggled anything before, and I could lose my job if I'm caught," David warned them. "I'm only doing this as a favor for my brother. If someone finds you, you're on your own."

"I understand," Colton said, ignoring Cassie's growl of displeasure.

"The loading crew looks like they're about to take off," David said, craning his head around to check. "Shall we?"

Cassie pulled Colton into a sudden, brief hug. "Come back with him, Colton."

"I will."

Brandon patted his shoulder. "Good luck, mate."

Following David to the airship, Colton wondered if this was how Danny felt when he'd boarded his own airship: strangely alone, his excitement tempered with dread. He looked over his shoulder and waved to the others. Cassie waved back, and Brandon gave a single nod of encouragement.

The airship loomed above them, its propellers lazily circling, the engines warming up. Colton would be in there soon, climbing toward the sky. Heading for India. Running from Enfield.

He took out the photograph of Danny's smiling face.

"I'm sorry," he said quietly. "I can't wait for you this time."

Suspicious people had been seen near the clock towers in both Meerut and Lucknow. One city was east of Agra, the other south.

"It's clear we need multiple eyes in both locations," Dryden said. "As much as I would like you three to stick together, I believe we need to split our forces. Perhaps Kamir—"

"Kamir is sick," Meena interrupted.

"Ah, well. I'll let you three decide among yourselves, then." The Major left to speak with his officers.

"I suppose Meena could go to Lucknow with Akash," Danny ventured, but Daphne shook her head.

"We should both be with someone who's more familiar with the surroundings."

"It would be better to go with either me or Akash," Meena agreed. "Danny, why don't you go with Akash to Lucknow? He can take the *Silver Hawk*—"

"No," Danny said. "Absolutely not. I'm not getting back in that godforsaken plane of his."

Daphne sighed. "*I'll* go to Lucknow. I don't mind the plane ride."

Danny didn't like the thought of Daphne and Akash alone, but he didn't like the thought of another plane ride more. He shared a look with Meena.

"I suppose we'll go to Meerut," she decided.

Major Dryden came back a minute later and seemed pleased with the result. He rubbed his hands together in excitement.

"Spiffing. Miss Richards, you'll fly to Lucknow with an escort. Mister Hart, you and Meena will take the train up to Meerut." Danny contained a sigh of relief. "I'll make arrangements immediately."

The next morning, they assembled before Major Dryden, who outlined their journeys and named the soldiers who would attend them.

"You two will be escorted by Captain Harris," he told Danny and Meena. To Daphne he said, "You will have Lieutenant Crosby."

Danny gave Daphne a triumphant smile. She grimaced back at him.

"This will likely take several days," Dryden warned. "Perhaps a week or more. You will report daily on what you find. In the meantime, some of my men will be on the lookout for that rebel airship."

The reminder sent a shiver down Danny's spine. At least he would be on the ground this time; the blessed, sturdy ground.

He caught up to Daphne when they left to pack their things. The sun was bright and hot, stinging his skin despite the new tan he had developed. Daphne joined him under the shade of an awning.

"Promise me you'll be careful," he said.

She rolled her eyes heavenward. "You are *not* my guardian."

"I'm aware of that, but if you don't recall, we were already attacked once on this assignment. In the air you'll be at more risk. If that ship comes after you—"

"I'm sure Akash can evade it."

Danny grunted. "We'll see."

Daphne eyed him a moment. She was close enough that he caught the faint scent of bergamot that always seemed to cling to her. "Be safe, Danny. No running off like you did last time. You have someone important waiting for you to return home."

"I know." He brushed a thumb against the cog in his pocket. "I don't spend a moment here not thinking about it."

Daphne gripped his forearm, and he returned the pressure. Standing there with her, Danny marveled at the distance they had traveled together. She seemed to be thinking the same thing, and managed a small smile that he couldn't help but mirror, as if they shared an unspoken secret. They went their separate ways to gather their things.

Meena found him an hour later. "The major asked if we'll be ready to leave soon."

"I'm ready." He was borrowing one of the spare packs from the cantonment supply house, since carrying his trunk would be too much of a bother. He gave the pack a light kick. "I have all I need."

They set off to report to Captain Harris. The captain's quarters were in a large building where bachelor soldiers resided en masse. Across the way was a similar building for officers with wives. There were no children here; British children were at home in the care of relatives and governesses. Danny and Meena passed by gardens tended to by the officers' wives, although their stubborn attempt to cultivate British flowers went unrewarded, the foxgloves and honeysuckles wilting in the heat.

A couple of wives sat in wicker chairs outside, lazily fanning themselves. They sent Danny and Meena disapproving looks as the pair passed.

"They do not like seeing me with you," Meena said. Danny heard a hint of amusement in her voice, verging on contempt. One of the older women, who had gray streaking her hair and a puckering set of wrinkles between her eyebrows, seemed to sense her hostility.

"Quai hai," she said loudly. An Indian servant appeared. "Bhisti, I require more water." The servant bowed and went to fetch the pitcher.

"They like doing that," Meena whispered, her amusement gone. "They enjoy reminding themselves who's in charge."

Meena took off her shoes before she walked into the bachelors' compound, adding them to the sepoys' shoes that lined the outside wall. Danny had noticed the Indians didn't like to enter buildings with clad feet. Danny and Daphne had once asked if they were expected to follow this rule, too. Meena and Akash had simply laughed.

Lower officers hung about in their shirtsleeves. Some smoked in a shaded compound behind the building. They glanced at Meena, but like Daphne, she ignored them.

"This is the one," she said, pointing to a door at the end of a hallway. Danny knocked.

"Captain? We're ready to leave."

He began to open the door, which was already ajar, but stopped immediately, frozen by what he saw. Captain Harris was inside, and clearly preoccupied.

He held another man in his arms—the Indian sepoy, Partha. They were kissing.

The soldiers looked up to find Danny and Meena standing stricken on the threshold. Captain Harris turned scarlet, and Partha pushed away from him, hiding his face in his hands.

"Come in," Harris whispered urgently. They stepped inside, closing the door behind them. Partha murmured to himself in his own language.

"Oh, God." Harris clasped his hands together pleadingly. "Please, please don't tell anyone about this. I didn't mean for you to see—for anyone to know—" The sepoy groaned and retreated to the corner. "Partha, stop that!"

"Captain, it's all right." Danny held up his hands, as if he could physically push down the tension in the room. "Your secret is safe with me." When Meena did not speak, he nudged her foot with his own.

"And me," she added in a low voice.

Harris licked his lips nervously, his gaze flitting between the two of them. "I'm so sorry."

"Please, don't be," Danny said. "We'll forget this ever happened." When the captain didn't look convinced, Danny tentatively tried to form a bridge between them. "I understand, Captain. I really do."

Harris met his eyes, and his own widened slightly. Danny gave him a faint nod. The man's shoulders lowered.

"Partha, it's all right," he called to the sepoy. "They won't tell."

"I'll be discharged if the major knows," Partha whispered. He was barefoot, like Meena, and this made him look even more helpless. "I'll be disgraced. I'll have no family."

"None of that will happen," Harris said, his voice getting stronger with each word. "We'll be fine." He turned to Danny with a small, sad smile. "I'll meet you at the auto."

Danny and Meena walked back outside, stunned and silent. Danny could tell that this had been more of a shock for her than for him.

He wanted to say something, but they were passing the disapproving wives again. The mechanics remained silent until they arrived at the autos, which were being loaded for the trip. A group of soldiers milled around, a mix of British and Indian.

Harris was committing two taboos: being with another man, and being with an Indian. In London, this wouldn't have been anything new. Here in India, the rules of living were harsher. Rules were lifeblood in the army.

And Danny could relate all too well, just replacing "Indian" with "clock spirit."

Captain Harris soon joined them, looking much more like himself in his uniform, save for the faint redness of his face. Looking at Danny and Meena made those points of color bloom.

Major Dryden wished them luck and imparted a few bits of last-minute advice. Danny, trusting Meena and Harris to remember it all, instead gazed around the yard in the hopes of seeing Daphne, but she had already left with Akash.

Please be safe.

As Danny and Meena were driven to the station, he kept thinking back to the terror on Harris and Partha's faces, a reflection of the terror that had rattled his heart when his father found out about Colton and him.

The fear that something was about to become undone.

The station was a sea of Indian and British passengers. Almost all of them were rushing to get to their destinations or else to escape the crush of people, the air malodorous with unwashed bodies, urine, dust, and smoke. A woman's red scarf fluttered wildly in the wind, and children running by tried to grab it before they were chased away by a man in uniform; their laughter escaped the roar of the crowd like birds taking flight. The homeless sat slumped against a far wall, one of them singing hoarsely for change.

"Our train is on Platform Three," Harris yelled above the noise, pointing to the far left.

They squeezed past the crowd toward the steam train, which was already sending up a coil of white smoke. The train was comprised of seven carriages painted black and red. A water crane was currently attached to the top of the boiler, refilling the steam engine's tank.

"We've reserved the first carriage for you," Harris told Danny and Meena as they hurried to the open door. "The soldiers will spread out. We don't want anything like the airship incident."

Meena and Danny climbed into the carriage, where the conductor punched holes in their tickets.

"Very happy to have you aboard," he said in an accent that was not quite Indian, but not quite English. For that matter, his skin was lighter than the other Indians Danny had seen so far. "Please make yourselves comfortable."

The front carriage was small but roomy. Danny and Meena stored their packs in the wire mesh above the burgundy felt-cushioned seats.

"We thought it would be best if you didn't sit with the others," Harris explained as he also stored his pack away. "In case someone's eyes and ears wandered."

"Are you sitting with us, Captain?" Danny asked.

"Just for the moment. I'll go inspect the rest of the carriages as soon as we're off."

He wants to be alone, Danny thought with sympathy. He would probably do the same, if his lover and he had just been caught. Remembering the time Cassie had done precisely that, his face grew warm.

Danny looked out the wide window and watched the steam roll lazily toward the sky. The whistle blew, the door to the driver's carriage opened, and two men stepped out to exchange a word with the conductor. A woman walked out after them and spotted Danny and Meena. She smiled and approached them.

"You'll be the ghadi wallahs, then? I'm Amala, part of the crew."

The woman's skin was more or less the same shade as the conductor's. Her dark hair hung in a heavy braid, and a blue cap was perched on her head. Her eyes were blue, her accent mostly English. Unlike Meena, who wore a pair of loose green trousers with a tunic she called a salwar kameez, the woman simply wore a pair of tan coveralls.

"That would be us," Meena replied.

"The ones going to Meerut?" Amala glanced over her shoulder at the men, then leaned in closer. "Is this about the clocks falling?"

Danny opened his mouth to reply, but one look from Meena and he shut it again.

"It's just that everyone's so curious," Amala went on. "First one tower falls, then another, and time not Stopping a tick. I lived in Burma as a child, and one of the clock towers there got fair banged up. Time skittered all over the place, and no one was allowed in or out until the tower was fixed. I wonder why it's different this time?"

"We couldn't say," said Meena curtly.

"I've crossed a line, I see. Why don't I make it up to you? I'll show you how the train starts up."

Danny was immensely interested, but Meena declined the offer. Danny said he'd join Amala in the operations room shortly, then turned to Meena. "What's wrong?"

"We can't talk about our mission to just anyone," she murmured. "It seemed as though she wanted to get something out of us."

"She was being nice."

"In any case, don't say anything about Meerut or what you saw in Khurja."

"I won't." Danny glanced at the conductor, who was now making his way to the other carriages. Captain Harris sat on the opposite bench, staring wistfully out the window.

Meena noticed Danny staring at the conductor and raised a sleek eyebrow. "They're half-castes."

Danny was hesitant to speak on the subject of castes. From what he had gathered in the books he'd read, it was a sensitive issue and best left unprodded. But now that Meena had raised the topic, he was curious.

"Half?"

"Many of your English men have . . . chosen . . . Indian women. Some mothers even throw their daughters at the higher officers, hoping to make a good match. The result . . ." She gestured toward the driver's carriage, where Amala had disappeared. "Half-castes. Unfortunates on the fringes of society."

"That's a rather rude way of putting it." Danny was startled by his own words, roughened with unexpected anger as he thought about Daphne and her father.

Meena shrugged, unruffled. "I take no offense with the people, only with their origins. Truthfully, I feel sorry for them. They do not belong in India, and they do not belong in your England. Many of them have formed their own caste. Most work on the railways." With a finger, she traced a diamond pattern on her kameez. "Viceroy Lytton does not oversee us well. Under his eyes, society has become unbalanced."

"I'm sure he's a busy man," Danny said, but Meena only scoffed. A wick of frustration was lit inside him, but he quickly doused it. Meena had every right to criticize his country.

Even so, it was still his.

Amala popped her head out and gestured to Danny. Meena's gaze warned him to be careful. He told Harris that he'd back shortly, but the captain only gave him a vague nod.

Inside the small carriage, Danny was impressed by the valves, knobs, and levers decorating the wall connected to the boiler tender. Amala explained that she was the support crew to the fireman, who made sure that steam pressure was released from the boiler to the steam chest. It was Amala's job to check the gauges and fuel levels when the fireman was preoccupied.

The driver pulled a small red crank and released the brakes. Amala tapped a gauge; the needle slowly arced over the numbers.

"You have to wait for the brake vacuum to reach twenty-one. Then you give a little throttle . . ." She pulled the large, red lever in the middle of the wall. "And we're off!"

The fireman pulled on a rope to give two sharp whistles. The pistons began pumping, the wheels screeching as the train crawled forward. Danny thought about how much Cassie would love to be here, getting her hands on the train's controls, asking endless questions about how it all worked.

When the train was well underway, smoke puffing from the chimney and the pistons making a loud *chug chug* sound as they sped along, Danny thanked Amala for the tutorial before heading back to his carriage. Meena sat looking out the window as

Agra slid by and dissolved into a grassy plain. Captain Harris was already gone.

"Who's that Kamir bloke, anyway?" Danny asked Meena, their earlier argument forgotten. "The mechanic you keep insisting is sick."

"A senior Agra mechanic. He once told me I had no business with the ghadi wallahs and that I should find myself a husband to wait upon. I knew he was going to be asked to assist you and Daphne, so I may have put something in his chutney that had him running for the outhouse for a few days."

Danny grinned and they passed into companionable silence, though it didn't last long.

"As long as we're asking questions . . . What did you mean, when you told the captain that you understood him?" Meena asked.

Danny tried not to let surprise show on his face. "Only that it would be unfortunate if people knew. I was helping him."

"Daphne said she wasn't your type."

"So?"

"You didn't seem very shocked about the captain."

"What the hell do you want me to say?" Danny snapped. Meena's lips thinned, but she said nothing more. Danny sat back, focusing on taking deep breaths. Harris's fear had somehow infected him, and it still crouched in his chest, waiting for the smallest trigger. When he looked back up at Meena, she only gave him a level stare.

"All right, fine," Danny said. "I'm just like him, so I

sympathized. You can be disgusted with me now, the way you were disgusted by him."

She looked down at her lap. Danny crossed his arms and glared out the window. After a long, uncomfortable moment, she finally spoke.

"Tell me about him."

Danny glanced at her. "What?"

"Daphne told me you have someone back home. I want to know about him."

Danny slumped down farther in his seat, somehow more uncomfortable now than he was a minute ago. "He's just . . . He . . . Why do you want to know?"

Meena sighed and tugged her braid forward, as if by pulling on it she could summon someone to come and make the situation less awkward. "I'll warn you, Danny: what you are is not accepted here. I don't know what goes on in your England, but here, it is not allowed. Please be careful."

He could have asked, *Why are you saying this? Aren't you offended?* but her words gave him all the answer he needed. "I will."

"So? Who is he?"

"Someone I met on assignment." Danny reached into his pocket, brushing his fingers against the cog. "We . . . talked. A lot. It was nice, just having someone listen. Someone who cared." He blinked a few times, then returned to the window. "I miss him." Meena had nothing to say to that, so they slipped back into silence.

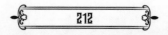

Danny dozed on and off, Captain Harris appearing once to check on them. Amala came to visit for a few minutes during her break, and though Meena was polite, she shot Danny a look reminding him not to divulge any details of their work.

They were halfway to Meerut when Danny sensed something was wrong. The train was quieter; the loud *chug chug* had dwindled to a less-grating *chuh chuh*. He wasn't the only one to notice the change, either. Meena was in the middle of a sentence when Amala frowned and moved toward the rear carriage door.

When she opened it, she screamed.

Danny vaulted out of his seat and caught her before she could tumble out the door. They both gaped at the long stretch of empty train tracks before them.

"They're gone!" Amala shouted in his ear. "Someone disconnected the carriages!"

She ran back to the operations room. Meena stared open-mouthed at the tracks rushing by, unspooling beneath the carriage like a strand pulled from a skein of yarn.

"Captain Harris and the others were on those carriages," Danny said leadenly as a weight sank to the bottom of his stomach.

It could have been an engineering defect, a weak coupling between the carriages. But Danny knew better.

This had been deliberate.

Meena swayed on her feet. "Close the door and get away from there, Danny." He didn't need to be told twice.

The door to the operations room was locked, and Amala

grunted as she threw her weight against it. "It won't open!" She pounded her fist against the door. "Oy, what's going on? Let me in!"

Danny opened one of the windows and stuck his head outside. The train was pumping along at the same speed, but it looked comically small without the rest of its carriages. The tracks stretched endlessly onward.

If they had no way to brake at the Meerut station . . .

"Maybe I can climb through the window in the driver's carriage," he called behind him. It didn't seem plausible, but he had read enough books where the main character ran about on the tops of trains like it was an everyday occurrence.

As he was turning to ask Amala, someone grabbed him around the neck and sent him crashing to the floor.

He tried to shout a warning to Meena, but he was breathless under the sudden weight on top of him, crushing him against the vibrating train floor. Danny managed to free his arm and elbowed his attacker in the chest, half-turning with the movement.

In that brief moment, he saw the man's dark-tinted goggles and the black kerchief tied around the lower half of his face.

"No," Danny gasped, but that was all he had time for before the man wrenched his arms up behind his back. Danny cried out in pain.

Meena launched herself at the attacker, distracting him just long enough for Danny to roll out of the way. The man back-handed her across the face with a sound like a thunderclap and she went down. He also smacked Danny for good measure,

stunning him. Grabbing Danny's wrists and straddling him so that he couldn't get away, the man began to tie him up, the rope's rough fibers biting at his skin.

"Stop!" Meena shouted, but the man ignored her. Danny heard a click before a shot rang through the carriage. The man grunted in surprise as a bullet grazed his arm, just above Danny's head.

Meena stood clenching a small gun in her hands. A trickle of blood fell from her split lower lip.

"Get away from him, and I won't shoot you again!" Meena yelled.

Danny could see where the bullet had torn through the man's jacket, but there was no blood. In fact, there was no flesh. Underneath the fabric was a glint of metal.

He opened his mouth to warn Meena, but the man grabbed him around the throat. She wasted no time, firing again and hitting the man's other side, near his collarbone. This time there was a yelp and a spurt of blood.

Danny used the distraction to kick the man off of him. Though his head swam and the world tilted dangerously, Danny got on top of his attacker and used his bound hands to get under the man's chin and hold him in a headlock, just as Matthias had taught him to do in what felt like another life.

"Don't move," Danny panted. The sweat on the man's neck was warm and slippery against his wrists. "Tell me who you are, and what you want with me." The man remained silent. *"Tell me!"*

Meena pulled back the hammer of her gun a third time. Before she could release another bullet, the man produced a knife from the inside of his sleeve and cut the bindings on Danny's wrists. He knocked Danny back and rushed for the open window.

"Stop!" Danny yelled, but it was too late. The man, trailing blood, launched himself outside.

Meena gasped and Danny swore. But the man hadn't leapt to his death. He'd caught a rope ladder that dangled from a small aircraft, which had been following alongside the train.

His attacker clung to the rope as the aircraft carried him away. Even through his dark goggles, Danny felt their eyes connect—a threat and a promise.

Danny slid back to the floor as Meena moaned something in Hindi. One of his wrists was bleeding, but the wound was superficial. All the same, the shock of crimson and the smell of the man's blood in the carriage made him dizzier.

"No!"

The cry came from the operations room. Danny scrambled back to his feet as Amala ran out. Through the doorway, which Amala had finally managed to open, Danny saw the limp forms of the driver and the fireman.

"They were knocked out," Amala said. "No one's been controlling the water level in the boiler!"

"What does that mean?" Meena demanded.

"The steam pressure's been building all this time. If we release it, the firebox is going to collapse."

"And if that happens?"

Amala mimed an explosion with her hands.

"Can we detach ourselves from the boiler?" Danny asked.

"We have to."

They helped Amala drag the unconscious yet still breathing bodies out of the operations room. Then Amala unhooked the couplings between the passenger and driver's carriages, and they watched the front of the train with its boiler trundle onward without them.

But their carriage was still moving forward at an alarming rate, blasting air through the open hole.

"How do we stop this thing?" Danny yelled as the wind whipped his hair and stung his eyes.

Amala searched for the brake cylinder. When she pulled it, the carriage shuddered and Danny and Meena fell onto the burgundy benches. The piston and wheels screamed and sparks flew from the tracks. They continued forward for another couple hundred yards before the carriage came to an exhausted halt.

A minute later, the chassis on the boiler farther down the tracks blasted apart, sending flames in all directions.

"Oh, God," Danny whispered.

They watched the flames gradually recede, leaving an unnatural quiet in their wake. The three of them shifted, taking stock of the situation. Danny had a lump on his head and a nick on his wrist. Meena had a split lip and the beginnings of a bruise on her cheek.

"I messaged for help when I got the door open," Amala said. "Someone from the city should be here soon."

Danny looked out the rear door. "I hope the others are all

right." He hadn't seen the large airship that had attacked the *Notus*, but that didn't mean it couldn't be out there, picking off Captain Harris and his men. Or maybe it was after Daphne.

The shock hit then, and he slumped to the floor. Meena put her hands on his shoulders and whispered something that sounded soothing, though he couldn't make out the words past the ringing in his ears.

About an hour later, the group spotted a caravan of autos heading in their direction. Danny had spent the entire time gazing at the sky, so worried about another aerial attack that he hadn't considered one from the ground.

But it wasn't an attack, it was a rescue. British officers from Meerut ushered them into their autos, warming them with blankets and the promise of tea.

Danny accepted the aid without speaking. A medic said he might have a concussion as he bandaged Danny's wrist.

Seated next to Meena as they were whisked away to the city, he couldn't focus on anything beyond breathing and blinking. Meena was all too happy to keep quiet.

As they approached the city perimeter, though, she asked him if he would be all right.

He took a deep breath and muttered, "I should have taken your brother's stupid plane."

Captain Harris greeted them when they were shown to their accommodations.

"Thank goodness! We felt the carriage break off, but we couldn't do a damn thing about it. Are you two all right? What happened?"

Danny told the captain about the man with the tinted goggles. Harris listened with an anxious frown.

"We've been on the lookout for that rebel airship. They must have known we would be searching, so they tried a different method." He put a warm hand on Danny's shoulder. "We'll get to the bottom of this, don't you worry. In the meantime, I'll set up a guard. Don't go anywhere without consulting me first. Is that clear?" They both nodded. "Good. I'll send a cable to the major and tell him the news."

When he was gone, Danny sank into an armchair and closed his eyes. He couldn't stop the loop in his mind: the smell of the man's blood, the sound of gunfire, Colton's face as he heard the news that Danny was dead or had been taken.

We'll be watching.

Danny's eyes shot open.

First the threatening note. Now someone was following him, attempting abduction.

He was an idiot for not linking them sooner.

Meena hesitated when a guard asked to escort her to her room. "You shouldn't sleep with a concussion," she said to Danny. She asked the guard in Urdu for some tea. "I have to keep watch over you for a few hours, at least." Danny was too tired to argue, and the sound of tea was tempting. He needed something to clear his head.

As she crossed the room, he heard the swish of fabric and remembered what she concealed in the folds of her salwar. Watching her, he added another person to the list of those he needed to keep an eye on.

XIV

The airship made a loud whirring sound as it cut through the air. The initial liftoff had sent an odd blend of fear and excitement through Colton as he looked out a small, round window, watching in awe as the earth fell away. He wasn't afraid of heights like Danny was, but he'd never been so far from the ground before. He liked it.

According to Brandon's brother, David, the journey to India would take at least ten hours. He'd snuck Colton inside the cargo hold and promised to sneak him back out when they landed in a place called Jaipur. Danny had never mentioned the name, so Colton didn't know anything about it. All he knew was that it was not Agra, which meant it wasn't where Danny would be. But he would figure out how to get to him.

He hoped.

I'll bet no clock spirit has done this before, he thought with a

hint of pride. It vanished as he reminded himself why he was making the journey in the first place.

"I'll save you, Danny," he whispered to his upraised knees. "Wait for me."

Tucked between two large boxes, he felt secreted away, safe from prying eyes. He would have to conserve his strength for whatever came next. With hours to go until they landed, and his body aching, Colton willingly slipped into unconsciousness.

Dirt collected under his fingernails as he dug through a mound of soil. The dirt was wet and cold, but there was something about it that soothed him—a richness that promised life.

He saw that life in a moment: the pale orange mound of a carrot. Pulling it up by its leafy stem, he shook away loose dirt and added it to the basket. Gathering vegetables was usually a chore he disliked, but today it helped take his mind off of the anticipation brewing in his stomach.

He would be going to the coast soon. His lessons were about to begin.

A few drops of rain hit the backs of his hands. He looked up and blinked when a drop kissed the corner of his eye. Quickly, he headed back inside.

A woman with long, dark hair stirred a pot hanging from a metal hook above the hearth. She smiled at him, but it was fleeting. "What's the fare, then?"

He showed her the basket of carrots and onions. She hummed sadly over the size of the onions, smaller than last year's.

A muffled cough sounded upstairs. Both he and the woman glanced at the wooden ceiling.

The bells of St. Andrew's parish chimed five. The front door opened a moment later, and a large figure shook rainwater from his dark hair.

"Curse this rain," the man grumbled. "At this rate, the river'll flood. How are you, boy?"

"Fine, Da."

"Ready for your trip?"

"Yes." He tried to contain his excitement, but the man grinned at the eager tremble in his voice.

The three sat down to a supper of stew and staling brown bread. Colors of taste flashed brightly in his mouth: sweet orange, savory yellow, black pepper, silver salt.

The woman began to ladle a bowl of stew, but he stopped her. "I'll do it."

He carefully climbed the stairs with the bowl steaming between his hands. The upper story was only one room, three beds partitioned by sheets that hung from the ceiling. He made for the one in the back corner.

His sister lay pale and gaunt, her brown hair fanned over the pillow. She had grown so thin. Her arms rested over the coverlet, her wrists twiglike under the cuffs of her nightgown.

He sat on the stool their mother normally occupied, and where their father perched when he told her stories. He liked to hear them, too, curled up in his own bed, listening to the low rumble of his father's voice through the sheet.

"Abigail," he called softly. Her eyelids twitched, bruised and puffy. When they opened, her blue eyes sought him, crinkling in the corners. "I have stew. Let's sit you up."

He helped prop her up against the pillows. Blowing on spoonfuls to cool them, he fed her while trying not to spill anything on her nightgown. Her eyes were half-lidded as she concentrated on chewing and swallowing.

After he washed the bowl downstairs, he returned to his own bed and crawled under the blankets. He listened to the rustle of his parents getting ready for bed, watching the flickering light of their lantern fade as it turned the sheet separating their beds from yellow to dark blue, like the sun vanishing beyond the treetops into night.

But he was too excited to sleep. In two days, he would go to the coast. Just thinking about it made his heart beat faster.

His daydreams were interrupted by a sudden fit of coughing. Before his parents could move, he was at his sister's side. Abigail eagerly drank the water he held to her lips, gasping when she was done. He swept her hair back and kissed her warm forehead.

"I can't sleep," she whispered. "Tell me a story?"

He curled up on the bed with her, moving her gently so he could fit. She snuggled into his side, closing her eyes. Stroking her hair, he recited the story their father often told about the bear who went to market. She laughed at all the right moments, but toward the end she drifted off to sleep, and he was left whispering the rest of the story to her dreams, all the while thinking about the call of the ocean.

Waves beat against rocks by the shore, frothing over onto the shoals of the beach. He stood hip-deep in the freezing gray water and shivered as the tide swept in and out. The waves pulled him backward and forward, unsure if they wished to take him or not.

"Center yourself," Instructor Beele called to him. Other boys and girls stood along the shore, observing. "Feel it in the water and expand from there."

He breathed in deep and closed his eyes. Feel it in the water. Could he feel it? Yes, there—just a bit, a little pinch of acknowledgment. He focused on that pinch and felt his awareness grow. Time swirled around him like the eddies in the water, twisting into complex patterns he couldn't possibly follow.

He lifted his hands. Water dripped from his upraised palms, rippling the pattern. That was his connection. That was him in time's grasp. Heart pounding, he submerged himself in the water.

His world was soundless and dark. Cradled in the cold and wet, he concentrated on the twisting vines around him. They drew in closer, the water pressing from every side. Reaching out, he plucked a single strand and time shuddered. He released a sound that came out as a bubble of air.

Deep in the water, far away and far below, he thought he felt something else. A presence, and a warning, and a blessing.

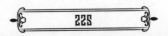

He broke the surface and drew air into his starved lungs. The others cheered from the shore. He turned to grin at them, water streaking down his face. Sand and silt clung to his bare feet as he stumbled back to shore, where Beele wrapped him in a thick blanket.

"Well done, Bell," the Instructor said. "And now what do you do?"

He faced the endless sea and bowed. "Thank you, Aetas, for showing a humble time servant your power. I will not misuse it."

The Instructor patted his shoulder and moved on to the next student, a girl who came from a nearby village. Many of these students would be sent to London, but he hoped he could stay at home, where he was most needed. God or no, Aetas had many time servants to assist him. His sister only had one of him.

He watched, shivering, as the girl slowly waded into the water. She was scared, yet trying to hide it. Someone tapped his arm, and he turned to see the tall boy who had gone before him. His dark hair was still wet, and he kept his blanket tightly wrapped around his shoulders.

"Well done," the boy said through chattering teeth.

"You, too."

"I'm Castor. I came from Enfield."

Bell smiled. "I know you. The cobbler's son."

"Yes. I know who you are, too," Castor rushed to say. His pale cheeks grew ruddy. "I mean, my father knows your father. Says he's a nice man."

They watched the girl disappear under the waves. He

wondered how long he had been down there; each of the students had been different. One of the girls had been down nearly a minute, and they feared she had drowned until she came bursting through the water.

"We're sorry about your sister," Castor mumbled.

Bell shifted on his feet. He wasn't used to talking about Abigail with strangers. "She's faring better."

"I'm glad."

The girl came up sputtering and they cheered for her. As she trudged back to the Instructor, Castor lowered his voice. "What did it feel like to you?"

He thought about the twisting vines and the power hidden beneath the waves. He pulled his blanket closer.

"It felt like life."

The May Day festival bloomed in greens and reds and yellows, and the maypole had been staked in the very heart of the village green. Children ran about while girls in white dresses twisted flowers into crowns.

Abigail sat on a chair outside in her nicest white dress, the breeze making curls of her long, brown hair. The doctor had said she was healthy enough for the festival. Her friends had already garlanded her with flowers and ribbons, and she sat like a young fairy queen overlooking the festivities. Her blue eyes were brighter than he had ever seen them.

"May I have some cider?" she asked.

"Of course." He kissed the top of her head, careful not to disturb any flowers, and found his mother behind a table laden with food and drink. She gave him a wooden cup of cider for Abigail and even snuck him a sweetmeat.

He sat with Abigail as the local musicians strung out song after song, laughing as a goat ate the mayor's handkerchief from his back pocket. Someone announced that the girls should assemble for the maypole dance.

Looking across the green, his breath caught. Castor leaned out from behind the church, beckoning at him.

"I'll be right back," he told Abigail. Careful not to be seen by his parents, he snuck around the church to where Castor waited, beaming.

"I have something for you," the boy said. Castor pulled out a green ribbon with a single rosebud tied to it, then wrapped it around his wrist.

"What if someone asks about it?" Bell argued, but Castor waved the worry away.

"Say it was from an admirer. I've seen you make eyes at Mary Baker before—say it's from her."

"You're too reckless." All the same, he took Castor's hand in his own. "I don't have anything to give you. I'm sorry."

Castor tilted his head to one side. He had a familiar shine in his eyes, the one that usually preceded trouble. "I know what you can give me." Castor tapped his lips.

"I-I can't do that here!"

"Why not?"

"We're in the open, and the church is right there, and—"

"No one can see us." Castor's brown eyes studied his face, taking in his reaction. "Sorry. I've made you uncomfortable. I'll settle for a smile, how's that?"

When Castor was involved, smiling was always easy, a natural instinct at the very sight of him. So Bell smiled, and it was a true thing. They stood there for a moment, listening to the music on the green, hands held fast together. The rosebud brushed against his wrist.

Slowly, he leaned in until their lips met. It was warm and soft, like the petals of the rosebud. Castor touched the side of his face, and when they broke apart, the shine in his eyes was brighter. Bell wanted to tell him that he smelled of grass and clean linen and the sea, all things he loved.

Castor led him back around the side of the church to rejoin the festival. The girls were dancing around the maypole now, tying the ribbons into a pattern almost as complex as time's. Abigail's friends supported her on either side as she joined them in the dance, laughing and trailing a blue ribbon behind her.

Their hands were still connected. He laced his fingers with Castor's and thought that this pattern was just as complicated, and just as wonderful.

Colton jerked himself awake as the airship shuddered around him. He wondered if something was wrong, but a glance out the porthole showed that they were merely descending.

He had wondered if he would have visions again, eager and afraid to learn more. The image of the sea was the most peculiar. He had never seen an ocean, although he knew what they were. As frightening as the vast waters had seemed, Colton thought them beautiful.

Even more peculiar was the boy who had walked into the ocean, the one who took care of his sick sister. The Instructor had called him "Bell." Colton didn't know anyone by that name. Beyond that, Bell's interactions with Castor made him uncomfortable. Bell was obviously infatuated with him, and those feelings had invaded his thoughts and almost felt like Colton's own. It seemed unfaithful to Danny.

Focus on getting to Agra, he reminded himself. *Worry about this later.*

But the visions left him in a strange mood. Not for the first time, he wondered if this was what people called dreaming. Danny had often told him of his own bizarre dreams. Humans seemed obsessed with the idea of them, and talked about them whenever they could.

"And then this big bird flew down and took the key right out of my hands," Danny had once said, "so I couldn't open the yellow door. But then I was sort of going through the keyhole, like I'd turned to smoke or something, and I saw that the room was filled with cakes."

Colton, trying to follow the narrative with no luck, had to interrupt: "Why was it filled with cakes? And why would the bird want the key?"

"I don't *know*, Colton, that's the point. It was just a dream. They're not supposed to make sense."

Were these dreams, then? But they *did* make sense, and besides, he had never dreamed before. Why start now?

He knew the answer would have to wait. He gripped Big Ben's cog and focused on the power it gave him.

The airship drifted down in a steady arc. Colton sensed the air shifting around the metal hull, almost the same way he could sense time moving. It had been a strange journey in that regard; his connection to Enfield had tapered off to little more than a faint flicker in the back of his mind. But here, time ran strong, shifting, shifting, until it settled around him like a snug coat.

The airship landed with a few bumps that rattled the floor. He stood and looked out the porthole. It was already evening, the skyline a swirl of purple and blue dotted with the outlines of strange trees.

The engines and propellers powered down. Fifteen minutes passed before the door connecting the hold to the rest of the airship clicked open. Colton braced himself, ready to run or hide, but it was only David.

"How was the ride? Are you feeling all right?"

"I think so." Colton touched his side, which gave off a pang. "Am I getting off now?"

David rubbed the back of his neck. "About that. You can't leave just yet."

"Why not?"

"I just got word that they're not unloading the cargo until early tomorrow morning. I thought I could sneak you out the passenger way, but even if I did, there's nowhere for you to go in the compound without getting caught. You're obviously not a soldier, or a crewmember. Anyway, the trains to Agra won't run again till morning."

Colton's shoulders slumped. "I'll have to stay the night in here?"

"Look, I'm sorry. I don't like it either. Brandon would have a fit if he knew"—Colton could not imagine Brandon having a fit of any kind—"but it's the safest place for you."

It was hard to argue, especially as once he stepped off this airship he'd be in a new world. He didn't feel ready to face it in the dark of night.

"I'll stay here," Colton agreed. "Will you come for me in the morning?"

"I will. Do you need anything for the night? Any . . . I dunno . . . blankets?"

Colton smiled a bit, reminded of Danny's mother. "I don't need anything. I'll be fine until morning."

He watched David, along with the crewmembers and soldiers, head into the large compound beyond. Suddenly, he missed Danny's bed. Making do with what he had, he curled up between two boxes and closed his eyes, trying to recreate Danny's image in his mind. The clothes he wore still smelled of him, but that would fade with time. Everything faded, eventually.

It was hard to concentrate on Danny when he still saw Castor behind his eyelids. Annoyed, Colton opened his eyes and glared at the box in front of him. What sort of story had influenced these dreams, anyway? Why were they all about Enfield?

It's like I'm reliving someone's life, he thought as night fell outside. *Someone from Enfield. Someone like Danny, who can sense time.*

"Who are you?" he murmured, unaware he'd spoken the thought out loud.

He was so tired. It didn't take much convincing to slip back into unconsciousness, curious to see if more dreams would appear. After all, he had an entire night.

And he wanted to know more about the sea.

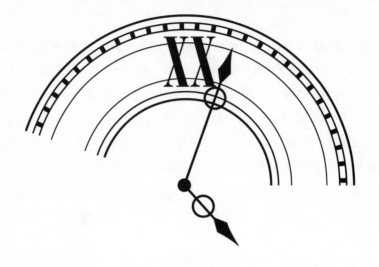

Instructor Beele was a thin, middle-aged man with ear and nose hair amusingly disproportionate to the hair on his scalp. As he paced before his students, lecturing on theories of time measurements, that wispy hair blew frantically in the coastal wind.

"Units of time have, of course, been guided by the sun for centuries," he said with a vague gesture upward. The sun was half-hidden behind brooding clouds, the sea restless, its soft roar underlying Beele's words. "Other methods included heartbeats and the blinking of the eyes. On a grander scale, years have been divided into recordable measurements: the saecula, the aion, the lustrum, the olympiad . . ."

Students sat on blankets along the shore. They did not take notes, as most of them couldn't write. This was a lecture they had to listen to and remember.

Which was why Bell glared at Castor whenever he flung little rocks at Bell's leg, or made faces when Beele wasn't looking, or leaned over to murmur in his ear.

"I wonder what unit of time is named after one of Beele's lessons," Castor whispered.

Bell couldn't resist. "A beelenium," he whispered back. They snickered as a couple other students gave them sidelong looks.

The Instructor stopped mid-pace. "Is there something you two find amusing?"

Castor cleared his throat. "No, sir."

"Stand up, Bell."

Flushed and ready to kill Castor as soon as they were alone, Bell stood and brushed the sand from his trousers.

Beele eyed him skeptically. "Since you've grown bored with time units, let's alter the topic slightly. Name the five Gaian gods."

Bell swallowed. "There's, er, Chronos."

"Who is?"

"Who's the creator of time. And there's Aetas"—he paused to bow toward the sea—"who was given the gift of time when Chronos could no longer control it."

"Keep going," Beele said.

"Oceana, the giver of water. Aetas takes refuge with her. It's said that they were born together. Then there's Caelum, the overseer of the sky and the heavens, who moves the sun and moon and stars. And Terra, the protector of earth, who grows our crops and raises mountains." He glanced down to see Castor clapping quietly.

"Very good. Now tell me, since you already seem to know

everything I have to say regarding time units, how Aetas came to be the Timekeeper?"

Bell chewed on his lips. Sheepishly, he shook his head.

"Sit down, then."

Bell plopped down next to Castor, who sniggered as Bell poked him hard in the ribs.

"Chronos," Beele said, resuming his pacing, "was born when the universe was breathing its first gasps. He is said to be the father of time. He understood how it moved and gave it shape. It had a will of its own, you see. Time is a flighty, complex thing; it will go in any direction, all at once, without control.

"Chronos saw this and set the earth on a straight track forward. One small slip, one pattern unraveled, and earth's time would tangle together like a ball of twine. We would go forward and backward, experience the same day in ten different ways, witness our births as we experienced our deaths. Chronos is the giver of time, the founder of what we know as history."

Beele stopped to stare out at the ocean for a moment, hands held clasped behind his back. "But it was too much, even for Chronos. Weary and losing control, he cut off four of his fingers, which grew into the four other Gaian gods. Aetas and Oceana were born first—in that, Bell, you were correct. Chronos gave Aetas power over time, and Aetas went to earth with Oceana to be closer to his new power."

Beele took a deep breath and turned back to his students. "What you all felt in the sea during your initiation was more than time. It was Aetas allowing you to see and sense it for yourself, as he does. Time is not a tapestry, cleanly woven; it is far more complicated. You will do well to remember and respect that."

Over the ground, Castor's hand had found Bell's, their fingers twined together.

"Sir?" A girl had raised her hand. "If Aetas is the one controlling time, then how come only time servants can feel it? My sister and parents can't, but I can."

Beele was rarely defeated by a question, and it showed in his frown. "That, we do not know. It's one of the great questions that has no answer. A theory, of course, is that Aetas requires only some of us to help him regulate time over all the world. It's too big a task for one being, even if that being is a god. So we offer ourselves to Aetas, aware of him always. That is what keeps this world turning."

Abigail had another fever. Their mother had gone to help an elderly aunt and their father was working late, so Bell sat by her bedside throughout the day, spooning broth into her mouth, returning to the hearth to boil water for tea. He went out to pick herbs, plants that his mother and her mother before her had been taught to use as cures for ailments.

When Abigail was awake, he told her stories of his lessons. She loved to hear about the ocean and the waves and how it felt to be immersed in the water.

"Time was everywhere at once, and it was so large, and so

frightening. And so lovely." He brushed the hair off of her forehead. "I wish you could feel it, Abi."

"Take me to the ocean, then."

"I will when you're better."

As the sun began to set, he heard a knock at the door. Castor waited on the other side, a small, wilted daisy in his hand. "It looked better before I picked it," Castor said, handing him the drooping flower.

"That's why they're supposed to stay in the ground." Bell took the flower and twirled it by its stem, grinning. "Would you like to come in for supper?"

Castor lifted a loaf of bread wrapped in cloth. "Baked this morning."

They made a meal of the bread, fresh butter, dried apples, and the last of the crumbly cheese Bell's mother had bought at market. He knew his parents wouldn't mind; the past two years had seen Castor come and go from the house on a regular basis.

If his parents knew the truth of their relationship, however, it would be quite a different matter.

Castor helped clear the table. "You know, I haven't seen you in a couple days. I'd hoped for another sort of greeting."

"Such as?"

Castor wrapped his arms around him. Bell returned the embrace, leaning in until they were cheek to cheek.

"I missed you," Castor whispered.

"It hasn't been that long."

"You're so cruel. It's been ages."

"A generation."

"A century."

"An olympiad."

"A beelenium."

They turned their heads and kissed. Bell felt Castor's smile against his own. He kissed him again and again until those lips softened and parted.

A small voice called down the stairs.

"Abigail heard you," Bell said, a bit breathless.

"I want to see her."

Castor was quite popular with Abigail. He made her laugh and usually brought small treats, like a sweetmeat or a game. Castor plucked the sorry flower from the table and bounded up the stairs, Bell following at a slower pace.

"For you, my lady." Castor knelt, presenting the wilted daisy to Abigail. She giggled and took the flower with a faint blush.

"I thought that was mine," Bell complained.

Castor raised his dark eyebrows. "You didn't appreciate it nearly enough. Now, if you'd had *that* reaction, I would have reconsidered."

"Stop teasing my brother," Abigail scolded. "Tell me a story instead."

"If you insist." Castor sat on the bed and Bell dragged over the stool. "How about the story of the three little pigs?"

"No."

"Rumpelstiltskin?"

"No! One I haven't heard before."

"Hmm." Castor rubbed his chin. Bell noticed that Castor sometimes had a vague shadow of stubble along his jaw and just under his nose. It made his upper lip feel prickly when they kissed, but he didn't mind. In fact, he rather liked it.

"How about I make up a story?" Castor gestured to Bell on the stool. "We both will."

Abigail clapped her hands in delight. "Yes!"

Their eyes met, each waiting for the other to start. Castor's eyes crinkled in amusement.

"There was once a boy . . ." he began.

"Who received a royal summons," Bell continued.

"To see the princess of another country."

"But that country was at war."

"So he became a soldier."

"And fought for whichever side needed him most."

"He tried to make it to the princess."

"Because she waited for him always in a tower of the castle."

"And she couldn't leave."

"For fear that he would never find her."

"But there was a battle in the very field that lay before the castle."

"And in that battle was the boy."

"A sword pierced him, and he fell to the ground, injured and bleeding."

"The princess saw, and feared for his life."

"She didn't want to leave the tower, but she knew now that she must."

"She dressed as a soldier and fought in the boy's stead."

"She stood over him, swinging her sword at anyone who came near."

"And when their side won, she dragged him into the castle to be healed."

"When the boy woke, he saw the princess splattered with blood, and looking more beautiful than he had ever imagined."

"The princess kissed him, and they were very happy."

The boys sat smiling at each other, Abigail almost forgotten until she cleared her throat. "And? Did they get married?"

"I suppose so," Castor said. "If you want them to."

"I want them to."

"Then they did."

Abigail said she liked the story very much. Castor tried to wheedle her into telling one of her own, but she fell into a coughing fit. Bell hurried to get her a cup of water. By the time he returned, her face was red with the strain. He stood staring at his sister's emaciated frame, taking in her hollow cheeks and thinning hair. Castor rubbed her arm and asked if she was all right. But all Bell could do was think about when they'd believed she was getting better, that maybe her body was becoming stronger.

All lies.

He walked to the dresser on his side of the room and, opening the top drawer, searched for a new handkerchief for her. There were no clean ones. He closed his eyes tight and held onto the dresser's surface.

When he opened his eyes again, he caught his own face in

the chipped mirror. Blue eyes, as blue as his sister's, stared back at him. A few freckles stubbornly clung to his pale nose. His brown hair was getting shaggy in the back; his mother would insist on cutting it soon.

Something moved in the mirror. Bell did not turn, instead watching Castor's reflection as it came closer.

"Come back," Castor whispered. "She needs to see you."

"But I can't see her. Not like this. Not anymore." Bell's eyes filled with tears, distorting their reflections.

Castor touched his arm. "She relies on you so much. You have to be strong for her. And I promise I'll help in any way I can." Bell watched as Mirror Castor leaned their heads together, arms encircling his body.

"I'll always look after her," Castor whispered. "I promise, Colton."

The world came roaring back, bringing a fresh wave of pain with it. Colton doubled over, choking on a scream. His side was on fire, his chest wound too tight. The cogs at his back flared, sensing his distress, and the pinprick of Enfield in his mind grew more distant than ever.

He rubbed at his chest with small, panicked moans. They echoed off the metal floor, surrounding him with the sound of his own fear. He didn't worry about anyone hearing him. In that moment, the enormity of the world was forgotten, and he was the only thing in existence.

Slowly, he sat up and leaned against the hull. He covered his eyes with a shaking hand, then his mouth, then his chest again.

He had wondered. Had tried to evade the thought—it had seemed too impossible, too absurd—but he couldn't ignore it any longer, staring him in the face the same way he'd stared at his own reflection.

They weren't dreams. They weren't memories of someone else's life.

They were *his* memories.

kash's hands were steady on the controls as he guided the *Silver Hawk* through the air. He had graciously offered Daphne the copilot seat, while Lieutenant Crosby and his soldiers sat in the back.

Daphne was grateful. She loved the open space between earth and sky, a space that felt honest, true. She would have gladly lived the rest of her life in the clouds, close to the sun.

"You look as though you're enjoying yourself," Akash commented.

"It's been a long time since I could relax on an aircraft. The last two times I was trying to keep Danny calm."

Akash laughed. It was a clear-ringing sound, all bells and confidence. "You're a good friend to him."

Daphne raised an eyebrow at her reflection in the window. "Friend." It was strange to think that she and Danny Hart had

become friends. But it would be cold—and untrue—to deny it. "I suppose we are friends."

Akash smiled. He had a strong jaw with a hint of dark stubble, and his aviator goggles sat perched above a nose slightly too large for his face. He'd offered her a pair before they'd taken off, but she had politely declined, wanting the full experience—glare and all.

She remembered Danny's warning that the rebel airship could be coming for her. She sat with her back straight, eyes often searching the surrounding expanse of sky. But there was no sign of that behemoth ship.

For now.

She watched Akash fly the craft with ease, like it had become more routine to him than walking. Lights blinked along the control panel, and Akash occasionally asked her to flip a switch.

"Would you like to try?" Akash gestured to the controls.

Daphne reined in her rush of excitement, keeping her face carefully blank. "Why not?"

"Excellent. It's really not too difficult, once you understand the basics. Now, let us say we want to go higher. If you—"

She pulled the center stick up and the plane pitched higher. She leveled it out and then gently pressed on the rudder bar, yawing them in a zigzag pattern. Releasing the center stick, she glanced over at Akash. His mouth was still open as if to give her instructions, but all that came out now was an incredulous laugh.

"You know how to fly?"

"Not by myself, but I've sat in cockpits before."

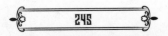

"Amazing, Miss Richards. I never would have expected someone like you to know about planes."

"Oh?"

He must have heard the frost in her voice, for his smile slipped. "I'm sorry. I meant no offense. It's just that here, in India, our women are not pilots. They may work on the rail lines or as ghadi wallahs, but even then, those women are often treated with disdain."

"I understand." It seemed that no matter where she went, working women would always invite scorn.

Akash nodded. "I tried to teach my sister how to fly, but she stuck up her nose at it. I'm fascinated by her work with clocks, but she never seemed to be at all interested in my planes. At first, I was hurt, but when I thought about it more, I suspect she wanted to avoid the scandal of being both a ghadi wallah and a pilot. She hears enough talk as it is."

Daphne thought of the looks Meena drew in the cantonment, the same looks Daphne herself had drawn when she walked down the halls of the Mechanics Affairs building. She felt a kindred frustration with the Indian girl, an anger that, despite constantly being buried, still grew roots.

"How did you learn how to fly?" she asked.

"Our father has a close friend who's in the good graces of the British officers. He learned to fly some years ago, and the British took him on as a messenger. He invested here and there, and came to own a small plane. When I was younger he took me and my sister up in that plane. Meena cried, but I loved being in the air, so he gave me lessons.

"I started working when I was ten, first for a merchant in the city. Then, when I was eighteen, as an aerial messenger for the cantonment officers. When I turned twenty last year I realized I'd saved enough to get my own craft." He patted the side of the *Silver Hawk* fondly. "With a little investment from uncle-ji and father, of course.

"And you, Miss Richards? How did you come to know so much of flying?"

She stared out the window at a shimmering river below, a serpentine vein in the earth's skin. "My father was a pilot. He took me up whenever he was off-duty."

She had always been happiest in the air, far from the ground and the worries that found her there. Her mother had balked at the notion of both her husband and daughter going up in an aircraft. Daphne remembered, even now, the crescent shapes her mother's nails had left in her skin, anxiously digging into her cheeks and arms.

After a brief pause, Akash asked, "Is he no longer with you?"

"He passed a few years ago."

"I am very sorry."

"It's all right." She kept her lips slightly parted, wanting to tell him: *He was one of you.* But she couldn't make herself say the words. It would feel like a lie, somehow.

An awkward silence brewed in the cockpit. Daphne listened

to the low murmuring of the soldiers in the back, wondering how much of the conversation they had heard.

"Urdu bol sakte hain?" Akash asked suddenly. *Do you speak Urdu?*

"Sirf thodi si." *Only a little.*

"Kyaa aap ko yahaan achchhaa lagaa?" *Do you like it here?*

"Haan." She paused to think of something else to say. "Meri Urdu . . . kharaab hai?" *My Urdu is not very good.*

"Not at all! You are very good already."

"I need to practice."

"We are practicing now."

They spent the rest of the trip speaking in fragmented Urdu and Hindi, Akash laughing at her accent and gently correcting her botched words. They tried to muffle their laughter when, at her insistence, he quietly taught her a few swear words. Daphne didn't want Crosby to overhear and have a conniption.

They landed outside Lucknow half an hour later, just before sunset. Daphne was disappointed that she wouldn't be able to go to the clock tower today. She had an itch in her belly that begged her to go as soon as possible. But when she climbed out of the *Silver Hawk*, ignoring Crosby's offered hand, she could tell that time was running smoothly. She could sense the fibers weaving in and out, straight and orderly. Time didn't feel sharp here as it had in Khurja.

Still, her scalp prickled when she remembered the report that suspicious people had been seen near the tower at night.

Horse-drawn carts called tongas were waiting for them.

Akash hung back to take care of his aircraft as Lieutenant Crosby led Daphne to their transport. As if Crosby could read her restless thoughts, he told her, "We'll get you to your rooms and settle you in. You can see the tower in the morning."

She knew it would be useless to protest. Taking a deep breath, she stepped into one of the tongas accompanied by Crosby and a sepoy—Partha, the one who was often in Captain Harris's company—and it took off for Lucknow. Craning her head around, she spotted Akash watching them trundle away. He waved.

Well, here I am, she thought as they rolled toward the massive city. *No airship attack*. She found that a little strange, but decided not to dwell on it, fearing doing so would somehow make it come to pass.

She had heard Lucknow called the Golden City of the East. Looking at the metropolis stretching before her, she could easily believe it. Sunset illuminated the endless rooftops, the light striking the tops of large, gleaming buildings in a display of dazzling colors. The roar of the crowds could be heard even at a distance. The river she had spotted from the plane ran through the city, dividing it in two.

"No doubt you've heard about this city back home," Crosby drawled at her side.

"Once or twice." She glanced at Partha, who kept his gaze fixed straight ahead. She cleared her throat. "It was besieged during the uprising."

"Yes, indeed. The infamous Siege of Lucknow. After that annoying business with the Enfield rifles, the Oudh and Bengal troops broke into open rebellion. The British troops had to defend the residency here in the city for quite some time, enduring all manner of attacks until the rebels could be driven out. They even had to fight underground through months of sickness and dwindling supplies. Since then, we've not had a problem." He glanced pointedly at the sepoy, who caught his look. "Disgraceful, isn't it, Partha?"

Partha bowed his head. "A vile time for your countrymen, sahib."

"Too right."

Daphne remained silent. She was painfully aware of standing between these two men—two sides of a war, two sides of her birth. There was a strangeness to her skin just then, as if it weren't actually hers. She wanted to scratch at it, see if it would flake off and reveal something truer. Something in-between, something like a mark, that would determine what to say, what to think, what she was.

In streets clogged with both people and animals, vendors hawked eggs and chickens and milk. Soldiers wearing hats or turbans meandered through the crowds, their hands on rifles and swords. They passed impressive mosques and shrines, the products of both Indian and European architecture. Urchins ran up to the tonga with palms held flat, begging for money. Daphne tried not to meet their eyes.

In a more deserted area of the city, they came upon a structure of red sandstone in what Crosby called the British quarter. Although Daphne saw laundry lines stretching between buildings and chimney smoke rising from roofs, the place felt abandoned.

Again, Crosby attempted to help her down, and again she ignored his hand. He moved his jaw like he was chewing his bad mood and pointed at the building before them. "These are our residences for the next several days. You are not to leave unless escorted by at least one soldier, and you must seek my permission first."

She tried to mask her irritation. "Is Mr. Kapoor staying here as well?"

"Who?"

"The pilot."

"Who knows." Crosby waved away the question. "Though the city has undergone quite the transformation since the Mutiny, there have been incidents in the past few months. Hostility toward our soldiers, a brief altercation at a mosque, what have you. This is why you need an escort, Miss Richards. The city may look inviting, but even behind a well-adorned wall you may still find mold. Partha, take her to her rooms."

The sepoy made to take her pack, but she shook her head. "I can carry it," she insisted.

He blinked at her, but silently allowed her to follow him into the building. Inside, the soldiers had carelessly left their doors open. Daphne saw men arguing, laughing, eating, sleeping. They passed an open sitting area where soldiers' wives drank tea near a balcony. A few noticed her and gave her outfit a disapproving glare.

Partha spoke to a servant in Urdu, who pointed him in the right direction. A minute later, they stopped before a red door. "This is your room, Miss Richards. Do you require anything?"

"I'm fine, thank you. I'll just wait until the lieutenant comes."

Inside she found a plain room with off-white walls and a chair so pouffed it looked like it was making up for the rigidness of the bed. A window faced the street, offering a view of flat rooftops. A shirtless boy crouched on one of them, whittling a block of wood as a monkey watched nearby.

Daphne stood at the window, unaware she was tapping her fingers against her thigh until she looked down. It was a habit she hadn't fallen into for some time, but she knew what it meant.

She opened the door and peered outside, starting when she saw Partha standing guard at the door. He seemed equally startled, his brown eyes large and almost doe-like.

"Yes, Miss Richards?"

"I, um. Never mind."

She made to draw back inside when he took a step forward. "Do you need something?"

Daphne studied his face. There was a sadness in his eyes, in the set of his mouth, that felt familiar. It reminded her of the way Danny looked when he thought he went unnoticed, when his gaze turned west, toward the boy he was missing.

"Do you . . . happen to have a cigarette on you?" she asked.

If he thought this was an odd request, he did a good job of hiding it. He darted a glance down the hall in both directions, then slipped a metal cigarette holder from his breast pocket. "Please do not tell anyone," he murmured. "I'd hate to be on the receiving end of those new words you learned."

So he'd overheard Akash teaching her swears in Hindi. Her face heated as she said, "I won't. Thank you."

She plucked a thinly rolled cigarette from the holder and silently handed it back to him. In the privacy of her room, she struck a match—she always carried them with her, on the off chance—and lit the end. The first inhalation made her cough, but the second was smoother and, almost at once, settled her nerves.

Daphne did not smoke often, but she'd taken it up shortly after her father's death. Her mother had screeched about the smoke and the smell, making it a rare indulgence. But every once in a while she felt the need, like when she was stranded in an unfamiliar city, the threat of a riot or kidnapping around every corner.

By the time Crosby came to her door with supper, the sun was completely hidden beyond the horizon. She had opened the window to let the air inside, hoping it would carry away some of the lingering scent of smoke.

"We've been planning out an itinerary," Crosby said. "We have all your visits to the clock tower scheduled. The first one is tomorrow morning, so mind you get some sleep."

"Excuse me," she said when Crosby turned to leave, "but what am I to do when I'm not at the tower?"

He looked vaguely uncomfortable, and she wondered if he had a wife, or even sisters. Her guess was probably not. Female company seemed a foreign concept to him.

"You'll be here, I imagine."

"Does that mean I'm confined to my quarters?"

"You may certainly leave with an escort if you wish, but as I said before, you must inform me first." At her frown, his voice grew colder. "Is that clear, Miss Richards?"

"Yes."

He left her to a lonely meal of rice, beans, and some potato dish in a brown broth. She only picked at it. Her mind was back on the *Silver Hawk* with Akash, in that open space between earth and sky where she didn't have to hide.

XXII

When they arrived at the clock tower midmorning the next day, Daphne found it disappointingly unimpressive. She'd spent the tonga ride searching for the tower above the rooftops, but the structure barely peeked above the buildings surrounding the circular clearing where it stood. The tower was mostly built of the same reddish sandstone as the officers' billet, with a wooden frame and a brick base. There was only one clock face at the top, the glass dusty and the numerals almost too small to read. Above the face was a simple spire that ended in a prong-like symbol. The clock tower seemed inadequate for a grand city like Lucknow.

"Dinky thing, isn't it?" Crosby muttered at her side. "I hear they want to rebuild it in the English style, but don't have the funds. What with all this strangeness of towers falling, maybe they won't have to."

Perhaps it was the casualness of his remark, but Daphne suddenly felt nauseated.

A groom helped her out of the tonga—she didn't mind offending Crosby, but didn't want to be rude to the Indian man—and she looked up at the building. She didn't know what the tower in Khurja had looked like, but if it was anything like this one, she wondered why it had been targeted. Did the terrorists have a strategy? Why not hit the largest cities first? Of course, everyone kept saying Delhi might be attacked, but not until New Year's.

Daphne's boots thudded against dark gray cobblestone as she circled the tower. Crosby had brought along Partha and another sepoy, but apart from their small contingent and the sepoys who stood at every entrance to deter anyone from coming near, the clearing was empty.

"What exactly are you looking for, Miss Richards?" Crosby asked after several minutes.

"Water."

"Ah. We did hear that the ground around the Rath and Khurja towers was damp after the attacks. Do you know what it means?"

"No clue."

There were no pipes or wells or pumps nearby. No grates, no sewers . . . no water. Bone-dry.

"Could you tell me what happened that made Major Dryden think Lucknow is being targeted?" she asked Crosby.

Frowning, the man scratched under his chin. "We usually have a guard around the tower, as you can see. They caught a few loiterers trying to get inside. Ran off before the guards were able to catch them, but no one knows how they got into the clearing in the first place."

Daphne pointed upward. "There are roofs just there. They could have rappelled down."

Crosby's mouth twisted into a sneer as he eyed the guards. "I'm sure they would have spotted something as obvious as that. Then again, they could have been drunk or asleep for all I know."

Anger flared inside her, but she tamped it down. This man wasn't worth a reaction. "Have there been any more sightings of trespassers?"

"I'll ask." He left her near the tower's entrance, flanked on either side by sepoys. Partha stood on her right, his eyes slightly swollen, perhaps from lack of sleep. Kept awake by the heat and nerves, it had taken Daphne a few hours to nod off the night before.

Partha caught her staring. "Yes, Miss Richards?"

"I was wondering if you were all right. You seem unwell."

He looked at her thoughtfully. Before he could respond, the tower entrance opened and two Indian men dressed in rough-spun white tunics and carrying bags over their shoulders walked out, stepping into the slippers they'd left outside.

"Yeh kyaa hai?" one of them asked.

Partha replied, but Daphne only caught the word *tower*.

They switched to English. "The tower has already been inspected."

Partha nodded in Daphne's direction. "She needs to inspect it as well."

The Indian clock mechanics narrowed their eyes, and she fought the urge to fidget. She met their gazes directly, but knew at once she'd made a mistake. They began to mutter in Hindi, too fast for her to follow.

"This is Major Dryden's order," Partha snapped at them. "We are looking at the tower, nothing more."

"She cannot go in by herself," one of the mechanics said. "We must go with her."

"Major Dryden's orders," Partha repeated firmly, placing a hand on his rifle. "She is to go in alone."

The mechanics muttered more until one rudely pointed at her. "Take off your shoes before entering," he commanded. "This is a sacred place. You bring bad luck already."

"What's all this?" Crosby had returned. "What's the holdup?"

"I was just going inside," Daphne said. She knelt to undo the laces of her boots. The mechanics eyed her for another moment, then wandered to one side.

"You don't need to take off your blasted shoes," Crosby snapped. "Just get inside and do whatever it is you're supposed to."

"I'd like to be respectful, sir." She carefully placed her boots beside the door and stood. When she met Partha's eye, he gave her the hint of an appreciative smile. She gave him one in return.

Once she was across the threshold, she closed the door behind her. Angry mechanics or no, she wanted to be alone.

Except that she wasn't alone.

And that was the whole point.

Up a short flight of stairs, she stopped on a wooden platform with a guardrail. It was part of a square-shaped walkway around the open space in which the pendulum swung lazily through the air, stirring the small hairs on her forehead as it passed.

Sunshine filtered through the glass clock face, illuminating the cables and pulleys and rope that extended far up into the rafters. Daphne took a flight of stairs leading to a higher platform, which gave her access to the iron-cast gears and cogs that turned in perfect synchronicity, powering the clock.

And Lucknow's time.

Although the tower was not what she'd call aesthetically impressive, she still felt the familiar awe of its presence sweeping over her body, up her arms, down her back. It aged her, reminding her of her past even as it planted her firmly in the here and now, even as the world evolved around her, without her. Putting a hand on the clockwork, her eyes watered until she had to close them.

"Something is happening," she said quietly, to herself or the clock, she wasn't sure. "I need to know what."

Daphne took a deep breath and opened her eyes. "Please, will you come out? I would like to speak with you. I'm worried that your tower is in danger, and if it is, I need to find a way to stop it. If you know anything, I'd like to help. Please, may I speak to you?"

Daphne tried to ignore the peculiarity of her words as she spoke them. As far as she was aware, she had only seen two spirits: Colton and the little girl in Dover. Before last year, she'd thought that clock spirits were nothing more than legend. Even after the disaster in Maldon, Daphne had never even considered that a spirit had been involved. Not until she had gotten tangled up in the drama of Danny Hart, anyway.

She allowed some of her power to trickle into the clockwork, checking the movement of the gears, the flow of time around the tower, whether or not any part was catching. All seemed well here. Time's fibers crisscrossed each other in pristine order, not a single thread out of place.

"I promise I won't hurt you," Daphne tried again. "I only wish to speak with you. Just for a moment."

Another minute passed, and then another. She sighed. At least she'd tried.

Turning back to the entrance, she jumped back with a small gasp. A young man stood at the top of the stairs leading down to the platform. He looked Indian, but his hair was a hazy silver, his skin bronze. Amber-yellow eyes stared at her, bright and wary. He wore a long white tunic with baggy trousers, and he was barefoot.

Although his features were not golden—maybe the type of metal used for the clockwork had something to do with that— his eyes were the same shade as Colton's and those of the spirit in the Dover tower.

Daphne licked dry lips, wondering what to say. She supposed there was only one thing *to* say. "Hello."

The spirit cocked his head to one side. "Kyaa mein aapki madad kar satkaa hoon?"

Of course the clock spirit spoke Hindi. Daphne racked her brain for the proper phrase, hoping she didn't mangle it.

"Do you speak English?"

He looked vaguely confused, then raised his hand in a so-so gesture, bobbing his head side to side. "English . . . little."

"Fascinating." She would have to tell Danny about this as soon as they were back in Agra. *What's your name?*

"Narayan. Aap kahaan sey hain?" *Where are you from?*

"I'm from England. I'm here to look at your tower and—" But he seemed confused again, unable to follow her English. She began tapping her fingers against her thigh. *"My name is Daphne. I am a ghadi wallah."* He nodded. *"Is your clock . . ."* Since she didn't know how to express it in Hindi or Urdu, she used her hands to convey something breaking apart. *"Trouble?"*

Narayan shook his head. He rambled in Hindi, but she only caught a few words: *time, city,* and *clock mechanics.*

"Nothing is wrong here? You haven't seen anything?" She pointed to her eyes, then to the clock face above.

"Nahi."

Daphne swore softly. If the clock spirit hadn't seen anything suspicious, then what was she doing here? Crosby had mentioned people skulking about the tower, but if they hadn't actually done anything *to* the tower, what was the point?

"I . . ." Narayan paused, thinking hard as he chose his words. "I see, here?" He touched his forehead.

"You saw something? In—your head?" He nodded. "What does that mean?" He began to speak in Hindi again, but she waved her arms. "No, stop! Bas. I'm sorry, but I can't understand you."

She made an aggravated noise and walked in a circle. Narayan watched her, as if fascinated by her behavior. She wished she had a translator, but the only ones allowed inside were the ghadi wallahs, and there was no way in hell she would ask for *their* help, not after how they'd treated her.

If they knew what she was . . . No, that might only make it worse.

Desperate, she tried to talk to Narayan again, but their words passed without meeting. Daphne finally had to admit defeat.

"I want to know what you mean, though, about seeing things in your head."

Narayan asked another question she didn't understand. Frustrated, he pointed down at the floorboards, then at the door. At first she thought he was ordering her to leave, but then he said, "You here, come back?"

Her lips relaxed into a smile. "Yes, I can come back tomorrow, if you like. Subah ko? In the morning?" He nodded eagerly. She wondered just how lonely he was here, reluctant to speak to the other clock mechanics, with no windows but the clock face to look out from.

"I'll come back," she promised. "You can teach me more Hindi."

He seemed pleased, but she couldn't help but be disappointed. Aside from seeing strange people in the clearing, there was nothing to indicate an attack was coming.

If that's true, she thought, *then why was I brought here?*

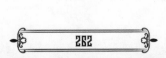

With arrangements made—her head spun at the idea of having a tutoring session with a clock spirit—Daphne left the tower and carefully retied her boots. Crosby descended on her within seconds.

"And? What happened? What did you find?"

"Nothing," she said truthfully as she stood. "If someone's planning on bombing the tower, they haven't acted yet. I would like to come back tomorrow, though, just to be certain."

"Yes, all right. Best to be sure."

They returned to the billet. Crosby instructed her to ask Partha if she needed anything, as he would be in meetings the rest of the afternoon.

She did want something—a way to learn more Hindi. She didn't trust the soldiers enough to bring them inside the tower, but she needed to know what Narayan was saying. A wasp of unexpected anger stung her. If only she'd learned from her father . . . though he hadn't known much of the language either, come to think of it.

Maybe there was an Urdu or Hindi dictionary nearby. She tried walking through the billet, but Partha kept at her heels. He reminded her of an old toy she'd had as a child, a yellow wooden duck attached to a string. She'd clutch the string and the duck would roll along behind her, following her every step.

"You don't have to come with me everywhere," she eventually said. "You should go rest. Have some tea."

Partha looked skeptical, but said that he would have someone posted to her door until he returned. Daphne rolled her eyes when he was gone. Finally, a moment to herself.

Maybe Akash would know where to find a dictionary. She asked a few servants if they knew where he was staying, but they shook their heads, eyes lowered, before they hurried on with their chores. Down another hallway, she nearly ran smack into a dark-haired Englishman in uniform. He gripped her arm to steady her.

"Here, love, I'm sorry about that."

"It's no matter." His hand lingered too long on her arm, and she glanced at it distastefully. "If you'll excuse me."

"Where you off to, love? Looking for some lunch?"

"I already ate," she lied.

"All right, be on your way, then. You ever want to play cards, my room's thirty-one on the first floor." He winked.

Making a mental note to never go near room thirty-one on the first floor, Daphne hurried up the stairs to her own room. Just as Partha had promised, another sepoy stood guard at her door, and let her in with a silent nod.

Once she was alone, she rubbed her arm and scratched vigorously at the spot the man had touched. She had learned to ignore the leers men gave her in London, the occasional grope on the streets. She'd been taught it was only men being men, that they couldn't help their urges. That she was only something nice for them to look at, to feel, as if that were her only purpose in this world.

She ripped off her bodice and looked for one with longer sleeves. Changed, she sat on the edge of her bed and yearned for another cigarette. Or tea. Better yet, sherry. But she was afraid to ask anything of the sepoy outside. She didn't want her door unguarded for even a second.

If only she could be doing something useful, anything to take her mind off these churning thoughts. But Crosby wouldn't dare let her out by herself.

She decided, suddenly, that she didn't need Akash's help after all. Or that of any of the soldiers. She would figure this problem out on her own.

Daphne squandered the day pacing her room and writing a long letter to her mother that she didn't plan to send. It would take nearly a month to deliver, and her mother would have difficulty reading it in any case. Still, it helped to steady her hand and her mind. She jotted down her thoughts, laying them before her as if they were pieces of a puzzle she had yet to solve.

Night fell and her restlessness returned. She wanted to visit Narayan again. She wanted to understand what was going on with the towers.

To blazes with it.

Daphne carefully opened the door to find that Partha had returned to his post.

"I'm going to take a turn around the billet," she lied. "No need to follow."

But as she walked down the hall, he did follow. She sped up her pace, and he lengthened his stride.

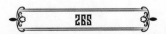

"Miss Richards, where are you going?" he finally asked. "I must tell the lieutenant—"

"Just for a walk, as I told you."

"I will still have to inform—"

She yelled in frustration, then took off running. Partha's boots pounded behind her. Startled soldiers turned their heads, and one of them laughed. Daphne rounded a corner sharply, barreling down the stairway toward the exit.

"Miss Richards!"

The night embraced her. She inhaled a lungful of cooler air and kept up her pace, running, running, directionless but lured by the pull of the clock tower.

"*Miss Richards!*" Partha grabbed her elbow and swung her around. She struggled, but he was far stronger. "Stop, please. Lieutenant Crosby will have my head if I do not keep you in the billet."

"I need to go to the tower," she growled.

"Why? Is it in danger? Do you know something?"

"No, I . . ." How could she explain it? How could she tell this man that in a place where she felt unwelcome, unappreciated, unprotected, she had only one comfort: the clock tower, and the complexity of its time? It was written on her bones. They ached.

"If there is no pressing need, I must bring you back," Partha said.

"Please," she whispered, half-ashamed when her eyes filled with tears. "Please, may I see it? Make sure it's all right?"

He wavered. There was something complicated in his expression, in the way his fingers twitched. He looked over his shoulder at the billet's glowing windows.

"Only if you cover up," he said at last. "Wait here."

She stayed in an alcove until he returned with a long muslin scarf, the sort that Sikh women wore. He helped her wrap it around her head, covering her fair hair.

They walked to the tower in silence. Daphne's legs were thankful for the exercise, her heart beating a slow, insistent rhythm. She wasn't sure why Partha had agreed to her request, unless he had reason to escape the billet himself. She'd noticed that he seemed distant, even lost at times.

"How long have you been in the army?" she asked him.

He lifted his gaze from the ground. "Five years."

"How did you come to join?"

Partha looked around, as if he didn't want anyone overhearing. There were only a few people on the streets in this quarter, including a couple men relieving themselves against a brick wall.

"My father was in the army," he finally said.

"Oh." She wasn't sure how to politely ask more.

He sensed the question, though, and answered anyway. "He took part in what the British call the Mutiny." He made a face at the term. "Unfortunately, he was caught and executed. The group of rebels he was part of were strapped to the front of cannons that were then fired."

A dark feeling stole across her chest, making her shudder.

"I'm sorry," he said in a low voice. "I shouldn't speak of such a thing."

"No, it's all right. I'm sorry for your loss. It's . . . terrible, what happened." The words were inadequate, but he nodded. "I'm sure Her Majesty becoming Queen-Empress doesn't help."

His face fell into that complicated look again, but he didn't respond.

"Are you going to the celebration in Delhi? Will you be helping guard the tower there?"

"No, Major Dryden does not want to spare many of his men. You and Mr. Hart are not to go under any circumstances. It might be dangerous."

She was about to ask more about the tower guard when they rounded a corner and saw a few British soldiers standing under a statue. As they got closer, she realized it was a depiction of the Queen. Her arm was held before her, a large jewel cradled on her stone palm.

The statue must be new, no doubt to celebrate the upcoming coronation. It seemed oddly out of place. Almost garish. Without realizing it, Daphne made a face.

The street was lit with torches, so Daphne could plainly see the faces of Lucknow citizens glaring up at the statue and the soldiers standing beneath it. The street felt like the string of a violin, taut and ready to sound. Partha sensed it, too, and put his hand protectively near Daphne's elbow. The soldiers laughed at something, ignoring the incensed crowd.

Then one man stepped forward and threw a head of rotting

cabbage at the statue. "Down with the Queen!" he yelled. "Down with the British!"

One of the soldiers grabbed his rifle. "What was that, now? I can barely hear you under that swill you call words."

The Indian man was small and stick-thin. He clenched his hands as the British soldier, large and broad-shouldered, stalked toward him.

"I asked you to repeat yourself," the soldier demanded.

The Indian spat Hindi at him, then literally spat—right at the soldier's feet. Before Daphne could blink, the soldier had knocked the man to the ground and pushed a boot to his neck. He aimed his rifle at the man's face.

"Say it again," the soldier snarled. "I dare you."

Some of the Indians put their heads down, walking faster. Others had stopped to watch. Now they roused as one, muttering and yelling and finding other things to throw: a shoe, a rock, a piece of garbage. The other two soldiers drew their guns, trading worried looks. They were clearly outnumbered.

The soldier pinning down the Indian man fired a warning shot in the air. The whole street fell deadly silent.

"Run to your homes, or whatever piss-stained alley you use for your beds," he ordered, "unless you want a hot bullet for your supper."

The Indians retreated slowly, malice flaming in their eyes. One man seemed to look in their direction, and Daphne stiffened, but he only gave a grim smile before he lost himself in the crowd.

The soldier let the skinny man up, and he scrambled away as

fast as he could. The soldier aimed his rifle as if to shoot him in the back, thought better of it, and shouldered it again.

Partha had dragged Daphne into the shadows, away from the commotion. When he gently tugged her arm, she realized she was shaking. "We must go back to the billet," he whispered. "Please. It's not safe."

A riot had almost broken out. Either the Indians would have been shot, or they would have torn the British soldiers limb from limb.

And she would have been helpless to stop it.

"Miss Richards, *please.*"

The fingers on her arm trembled. She looked into Partha's eyes. They were wide, frightened, but shone with the same fervor of the crowd, a current of hatred under subservience.

At least they had something in common, then.

"I'm so sorry," she whispered.

He swallowed and swung his head from side to side. "Do not worry yourself. But we must go. Now."

The clock tower. Was it all right? Had this been a distraction to attack it? As they walked back in the direction they'd come, she focused on the energy of Lucknow's time and found it unchanged. Narayan Tower was still functioning.

"Please do not tell the lieutenant," Partha said.

"I won't. You have my word." But even if she never spoke of this to another soul, it would still play through her mind in grim horror, searing a brand that she would carry forever.

The next day, Daphne all but ran to the clock tower and found Narayan waiting for her. She tried to speak to him again, but had no more luck. The most she could make out was that he had seen more visions.

She needed a translator.

Back in her room, she sat stewing in her own irritable thoughts, hating her circumstances, until a rap at the window made her jump. Akash waved at her from the other side of the glass.

Her room was on the second floor.

Her heart leapt as she flung open the window. "What are you doing? How—?"

"Don't worry, there's an overhang here. See?"

Daphne leaned out and saw that he was, in fact, standing on a slanted ledge. "You're going to fall and break your neck. How did you even get up here?"

"Meena and I used to run across rooftops when we were little. We stole kites." Daphne raised an eyebrow, and he grinned. "I don't think the sepoy at your door likes me," he went on. "He wouldn't let me in."

"Oh. I'm sorry. I would have welcomed the company." But then the events of last night returned to her, biting and surreal. No doubt they bit at Partha, too.

"Since the lieutenant won't let you out without an escort, I will gladly be your escort if you would like a tour of Lucknow," Akash said.

"Thank you, but maybe some other time."

His smile dimmed. "Are you feeling well, Miss Richards?"

"Honestly, I just want some tea."

"I can bring you tea."

"How?"

"I will think of a way."

"Don't you dare climb up here with a teacup on your head."

"I climbed *down,* actually. And I could hold the saucer between my teeth, if you prefer." He flashed those teeth in another brilliant smile.

She scoffed. "Good luck with that. I can't wait to see your shirt soaked with tea."

"Then I will return quickly."

"Wait wait wait!" He had actually started climbing back up to the roof, as if he had every intention of delivering piping hot tea to her window. "Are you mad?"

"Meena usually says so."

"Well, Meena must be right. You're not bringing me tea."

"All right." He put his hands on the windowsill. "Then come out here with me, and we'll get it from a chai wallah down the street."

Daphne considered her options: stay trapped in her room, eaten away by fear and loneliness, or go outside and risk seeing another episode like last night's. She might be able to find a Hindi dictionary, though. And there *was* the promise of tea.

Carefully, she climbed out the window and onto the roof, balancing beside Akash. He grinned at her, as excited as a little boy. A spark of that excitement caught flame inside her. She wanted to run, but not from Akash; from this building, from herself, from everything she had ever known.

"Teach me how to climb," she heard herself say.

"Haan, Miss Richards."

The chai was sweet and hot, and Daphne closed her eyes in bliss after the first sip. The chai wallah's cart was busy, so to avoid being jostled by impatient customers, Daphne followed Akash as he weaved through the crowd. Although it was warmer, Daphne was glad she had changed into her long-sleeved bodice, even if she still attracted stares. Mostly, it was her fair hair and skin that drew curious eyes. She wondered what it would be like to blend into the crowd, to immerse herself without fear of standing out.

"Do you like the chai?" Akash asked. She hummed her approval. "Are you at all hungry?"

"Not at the moment."

"Then what would you like to do?"

"I'd just like to walk."

Akash didn't exactly lead her. He didn't know the city well, though he said he had been there a few times for deliveries. But he walked at her side, sometimes choosing which way to turn, sometimes letting her steer their course. Daphne was amazed to realize that aimless wandering with tea in her hand was exactly what she had needed.

They saw a sign for the botanical gardens ahead. They exchanged a look.

"Would you like to go?" he asked.

"I would."

Daphne had been to the gardens in London and found them beautiful, if boring. It had been more fun when she had gone with her mother and father. They would spread a blanket on the grass of Regent's Park and feast on a picnic, watching bumblebees hover over bright blooming flowers as swans drifted easily over the water. She had dared her father to race her, crowing in victory every time she won, though she knew now that he had let her win, dramatically staging despair at losing only to make her grin.

The gardens of Lucknow were laid out neatly, interspersed with bright emerald patches of grass and dark, leafy trees. Sometimes the paths curved, following a hedge or a large planter filled with multicolored flowers. Tiers of plants were arranged like a stage, showcasing the Indian breeds of flora and fauna. Indian and European visitors alike chatted around them, some heading home as evening approached, others taking their time lounging on benches or on the grass.

"It really is a beautiful country," Daphne murmured, "though often a sad one."

"There are many unpleasant parts of India. If you can still see the beauty, then I am happy."

"I do see it." She brushed a flower with her fingertips. It felt good to breathe warm air and have her body sing with exercise. She wanted to sweat out the impurities of her body and mind. To be clean, inside and out.

"My father was half." The words spilled out of her before she could staunch them, and suddenly the evening air was popping and electric, her heart pounding a ragged rhythm. It was foolish, she told herself. She was being foolish.

But when she managed to look at Akash, he was waiting for her to continue.

"Half-Indian," she clarified. "I don't look it, I know. And I . . . honestly, I don't *feel* it. But here, I . . . I don't know. It's a little closer to me, I think. I can understand it in some way."

The world was quiet around them again, quiet save for her heart. She had been too afraid to voice her feelings before, too scared to bare this sliver of herself that no one else could possibly understand. Some days, she was sewn together like bits of cloth, squares and threads unraveling in different places. Some days, she wondered what comfort meant, and if it was something she would ever learn.

She had decided long ago that being what she was meant living in a constant state of unknowing. It was yearning for a world that was not meant for you.

Akash didn't dismiss her words. He didn't exclaim about how British she looked. He didn't even ask about her father.

Instead, he said, "Thank you. I'm glad I know this."

Relief flowed through her. "You are?"

"Yes. I think I understand you a little more, now. I always feel as if you care more than the others. Now I know why." He glanced at her shyly. "May I ask you something, Miss Richards?"

"Please just call me Daphne." She had been begging him to call her by her first name for weeks. "What is it?"

He tapped the spot next to his temple. "This mark. What is it?"

Daphne touched the diamond-shaped tattoo. She'd expected a much different question. "Oh, that. It's only a tattoo."

"Yes, but why that symbol?"

She lowered her hand and slipped it into her trouser pocket. Danny had asked her the same question, and she hadn't answered then. But something about Akash made her want to tell him. She needed at least one person to understand her reasoning, silly as it seemed now.

"The diamond means invincibility. I was at a point in my life where I wanted to be invincible, so I got the tattoo to remind me. I had to be firm, unbreakable." She breathed in deeply. "It was a way to face my fears."

Akash took a moment to think this over. "Did you know that diamonds were first discovered in India?"

Something soft pulled her lips upward. "No, I didn't."

"There is a symbol here called the diamond throne. It is a symbol of infinity, the meditation spot of the Buddha himself. It is thought to be the center of the universe, where things are quiet and enlightenment may come."

"That sounds nice. I could use some enlightenment at present."

"That may be true of everyone. You're ahead of all of us, I think." Ever so lightly he brushed a fingertip over her tattoo. Daphne flinched and he lowered his hand at once. "I-I am sorry, Miss Richards. I'm sorry if I touched you inappropriately. Please forgive me."

She almost wanted to laugh. If *that* was inappropriate, she'd hate for him to know where else men had let their hands wander. "I just wouldn't like to be touched right now."

He ducked his head. "I'm sorry."

"It's all right."

The sun was setting and clouds rolled in from the plain as they continued to walk. Daphne wondered if Partha had looked in on her only to find her gone.

"What did you mean by needing enlightenment?" Akash asked. "Is there anything I can help you with?"

She hesitated. As much as she wanted to figure out Narayan herself, she was coming to realize she couldn't do it alone.

Daphne swallowed her pride. "If I tell you what I've seen at the clock tower, will you keep it secret?"

"Yes, of course."

So she told him of Narayan and her promise to return. She wanted to know more about the tower and what the spirit had seen. Akash listened, his eyebrows drawn into a V as if he was struggling to decide if she was joking or not.

"What do you mean by spirit?"

"They're the forces that keep the clock towers attached to time. In a sense, they're a manifestation of the clock, but they appear as humans, like us. I spoke to a couple back home, and so has Danny. Hasn't Meena mentioned them before?"

"A couple of times, but only in stories."

"Will you come and meet him with me tomorrow? Will you act as my translator?"

"I wish I could, but they won't let me in the tower."

"Even if I say that it's all right for you to join me?"

"Even then," he said. "Though I would gladly be your translator, the ghadi wallahs will chase me away."

"Has that happened to you before?"

"Meena has always dragged me to clock towers. Sometimes I've been lucky enough to see her work. Other times, I've been smacked or shoved out. Once, I was chased away with a broom."

Daphne's mouth twitched. "Well, that's too bad. I hoped you would be able to tell me what he's been saying."

"Why not use one of the other ghadi wallahs?"

"They don't trust me. And, to be honest, I don't trust them either."

A grin spread lazily across his face. "I am glad to hear that you trust me."

Her blush was almost painful. "Er . . . good." She cleared her throat. "Could you teach me some phrases in Hindi for tomorrow, then? I'd like to ask the spirit a few things."

They spent the walk back to the billet repeating Hindi words, continuing to draw stares. But Daphne tuned them out, focusing only on how Akash shaped the words on his lips and the way his voice resonated on each vowel.

Back at the sandstone building, Akash showed her how to use the low-hanging awning of the next building over to jump onto the roof. She followed him across and dropped down at her open window. Daphne looked inside, but the room was dark. She had half-expected Lieutenant Crosby to be waiting for her with teeth bared and whip in hand.

Akash dropped down next to her. After she climbed through the window, they stood staring at each other, their hands resting on the sill. One white, one brown, only six inches away from touching.

"Akash?" Daphne had to swallow; all that talking had dried out her throat. "Tomorrow afternoon . . . come back to my window?"

He smiled slowly. "Haan, Miss Richards."

XXIV

*S*omeone screamed in the darkness. It struck Danny like a lightning storm, but a barrier stood between him and whoever was in trouble, gray and impenetrable and terribly familiar.

Who was crying for him? Danny banged his fist on the barrier and shouted back. He told them to wait, that he was coming, that he would save them.

"That's a laugh," drawled a voice above his head. He turned to find the man with dark-tinted goggles leveling a gun at his head. "You can't even save yourself."

Danny surged out of the dream in a sweat, the echo of a gunshot still ringing in his ears. His legs were tangled in the sheet;

he had thrown the rest of the bedding off during the night. He'd squirmed out of his nightshirt as well, and was now lying only in his drawers. The arched window, open the whole night, had done nothing to lessen the heat in the room.

He heard the scream again and sat up. He untangled himself from the sheet and hurried to the window. But the more he heard the cry, the more he realized it didn't sound human.

Danny leaned out and looked down the street. A bright blue bird, about as big as a pheasant, was strutting around in a pen. As it shuddered, its impressive plumage lifted from the ground into the air. A bloody peacock. Right on cue, the bird made its shrill cry, as if it knew Danny was watching and laughed for having tricked him.

Grumpy, Danny dressed, leaving his shirt untucked. He examined himself in the mirror. His hair was a rumpled mess and the skin under his eyes was dark and puffy. Danny thumbed the scar on his chin. He looked tired. Haunted.

As he tugged a comb through his hair, he wondered who had been on the other side of that barrier in his dream, that person he couldn't reach. He immediately thought of Colton, and the resulting dread stole his breath away. Compelled by longing and something darker, he took Colton's picture from his pocket.

Looking at it was both painful and sweet. Over the last few weeks, Danny had taken to drawing inward, finding solace in his memories. As if, by standing still enough, he could feel Colton's lips on the hollow of his throat, on the curves of his closed eyes.

He would have given away all he owned for the sensation of Colton's thumb trailing a path over his jaw, or the sound of his voice conjuring his name from the air.

He missed his touch like a sky misses a firework, a spark as brilliant as it is brief.

Feeling a little foolish, Danny put his lips to the charcoal ones on the page. Lord, he was losing it.

A knock sounded at the door. He quickly stuffed the picture in his pocket as it opened to reveal Meena frowning in the doorway.

"I thought you would look better come morning, but I don't think that is the case." She pushed the door open farther to reveal the breakfast tray she was holding. "I've already eaten, but I saved you some food."

"Oh, thank you." He took the tray from her, placing it on the bed. There was fruit, a thicker bread than the chapatis he'd grown used to, and hard-boiled eggs. He reached for the tea first. It was not chai, but a full-bodied English blend, and he nearly moaned in appreciation.

"How do you feel?" Meena sat on a chair beside the low wooden table where his water pitcher had been placed the night before.

"I've certainly been better." He downed the rest of his tea. "What about you? You were hit rather hard."

She touched her puffy lower lip. "Not as hard as you were." The medic had insisted that Danny had a slight concussion. Meena had watched over him until she had started dozing on the very chair she sat on now, at which point Danny had kicked her out and fallen into bed.

He touched the spot where the man on the train had smacked him. It was still sore, and he had the remnants of a headache.

He could see a question forming in Meena's eyes, but she was interrupted by another knock. Captain Harris greeted them when he opened the door.

"Good morning. I wanted to see how you were holding up."

"Well enough," Danny said.

"I'm glad to hear it. I still need to file an incident report for the major, so I need to go over the attack with you again."

Meena left nothing out, not even the use of her gun. Harris's fingers twitched, but he otherwise masked his surprise well. "At least if this man tries to attack us next time, we'll know a little more about how he operates."

"Do you think there'll be a next time?" Danny asked, not bothering to hide the trepidation in his voice.

"It seems this man wants you for some reason."

Danny's earlier revelation coiled around his throat, constricting it. How much could he divulge? What if he was wrong?

"He's hurt, though," Meena pointed out. "It may be a while until he strikes again."

"Maybe." Harris gathered his notes. "Anyway, you two are due at the tower. Shall we leave in half an hour?"

Meena stood. "May I make a request, Captain?"

"Of course."

"I would like to visit the temple first. I must perform puja."

"That can certainly be arranged."

She left to prepare, leaving Danny to frown quizzically at Harris.

"Puja?"

"A Hindu prayer ritual," the captain explained. "Normally, they perform it with a household icon. The Hindu sepoys have their own icons. Partha keeps his in his room." Harris froze, his grip tightening on his pen.

Danny fiddled with a piece of bread, dropping crumbs on the floor. "I meant what I said earlier, Captain. I'm not going to tell anyone. You have my word."

Harris managed a small, tight smile. "I believe you, Mr. Hart." He hesitated. "Partha and I . . . we've been worried, of course. About someone finding out. But if that someone is you, I don't think we need worry."

Danny briefly thought about his conversation with Meena and decided not to remind the captain that she, too, knew his secret. "I'm glad, though. That you found each other."

There it was: a small flash of happiness, a glint of gold at the bottom of a riverbed. Harris looked at the floor, but the corners of his lips were still turned up. Danny also knew that slow walk to joy, how it turned his heart heavy and light in turns.

"I don't know how long it can go on," Harris said, "but I plan to stay in India. With him." He cleared his throat and ran a hand through his hair. "And you, Mr. Hart? Is there a certain someone?"

Now it was Danny's turn to examine the floor. "Yes."

"And it would be undesirable for someone to find you two together?"

Danny nodded.

Harris sighed. "It's a strange world, Mr. Hart. I'll always fight for the promise of an easier tomorrow. Right or wrong, selfish or not, this is what we want." He nodded to himself. "And that's enough. Whatever it takes."

"Whatever it takes," Danny agreed, touching the cog in his pocket.

The tonga stopped in front of a stone temple that bustled with colorfully dressed men and women in saris that ranged from canary yellow to cornflower blue. The street was clogged with worshippers and shoppers who flitted among the carts strategically placed around the temple.

Meena hopped down and gestured for Danny to follow.

Danny turned to Captain Harris. "Will you be coming with us, Captain?"

"I wish I could." Harris glanced sidelong at the escort of mostly British soldiers, some already sweating under their hats. "But I don't want to cause a scene. You're not a soldier, so they'll be kinder toward you."

Since the captain seemed intent on waiting outside, Danny trailed after Meena. She'd changed into a freshly laundered sari

of dark green before leaving her room. Even her hair was washed and had been wetly tied into its usual braid.

"I didn't bring any offerings, so we'll have to buy some," Meena explained. "Have you taken a bath?"

"Er . . . No. Was I meant to?"

She flipped her hand. "No matter, you're a foreigner. Now you know for next time. Are you at least wearing clean clothes?"

"Yes." His clothes had been laundered just before leaving the cantonment.

Meena steered him toward a fruit vendor who insisted that they buy his mangos. She bartered with the merchant, their voices rising until they came to some sort of agreement. She reached for her money, but Danny stopped her.

"I want to pay," he said, "since this is my first time visiting your gods and all."

She gave him a funny look, but allowed him to pay for a couple pieces of coconut and, just to make the man stop shoving them under his nose, a mango. The vendor thanked them, bowing his head a few times before turning to the next customer.

"Are you planning to offer the mango, or eat it?" Meena asked.

Danny slid it into his pocket with a sigh. "I suppose I'll eat it later. I've never had mango before. Think I'll like it?"

"They're my favorite fruit. You'll love it."

They joined the queue leading up the stairs. Danny heard giggling and realized the women were laughing at him.

Meena grinned. "You're in the wrong line. Go over there."

She pointed to a line a few feet away made up of only men. Face burning, he made himself walk slowly to the end.

"What are these for, anyway?" he asked, holding up the piece of coconut Meena had given him. It was sticky and warm from lying in the sun.

"An offering to the gods. We don't have time to visit all five, so we're only praying to Shiva today."

"Who's that?"

The lines moved, and they moved with them. "Shiva," Meena explained, "is the Supreme God. He is the creator, the destroyer, and preserver of all, though other gods may play these roles as well, depending on which temple you visit."

"Sounds like a stressful job."

She glanced at him, unimpressed. "He is All. It's simply his nature to be these things."

"But how can someone be both a creator *and* a destroyer?"

"He dances."

Danny tried not to laugh, but it came out as a muffled snort. Meena scowled.

"He dances the tandava," she said, "which started the cycle of creation. When he dances it again, it will destroy the universe he's built."

"But why? Why ruin everything you've created?"

"Because everything that is born must eventually die," she said simply.

When they reached the main chamber, Meena took off her slippers. The other men and women were doing the same, lining their shoes up neatly across the stone floor. Danny pulled off his boots and padded into the chamber in his stockinged feet.

The chamber was wide and drafty, lined with stone statues. Adorning the walls were murals in faded ink of gods and goddesses he couldn't name. One of them rode a tiger.

Beyond the lines, Danny could see an inner chamber where a stone idol sat upon a dais. His hair was long, his eyes closed, and his lips were turned up in a benevolent smile. This must be Shiva, the creator/destroyer.

Bit cheeky for a bloke who'll blow up the universe, Danny thought. The idol sat in a meditation pose—a rather uncomfortable-looking bending of the legs—with hands held open in his lap. Two snakes were wrapped around his biceps, and a larger one had wound itself around the god's neck. His hair was piled atop his head like a hill, a crescent moon-shaped disc sticking out from one side. Beads hung from his neck, resting on his bare chest.

An old priest dressed in an orange robe sat outside the inner chamber. Though bald, the hair near his ears was wispy and white. His shriveled lips curled into his mouth, making his chin jut out. At Meena's instruction, Danny handed the priest his piece of coconut. The priest pressed his thumb into a copper bowl of vermilion and crooked a finger at him. Danny leaned down, allowing the man to draw a line between his brows with the red powder.

Then the priest handed him four cashews. Since Danny hadn't expected to be given anything, he said, "Thank you." A few people turned to glare at him. The priest opened one eye, looked at Danny, then lowered his eyelid. Danny thought he caught a tremor of a smile pass over the man's inverted lips.

Sufficiently mortified for the day, Danny stuck as close to Meena as he could. When they approached the idol of Shiva, she nudged him.

"Do this," she whispered, putting her hands together in prayer. She bowed over her hands toward the idol. Danny followed her instruction as others kneeled on the floor and bowed to the god while they chanted in Hindi.

Meena signaled with her eyes, showing Danny where to stand while she joined the devotees. Her voice rose strong and sure as she chanted Shiva's name and the prayer that filled the inner chamber where the idol sat, smiling at his followers. There was something oddly peaceful about him, although Danny had to imagine that a god who could end the world came with a temper.

Briefly, he thought of Aetas—and of Chronos, waking enraged from his sleep to slay Aetas for what he'd done. That had nearly been the end of the world. Maybe Shiva had danced then, and made the earth tremble.

The earth was trembling now. Perhaps Shiva was beginning to dance again.

When Meena was finished, she gestured that they could leave. Outside, they put their shoes back on.

"You can eat the prasad now," she said, and popped her own cashews into her mouth. Danny followed her example.

"What were you saying back in Khurja, about the ash . . . ah . . . something about the Indian Gaian gods?"

"The ashta vasus?"

"Yes, those. Does India have its own story about how Aet—I mean, how Agni died?"

"Not specifically, no. The story goes that all of the vasus were caught stealing a cow from Vashishta, a sage, who cursed them to be born again as mortals. They asked the goddess Ganga to be their mother, and to relieve them of their mortality as soon as possible. So Ganga Devi gave birth and drowned the vasus to free them of mortal life, so that they could return to the heavens. Only Dyaus survived in his incarnation, trapped as a mortal."

"Where I come from, there are several stories of how Aetas died. No one can agree on how exactly it happened. I was curious if any of your stories lined up with ours."

She shook her head, her braid swaying. "I don't think so. But the vasus are still important. They're still in everything we see and touch. Shiva," she said, nodding back at the temple behind her, "keeps the cycles and the elements moving. Now come on, Captain Harris must be burning under the sun."

Danny followed her down the stairs and into the road. He looked around and was surprised by how many beggars had congregated at the temple. They sat slumped against the walls or nearby trees, dressed in rags or loincloths, some with fabric wrapped around their heads, all of them barefoot. Danny slowed to a stop.

"Leave them, Danny," Meena said.

He saw a man walk up to a beggar and hand him a banana. The beggar thanked him. Down the street, another beggar sat with a child propped against his chest, his dark eyes bloodshot.

"Danny," Meena warned, but he ignored her, approaching the beggar with the child. The child noticed him first and looked up.

Without a word, Danny handed them the mango from his pocket. The beggar looked him over, then took it carefully. He put his hands together in the same way Danny had in the temple, the mango between his palms, and bowed his head.

Flustered, Danny turned back to Meena. She was giving him that funny look again.

"Captain Harris," he reminded her, walking past. She followed without a word. When he caught a glimpse of her face, she was smiling slightly.

The clock tower stood in the very heart of Meerut. Danny had not known what to expect, as the only tower he'd seen in India so far was the one in Khurja, and that had been a pile of rubble.

The Meerut tower was about as tall as Colton's in Enfield. It was constructed mostly of limestone, though the clock face was made of a beautiful green glass. Meena told him the face glowed emerald at night.

"Hopefully we can witness it," Captain Harris said as they were helped out of the tonga by a groom. "I hear the guards don't let anyone except mechanics near once the sun goes down. Understandable, considering what happened to Khurja and Rath. Major Dryden's orders were passed down from Viceroy Lytton himself."

"Orders to guard the towers?" Danny asked.

Harris nodded. "They weren't always this protected, but now the viceroy wants every Indian clock tower manned by soldiers. Seems a bit strange, though, doesn't it? To protect the towers even though time's still running in Rath and Khurja? Makes you wonder what the point really is." He noticed Danny and Meena staring at him. "I meant no offense."

"Many have been saying the same in Agra," Meena said as they walked to the tower. "It is unnatural. But then again, people are redefining what they consider unnatural."

Time running itself, Danny thought, *is not natural at all.*

Sepoys stopped them before they reached the entrance. One guard with eyebrows nearly as thick as his mustache eyed Danny and Meena before asking, "Why are these children here?"

"These *children,*" Harris said, "are clock mechanics sent by Major Dryden."

The sepoy's tall partner, who wore a turban, said something in Urdu. The other replied with a displeased hum.

"The other ghadi wallahs were here this morning," he told them. "They were not happy to learn they were excluded from this . . . assessment."

"They're not affiliated with the army," Harris said. "These mechanics are. If you'll excuse us?"

Harris led Danny and Meena to the tower. The sepoy called after them, "Make sure they take off their shoes!"

"I know that," Meena growled. "Do they think I am a new ghadi wallah?"

"How long have you been one, anyway?" Danny asked as he once again unlaced his boots.

"About two years. And you?"

"Uh . . ." He looked away. "A little less than that. You're nineteen?"

"Sixteen."

Danny coughed in surprise, though the thought was immediately driven from his mind as they walked into the tower. He breathed in the musty air, feeling the power in the building all around them. Time spread outward from this one point, dominating all of Meerut and its people, covering the city in a tightly woven tapestry.

"Captain Harris said there's been no water around the tower," Meena whispered as they walked up a flight of stone steps. "But they saw someone on the roof a few nights ago."

"What happened?"

"I don't know. Perhaps the person jumped. If that's the case, no body was found."

At the top of the stairs, a thin wooden railing divided them from the stem of the pendulum. Danny looked down and saw it far below, swinging back and forth. The gear train sat beneath the clock face, smoothly whirring.

He thought about Colton's tower, and the familiar embrace of time that welcomed him whenever he walked inside. Time did not feel the same here. In Meerut, in this tower, time was colder—harder. Perhaps it was only Danny's connection with Colton that made Enfield feel different. He felt discouraged, like he wasn't wanted here.

Meena walked down a short flight of stairs to get to the clockwork underneath the gear train. "I do not sense anything wrong," she murmured, her voice echoing above the loud *ticktocks*. She touched a finger to the bronze central cog, which turned steadily in the framework of the clock's skeleton. Danny thought of it severing, of time instead being a hollow, airy thing he couldn't grasp.

"I don't, either." Danny walked around the higher platform, looking through the green glass of the face. Meerut appeared warped on the other side. There was a small door next to the face, but no scaffolding. Just as well; he wouldn't want to go outside, especially with all those soldiers watching his every move. But then how had this mysterious person gotten to the roof?

In his mind, he saw a flash of silver: the metallic rope the man with tinted goggles had used.

Danny took a deep breath. "There's only one person who would know for sure."

"There is? Who?"

Danny looked up at the rafters with a flutter of anticipation before he cleared his throat. "Hello? Can you please come out? Er, maazirat . . . chahta . . . hoon?"

"What are you doing?" Meena asked warily.

"Hello? Salaam? Namaste? We would like to speak to you, if only for a moment."

Meena bounded up the steps, making the bangles on her wrists clatter. "Have you gone mad? There's no one here!"

"There is." He took the small cog from his pocket. Though it didn't hold much sway here, he held it up and poured some of his own power into the metal. Nothing stirred, not like it did when he was in Enfield.

Meena lowered his arm to look at the small cog. "Where did you get this? Danny, please tell me what's going on. You're not making sense."

"I'm trying to talk to the spirit of the tower."

Her face hardened. "What?"

"They can tell us if anyone strange has been at the tower."

"Danny—" She checked her tone, then began again. Slowly, calmly, as she would talk to a child. "There are no clock spirits."

"Yes, there are."

"No, there *aren't*."

"You believe in Shiva and the vasus, but not clock spirits?"

Meena's mouth twisted.

"Hello?" Danny called again. "Please show this young woman you exist."

"Danny, enough! I want to leave. Let's just talk about what we've seen—"

"Hold on." He walked around the platform and hurried down the stairs, toward the clockwork. He removed the bandage around his wrist. A soft scab had formed over the cut where Goggles had nicked him, which Danny now painfully scratched off, letting a dark bead of blood well on his wrist.

Holding his breath, he pressed a drop of blood to the central cog.

Time pulsed and lifted all around him, a feeling so similar to falling that he nearly threw up. It was almost like Khurja, almost that same sharpness, but not quite. Intoxicated with the power, Danny tried to reach for the time fibers. To pull them and morph them into a different shape.

A scream tore through the air, and Danny was yanked away from the clockwork. He nearly toppled over the railing into the pendulum pit below. He held onto the railing and gaped as a middle-aged woman wiped his blood off the central cog.

She spun around and glared at him, swearing in a different dialect than Urdu. Her golden hair was tied back into a loose bun, her body round, her face puffy around the cheeks. Her skin was a dark tan, more bronze than brown, and her eyes were amber. She wore a faded yellow sari.

"I'm sorry!" Danny tried to say around her yelling. "I'm sorry—maaf kijiye!"

She stopped at last, her jaw clenched. Danny righted himself and wiped the last speck of blood from the cog. He shuddered to his toes, and the world shuddered around him.

"I wanted you to come out," he said. "It was the only thing I could think of."

She huffed and looked up at Meena. The girl stared down at them, mouth agape, the whites of her eyes more visible than her dark irises.

"Meena? Please come down," Danny called to her. "I don't speak her language very well."

"Who . . . Who is she?" Meena croaked.

"The spirit of the tower." Then, because he couldn't resist: "I told you they existed."

After getting over her initial shock, Meena acted as a translator between Danny and the annoyed spirit, occasionally interjecting her own responses. The spirit's name, like her tower, was Aditi.

"She says she has been the guardian of this tower for too many years to count," Meena said, her eyes never leaving the golden woman. The spirit stood with her chin up, as if she enjoyed the attention. "She does not like that you forced her to come out. What did you do?" That last question was solely Meena.

"Uh." The wrist wound had clotted, and he hid it behind his back. "I can explain later. Please ask her about the intruder."

What followed was a long conversation in Hindi that Danny could barely understand. The women glanced at him a couple of times.

Meena switched to English. "She says she doesn't know. She remembers someone on the roof of her tower, but by the time she went up to confront the intruder, they were gone."

"And there's nothing altered in her tower? Nothing out of place?"

Another exchange, and Aditi shook her head.

"Odd." Danny rubbed a hand over his thigh, thinking. The other two carried on without him. He was happy to let them, until he heard his name.

"She wants to know how you knew she was here," Meena said. Judging by her narrowed eyes, she wanted to know the same thing.

"Tell her—" What could he say? "Tell her that I've spoken with others of her kind. Maaf kijiye," he said again to the spirit.

"She says it is all right," Meena translated under Aditi's words, "but that you should show more respect in her tower." Meena arched an eyebrow at him, and he shoved his hands into his pockets.

"Fair enough. Ask her again about the trespasser. Any idea of what they were doing on the roof?"

They went around in circles until Aditi grew tired of them and made a shooing gesture. Meena asked if they could come back, and Aditi agreed, but only if they gave her an offering.

"An offering to a clock," Meena murmured as they left. "How strange." She stopped Danny before they walked through the door. "You owe me answers."

He swallowed. "When we're back at headquarters."

They reported to Captain Harris that they had seen nothing amiss. He asked the question running through their own minds: If time still ran strong through Aditi's tower, why were they here?

A *diversion, maybe?* Danny's stomach began to squirm as he thought about Daphne farther south.

Harris reminded the pair to take an escort if they decided to roam around the city. Danny just wanted to lie down, but Meena's persistence kept him from his desired nap. She came to his door barely five minutes after he had returned to his room.

"Can't I get a half hour to myself?" Danny complained. "Concussion, remember?"

"I've never seen anything like that before," Meena whispered. "You just *knew* she was there. You knew how to make her come out. How?"

He sighed and gestured to a chair. Meena took the seat, but didn't take her eyes off him.

Danny sat on the edge of his bed and clasped his hands together. "Like I said, I know a few clock spirits back home."

"How many have you spoken to?"

"Three."

"Are they all like her?"

"No, not really. They all look different, and have different personalities. One is a man, another is a woman, and . . . another is a boy. About as old as me."

Meena studied his face, and he worried what she saw there. "Tell me about them."

He told her about Big Ben in London, and about Evaline and the disaster involving his father in Maldon. By the time he described Colton, Meena sat mesmerized, her mouth slightly parted.

"I've mostly spent time with Colton, the spirit of the tower I watch over back home. He's always curious, and asks a lot of questions. Not like—" He nodded in the direction of Aditi's tower. "I don't think any two spirits are the same."

Meena played with a fold in her sari. "I always thought the spirits were just stories. Something the older ghadi wallahs told the young ones for fun."

"I thought the same, once. Colton was the first spirit I ever saw. Well, I saw Big Ben when I was younger, but I didn't know he was a spirit until later. But Colton decided to show himself to me." Danny stared at his fingers. "I was grateful that he trusted me enough. That he spoke to me like he cared about my life."

After an uncomfortable silence, Danny looked up and met Meena's eyes. Her face no longer held wonder, but suspicion.

"Danny," she said slowly, taking something from her satchel, "you admitted there is a boy you love back home." She unfolded the paper in her hands. "Is this boy also a clock spirit?"

Danny's heart sank as Meena held up the drawing of Colton.

"You dropped it in Aditi's tower," she said.

Damn it. She stared at him, waiting for an answer.

"What would you do if I said yes?" he asked softly.

Meena stood and dusted off her sari, then pierced him again

with dark, intelligent eyes. "I am not Danny Hart, so I cannot make decisions for you. But if I *were* you, I would stop this. I may have only just learned about the spirits, but I know enough that they should not be tampered with."

"It's not tampering—"

"This sort of union cannot end happily. You must see that. And if you can't, then I will pray until you do."

"Meena . . ."

She waited to hear what he had to say, but he had no words to offer, no defense to build around himself. He knew the consequences; knew them better than she did. He thought of the way time altered when Colton felt too much—felt because of *him*. If Harris worried about being selfish with Partha, he didn't want to know what the captain would think of this.

It reminded him unpleasantly of what his father had said before he left: his warning that Danny putting Colton before all else would only lead to disaster. That the barrier between *want* and *need* was hard and unforgiving.

Danny lowered his eyes to the floor, where they caught a glimpse of black. He blinked, but the spindly leg he saw peeking from under the chair disappeared with a faint whir.

Meena sighed and put the picture on the table. "We should focus on one problem at a time. First, this spirit. Then you can worry about your own."

She didn't realize that he never stopped worrying.

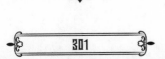

They visited Aditi several more times in the next week. Every day, Danny grew more and more convinced that something wasn't right in Meerut. Each night ended with uncertainty and each morning dawned with anxiety. He was missing something, he was sure of it.

And he had heard that whirring, clicking sound again. He'd searched all over his room, even told Captain Harris about it, but not even the soldiers could find the source of the sound.

He remembered the mechanical spider he'd seen at the Taj and shuddered.

Danny and Meena's visits to the clock tower provided only more frustrating clues. The scaffolding Danny originally thought was missing actually lay broken at the bottom of the tower. They asked what had happened to it as they performed routine maintenance on the clock.

"She doesn't know," Meena translated. "There are blank spots in her memory, as she sometimes focuses on other places in Meerut besides her tower. One day, the scaffolding was beside the clock face, and the next, it was broken. The ghadi wallahs made a fuss, saying someone needed to pay for the repairs, but no one came forward."

Danny combed the tower for clues, but there was nothing to suggest a stranger had been there. Aditi was of little help; she liked to gossip with Meena while Danny prowled around. Their laughter was grating, and once Aditi even pinched his cheek. Meena insisted it was an act of fondness.

"She says you are too thin. You need to eat more."

"I eat plenty." He sat cross-legged in front of the clockwork. Sunlight shone through the clock face and turned the platform a bright emerald.

Aditi said something, and Meena called down, "She would like to know where the small cog in your pocket comes from."

He hesitated. "Tell her another of her kind gave it to me. As a gift."

Meena's eyebrows rose. Blushing, Danny turned back to the clockwork. He thought of his father and how much Christopher would have loved to be in this tower with him, comparing Indian and English designs.

As the other two prattled on, Danny carefully reached for the time fibers around him. Bright and steady, as they had been every day so far. Once in a while, he caught a tiny tremor. He followed the anomaly to the central cog, to the spot his blood had touched.

He so vividly remembered that day at Enfield, using his blood to control time, how the pattern had shifted just for him. In some way, that was what had happened in Khurja, too. Time had unraveled and then reformed into a new, more complicated pattern. Something abnormal, and yet . . . familiar.

"Danny," Meena said, "Aditi has been having dreams, and wonders if this other spirit you know has them as well."

He turned around and edged out of the green-tinted sunlight. "Dreams?" He thought of his past conversations with Colton. "No, I don't think they're capable of having dreams. They don't even sleep. Can she explain them?"

Aditi unleashed a long stream of Hindi. "Let me see if I can translate all of this," Meena said. "She says that in the dreams, she's like you and me. She walks around the city, but it's not how it is today. It's older, with fewer buildings and people. In one dream, she's buying a goat. In another, she's in a hut preparing milk for butter. She rides in a cart, and she knows she's traveling south, toward the sea.

"But the strangest one she's had so far is of men screaming in the street, yelling about finding a solution to something. She can't tell what they're talking about, and because she's scared, she tries to run and find a man—" Aditi interrupted, and Meena nodded. "She tries to find a man she calls her husband to ask him what's happening. And then the dream ends."

Danny tried to imagine the dreams as Meena described them. "I might know what it is."

Meena looked surprised. "You do?"

"Colton—rather, spirits in general—have different senses. They can see and hear things all over their towns and cities. They get to see thousands, if not millions, of people during the years. It could be that she's remembering others' lives."

Though Colton had never had visions like these, so far as Danny knew. Now he suddenly burned to ask him more.

Meena's brows gently furrowed, framing the red bindi between them. "I'm not sure, Danny. This doesn't sound the same."

The door to the tower opened below. Danny looked up, but Meena was now alone on the upper platform.

A ghadi wallah climbed the stone steps and gave them a cool stare when he reached the top. He said something to Meena. She replied in a tone even frostier than his. It wasn't unusual to be sent away if the ghadi wallahs thought they were taking too much time in the tower. Danny figured they had a right to be suspicious.

But the quiet, to him, was even more troubling.

Too anxious to be on his own one afternoon, Danny decided to ask Meena if she fancied a walk. They had made it a habit to discuss theories as they wandered the city. Once, they had found a snake charmer near the temple. Danny's eyes had followed the swaying head of the cobra, hypnotized by the charmer's music.

Danny felt very much like that snake, ensnared by a force he couldn't understand.

He knocked on her door and heard her faint "Come in!" He pulled up short when he saw the small handgun she'd used on the train lying on the bed's counterpane, sunlight glinting innocently against its steel casing.

"Does it frighten you?" she asked, noticing where his eyes had landed.

"No." He closed the door halfway behind him. "Maybe a little."

"It scares me, too. But Akash makes me carry it."

"Why? Does he have one, too?"

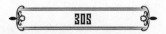

"I think he does, although he's never shown me. As for why . . ." She touched the gun. "He worries."

Danny knew better than to ask questions. "I suppose it did come in handy."

Meena stored her handgun away in its secret pocket in her salwar. He wondered if she ever worried about accidentally shooting herself in the backside. "Let's walk."

They asked a sepoy to escort them. He had won against Danny in cards the night before, so he was willing to make up for it by trailing behind the two mechanics. People stared wherever they went, but other British settlers were given the same treatment, so Danny didn't take it personally. Still, it didn't help his nerves that people here were painfully aware of his existence when he was so used to being invisible in a London crowd.

It could have been worse. One day he'd noticed a sign above a dining establishment that read NO INDIANS OR DOGS ALLOWED. He had inhaled sharply at the implication of it, but if Meena had seen, she'd pretended she hadn't. By some unspoken agreement, they had not walked down that street since.

They barely realized they were walking in the direction of Aditi's tower until they saw the top of the spire over the nearest rooftop. By impulse or resignation, they turned toward it.

"There's still something I don't understand," Meena said, voice low so that no one could overhear. The sepoy loped a few paces behind, squinting against the last rays of sun. "When we first arrived, you did something to Aditi's cog that upset her. What was it?"

"Oh, that." His heart beat a little faster. "It was just an experiment."

Meena would have asked more, but as they walked into the circular clearing where Aditi's tower stood, something pricked against Danny's senses. The air felt . . . sharp. It warped around him, and his skin broke out in gooseflesh. He could *see* it, a distortion in the air like heat rays in summer.

Looking down, he realized the cobblestones under his feet were dark with water.

"Meena," he whispered. She saw the water and gasped.

"Where are the guards?" She ran into the clearing, but no one was there.

The sepoy, sensing their distress, rushed forward. "What's wrong?"

Danny spun in a tight circle, not sure what he was looking for. And then he found it. A black line ran up the side of the tower, toward the clock face. It was smoking.

Hickory dickory dock.

The smoke rose higher.

The mouse ran up the clock.

As he followed the spark with his eyes, he noticed a figure beyond the thick glass of the clock face. The spirit banged on the green barrier, yelling soundlessly, trapped.

The clock struck one—

"Meena, get away from there!" he shouted.

The tower exploded.

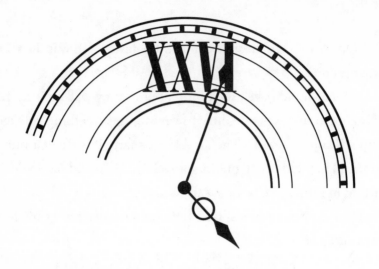

Colton was quiet as David drove him to the train station in the city called Jaipur. David had managed to filch an auto from the caravan the soldiers used, but insisted it had to be returned as soon as possible before an officer realized it was missing.

"The train that'll take you to Agra comes in an hour," David explained as he fumbled for something in his pocket. "I believe it's called the Jabalpur Express. Can you remember that?" Colton said he could. "Here, you'll need this."

David shoved a wad of crumpled paper at him, along with a dozen or so silver and bronze coins. Colton sat with the pile in his lap, trying not to drop any of it.

"What's all this?"

"Rupees and annas. Indian currency. You can't get too far with pounds and pence in this country, so stick to what I just gave you."

Colton stared at the young man. He knew enough about humans to understand that this was a substantial gesture. At a loss for words, he looked out the window at the passing buildings. Strangely, they were pink. "I've never seen buildings like these before," he said.

"The Prince of Wales visited Jaipur earlier this year. They painted everything pink to welcome him."

"Oh." Colton supposed that was nice of them. As they rounded a corner, he jolted in his seat. Jaipur's clock tower loomed nearby.

"Stop the auto."

"What? No. We have to—oy!"

Colton had already opened the door, and David was forced to pull over to the side of the road. Colton nimbly stepped over a mound of cow dung and made his way to the tower, drawn to its force. People glanced at him, but he didn't care. He felt braver in the dawn light.

He climbed a short wall and stood on the top, taking in a sight that made his eyes go wide. A vast courtyard stretched before him, empty save for giant curving structures. One was immensely tall, in the shape of a flight of stairs that led nowhere. Another was a half-circle lined with marks. There was also a pit in which a pendulum swung.

"It's the conservatory," David called from below. "The king of Jaipur built this a long time ago. They're all time-telling devices."

Colton could sense it, now. The tall stairs leading to nowhere

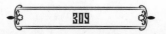

actually formed a sundial. Time fibers wove around the structure, strengthening the connection to the clock tower tenfold.

Something made him turn his head. On top of the yellow clock tower stood a slight figure. When their eyes met, the figure disappeared.

He reappeared in front of Colton, who stepped back in surprise.

The boy was shorter and younger than he was. He had bronze skin and dusty yellow hair. His amber eyes flashed as he tilted his head to one side. Colton found himself mimicking the gesture.

"You are like me," the boy said in a heavy accent.

"Yes, I think so." Colton thought back to his visions—his dreams—his memories. Honestly, he had no idea what he was. "Don't worry, I won't be staying long. But may I ask you something?"

The boy considered, then nodded.

"Do you have visions of a life before this one? A life that makes no sense?"

The boy's gaze wandered toward the conservatory. "I see . . . a woman. I call her mother. She feeds me roti and smacks my arm when I misbehave."

Colton's throat constricted. He thought of the woman in his own visions, the tall one with the long dark hair. *Mother.*

"Colton!" David called.

"I have to go," he whispered. "Goodbye."

"Goodbye," the boy said. He disappeared into his tower.

Colton climbed back down the wall to where David waited

below. The young man's eyes darted around warily as he pulled Colton to the auto.

"What the bloody hell was that?" he demanded. "Actually, no—never mind. The less I know, the better. Let's just get you to the station."

They drove the rest of the way in silence. When David pulled up beside the train station, Colton took what was left of the British money from his pockets and handed it to David.

"Don't bother, mate. I don't expect anything in return."

"Please," Colton said.

David took the money half-heartedly. "I'll keep hold of it for you. Brandon can give it back when you return." David looked him up and down. "And you better return. Having Brandon for a brother, I know how important you spirits are to the clock towers. I know how important you are to Enfield. Don't leave us with another Maldon, all right?"

Colton slowly put the Indian money away, unable to meet David's eyes. "I won't."

David directed him to the stairs leading to the platform above, where passengers congregated.

"Be safe, then. And good luck."

"Thank you for your help."

David only nodded before he returned to the auto. Colton understood that David needed to go, but all the same, he wished he would come with him, even just to the platform.

Colton watched the auto pull around and head back for base. He was on his own again.

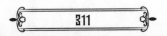

His legs buckled under a sudden spell of weakness, but he gripped Big Ben's cog and fed on the power from the cogs on his back, as well as whatever the conservatory could spare. He wanted to sit and think, but getting to Danny was more important. Only a train ride separated them. This, more than the cogs, gave him the strength to walk to the stairs.

His determination was short-lived, though, as a guard with olive skin stopped him. "Ticket?" he asked.

Colton wearily looked at him, hoping he would explain. Eventually, the man sighed and pointed at a kiosk on the right.

"Tick-et," he said slowly, raising his voice as if Colton was hard of hearing. "To ride the train."

"Oh, I'm sorry. I've never ridden a train before."

Finding that Colton spoke English, the man returned to his normal voice. "Go on then, get one and we'll let you through."

Colton approached the man at the kiosk, who only gestured to a list above his head. Colton scanned the board and tried to figure out what he wanted, but he couldn't read the words. "Um, a ticket to Agra, please? The Jabalpur Express?"

The man did something behind the kiosk. He brought out a rectangular bit of paper and stamped it, then held out his hand. Colton, growing increasingly frustrated, shrugged.

"Money," the guard from the stairs called. He'd been watching the transaction. "A ticket to Agra's gonna be eight annas."

"Right. Money." He fumbled with the notes and coins in his pocket, trying to determine which were annas and which were rupees. The coins clattered onto the surface of the kiosk as he separated them. This was even more confusing than English currency.

The man behind the kiosk grunted impatiently and swiped the necessary coins from the pile. Colton tried not to feel incompetent as he put the rest back in his pocket, suddenly thankful Danny wasn't here to witness this. He would never hear the end of it.

Colton showed his ticket to the guard, who pretended to applaud. Frowning, Colton swept past him and up the stairs to join the other passengers waiting for the Jabalpur Express.

There weren't many people here, but enough to make him nervous. London had been different. Everyone had been constantly moving, their eyes focused elsewhere, pretending no one around them existed. Here, people noticed him, and it made him feel as if he held a sign that told them what he really was.

He found a small wooden bench near the empty tracks. Well, not completely empty; trash littered the sides of the tracks, and small gray mice scurried along the ground below. They looked like the ones that sometimes snuck into his tower. Colton had spent long hours watching them, how they balanced on the beams and the way their noses and whiskers twitched. He wanted to climb down and help them off the train tracks. He couldn't imagine it was very safe down there.

Since he was alone on the bench, he dug through the small pack he carried until he found the photographs. He looked at the one with the gun pointed to the back of Danny's head.

"I'm almost there," he whispered. "Wait for me."

A clock that hung above the platform read 8:50. About ten more minutes until the train arrived, and forty until they departed. He had never been this impatient until he'd met Danny. Now, every minute was an eternity.

He rubbed his right side, feeling the scar underneath his clothes. What would Danny say when he saw it? For an instant, it wasn't Danny's worried face he saw, but Castor's.

The ache grew, and his face scrunched up in an effort not to cry out in pain. He had known Castor after all; had known him in the same intimate, indefinable way he knew Danny.

All those people—Castor, Abigail, his mother and father—who were they really? Colton had been a spirit for as long as he could remember. He was the product of time. He *was* time.

But now these dreams, these memories, made him doubt himself. For the first time since he could remember, he didn't know who Colton was.

An elderly woman shuffled up to him and held out a wrinkled hand. Her lips were barely perceivable, and a few white hairs grew from her chin. She mumbled something to Colton, but he couldn't understand her.

"I'm sorry?"

She mumbled the same word again. He recalled a man dressed in rags who had wandered Enfield for a month or two before dying of exposure. He had been seeking money and food. If this woman was doing the same, then she was likely a beggar.

He took a paper rupee from his pocket and gave it to her. She pressed her hands together, as if in prayer, before meandering off.

An Indian man in a blue suit shouted that the train was arriving. Colton looked around at the impatient crowd. A little British girl cried that she wanted water. An old man rested most of his weight on a thin cane.

"Hoy there, you lot!"

Colton whipped around. A British officer in uniform descended on two Indian children. They yelled and squirmed, but the officer held them up by their collars and shook them. "Drop it! Now!"

The children dropped the coins and rupees they'd been clutching in their small, dirty fists. The officer let them go and they raced off, ducking and weaving through the crowd, which parted as if the boys were diseased.

"Disgraceful," the officer muttered as he picked up the money. Then, to Colton's surprise, the man turned and handed it to him.

"They took this from you."

Colton checked his pocket. "How—?"

"Thieves. They were working with the beggar woman. She sees where you take out your money, then the urchins nick the rest. Anyway, make sure you keep that safe."

"They could have had money if they needed it," Colton said with an edge in his voice.

The officer frowned under his bristling blond mustache. "The money wouldn't go to them. They would have to take it straight to the woman, and who knows what she would have done with it. Probably spend it on drink and hookah."

"You still didn't have to treat them so poorly. They're just children."

Anger brewed on the man's face, and Colton checked himself. He couldn't draw attention, and unfortunately, there were now many eyes upon them. He ducked over his pack and put the money inside.

The train pulled up, sparing him from further argument. It was a noisy thing that blew smoke into the air as it rolled in. Colton kept a tight grip on his ticket.

The doors opened and everyone rushed to get on at once. Colton waited his turn to board, finding himself in a long corridor with seats along barred windows.

The ticket inspector reached him, punched a hole in the corner of his ticket, and continued on. Colton wondered what to do now. The thought of sitting among all these people—who were Indian, which meant the English probably sat elsewhere—made him even more nervous, thinking of all the ways he could invite their gazes. Though Colton was often lonely in his tower, he'd grown used to solitude, and right now that's all he longed for. He wanted to put his thoughts together before he found Danny.

A young Indian woman bumped into him from behind. She looked lost, and not a little scared. When the ticket inspector turned to the new passengers, her eyes grew large.

"Are you all right?" Colton asked. The man punched someone else's ticket and she winced. "Do you not have a ticket?" She shook her head.

He handed her his own. She stared at him, then snatched it

from his hand. Just in time, too, for the man turned to her next. She showed him the already-punched ticket.

"Sorry, miss. Must've already done yours."

When he was gone, she tried to press the ticket back into Colton's hands.

"Keep it. I don't need it anymore."

He turned to find a quiet place. An open door led to another carriage, this one even louder than the one he'd just left. His side ached, and his head swam. He felt weaker by the second.

He passed through two more carriages until he found a closed door. Testing it, he found it wasn't locked, and opened to a darker carriage filled with luggage and crates. Colton waited until the men loading the compartment jumped off and closed the main platform doors. Then he snuck inside and closed the door behind him.

The carriage was blessedly quiet. All he could hear was the hiss and rumble of the train. He wandered through barrels and boxes, smelling strange aromas and reading strange words. *Tallow, oil, ink, spices.* If he were human, he wondered if he would sneeze. Danny would sometimes sneeze in the tower if it got too dusty. Colton once told him he looked adorable when he sneezed. Danny, flustered, hadn't been able to speak for five minutes.

The pain flared again and he leaned against the wall, sliding to the floor. Wedged between a box marked FRAGILE and another smelling of mint, Colton closed his eyes and tried to decide what to do.

He had to dream again. When he'd looked in the mirror,

he had seen himself, the same face he'd seen in Danny's mirror and in the sketch Danny had drawn. But the colors had been all wrong, his skin paler and dotted with freckles, his hair dark, his eyes blue. He'd looked . . . human.

Maybe it wasn't me, he thought. *Maybe it was someone I knew when my tower was built. Someone I wanted to look like.*

But the Jaipur clock spirit had said he'd experienced the visions, too.

The only way to find out was to dream. But, despite his weakness, Colton couldn't get to that place of unconsciousness. It seemed he had stocked up on rest during his night on the airship.

The train began to move forward. Colton realized what he had to do. With a pinch of trepidation, he slipped the cog holder off his shoulders and leaned it against a box. Almost immediately the weakness tripled, his head swimming and his vision doubling.

Closing his eyes, he fell into sought-after darkness.

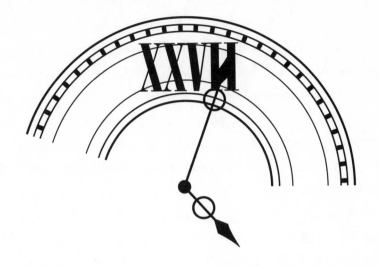

XXVII

They lounged in Castor's bed for most of the afternoon. The sheets were thick and somewhat itchy, but the two of them barely noticed, too distracted by each other.

The wind howled outside, but they were warm and safe in bed. Colton felt heavy and happy as Castor hummed low in his throat. Their fingers skimmed over skin, their eyes sometimes meeting with a secretive smile.

"So?" Castor asked. His voice had fallen into a comfortable baritone in the past year, and it made Colton shiver when it hit its lowest notes. "What do you think?"

"About what?"

"What we were talking about before."

"You mean before you shoved me onto the bed?"

"Yes, that."

"I can't remember that far back."

Castor scooted farther in, resting a warm hand on Colton's back. Colton pressed his own hand against Castor's chest. "When we were talking about London," Castor said.

"Oh." The bliss faded a little, making him more aware of the cold air outside. Colton idly drew circles over Castor's chest, but wouldn't look at his face. Lowering his voice, he said, "I don't think it would work."

"Why not? You said you loved the city when we visited last year. So did I."

Colton bit his lower lip, and Castor brought his hand back around to run it up his side.

"I want to live with you," Colton said softly, "but I can't leave my family. I can't leave Abigail. You know that."

"I do. Which is why"—Castor paused to kiss the tip of Colton's nose—"she'll be coming with us."

Colton drew back. "What? She can't go to London. She's still unwell. Enfield is good for her. Fresh air, fewer people, a doctor who knows her condition—"

"But she can be with her big brother and his handsome friend who know how to care for her. Maybe London life will do her wonders, and she'll grow strong enough to go out into the city and enjoy herself. Make friends, see plays, dress up."

"We haven't the money for that."

"Not now, but that can change."

"You just want to spoil her."

"Maybe. But you do, too."

"I don't think our parents would ever allow it."

"They're not nearly as protective as you are. I'm sure they'd listen to you."

"Castor . . ." The boy's brown eyes were warm and deep, and he made the mistake of looking into them. There was little to no chance of denying him when he looked so sincere.

"Just consider it." Castor drew Colton closer until their stomachs touched. Colton closed his eyes as Castor kissed him, lightly at first, then deeper. They were reaching under the sheets again when they heard the front door slam.

"Castor!"

They sprang apart like spooked cats. Colton fell to the floor as he scrambled for his clothes, counting the heavy footsteps approaching Castor's door.

"Castor? Are you in there?"

"Yes!"

The door opened with a creak and Castor's father peered in. Castor sat fully dressed on his bed while Colton took up the wooden chair in the corner. Both boys tried to hide the fact that they were breathing heavily.

"Beele is looking for you two. He's by the shrine."

They exchanged a look. Beele hardly ever asked to see them outside of classes, and their next trip to the coast wasn't for a few weeks.

"Thank you, Mr. Thomas," Colton said.

The boys silently walked across the village green. Castor's face was still bright pink. Colton hoped he would forget about London for a while.

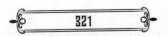

Beele stood lingering beside the Aetas shrine near the church. The statue depicted the god with palms supine, standing strong upon a dais of a clock face. His face was cut in clear detail, from the straight line of his nose to the deep facets of his eyes. Colton glanced at it, feeling both drawn and disquieted by the figure.

When everyone was assembled, Beele told them they were making a special trip to the coast as soon as possible. Murmurs and puzzled looks swept through the students.

"Sir, has something happened?" Castor asked.

"Well . . ." Beele's eyes swept over the group, the older boys and girls and the younger ones who had just been initiated. "Something must be looked into, and I'd rather everyone be there."

"What needs to be looked into, sir?" asked a tall boy.

Beele cleared his throat. "I'm not meant to say, but . . . we must check on Aetas."

More looks, more murmurs. "On Aetas?" a girl repeated as they all looked up at the shrine before them.

"Yes. We need to see if he can still hear us."

The ocean raged under the iron-gray sky as time servants stood along the shore, cold and confused. Most assembled had no idea why they were here. A few stared across the water with trepidation.

Colton stood close to Castor. Both shivered as the wind

played with their hair. More than anything, Colton wanted to hold Castor's hand, but practicality made him stay still. They watched the churning ocean, mesmerized by its white-crested waves, the sinuous arcs they made before the water crashed down with a frightening roar.

"Something is wrong," Beele said somewhere on Colton's right. Other instructors and their students from neighboring districts were gathered nearby. The adults shifted on their feet, glancing warily at one another as the students looked on.

"Hancock, why don't you go in?" one of the instructors suggested to a stocky middle-aged man with dark sideburns. Hancock drew a deep breath and nodded. He removed his coat and timepiece, then made his way to the ocean.

Everyone watched as the instructor stepped into the surf. It nearly dragged him under, and a few younger children gasped, but Hancock righted himself and submerged before a wave could topple him.

Colton began to nibble on his thumbnail. Castor hated the habit, but refrained from pulling Colton's hand away as he normally would. Instead, he stared out at the water and waited like everyone else.

A moment later, Hancock came up sputtering and fighting the tide. Beele and another instructor ran to help him out of the water.

"What did you feel?" Beele demanded as they toweled him down. Hancock shook so violently that his teeth chattered loud enough for Colton to hear.

"I—" Hancock couldn't speak at first, breathing hard through his mouth. Swallowing, he forced the words out. "I didn't feel anything. I tried speaking to Aetas, but he didn't answer."

The look the adults gave each other formed a pit in Colton's stomach.

One by one, each instructor waded into the ocean. Then the children stood ankle- or knee-deep. All arrived at the same conclusion: Aetas could not be felt. The twining pattern of time was barbed and static—they feared touching it.

"What does that mean?" Colton whispered. He wanted to race into the water, but Beele had warned him not to wade too far.

"I thought I felt something strange the other day," Castor whispered back. "In Enfield. Like an ache in my belly."

Colton had felt it, too.

The students demanded answers, but for once, their instructors had none.

"Perhaps Aetas is distracted and needs us to work even harder," Beele suggested. "When we go home, make sure you meditate twice a day, once in the morning and once at night. Focus on Aetas and the strings of time around your home. Make sure they are running true."

It was a long wagon ride to the coast, and by the time they were trundling back to Enfield, most of the children had fallen asleep in the back. Colton and Castor sat near the front, listening to the clop of the horses' hooves. Because of the wagon's cover, they couldn't see the stars, but moonlight filtered through the slit near the driver's bench. They spoke in whispers until Castor nodded off, resting his head against Colton's shoulder. Colton couldn't bring himself to move him away. None of the children would see, anyway.

Beele and Hancock were speaking on the driver's bench, their voices low.

"There must be something we're missing," Beele said. "Some piece of the puzzle. First the south of Africa, and now us. What's the cause?"

"It's almost as if time is rippling. It makes my skin crawl."

"Do you think there's anything we can do?"

Hancock was silent a while. Colton was about to drift off when the man spoke again.

"I think there is more to it than we originally thought. Have you ever tried . . . to control it?"

"What do you mean?" Beele asked, his voice even lower.

"Time. Have you been able to control it?"

Beele didn't respond.

"It's one thing to meditate," Hancock went on, getting more excited with every word, "but I think I've found—some of us have found—that time may run deeper than we suspected. The other day, when I was cleaning my timepiece, I nicked my thumb. A bit of blood got onto the gears and, well, it felt strange. I played with the sensation a bit. It was as though the time of the watch was directly connected to my thoughts."

Beele laughed softly, but he didn't sound amused. "You must have swallowed seawater."

"I'm serious. I don't think Aetas merely wants us to watch over time. He wants us to *control* it."

"Enough," Beele muttered. "You're talking nonsense."

"You'll see soon. We're about to make great discoveries. Perhaps Aetas is simply telling us we need to stop relying on him and finally take the matter into our own hands."

"I said that's enough."

The men fell silent, but Colton was wide awake. He watched a sliver of moonlight fall onto Castor's pale cheek, turning it white.

Over the next few days, strangers arrived in Enfield. Men from London, who spoke with refined accents and insisted that they were here for anthropological research. The townspeople gave them a wide berth. Colton kept an eye on the strangers, wondering if they'd come because of the Aetas matter. Instructor Beele's uneasy behavior all but confirmed it.

Colton and Castor spoke about the latest news in quiet voices. None of the other time servants could figure out what was happening, and the authorities in London were helpless. It was only the servants' constant meditation on time that kept the complicated weaves safely blanketed over Enfield.

Colton sat outside his house one morning, eyes closed, focused inwardly. Neighbors usually left him alone when he did this, but today someone bumped into him, shattering his

concentration. Colton opened his eyes with a small growl of frustration.

One of the London men looked down at him, frowning. "What are you doing?"

"I'm a time servant. I'm channeling Aetas."

The frown deepened. "Don't have to do that in the middle of the road, do you? Or do you lousy churls not have chairs? Tell me your name, boy."

"Colton Bell, and I'll meditate wherever I please."

The man bared his teeth, but didn't press the matter further, turning with a flip of his long green coat before strolling down the road that led to the village green.

The encounter sat oddly with him, as had everything that had happened in the last few days. Even well into the night, he couldn't stop the nervous squirming of his belly, or the dull, frightened thudding of his heart.

It was nearly midnight and Colton sat in the middle of his bed, unable to sleep. Ever since the trip to the coast, Hancock's words had been rolling around his head like marbles. There was something he had to try.

He looked to his right, to the sheet dividing his bed from his parents'. His father's snores sawed through the air and his mother's lighter snores whistled in harmony. On his left, past the other sheet, Abigail was quiet as usual.

Colton took a deep breath and slipped out of bed, trying not to make a sound. He bypassed the creaky step near the bottom of the stairs and lit a lantern, which he placed on the table. He sat within the lantern's buttery glow and opened his hands to reveal the timepiece he'd been clutching.

It was his father's, and it was very old. The silver exterior was carved with a scalloped design, almost like a seashell. It was the most expensive thing they owned.

Colton laid his tools out before him on the table's surface. Carefully, quietly, he pried the timepiece apart to get to the gears within.

When he laid eyes on the smoothly turning mechanism, his heart started to beat faster. The parts were so tiny, so beautiful, so mysterious, that he couldn't help but stare.

Colton grabbed the pocketknife his father had given him on his tenth birthday. He pricked his thumb, watching as a small bead of blood rose to the surface. Swallowing, Colton wondered if he should abandon his plan, put the timepiece back together, and forget what he had heard on the wagon.

But he had to know.

He pressed the bead of cooling blood to the gears. Something sharp ran through his chest and he had to slap a hand to his mouth to stop himself from crying out.

Time writhed around him. He felt it intimately on his skin, the way Castor's fingers felt when they traced the lines of his body. He shuddered, his hands hot as they clutched the faintly glowing timepiece.

He replaced the face. Focusing on the awareness that raised the hairs along his arms, he silently commanded the timepiece to stop. The hands slowed, the ticking ceased, and the small bubble of time around him froze.

He couldn't breathe.

Start. Start.

The hands resumed their journey, and the faint *ticks* of the second hand came back to life. He inhaled.

"Hancock was right," Colton whispered. "We *can* control time."

A rustle made him jump. He looked at the front door, then the window beside it. It could have been his nerves, but he thought he saw the flash of a pale face before it disappeared into the folds of night.

Colton was about to run to the door when he heard Abigail whimper upstairs. He hesitated before he put the timepiece down and hurried to her instead. She was tossing under her sheets, frantic and perspiring.

"Abigail." He cradled her face with his hands, smearing blood on her cheek. "Abi, wake up. It's just a dream."

Her eyes moved under her lids, then opened slowly. Although her forehead was coated with sweat, she shivered.

"Colton," she whispered hoarsely, her fingernails driving into his skin. "Colton, you're here."

"Of course I am. I'm always here."

"You were gone. I couldn't find you."

He gently swept her hair back. "I'll never leave you, Abi. I promise you'll always be able to find me."

When she was calm again, he wiped the blood from her cheek and gave her some water. He thought about the timepiece downstairs, and how he had to dismantle it to clean the gears before their father woke up. But Abigail couldn't find sleep again, so he held her, wondering what he should say to Instructor Beele.

This discovery was going to change everything.

When Castor came over the next day, Colton led him out back to the garden. As they tilled the soil in preparation for the spring planting, Colton told him about his experiment the other night.

Castor listened intently as he worked, but when Colton reached the part about his father's timepiece, he stopped and leaned against the hoe, eyes wide. "Colton, how could you do something so reckless?"

"I had to try. Hancock said it himself: time is changing. The way we sense it will change, too, if Aetas stays unreachable. Maybe he *is* doing it for a reason."

"We can't control time!"

Colton shushed Castor and looked around to see if anyone had heard. He saw no one, but felt a prickle of apprehension, as if someone were watching. He still wasn't certain if he'd imagined the face in the window the night before. "We're time servants. We work directly for Aetas. Who's to say that we can't do what he can?"

Castor shook his head. "That's misusing our power. If we can control time with our blood, we'd all be at war within a second. Don't you see that?"

"Of course I do. But that doesn't mean—" The air shifted, and Colton turned his head. For a moment, he thought he could smell the sea. "Castor?"

"I feel it, too," Castor said. "What—?"

Everything twisted

The world spun upside down, the sun and moon collided, and Colton fell to the ground. Pain ripped through his body and he screamed. He felt like he was being flayed alive, like thousands of thorns tore into his flesh, burying into his bones.

Castor screamed beside him. The ocean roared. The earth trembled.

Then the pain ebbed like the tide, and Colton looked up to see the sky shrouded by an ominous gray barrier. Within a blink it was gone, replaced with watery sunshine. Another blink, and the barrier returned.

"What's happening?" Castor yelled.

Colton struggled to his hands and knees, retching. He was being turned inside out. His guts writhed like snakes.

When he looked up, he gasped. The tilled earth sprouted crops not yet planted, carrots and beans and potato flowers. They grew at an impossible rate. Then, just as quickly, they shriveled and died.

"What is this?" he croaked. "Castor?" But another wave of

pain hit, and he dropped to the ground. He curled into a ball and sobbed. Time s^{q}u^i^{r}m^e$_d$ and snapped and b^i^{t} .

"Colton! Colton, get a hold of yourself. We have to find Beele."

He looked up at Castor, his face pale and frightened, his brown eyes round, his hair in disarray.

And then he was looking at someone else, someone he didn't know. Another boy, his face sharper and his hair darker, his eyes not brown but bright popping green. There was a slanted scar on his chin.

"Colton, what's wrong?" the boy demanded in an entirely different voice. "Colton!"

"Who are you?" he rasped. "Where did you come from?"

But the boy had changed back into Castor, and helped Colton to his feet. Colton swayed and leaned into him, but he managed to stay upright. They hobbled around to the front of the house and froze.

The roads were lined with more houses than had been there this morning, crowding the countryside. Huge, clunking beasts of metal trundled down the streets on wheels.

"What are they?" Castor asked. A second passed, and then they were looking at their own Enfield again. Another second, and it was nothing but a grassy plain extending toward a forest.

Everything was spinning and

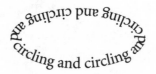

Colton turned and nearly ran into the side of his reappearing house. A scream tore through the air above their heads.

"Abigail!"

They hurried inside, where his parents had been knocked out by the force of time unleashed. They hurried up the stairs to Abigail's bed, where she sat rocking back and forth, holding her head.

"Abi, what's wrong?" When he reached for her, she disappeared. Colton whirled around. "Abigail! *Abigail!*"

She returned, still rocking, still holding her head. Colton wrapped his arms around her, determined not to let go.

"What's happening?" she cried. "Make it stop! It hurts so much!"

"Aetas," Castor said. "It has to be. What if he's disappeared for good? What if time's running free?"

"Please make it stop," Abigail begged, holding onto him. "Colton, please."

"I will, Abi. I promise I'll make it stop."

Before they could determine how, they heard a commotion on the stairs. Men burst into the room and grabbed Castor. One of them dragged him away from Abigail, still screaming as she held out her hands for him. He tried to free himself, but his captor smacked the side of the head, then yanked his arms up behind his back.

"Let go of my brother! Let him go!"

Colton and Castor were hauled downstairs, where his parents were rousing. When his father got a look at what was happening, he gained his feet with fearsome speed.

"What are you doing with those boys?"

The men kept his parents at bay, though Colton managed to lock eyes with his mother, her hand frantically reaching for him.

"Colton!"

Abi had stumbled down the stairs, wheezing and flushed, clutching desperately at the walls. Their mother caught her before she fell, and Colton heard her scream his name again before they were shoved outside.

"To the church," one of the men said.

The boys were dragged to St. Andrew's. Inside, wooden pews had been pushed up to the front altar, leaving the nave mostly barren. They were herded to one side and forced to sit with their backs to the wall.

"We haven't done anything!" Castor yelled. "We're time servants!"

"Exactly," a man snapped. Colton recognized him as the one who had disturbed his meditation the day before. The mayor's aide, Lucius, stood awkwardly by the man's side. "Sit down and stay silent."

One by one, more time servants were forced into the church and made to sit along the wall. Old, young, it didn't matter. Colton's skin tightened with unease, Abigail's screams still echoing in his ears.

Eventually they were all assembled, even Inspector Beele, his face red and his expression indignant. Colton couldn't remember a time when time servants had been treated this way, not since the dark ages when they were thought to have been witches. The thought only made Colton shiver worse.

The man from London stood before them, hands fisted at his sides. Time warped through the air like heat off of a bonfire. The church **blurred** around them, becoming a pile of rubble, filling up with pious churchgoers, then returning to the present.

"We were warned something like this might happen," Lucius told them. "The time servants in London have been looking into this matter for weeks." He glanced at the man in the green coat, then coughed. "Mr. Archer?"

The man, Archer, drew himself up taller. "It has been reported the country over that our connection with time—with Aetas—has possibly been severed. I'm here to tell you the truth. Aetas cannot be felt because he's no longer here.

"Aetas is dead."

The time servants sat in stunned silence. Then two little girls began to cry, and the others broke out in shouts.

"*Silence!*" Archer waited for their attention to return to him. "Aetas is dead! It has been reported by the Gaian priests that Chronos has killed him, likely for the sin of giving humans power over time. Now, because of your god, we all have to pay the price of Chronos's wrath."

The time servants didn't call out this time. They just gaped in horror.

"This world will end if we don't find a way to control time," Archer went on. "And soon."

"You had to manhandle us to relate the news?" Beele spat. "We may help you if you allow us to discuss the matter, but we can't do anything useful if we're tied up."

Archer shook his head with a tiny, pitying smile. "You time servants think that your god will always protect you, that your power is mightier than the rest of us. Not this time. We have our own ideas."

Beele paled. "What do you mean?"

"There have been experiments going on in London. One worked better than we ever dreamed. Now, we have finally settled on our best chance of survival, and we will grab it with both hands. If Aetas is dead, your powers alone won't be enough."

"Now, listen here—!"

But Archer ignored Beele, ignored everyone's cries. He set men to guard them. Lucius wavered, looking like he wanted to give them reassurance, but he avoided everyone's gaze and followed Archer out. Colton tested the rope around his wrists, gritting his teeth.

"What are they talking about?" Castor's voice shook. "Aetas, dead? Is that true?"

"I don't know," Beele said bleakly. "But this is *our* duty, and our right. Whatever happens, we must stick together."

Castor was breathing unevenly. Colton moved a little closer.

"Stay where you are!" a guard warned him.

"What do you think they're going to do?" Colton whispered.

"I don't know. Damn it, I'm scared. I've never been this scared before."

"Calm down. We'll find a way out of this."

Lucius returned as the sun was setting. The time servants could hear angry voices outside the church, but the London contingent had set up a protective ring around it, preventing anyone from getting inside.

Archer followed behind the mayor's aide. He walked up and down the line of time servants, eyeing each one critically. "You all hold the power to connect to time. Some might even say the power to *control* time." Colton heard Beele's sharp intake of breath. "This power is pivotal to us all, now. If time runs rampant, it'll only be a matter of days until we destroy ourselves." Suddenly, time warped and Archer was an old man—a skeleton covered in a leathery wrapper of skin. Some of the children yelped.

Then Archer was himself again, slightly off-kilter. He shook his head to clear it before continuing on. "I only need one of you to put our plan into motion. Does anyone volunteer?" None of the time servants moved. No one made a sound. "It'll be much easier with a volunteer."

Castor stirred, but Colton nudged him hard with his elbow. Their eyes met, and Colton shook his head. Castor bit his lip.

"Lucius," Archer drawled, "you know these people well. Tell me, which do you think is the best choice?"

The mayor's aide shrank back, shaking his head. "I-I'm sorry, but I—No. I'm sorry."

"What about you?" Archer swung his gaze to Beele. "Who would you say is your best student?"

Beele's eyes flickered to Colton, but the Instructor said nothing.

Archer gave a dramatic sigh. "I suppose I'll have to choose myself." He went down the line again, his eyes skimming over the smallest of the children and the oldest of the seasoned time servants before falling on those in between. Everyone dropped their eyes, trying to disappear into themselves.

Only Colton defiantly met Archer's gaze. The man stopped before him, his upper lip curling. No doubt he was remembering their run-in the other day.

"I've been told," Archer said, as if to Colton directly, "that one of you shows great promise in this particular field. So much so that there have been experiments of a sort happening right here in Enfield."

Colton felt the blood drain from his face. Out of the corner of his eye, Castor turned to look at him.

"I've been informed that he was strong enough to connect to time on his own," Archer explained, kneeling before him. "We need someone strong if this is to work."

Colton's lips trembled. He pressed them together, forcing himself to keep looking Archer in the eye. The man was oddly somber now, his earlier sneer wiped from his face.

"Colton Bell, was it?"

Slowly, Colton nodded.

"If you volunteer," Archer said softly, "you'd be saving your town, Mr. Bell."

His breaths were shaking as they left him, but still he didn't look away from Archer. "How? How could I possibly stop what's happening?"

"There is a way. I can't say any more than that."

Colton licked his dry lips. Time rippled up and down his arms, as if rubbing them in comfort. He leaned into the feeling, opening himself to the fury and the fire of time without Aetas's control.

He thought of Abi in her bed, begging him to make it stop. His promise that he would fix it for her.

Colton gritted his teeth and again met Archer's gaze. Stiffly, he nodded.

"No!" Castor made to get up, but the guard coming to take Colton kicked him, and Castor crumpled back to the ground. "No, stop! Take me instead! Don't take him, take me!"

Colton was seized by a sudden panic. Something wasn't right. He tried to elbow the guard holding him in the face, but a second man grabbed his other arm, and together the two of them dragged Colton through the church, toward the open doors.

"*Castor!*" he screamed. His own name was cried back, but he couldn't see Castor's face. Just heard his name, over and over.

"Castor!"

"*Colton!*"

"What are you doing?" the priest demanded as the flood of angry voices grew louder. "Release this young man at once!"

"Please say a prayer for us, and for him," Archer said.

Colton fought again, frightened tears streaming down his face. "*Castor!*"

His name reached him one last time before the doors closed, and then he was out in the road, the men pulling him toward the village green. Shouts rang out through the dusk; he thought he heard his father above them all. Lucius ordered for him to be restrained.

Past the village green, Colton saw a glint of bronze. Someone had blocked off a square of unused land, where scraps of metal lay.

No, not scraps.

Cogs and gears.

Colton squirmed against his bonds, breathing heavily. The men forced him into the plot where he fell on his side, on top of the clock parts. Someone rolled him over onto his back, and his legs and shoulders were pinned down. The spokes of the gears bit into his skin.

"Let me go!" he shouted, struggling still.

"You agreed to help us, Mr. Bell," Archer said above him. The last of the sunlight lit his hair like fire, shadowing his face.

"Not like this! I *can* help you, but there must be another way—"

"This is the only way," Archer said. Now the man was the one avoiding his eyes. "Believe me, we don't want this. We're only doing what we must. I'm sorry, Mr. Bell." He turned to the man on his left. "It has to be all his blood. Every drop."

The knife gleamed red in the last rays of sunlight. Colton's entire body froze with fear. He whimpered, making one last, feeble attempt to escape as the knife rose above him, a single stretch of a heartbeat.

And then the knife plunged in.

He grunted. The pain lanced through his chest, down to his feet, up to flood his brain with agony. Screaming—someone was screaming. His mother? Abigail? Castor? Blood pooled underneath him, soaking his shirt, running over the cogs and gears that lit up brilliantly at the taste of his blood.

"The throat, too," Archer ordered.

Someone grabbed his hair and craned his head back. The knife left him with two mouths that gaped at the crimson sky above.

He twitched and jerked. The cogs grew hot. He choked on blood. His heart fluttered.

Time compressed around him, focusing on this one point of existence. It fed on him. It made him bleed faster, greedy for his life. Greedy for the power within his body that Aetas had planted so long ago. The complex knot of time unraveled, weaving into a new pattern. No more chaos. Now, there was order.

Death. And life.

"It's working!"

It was the last thing he heard before death pulled him under like a hungry wave.

Colton woke to the smell of mint. He sat propped against the box, staring into the heart of nothing. His body was shaking. His throat began to convulse.

He dragged the cog holder nearer, clutching it to his chest. A thin, whining sound escaped him. He tried to stop it, but the keening grew louder, and longer, until he broke into tearless sobs.

He banged a fist against the box marked FRAGILE, screaming and scratching at his throat and chest.

I died. I was human. They killed me.

It didn't take long to remember the tower they'd built on the grave they had dug for him in that plot of land. The blood-soaked cogs had been installed in that tower. The cog directly beneath him had become the central cog, the main life force of the tower that ran Enfield's time.

For hundreds of years, he had been walking on top of his own bones.

The compartment door slid open. "Hey! What are you doing in here?"

Colton stopped screaming. He stared at the officer with the blond mustache, the one who had patronized him at the station. There were other officers behind him. Slowly, Colton stood, his legs weak but sturdy enough to support him. He slipped on his cog holder.

"What are you doing in here?" the officer asked again. "Where's your ticket?"

"I don't have one." Colton could barely hear himself. Barely feel himself. He was only that: *barely.*

"Stowaway," another said.

The officer reached for his pistol. "Don't make a scene, boy, and we might let you off easily."

Without thinking, Colton turned and ran to the door on the opposite side of the carriage.

"Grab him!"

Colton darted into the next carriage, the one reserved for

British passengers. Everyone turned their heads to see what was going on. Colton noticed an open window, one without bars. He dove toward it, shoving people out of his way. A woman screamed and smacked him with her parasol.

The soldiers followed. "Don't let him jump!"

Colton had no intention of jumping. He instead climbed out of the window and onto the side of the speeding train. The wind almost knocked him off, whipping his hair into his eyes. Colton reached up to the top of the window, but one of the officers grabbed his ankle below.

Grunting, Colton kicked the man in the face until he let go, then scrambled up. He was so used to climbing his tower that the train felt easy in comparison. He hoisted himself onto the roof and stood there a moment, bracing himself against the wind. The train whistled, and if he squinted through the steam, he could see a river up ahead.

A small door in the roof banged open and soldiers poured out. Bullets flew around him, and one ricocheted off of his central cog. He stumbled forward with a pained cry.

"Stop right there, lad! There's nowhere to go!"

Colton still ran, jumping onto the next carriage's roof and ducking under their gunfire. The train just had to get close enough—

"Oy, lad! Stop!"

He hugged the pack to his chest and looked down as the train passed over the river. Glancing over his shoulder, he dodged two more bullets before jumping over the side.

The wind drowned out the soldiers' shouts until he hit the water. The cogs at his back dragged him down to the bottom, and he let them. He sat on the riverbed, looking up through the murky haze as the dark shadow of the train sped by. He waited until it was long gone, waited several more minutes just to be sure, and started climbing up the riverbank.

Emerging from the water, he spat out a mouthful of muck. An old, brown-skinned man in a loincloth sat at the river's edge, beating laundry against rocks. He stared openmouthed at Colton.

Colton walked onto land, wringing his clothes and shaking water from his hair. There was no sign of the train. Now what?

He walked until he found the train tracks. The best way to get to Agra, he supposed, was to follow them.

He stood under the Indian sun as his clothes steamed in the heat. He stared into the distance, feeling hollow. Feeling nothing. He could still hear the screams, those of his sister, Castor, and his own. He still smelled coppery blood.

His tower had been his sanctuary for hundreds of years, the clock the beating heart of Enfield. But now he knew the tower wasn't his home.

It was his tomb.

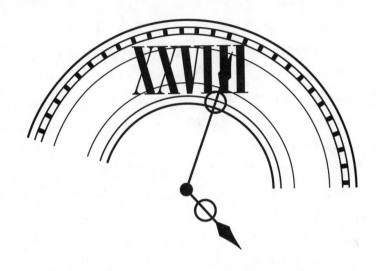

XXVIII

Lucknow had almost become Daphne's prison. She'd arrived in low spirits, sinking farther with every blow the people around her inflicted: the disapproval of the other women, the leers of the men, the distrust of the Indians. Aside from Partha, only two people had shown her kindness. Thankfully, she could spend most of her days with both of them.

Her mornings were given to Narayan in his tower. They spoke in broken Hindi, but Daphne could understand most of what she didn't grasp through his gestures. Though he was more forward than she would have expected, she didn't mind. She preferred his company to the soldiers'.

And thanks to Akash and her expanding vocabulary, she finally understood what Narayan had been trying to tell her that first day.

"Dreams," she said. He nodded. "What do you dream about?"

A boy being bitten by a snake, then lying in a fever. A pretty girl carrying a clay pot of water on her head. And the dancing. He danced in his dreams, kicking up dirt and tossing his head to battering drums, women with bloodred scarves and jangling ankle bells around him.

Daphne had no clue what it all meant. But every day Narayan claimed to have more dreams, and each one seemed more confusing.

She passed the afternoons with Akash, who dedicated his mornings to discovering activities for them to do. By lunchtime he was at her window, tapping three times like a clockwork bird.

They had started with walking aimlessly about. On the second day, he'd taken her to a small dancing festival across the city. Men and women had spun and flung their arms in sinuous motions to the music of drums and a sitar. Daphne had loved watching the women's skirts twirl, listening to the rattling jewelry on their ankles and wrists as she tried to imitate the women's intricate hand gestures. It was just how Narayan had described his dream—men and women losing themselves in the music, blending the border between living and pleasure.

When she expressed interest in the women's clothing, Akash used their third day to take her to a tailor.

"Oh, no, I couldn't possibly," she argued, but he insisted.

"The prices are very good."

"Won't it be offensive?"

He frowned. "Why would it be offensive? You're one of us."

She stared at him, lips parted, heat welling through her body

until she felt an uncomfortable pressure behind her eyes. She had to turn away, unwilling to show him just how much those simple words meant.

So she had spoken with the tailor—with Akash translating—about what she'd like. The woman had smacked her lips together as she made her measurements.

By the fourth day, Daphne was the owner of her very own salwar kameez. It was comprised of a long silk tunic, dark blue with gold-colored brocade around the hem, and matching trousers that were surprisingly airy. There was a scarf as well, but Daphne carefully put this in her bag. She didn't want to ruin it.

At first, in the mirror, she only saw the contrast: fair girl, foreign dress. She saw the stitches between the fabrics of her body, the mismatching patchwork. Then, slowly, it all started to come together. The fabrics overlapped, and she felt as if she were discovering a new Daphne.

A girl trying to patch up the holes within her.

She modeled her new outfit for Akash. He clapped, showing a large, bright smile.

"Stunning," he said, and she blushed.

The outfit, of course, needed to be kept hidden from Crosby. But coming back through the window, Daphne tripped and stumbled into her room, knocking over a cup. The door opened slightly and Partha peered in. He took in the outfit, eyebrows raised. Meeting her eyes, he bent his head as if to say *very well*, then gently shut the door again.

On the fifth and sixth days, Daphne knew something was

wrong. While she enjoyed visiting Narayan's tower, the fact that there was nothing out of the ordinary made her question once again why she was here. The spirit seemed wholly unconcerned.

"But you would tell me if something was wrong?" she insisted. He nodded, then pointed impatiently at the wooden mancala board sitting between them. He'd hidden it in his tower for years after a couple of ghadi wallahs left it there.

She took her turn, studying Narayan as she moved the dried beans around the slots. The spirit smiled, blindingly innocent.

"If nothing's wrong with your tower, I'll probably have to leave soon," she said.

He looked up at the word *leave*, his smile gone. She tried to explain that she couldn't spend the rest of her time here in Lucknow, not when there were so many other cities in India that could be attacked.

Again, she wondered if her assignment here was nothing more than a diversion. Her stomach curdled at the thought.

Narayan picked up her hand. "You here, come back?"

"Yes, I hope to come back and see you again. Then you can tell me more about your dreams."

Her heart was heavy as she ate lunch alone in her room, thinking about what might happen if the terrorists struck Lucknow before she could act, or if they struck elsewhere while she was distracted, useless.

Three taps at the window. Right on time. Pushing her plate away, she crossed the room and opened the latch. Akash leaned against the windowsill, smiling. He looked boyish when he smiled like that, his black hair swept casually across his forehead, and for some reason this made her happy.

"Shall we walk?"

"We shall."

Their method was aimless, their destination unknown. It was nice just to walk and look, memorizing as many details as she could to take to her mother back home: the lizards on the ceiling of her room, the little shops hidden in narrow alleyways, how rich the milk tasted.

"You should have worn your new clothes," Akash said.

"I suppose I'm still nervous about it."

"There's no need. Wear it tomorrow, please? Please?"

"I don't know . . ."

"Pleeee—"

"Stop that."

"—eeee—"

"For heaven's sake! I'll wear it."

He laughed and ruffled his own hair, then smoothed it down again. "Very good, Miss Richards." Like it had been her idea in the first place.

"I told you, call me Daphne." But he was looking across the street now, eyebrows furrowed. "What is it?"

He hesitated. "I haven't eaten lunch. Are you hungry?"

"I already ate." Although she had only taken two bites of her kedgeree. "I suppose I could eat something more."

They moved toward a vendor selling chapatis, which smelled wonderful. They came right off the pan, hot and steaming and

slathered with a type of clarified butter Akash called ghee. There was a small line in front of the vendor and his daughter. The former made chapatis behind a wooden stall while the latter handed them to customers and accepted their money. As Daphne and Akash joined the queue, she drew out a couple of annas.

"*Allow me*," Akash said in Urdu. Daphne began to protest, but Akash held up a hand. She rolled her eyes.

He paid for two chapatis, then said something to the chapati maker in Hindi, which Daphne couldn't make out. The man looked up from his work, nodded solemnly, then bent over his pan again.

A minute later, the girl handed them their food. Daphne smiled at her, but the girl only looked back with fear in her large, dark eyes. Unsettled, Daphne turned to let the next customers order.

She bumped into a man who had been hovering behind her. Both their chapatis fell to the ground.

"I'm so sorry!" She stooped and picked them up, trying to brush off the dirt. "I'm really—here, I'll pay for another. Is that all right?"

The man nearly ripped the bread from her hand, cursing. Spittle landed near her eye and she winced.

Akash put a hand on the man's shoulder, steering him away. They argued loudly until the man stormed off.

Daphne clucked her tongue at his back. "I offered to pay for another."

Akash shrugged. "It was nice of you to offer. Shall I get you a replacement?" He had already wolfed his chapati down, leaving behind nothing but greasy fingers.

"It's only a little dirt. I'll be fine." She rubbed the surface of her chapati, then frowned. "There's something written on it."

Sure enough, there were words stamped into the bread. Not the letters of any Indian alphabet, but letters she could identify. The language, however, was not English.

"Feu-de-joie," she said slowly.

Akash was staring at the chapati as if it were covered in more than just dirt. "That's French, isn't it?"

"It is. I think joie means joy, but the phrase itself, I'm not sure." She glanced up, but he was still staring at the bread in her hands. "What is this about?"

He shook his head slowly. "I don't know."

"Do Indian people usually stamp messages on their bread?" Akash shook his head again. "Strange."

Suddenly, someone grabbed her arm. She instinctively swung out, hitting her assailant in the ear. He released her with a howl of pain.

It was the same man she had accidentally run into. She thrust the chapati at him. "Look, just take it, all right? Take the bloody thing and leave me alone!"

The man snatched the bread, bloodshot eyes watering from the pain in his ear. He looked at the chapati, then began to breathe like a bull.

"You! This not for you!"

"I'm sorry! Please, leave me alone."

Akash tried speaking to him, but the man shoved him away and charged at the vendor. Those waiting in line scurried away as the man shook the bread in the vendor's face and shouted, a vein bulging in his neck.

"What's going on?" Daphne demanded.

The man reached around the cart and pulled the girl away by her thin wrist. She shrieked.

"Let her go!" Daphne yelled, but no one paid her attention. "Hey!"

Something clicked on her right. Looking over, she gasped and backed away from the pistol Akash aimed at the man.

"*Drop her!*" Akash said in Hindi. "*Step away!*" His voice shook, but not with fear. Daphne had heard the same rage-filled timbre in her mother's voice enough times to know the difference.

The man saw the gun and slowly released the girl. The vendor ushered her back around the cart, where she clung to him, sobbing loudly into his apron. People looked on, too riveted to leave, too scared to interfere.

The man muttered something, spat at their feet, then turned and stalked down the street. When he was gone, Akash lowered the gun. Daphne hurried to the girl.

"*Are you all right?*" she asked. The girl kept crying, her thin body shaking.

"Leave them," Akash murmured. "They'll get over the shock sooner if we're gone."

Daphne wavered, then dug inside her pocket. She took out

the two pills she'd kept there since the *Notus*'s crash and handed them to the father, who took them uncertainly.

"Please give these to your daughter. They'll calm her."

Footsteps pounded down the street. They braced themselves, but it was only Lieutenant Crosby.

Sweat rolled down his face as he panted out, "What in the devil's name is going on here? Miss Richards, what on earth—?" He stopped, frantically waving his hands about. "No, you can tell me later. I must speak to you both."

"What's happened?"

"We've received word from Meerut."

Judging by his tone, it wasn't good news.

Daphne made sure she packed everything before going to the tonga that waited outside. As she and the soldiers rode through the city, she held her stomach, feeling sick.

The Meerut tower had been blown to bits, and time continued on. Thoughts assaulted her one by one, thoughts of Danny and Meena, Captain Harris, the Meerut tower, the crying girl, and leaving Narayan without saying goodbye.

Crosby ushered them into the *Silver Hawk*. If Daphne didn't know better, she would have said he was frightened. But that didn't make sense coming from the man who'd said the towers might as well fall if time wasn't Stopping.

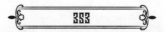

In truth, none of this made sense.

Akash was already in the pilot's seat; he looked at Daphne with a silent plea. She asked Crosby if she could sit in front, to which he gave an annoyed "Yes, whatever pleases you" before he shut the door behind them.

Once they were safely in the air, Akash turned to her. "I'm sorry for what I did today."

She was confused until she remembered him leveling his gun at the angry man. The news from Meerut had temporarily driven it from her mind. "You did what you had to."

"No, I feel as if I must give you an explanation."

"You don't." She shifted in her seat, then glanced at him. "I didn't expect something like that from you, though."

"I'm sorry." He paused, collecting his thoughts. "When we were younger, Meena and I would go into the city without our parents. We thought it was daring. Sometimes, people mistook us for urchins. Maan would get so angry when we came home dirty and covered in scratches and bruises, but it was how we liked to play.

"One day, we were out too late and it was raining. It was so dark we got lost. Meena started crying and ran into an alley. I tried to ask directions, but passersby ignored me, thinking I was a beggar. Then, I heard Meena scream.

"I ran into the alley and—" His voice was now almost impossible to hear over the drone of the plane. "A soldier was there. British. He was looking at her like—like a fox who'd caught a rabbit. He came closer, and Meena couldn't speak, she was so terrified.

"I yelled. I didn't know what else to do. The sound brought

over two sepoys, who convinced the man to leave. But he was smiling, as if he'd won something."

Akash clenched his jaw. "We used to spend all our time together, but now with her work and my deliveries, that's impossible. I can't always be there for her, and she can't always be there for me. So I make her carry a gun, and I carry mine, because I don't want that to happen again. Meena lives a dangerous enough life as it is." His hands tightened on the controls.

Daphne remained silent, but she knew he didn't want words. She let her hand touch the back of Akash's, and he briefly held it, out of view of the others.

They landed near the Agra cantonment sometime later. Daphne left her pack behind and hurried inside.

She found Major Dryden outside the counsel building, talking sternly to a few sepoys. They all said, "Yes, sahib," before hurrying off. Dryden turned and started when he saw her.

"Miss Richards! Thank goodness you're safe. Dreadful news. Simply awful. I'm dispatching troops to Meerut at once, and we have men going to Lucknow as we speak. It's better you stay here."

"Lucknow?" She had only just left. It didn't make sense that the major would send more soldiers so soon.

Dryden sighed wearily. "You must have been in the air when it happened. The tower at Lucknow was also targeted. We just received a wire that it, too, has fallen."

At first her mind refused to accept what he'd said, so she merely stared at him, uncomprehending. It didn't make sense. She had *just been there.*

And she hadn't been able to stop it.

She had failed Narayan.

Her eyes burned, and her throat ached. She should have known that that riot was a distraction. Because she hadn't done enough, Narayan and his dreams of dancing were gone forever.

The major cleared his throat, uncomfortable at her sudden display of grief. She gathered herself and whispered, "Where are the others?"

A flicker of unease crossed his face. "On their way back. They won't arrive till evening."

So Daphne was left to fret with Akash. She shed a few tears in her room for Narayan, then sat silently in the mess hall. Eventually they wandered outside the cantonment. Daphne drank two cups of tea. Akash only stared north.

Finally, just after sundown, they spotted the autos. They rolled down the dusty streets before stopping within the ring of buildings.

Captain Harris emerged from one, haggard and pale.

"Where's Meena?" Akash demanded.

"Right here. Just a moment."

Harris opened the back door and helped Meena out. Daphne stifled a gasp; the poor girl was bruised and scratched, and there was a burn across her face that had been covered with gauze. Even some of her dark, sleek hair had been burned along one side.

Akash cried out and made to grab her, then thought better of it. Instead, he gently put his hands on his sister's shoulders and kissed her forehead, right over her bindi.

"*Are you all right?*" he asked. Meena's mouth trembled and she shook her head. "*What happened?*"

A few soldiers and sepoys stepped out of the autos. Daphne saw Partha run up and grab Harris's arm, leaning in to say something quietly in his ear. Harris replied, then gripped his forearm tightly. Something raw passed between them, stark relief and trepidation.

Daphne scanned the rest of the convoy. Heart pounding, she returned to the siblings and touched Meena's arm. She looked up, eyelashes spiked with tears.

"Meena," Daphne whispered as her throat tightened, "where's Danny?"

The girl let out a faint sob, pressing the back of her hand to her mouth. When Akash reached out to hold her, she pushed him away.

"When I woke," she said, "I was on the ground, and the tower . . . Aditi's tower . . . it was broken. So broken. Everything was—fire and stones and—such a terrible sound."

"But Danny," Daphne said louder, dread rising like water in her lungs, drowning her. "Where is Danny?"

"No one could find him. When the captain came . . . he was gone." Meena held back another sob. "He's gone."

A dull ache traveled from Danny's forehead to the back of his skull. He groaned, but didn't open his eyes yet. He was still drifting, weightless, hardly existing save for the ache in his head.

Eventually something penetrated the thick shell of his unconsciousness: a sound like bees droning.

Danny slowly opened his eyes. He had to blink several times, the light sharpening the dull ache into a stabbing pain. He groaned again and rubbed his face. At least he was lying in a bed.

That made him sit up with a jerk. *Bed?*

Holding his head as it rang with a fresh peal of pain, he took in his surroundings. Yes, he was definitely lying in a bed in the middle of a stark room, facing a closed metallic door. To his left was a round window, the source of that nearly blinding light.

Dizzy, he tried to think back. He had been walking with Meena. They were going to Aditi's tower. Then—

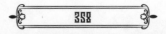

"The tower fell," he whispered to his clammy palms.

His body was battered, his limbs stiff and sore, but he had to find out what had happened.

Biting back curses, Danny moved to the edge of the bed. His clothes had been replaced by a nightshirt that came down to his knees. There was no sign of his belongings.

The cog, he thought frantically.

He lurched to his feet, then promptly stumbled into the wall. Inching his way to the door on unsteady legs, he fought off the darkness creeping across his vision. He needed answers. Where was Meena? Why wasn't he back at the cantonment? What had happened to Aditi?

Danny yanked at the knob with both hands. The door remained firmly shut. He was locked in.

"Hey!" His voice broke with fatigue. He banged on the door. "Hey, let me out!"

There was no answer. Danny stepped back and stared at the metal surface, shivering. He hugged the nightshirt closer to his body.

The window—he could at least try to figure out where they were. He stumbled toward it, eyes squinting in the sun's glare.

He expected to see palm trees and buildings.

Not the vast, chilling expanse of a cloudless sky.

Danny stumbled back until he hit the side of the bed on his way to the floor.

An airship. A bloody *airship*.

A key rattled in the lock. Swinging his head around, Danny

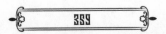

found himself staring at a young man not much older than himself, looking at Danny as if he'd all but expected to find him on the floor. He was tall with wide shoulders and a jaw shadowed with afternoon stubble, his light brown hair combed neatly above a smooth, high forehead.

"You're awake," he said in an English accent. "Good."

"Wh-Who the hell are you?"

"We can have proper introductions later. First, I need to check your condition."

"Don't come near me!" Danny used the bed to scramble to his feet, nearly wrenching the sheets off in the attempt.

The young man raised his hands, still holding the brass key. "I don't wish to hurt you." As he came forward, Danny backed into the wall. Now he could see the stranger had gray eyes, so light they were almost silver.

"I just want to help," the young man said, holding out a hand.

It was made of metal.

Something fluttered in his memory—a glimpse of metal underneath a sleeve torn by a bullet.

"You!" he gasped. "Don't come any closer! Stay the hell away from me!"

"Daniel—"

Danny threw the sheets at him and darted past, veering woozily toward the door, but a large Indian man wearing a turban blocked his path. He grabbed Danny and pinned him to the floor.

"Don't hurt him," the young man ordered as he ripped the sheets away. "Liddy!"

Danny squirmed and bucked as a ginger-haired girl rushed inside and knelt beside them. The Sikh man held out Danny's right arm, and she pushed the sleeve up. Danny couldn't fathom why until he saw the glint of a needle in her hand.

He screamed and thrashed.

The girl named Liddy cursed. "Hold the bleeder still!"

The gray-eyed man crossed the room to help. Danny felt the needle slide into his vein and groaned through gritted teeth.

"This'll knock him out," Liddy said. "Sleep tight, mechanic." He tried to take a swipe at her before the dizziness overtook him, but his hand barely left the floor.

He was out within seconds.

"Now, let's try this again. Slowly this time."

Danny was back in bed. His head felt as though someone had stuffed it with wool. He blinked his eyes open, calm and pain-free.

The light in the room was dimmer than it had been when he'd first awoken. The young man sat on a chair a couple feet from the bed, watching him. This would have ordinarily sent Danny into a panic, but still feeling the effects of the tranquilizer, he only noted the gray-eyed man's presence with mild surprise.

Danny took his advice, sitting up slowly as blood pulsed against his temples. Leaning against the wall, he cast an eye over his captor.

"Who the hell are you?" he murmured.

"My name is Zavier."

Danny waited a moment. "That's it? You chase me across India and the only thing you can say is 'My name is Zavier'?"

"Zavier Holmes, then, if that makes it better."

"I'm fairly certain it doesn't, no."

The young man held up a finger. He went to the door and returned with a tray. "You're going to be hungry in a minute or two. This conversation will be easier if you've eaten."

He set the tray on the bed and Danny blearily studied the offerings. Toast with little dishes of butter and jam, hard-boiled eggs, slabs of bacon, and a cup that was covered with a napkin. He lifted the napkin and mercifully found tea.

"Trying to win me over, are you?" All the same, he picked up the cup and sipped carefully. The contents were lukewarm, but better than nothing. He hoped it would clear his mind; he didn't like feeling so disconnected.

Zavier returned to his seat. "We don't want to make this harder for you."

Danny snorted weakly. "Threatening me with a gun, trying to abduct me, *succeeding* in abducting me, drugging me . . . Sorry, mate, but you've already made it rather difficult for me to trust you. A bit of toast and bacon won't change that."

"I didn't intend it to. But after hearing what I have to say, I hope you'll consider our side of things."

"And what would that be, exactly?" But even as Danny said it, his mind began to whir back into motion. "You *are* the terrorists, aren't you?"

Zavier flinched. "Please don't call us that."

"That's what you are! You bastards have been destroying towers without even thinking of the consequences. What do you think—How can you even—?" His mind had started up too fast, and now it was stalling. Danny put the cup down and breathed deeply through his nose, eyes screwed up tight.

"If I promise to explain," Zavier said, "will you promise to listen?"

Danny opened his eyes to glare at him. "Why do you even want me to listen? What am I to you?"

Zavier scratched behind an ear using his metal hand. The likeness of the arm was good, but the fingers were vaguely skeletal. He used them to gesture at the breakfast tray. "Please, eat. This will be easier if you have some food in you."

"I doubt it." Still, Danny couldn't ignore his light-headedness. He reached for a piece of toast.

"Listen, Daniel—"

"Danny," he corrected, spreading butter over his toast before taking a bite.

"Danny," Zavier tried again. "I understand my methods were extreme. But you have no idea how badly we need you right now. I may have been . . . overzealous."

"You know," Danny said after swallowing, "you could have— here's a novel thought—*asked*."

"Trust me," Zavier said, "you wouldn't have come if I'd asked. I had to find the right opportunities, which wasn't easy. But we've been keeping an eye on you, to make sure you stayed safe."

Danny barked a laugh. "Safe! Pointing a gun at me and trying to launch me out of a train? That's safe to you?" He glanced at the young man, who didn't look so sheepish anymore. "How's the shoulder?"

Zavier lifted his eyebrows. "Healing. You choose your friends wisely, I will say that. I think I still have a lump where Miss Richards hit me."

Danny put his mostly eaten toast down. "You know about Daphne?"

"Yes. We know about the events of Enfield last year, when Miss Richards stole the central cog from the tower and you brought the Enfield spirit to London. We know about the spirit, too. Colton, is it?"

A shard of cold fear stabbed Danny's stomach. They eyed each other, both wondering who would crack first.

In the end, it was Danny. "How could you know about that?"

"We planted spies in London during the construction of the new Maldon tower, hoping to glean something from it. One of our contacts is a constable who overheard your confession when you and Miss Richards were brought in. We also know about Matthias, and how he was connected to Maldon and your father's imprisonment there. And if you think we didn't have people watching you in India, you're sorely mistaken."

Danny thought about the people he'd come to trust over the past few months. The things he had told them.

"How do you know about Colton?" Danny asked, his voice barely louder than a whisper.

"After the Enfield matter, we kept an eye on the town. You were seen with him a few times. The witness reports were enough to confirm what we suspected." Zavier leaned forward, resting his elbows on his knees. "It seems that you are in a very risky, very illegal relationship with the Enfield spirit. We can't do anything about that, of course. It's not our place. However, if you don't agree to help us—"

The tray upended with a loud clatter as Danny launched out of bed and grabbed Zavier's collar.

"Don't you dare lay a hand on him," Danny growled, twisting the cloth in his hands. "Don't you dare touch him!"

Zavier's eyes widened slightly, and he coughed against Danny's knuckles. "We haven't laid a finger on the spirit. Please, calm down."

Danny stood there, panting, fingers so tight in the fabric of Zavier's shirt that he couldn't feel them tremble anymore. Slowly, he let go and tottered back to the bed, all his newfound energy spent.

"But you will if I don't agree to help you."

Zavier nodded, touching his throat. "Leverage."

Danny rubbed his hands over his face. "What exactly do you want from me?"

"We know that something uncanny happened in Enfield on the day you stopped Matthias from harming the tower." Zavier stood and began to pace the room. "From the reports, he'd taken possession of the tower's central cog. And then, suddenly, you were reinstalling the cog in the tower. No one knows what happened between those two moments. Except for you."

Danny's mouth was dry, but he'd spilled the last of the tea, a spreading stain on the sheets that soaked the pallet underneath.

"I don't mean to offend," Zavier went on, "but I wouldn't think someone like you could overcome a man like Matthias so easily. Did you have help? Did you trick him? No one seems to know.

"And here's another curious thing: our contact also overheard a conversation between you and Miss Richards. Not the whole thing, but enough to be of interest to us. You told her that you had Stopped time. That you were able to control the fibers in Enfield, if only briefly."

Zavier came to stand before Danny, who looked up wearily.

"How?" Zavier demanded.

Danny moved his hand to his hip, where the small cog would have rested in his pocket.

"You hold a secret that can influence not just the clock mechanics, but everyone on this earth," Zavier said. "We need this information if we're to succeed in our mission."

"Which is?"

"To bring back time. To let it run freely. It will be difficult, but if you help us . . . If you tell us how you manipulated time in Enfield . . . Danny, this is a secret long since written out of history books. Our ancestors didn't want us to know it, but we *must* if we're to liberate ourselves from the towers."

"Liberate? The clock towers aren't our masters."

"Oh yes they are. Without them, we can't even function on the most basic level. They hold all the power in this world."

"If you even knew how hard the spirits work—!"

"The spirits? They don't have a care for what happens to us. Just take a look at your Enfield spirit, deliberately manipulating his tower again and again in order to get you permanently assigned there."

Blood rushed to Danny's face, bringing with it the uncomfortable heat of rage. "You know my answer already, and it's not going to change. I'm not going to help you destroy towers."

Zavier watched him a moment. Danny forced himself not to look away. Eventually, Zavier sighed and turned for the door.

"I'll give you some time to think it over. Someone will change your sheets later."

"Wait—!"

But the door was already closing. Danny heard the telltale scrape of the lock, once again shutting him inside his prison above the earth. He thought he was going to be sick. The drug's aftereffects were making him woozy and nauseated, and he laid down for a few minutes, careful not to lie in the puddle of tea.

The nausea gradually gave way to the hunger Zavier had promised would come. Danny reached for a rasher of bacon that had landed near the foot of the bed. Nibbling on it, he wondered where the ship was flying over—trying not to think too hard about the "flying" part—and how he could possibly get back to Agra or Meerut.

Meerut. Aditi's tower. Pain spread through his chest, and he turned to hide his face in the pallet. That poor spirit. To be so helplessly trapped in her tower, not knowing she was about to be wiped away forever . . .

Clenching his hands into fists, he took a shaky breath and got up. He walked to the door and knocked as loudly as he could.

"Can I have my clothes back, at least?"

It opened a moment later to admit a young man and woman, both around Zavier's age. The woman was Indian, her wrists adorned with bangles, her long black hair falling loosely down her back. The man wore his brown hair nearly to his shoulders, and he was the tallest human being Danny had ever laid eyes on. He stooped a little, like he was making an unconscious effort to take up less space.

Danny blushed when he noticed the woman held a pile of his clothes.

"Bit chilly in here, eh?" the young man said in an accent common in southeast England. "Go on, then. I'm sure you'd like your trousers back."

Something about the young man pulled at Danny's memory, and he stared at him until it finally registered. "You were part of the protests last year, outside the Mechanics Affairs building." Danny glowered. "You stole my scarf."

The young man grinned. "Got it back, though, didn't you?"

Danny's head was spinning. Now that he thought about it, the ginger-haired girl had been in the crowd as well, protesting the construction of the new Maldon tower. He still heard their words, just as sinister now as when they were first spoken: *Don't think this is finished.*

What had he gotten himself into?

The woman handed Danny his clothes and politely looked

elsewhere. When it became clear that they weren't going to leave, Danny blushed harder and began to dress. He noticed a bandage around his elbow where that ginger-haired girl had stabbed him with the needle. He ripped it off, revealing the mottled bruise underneath.

"Zounds, what happened?" the man asked, nodding at the messy sheets. "Was the bacon burnt?"

"Leave him alone, Ed," the young woman chided. Her voice was lower than Meena's, and her skin was darker, like those from southern India. As he tugged on his trousers, Danny inhaled sharply.

"What's the matter, something stuck?" the man, Ed, asked with a smirk.

"Meena," Danny said. "What happened to her? Is she here?"

The two exchanged a look. "We didn't bring the girl," Ed said slowly. "Just you."

Danny hoped that Meena was safe. Maybe her Shiva had protected her.

Finally, dressed and feeling a little more like himself, he checked his pockets. No cog. Someone had definitely taken it, and he thought he knew whom.

"Right, then," Ed said, turning the young woman back around. "Introductions. I'm Edmund. This is Prema. Welcome aboard." When Danny didn't respond, he leaned in. "Psst, this is where you say your name."

"We already know his name." Prema sighed. "Hello, Daniel. It's nice to meet you."

"It's Danny, actually." He licked his lips, and his eyes strayed toward the window. "I, uh . . . What *are* you people?"

His captors exchanged another look. "We work for Aetas," Edmund said proudly.

Danny blinked three times, waiting for a further explanation. When he received none, he asked, "What on earth does that mean?"

"Ed, you're being too blunt. Anyway, Zavier said he wanted to be the one to tell him."

Danny jumped on the opening. "I want to speak to him."

"Of course. It's just . . ." Prema hesitated, and Edmund shifted on his feet.

"What?" Danny snapped.

"Could you hold out your hands?"

Fighting the nervous energy in his chest, he stiffly held his arms out. Prema gave him an apologetic look before she handcuffed his wrists.

"Can't have you getting into mischief," Edmund said cheerily.

As they walked him along a few corridors, Danny wondered just how big this airship was. He recalled the massive shadow beside the *Notus*, like a leviathan floating up into a kingdom of clouds.

A few doors were open, and he glanced inside the rooms as they passed. He didn't see anyone except a girl who was practicing throwing knives at a pallet she'd leaned against the wall. When she noticed him walking by, she sneered.

They eventually stopped at a metal door with a red *Z* painted on it. Edmund knocked and opened the door.

"Good, I was hoping you would find me," Zavier said as they entered. He was sitting on the edge of a wooden desk, a book in his hand.

Zavier nodded once, and Prema gave Danny a small smile as she unlocked the handcuffs. Once the other two had departed, Zavier stood and closed the book. Glancing at the cover, Danny swallowed his surprise. Greek myths.

"Look, Danny, I'm sorry if I got you worked up earlier. I've been hoping you'd join us for so long now. I may have overstepped."

Danny rubbed his wrists and cleared his throat. "No amount of pleasantries is going to put me at ease, you know. I'm your prisoner."

"That's true enough." The bastard actually admitted it. "But we won't hurt you."

"It's not just me I'm worried about. You're threatening Colton. You're destroying clock towers. Don't you think that affects people?"

Zavier drummed his metal fingers against the book cover. "Yes, and I think it affects them for the better. They shouldn't be pawns in this war on time. But," he said when Danny opened his mouth, "I don't believe this is the right path to take for this discussion."

"What is, then?"

Zavier gazed down at the book, then held it up for Danny to see the cover depicting a Trojan soldier on horseback. "Are you familiar with Greek myths, Danny?"

"I thought your little spies told you everything."

"Don't be cheeky."

"Yes, I know some of them. What does that have to do with anything?"

"I have something I'd like to show you," Zavier said. "Then I'll tell you the whole story."

"Will I be wearing handcuffs again?"

"That was Ed and Prema being cautious, but I see no reason for them. There's nowhere for you to run on this ship."

He thought of the girl throwing knives in her room. "I could grab a weapon."

"You wouldn't know how to use it."

"You seem to have very little faith in me."

Zavier smiled, half amused, half considering. "No, Danny. I have all the faith in you." His eyes dropped back to the book. "Just for something different."

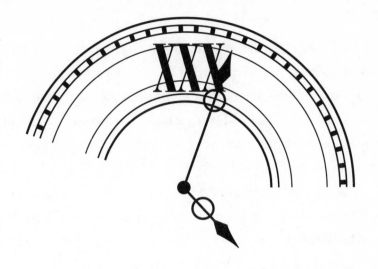

Zavier led him back into the barren corridors. His boots thudded against the metal floors, but Danny was only in his socks; they hadn't allowed him his shoes. The cold metal leeched through the thin fabric, numbing his toes.

"By the way, I'd like my trinket back."

"Trinket? You mean this?" Zavier pulled the cog from his pocket. Danny tensed. "It's curious that you carry it around so openly. What if someone were to see you with it?"

"That's just a risk I take." He reached for it, but Zavier held it at arm's length.

"It's illegal to own pieces of the clock towers. You never know what sort of power they might still possess."

Danny clenched his jaw as Zavier put the cog back into his pocket. "What do I have to do to get it back?"

"First, you listen. Then, we speak."

They came to a set of wide doors that opened to a view of a plant nursery. A garden in the sky. Danny had once read that these were used to generate more oxygen throughout the larger airships. As they passed, Danny caught the aroma of basil and mint. It brought him back to his family's garden on rainy days, when his mother plucked herbs for cooking.

The simple thought of home, of his mother, hit him hard, and his eyes began to burn. It struck him in that moment just how far away he was, how helpless, how alone. He crossed his arms over his chest and tried not to shiver.

The boy beside him was his enemy. No matter how calmly he spoke, or how much patience he showed, Danny couldn't let himself forget that.

They walked down a set of steps, and Danny heard the ringing of metal.

"A quick stop." Zavier led him to a set of thick double doors. Though they were closed, Danny could hear the clang of a forge. "I think you might enjoy this."

When Zavier opened the door, Danny's lips parted in surprise. The walls and floor were covered with scraps of metal, some of them twisted together into awkward-looking machines, some molded into weapons. Something kept making tinny noises, random bits of light blinked here and there, and a little automaton in the corner was twirling in useless circles.

A boy at the forge stopped hammering and raised his goggles, squinting toward the door. It was alarmingly hot in the room, and

Danny saw rivulets of sweat rolling down the smith's olive-toned face and bare arms, matting his dark, curly hair.

"Zave, I've just gotten the metal at the right temperature. Can't this wait?"

"Sorry, Dae. I wanted Danny to see the forge."

Indeed, the forge at the smith's back was impressive, a gaping mouth filled with glowing coals and spiraling embers. Dae gestured at it impatiently.

"There, he's seen it."

"Danny, this is Daedalus, but he goes by Dae. He helps with the technology we use on the ship."

"Like those strange contraptions you used before? Those metal ropes?"

Zavier nodded, ignoring Danny's accusing tone. "He's built a number of useful devices."

"Those spiders, too?"

"Yes, those, too." Zavier walked farther into the room and picked up a large chrome spider. From a distance, it looked deceptively real, but Danny could now see the pinions and screws. Unsettled as he was, Danny couldn't quash his fascination, taking a step forward for a better look.

"It transmits sound," Zavier said. "Not terribly well, but well enough. We've been using them to help keep tabs on you and Enfield."

The spell broke, and Danny backed away again. "Of course you have." He glanced at Dae only to find that the smith was staring at him. Danny drudged up whatever false bravado he possessed and managed a sneer.

"You're an inventor, and your name is Daedalus?"

The smith frowned. "Yeah, ha ha, right bellyful of laughs that is. Can you guess what my father's name was?"

"Hephaestus?"

"No. George." He shoved the metal he was working on back into the forge.

Zavier gestured for Danny to follow him out.

"How did you come by all these people?" Danny asked, wiping sweat from his forehead.

"Some of them approached me, and some, like Dae, I was lucky to find and talk into joining. We need certain skills for this sort of mission."

"But they know what you're doing, and they're all right with it? Why?"

"Because they know the truth."

Zavier and Danny arrived at an observation deck, the wall fitted with a bubble of industrial-thick glass, beyond which stretched endless sky. They sailed an ocean of clouds.

Danny stopped at this horrifying picture. Zavier sensed his reluctance to follow. "Don't like flying?"

"Funny you should ask," Danny muttered, "considering our last encounter on an airship."

Zavier rubbed the back of his neck. "Let's sit a moment."

Danny grabbed a chair and angled it away from the glass. "Where are we, anyway?"

"Right now, we should be flying over the Maldives."

Danny sat down hard. "The Maldives? As in the islands? As in, not India?"

"Correct."

"I—" Danny stopped himself, knowing it was useless to raise a fit. He rubbed his eyes, trying not to imagine the ship crashing into the ocean far below.

"All right," he said when he'd gained control of himself. "You said you would explain. So, explain."

Zavier sat with his legs crossed, hands resting on his thighs. It would have appeared casual had Danny not noticed the tension strung across his broad shoulders.

What in the hell does he have to be nervous about?

"This mission is about something far bigger than tampering with clock towers," Zavier began. "This is about gods and the world as we know it—and as we once knew it. Do you know the story of Aetas?"

"Of course I do. He was created from Chronos, he gave us power, Chronos killed him, and in order to run time ourselves, we built the towers."

"In essence, that's all we know. But there's a lot more to it." Zavier looked out the window, gathering his thoughts. "Aetas was only supposed to hold time, to make it move forward. But it's a heavy burden, and even a god can't be expected to control something that immense. So Aetas did something tremendous. He gave some humans the power to manage time on his behalf.

"But, as you know, Chronos found out what Aetas had done."

"And killed him for it," Danny finished.

Zavier hesitated, the skeletal fingers of his mechanical hand twitching. "That is . . . what many believe."

His tone had shifted to something darker, something more uncertain. It walked fingers up Danny's spine, raising the hairs along the back of his neck.

"What are you trying to say?" Danny demanded, but his voice came out soft, ragged.

"What I'm saying is . . ." Zavier met his eyes, glinting silver like coins at the bottom of a fountain, forgotten wishes and nameless magic. "In his wrath, Chronos opened a prison deep within the earth, beneath the bottom of the ocean. Instead of killing him, Chronos banished Aetas inside, sealing him off from the world and time itself.

"What I'm saying is: Aetas is not dead."

Zavier let this statement hang in the air, final, definite. His uncertainty was gone, but his shoulders were still stiff, his gaze still locked on Danny's, as if waiting for an explosion.

Instead, Danny laughed.

"You're barking," he said, his voice hollow. His situation had become that much worse. Not only had he been kidnapped, but kidnapped by a madman.

Zavier's shoulders finally lowered, slumping in disappointment. "I figured you wouldn't believe me at first. But I'm telling the truth—and that's why we're here. Why *you're* here."

"And how do you figure that?"

"When Chronos imprisoned Aetas, time spiraled out of

control. The only way to fix it was to build the towers. Chronos let us believe the god of time was dead. He wanted nothing further to do with the human race. We were on our own. We still are.

"Yet, if Aetas is released . . . just think of it. A world where time runs freely again, where the clock towers aren't necessary. No more mishaps. No more Maldons." Danny flinched. "If we free Aetas from Chronos's prison, we can be a whole world once more."

Danny licked his lips. They were cracked and stinging, and he focused on those small points of pain to keep his head clear. "Let's say you're telling the truth. How could you possibly know all this? Where would you even get such information?"

Zavier finally looked away. "It wasn't uncommon for a follower of Aetas to also be devout to Oceana. After all, what's the one thing that connects the world? Aetas used the oceans to control time in every corner of the earth. I was fed stories of the Gaian gods when I was little, and visited the ocean whenever I could. To . . . speak to her, I suppose. To speak to them both."

Zavier's breathing had turned deep and even, a look of wistfulness—of devotion—softening his face, reminding Danny just how young he was.

"One day," Zavier whispered, "she spoke back."

Danny dug his fingers into his thighs. "Who?"

Zavier swung his gaze back to him, calm and almost glassy. "Oceana, of course. She appeared in the surf and the foam. So inhuman, so much *more*. She told me everything."

Danny laughed again. "All right. Oceana spoke to you and

told you Aetas was trapped in a prison Chronos created. That doesn't explain why time is still running in Rath and Khurja and—and Meerut, after their towers fell. Did Oceana explain that while you were chatting by the seashore?"

"Not in so many words," Zavier said as the distance left his expression. "Scheming against Chronos would be dangerous for her. But she gave us clues, and led us to Aetas's prison. Although his power is trapped, it still leaks through the edges of his cell, infusing the water above. We've found that if we use this water on the cities we wish to free, and then destroy the towers, time continues on.

"But we can't use this method for every tower in the world. It would take years. We need to free Aetas so that he can help us do away with the towers for good."

Danny stood and walked the length of the room. He stopped before the window. "That can't possibly be true," he said to his reflection in the glass. "It can't."

Zavier joined him. An extension of the airship, possibly the bridge, could be seen above the window. Without a word, Zavier pointed up to it, and Danny's eyes followed. Big block letters spelled out a name:

PROMETHEUS

"We need to help him, Danny," Zavier said quietly. "He relied on us once, and Chronos locked him away. We have to free him. We have to break his chains."

"Why are you so fixated on this idea?"

Zavier clenched his jaw. "I have an interest."

Judging from Zavier's tone, he had much more than a simple interest. There was something disturbingly familiar in Zavier's eyes, but Danny couldn't identify it.

He waited for Zavier to explain. When he didn't, Danny pressed his cold palm to his forehead. "You think you know everything, but you don't know a thing about the clock spirits. If you keep destroying towers, the spirits will die. Did you know that the spirit in the Meerut tower was named Aditi? She's gone now, because of you."

"Meerut and Lucknow were both essential to our plan. I'm sorry it had to be that way, but—"

"Lucknow?" His heart gave a sickly jolt. "You hit Lucknow, too?"

Zavier interpreted the dread on his face. "We waited until Miss Richards was out of the city."

Thank God. "That . . . That still doesn't excuse what you've done. It's only another death to add to your growing list. Can you really have that on your conscience?"

"You're being overly sentimental, letting the Enfield spirit cloud your better judgment. You must realize that your relationship with the clock spirit is not real."

Not real.

Danny grabbed Zavier's shirt and slammed him against the glass, hoping it would break, wanting desperately to push him out into that endless field of clouds.

"Not real?" he snarled. "What the fuck do you know about what's real or not? You may be an expert on Aetas and Chronos and all that nonsense, but I know about clock spirits, and I know that you can't do this without destroying them."

Without destroying Colton.

Zavier put a hand on Danny's, trying to pry it off of him. "You're blinding yourself to the bigger picture by limiting the scope. What would you do if Colton was gone, Danny? You'd keep on living. The world would keep on turning. With Enfield already—"

He stopped suddenly, gray eyes shifting.

Danny's stomach dropped. "Already what? What did you do?"

Zavier sighed. "Not us, Danny. Someone attacked Enfield. The town is Stopped, at least until we free—" He grunted as Danny shoved him against the glass again.

"What happened to Colton?"

"Danny, listen—"

"What happened?"

"The tower was hit. Time Stopped. We . . . don't know where Colton is right now."

Panic, hot and searing, rose up Danny's throat. He spun around and lost his bearings, tripping over his chair. "I have to go," he panted. "I have to—"

He broke out into the corridor and ran. But he was still weak, and it only took a few seconds for Zavier to overtake him. He struggled, nearly freeing himself before another pair of hands seized him.

"What've you told him?" Edmund's voice.

"Only the truth. Hold on, I'll need to sedate him again."

"No!" Danny screamed.

But his sleeve was pulled back and the needle slipped into his arm once more. He tried to say Colton's name before he was carried away by greedy darkness.

Meerut had been combed over, the surrounding areas searched, but there was still no sign of Danny. It had been a few days, and with each passing one, Daphne felt the lump in her stomach grow harder and heavier.

There wasn't much to go on. Meena said they had arrived at the tower, found the water around it, and then the tower exploded. She had awoken as she was being carried away from the rubble.

"The last thing I remember of Danny," she'd said, "was him yelling at me to get away from the tower."

Meena was still in a daze, still processing everything that had happened. Akash could usually be found at her side or hovering nearby. Today, though, his protectiveness had begun to infuriate her, which was a good sign. If she had enough energy to get angry, she'd be all right.

Daphne remembered when the new Maldon tower had fallen. How it had crushed Lucas, but not before a gear had buried itself in his chest.

The thought was too close to her own private horror. The Dover tower might not have been leveled, but she could have died that day. The clock spirit helped her restore Dover's time before her own ran out.

Dryden, Harris, and Crosby were frazzled. It was bad enough that towers were falling and no one knew why. Now an English mechanic was missing.

How would Danny's parents react to the news? Or Danny's friends?

Or Colton?

It was obvious now that she and Danny had been forced to split up for a reason.

She was such an idiot.

Taking a deep breath, Daphne tried not to wallow in those thoughts. They would find Danny. *She* would find him.

At least they'd brought back his things, which had been dumped in his cantonment room. Kneeling, she opened Danny's pack and rifled through the clothes that needed washing, the shaving gear, the jar of aloe he'd used to protect his skin from the sun. Daphne's hand brushed a piece of paper. She drew it out and unfolded it, her breath catching. It was a drawing of Colton. Danny must have done it; she recognized his lines from the clockwork sketches in his case reports.

A sudden sadness passed over her, and she carefully put the

picture away. The look Danny had captured in Colton's eyes was not for her to see.

She sat on the bed and stared at the far wall. *Why would they take Danny? Why would they single him out? Where would they take him?* It didn't seem real. It felt as though Danny would come strolling into the cantonment at any moment, asking why everyone was so worried.

They needed a plan. So far, Dryden's only idea had been to lure the terrorists with something, but what could possibly draw them out of hiding? They could have their pick of any clock tower.

Daphne's only contribution had been to look up the French phrase she'd read on the chapati in Lucknow: feu-de-joie. "Furious joy." A code of some sort?

It has to mean something. Why else would that man have gotten so angry about me seeing it?

Her head whirled in restless circles until she was interrupted by a knock at the door. Shaking herself, she got up and answered.

The private on the other side tipped his hat. The burnt orange sky behind him was blurred with navy blues and rich purples. "Evening, Miss Richards. Someone said I might find you here."

"Does the major need me?"

"No, miss, nothing like that. There's a messenger for you. Asked for you by name."

Frowning, she opened the door wider and saw a boy standing behind the private. He was dressed in the English style with a white dust-stained shirt and dark vest, his cap pulled down low so that she couldn't see his eyes. He studied his feet, refusing to look up.

"Is that all right, miss? Or do you want me to get an officer?"

"No, it's fine. What message—?"

The boy finally met her gaze, and the words were stolen from her throat. He looked at the private, then back at Daphne, amber eyes pleading.

"I . . ." She slowly cleared her throat. "Thank you, private."

The soldier saluted and went on his way. They waited in tense silence until he was around the corner, then Daphne frantically gestured the boy inside.

Once in the room, she forced herself not to slam the door. When she turned around, he'd removed the cap and held it between his pale hands, hands that had once been tinted bronze.

"Colton," she whispered.

He tried to smile. "Hello, Daphne."

"What—you—" Breathing had suddenly become difficult. She walked past him and sat on the bed before she passed out. "I've gone mad. The Enfield clock spirit is in India."

"You're not mad. I've come looking for Danny."

"This shouldn't even be possible. How are you—?"

He turned around, showing her a flat, leather-covered pack on his back. "It has my central cog. A few smaller gears, too." He looked over his shoulder at her. "Please don't steal it again."

"Colton . . ." He turned back around, desperation filling his eyes. "You need to explain. From the beginning. How are you here, and why?"

"The beginning? It's a long story."

"I need you to tell me." She scooted over, and he sat next to her, dropping a small pack at his feet.

"Can't you just tell me where Danny is?"

"I need you to explain this first."

He looked up at the ceiling. "All right. From the beginning."

She heard it all: the attack on his tower, his trip to London, the threatening letter, the flight from England, the train ride halfway to Agra, being shot at, and the walk the rest of the way. He was dusty and weary, his voice slow and methodical, like an automaton on its last gust of steam.

Even with all this information, even with the incredible details Colton wove into his story, she sensed that he was keeping something from her. There was a muted quality to his eyes, as if he had seen something that went beyond words.

When he was finished, he sat watching her expectantly.

She opened her mouth a couple of times before she found what to say. "Why would anyone attack the tower, then keep the town Stopped? Time is running freely in every other place that's been attacked. Why not do the same to Enfield, if that's their goal?"

"That's why I need to see Danny. The other part—" He searched through the pack and showed her the letters and the photo. "He's in danger. You probably are, too. They warned me that if I didn't come here, something was going to happen to him. I asked for him when I got here, but the men said he wasn't available. What does that mean? Daphne, can't I just talk to him? Where is he?"

A lump formed in her throat, and she swallowed it away with effort. "Colton—"

"I tried to get here as soon as I could." He began talking faster, growing more distressed. "The note said they would do something if I didn't come, so I—Daphne? Where is he?"

She closed her eyes tight. "He's missing, Colton. There was an attack, and in the commotion, he must have been taken. We don't know where he is. I'm sorry."

The room was silent. She opened her eyes, afraid Colton had left. But he remained sitting beside her, absolutely still, staring at nothing. Slowly, he curled toward his knees and put his head in his hands. He had come too late.

Daphne knew how to fix broken clocks. She didn't know how to fix a broken spirit.

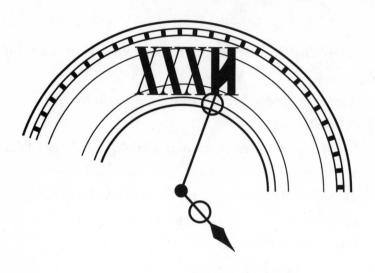

XXXI

Danny woke to the smell of kippers. For a moment, he thought he was back home, his mother fixing up a full breakfast downstairs. The thought was so comforting that he smiled into his pillow. He would have a large breakfast with his parents, drop by Cassie's place, then drive back to Enfield.

Enfield.

His eyes snapped open. He touched his aching elbow, where they had wrapped a new bandage.

Now he remembered.

"Ah, there you are. I thought some hot food would wake you."

Danny sat up. He felt curiously hollow, as if all his insides had been scraped out. A woman sat in a chair beside his bed, one finger marking her place in the book she'd been reading.

She set it down and reached for the breakfast tray at her feet, placing it before him and settling back to assess his reaction. He looked her up and down. She was middle-aged, and looked quite fit. Her light brown hair had been tied into a simple chignon, revealing an angular face with hazel-green eyes.

"You need to eat, love," she said. "They gave you a much higher dosage than was necessary, and you've been in and out for nearly two days. Poor thing, you're too thin already." She clucked her tongue. "Don't worry, I gave them a tongue-lashing. Won't happen again."

Danny studied the tray. Tea, toast, kippers, mushrooms. His stomach rumbled, but he was too faint to reach for any of it.

"Who are you?" he croaked.

"Josephine Davis. Jo for short, if you like. I'm Zavier's aunt."

Danny blinked. *Aunt?*

"I'll save you some questions and explain, but only if you start eating." She pointed sternly at the tray. Danny slowly picked up the fork and speared a mushroom. It was chewy almost to the point of being rubbery, but the flavor flooded his mouth with an almost painful intensity.

"There's a good lad. Now, let's see. To start with, this is my husband's ship. He passed away a few years ago, so for the moment, it's unregistered. Zavier's father passed from a mining accident when he was fifteen, and his mother, my sister, is—gone." There was a curious lilt in her voice at the word *gone*. "He's been with me ever since. He's a good boy, if a bit narrow-sighted.

"I help pilot the ship. Zavier takes care of operations. It was just him and a few others at first—Ed and Liddy, if you met them; they're his friends from back home—and they had to work to convince me to let them use the ship, but in the end they won me over."

Danny forced down a bite of kipper. "I'm not planning to join—"

"I know, I know. That's between you and Zavier."

"Then why are you here, if not to recruit me?"

"To give you a proper welcome to the *Prometheus*. And to apologize for my nephew."

Danny took a long sip of tea, wondering what to say. She didn't make him anxious like the others did. There were no pretenses here, no masks, no suspicion.

"You actually believe in this cause?" he asked at last. "Destroying clock towers?"

"I do. Zavier has always known what he's doing, and, by God, that boy is clever. I believe him about Aetas. About all of it."

"Why?"

She shrugged. "I'm sure he's told you about Oceana. It was like a dream, but we all saw her." Jo's eyes glazed over, as though recalling something far away, unreachable. "It's a little hard to not believe in something you've seen with your own eyes."

"You realize that you're a terrorist."

Jo smiled. "Call it what you will, but you can't deny the world as we know it is changing. Nothing can ever stay exactly as it is. Best get on the wagon before it leaves you in the dust." She picked up her book again. "Eat, love. Then I'll take you to see Zavier."

Danny's stomach had shrunk while he slept, but he ate most of the breakfast, which appeased Jo enough that she was willing to give him his clothes back. She stood facing the wall as he dressed, then turned back to hand him a comb.

"You can have a bath today, if you like," she said in a tone that plainly meant he needed one.

"Thank you." He couldn't believe he was thanking one of *them*, but she'd been decent, unlike the others. No jokes, no ultimatums, no handcuffs, and best of all, no needles.

She took him to Zavier's office and, after a quick knock, opened the door.

"Danny's awake. I've brought him to see you."

Zavier had been talking to Dae, who took this as his cue to leave. The smith gave Danny a once-over as he passed.

"Please come in, Danny. Thank you, Aunt Jo."

She gave him a pointed look before she closed the door, and then it was just Zavier and Danny and silence. Zavier had a metal, rod-like device in his hands. He turned it over in his fingers before setting it on the desk behind him. It looked new. Dae must have brought it to show him.

Zavier cleared his throat. "I apologize for what happened. We won't resort to such methods again, provided you can remain calm. If not," he said, touching the metal rod, "we have other methods. Less harmful, but still effective. Please don't make us use them."

Danny stared at the desk, eyes roaming over the strange rod and the papers Zavier had been reading. Even upside down, he could tell that one of the sheets was written in French. He saw the phrase "feu-de-joie" underlined three times.

"I won't make you use them," Danny said, voice cracking with weariness, "if you tell me what's happened to Enfield."

"I've already told you. Now, I've been thinking. Since you don't believe us about Aetas, I thought we could show you, so you can better understand. We still have a little water left after Meerut and Lucknow."

Danny's heart began to pound painfully fast. "You're going to destroy *another* tower?"

"Just a small one in Edava. It's a town on the southern coast of India. The tower there is already falling apart."

Danny thought of Colton's tower, and how it had been falling apart from neglect when he'd first seen it. "You can't just knock down a tower because of that!"

"Not because of that, Danny. Because we're freeing time. We've tried using the water without resorting to this, but found the power wouldn't take over until the influence of the clock was removed. We're doing these people a favor. Instead of worrying about their tower Stopping, we're liberating the people of Edava from the tower's wretched hold on them." Zavier's eyes flashed. "You more than anyone should know what a liability a tower can be."

There were too many words begging to be yelled, too many ways he wanted to smack the self-righteous look off Zavier's face. Breathing hard through his nose, Danny said, "I won't help you if you do this."

Zavier examined him a moment. He took Colton's small cog from his pocket, making sure Danny saw it. "If you really want to know what happened to Enfield, you'll let us show you."

Danny bared his teeth. Zavier took his silence as agreement and slipped the cog from sight.

A knock interrupted their icy standoff. The door opened to reveal Edmund.

"Za—oh, hullo there, Danny. Sorry about the whole . . . well." When Danny only glared at him, he turned to Zavier. "The others have come back. When should we detonate?"

"In a moment." He glanced at Danny. "Remember what I said." He slipped the metal rod through his belt, and Danny swallowed.

At the observation deck, joined by a couple others, Danny's stomach flipped. Before, his view had been an ocean of gray clouds. Now, he could see the sparkling azure of the Arabian Sea below, and where it met a rocky coastline crowded with palms. A town was nestled there. Quiet. Unsuspecting.

"Some of the others rigged up explosives we got from Dae," Zavier explained as they took their places before the window. Danny was flanked by Zavier and Edmund, the others—Prema and the large Sikh man—positioned slightly behind, probably in case he tried to run again. His elbow throbbed, a painful reminder of how poorly that had ended for him last time.

"Dae found a way we can detonate the explosives from a distance, but we still have to be within ten miles for the transmitter to work." Zavier held out a hand and Edmund passed him a metallic box. Zavier opened it to reveal a control panel inside.

A small aircraft suddenly flew out from below them, toward Edava. Danny hoped, if only for a moment, that it was someone else—someone who had seen the airship and was rushing to get help. But then he quickly realized it was the same aircraft that had rescued Zavier from the train. It must have been docked on the airship.

Danny held his breath as the plane circled the town in the distance, as the air beneath it began to shimmer.

"He's dropping Aetas's water over the tower," Zavier explained. "It'll soak up the time of Edava, rendering the tower obsolete."

The plane turned and headed back for the *Prometheus*.

"Watch, Danny. *This* is the power of Aetas."

"No," he said quickly, even as Zavier reached for a button on the control panel. "No, you can't! *Stop!*"

He tried to lunge at him, but the large Sikh man held him back. Zavier pressed the button, and at first, nothing happened. Then Danny saw a plume of wild smoke rising from the middle of the town. He lurched forward.

"You bastard!"

"Watch, Danny!"

Danny was let go, and he pressed his hands to the glass. He waited for a gray dome to block the town from the world, Stopping time the way Maldon had Stopped nearly four years ago, the way Enfield had Stopped the year before.

Nothing happened.

A ripple ran through him, through the very air, and he could have sworn even the airship shook. Sharp, crisp, just like Khurja.

Edava began to glow, faintly at first, and then brighter,

brighter, until the glow disappeared with a blinding blink. People appeared along the coastline, pointing at the *Prometheus*. They were free. Time was still running.

And the Edava spirit was dead.

"We know you want to preserve the towers," Zavier said softly. "But sometimes, you have to sacrifice what you want for what's right. Surely you must understand. And if you don't yet, you will."

Danny didn't realize he was crying until he saw his reflection in the glass. He closed his eyes and slid to the floor, weeping for a soul he had never known, and weeping for a soul he did know. One that these people were trying to erase from his life for good.

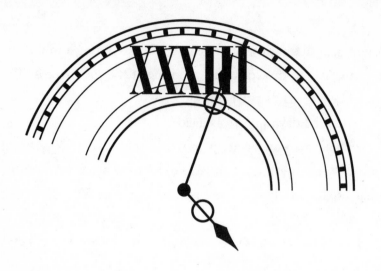

Daphne knew she couldn't hide a clock spirit in her room. Nor could she hide him in Danny's, as it was regularly cleaned by Indian servants despite not having an occupant. She thought about her options, but when she started plotting how she might smuggle Colton into the Taj Mahal, she knew she'd run out of plausible ideas.

So she went to Captain Harris—of all the officers at the cantonment, she trusted him most—and made an uncomfortable request. "I was wondering if, perhaps, I might have access to another room. A private one that's out of the way."

Harris frowned. No doubt he'd been expecting yet another request to join the search for Danny, to which she had been repeatedly told no. "You already have a room, Miss Richards."

"Yes, it's just, uh . . ." A flush crept up her neck. "I need it to practice."

"Practice?"

"Yes. I . . . sing. Apparently."

He brightened slightly. "You do?"

"It's the only thing that calms me. During this, um, difficult time, I'm in need of quite a bit of calming."

"That's certainly understandable. But why would you require another room?"

"Mine's right in the middle of everything. I don't want anyone to overhear. It's terribly embarrassing, but if I had a room that was out of the way . . ."

"Ah. Let me see what I can do."

After conferring with the major, he gave her the key to a room in a lonely corner of the cantonment. After all, the major said, they didn't want her becoming hysterical during this rough patch. Daphne gritted her teeth.

"Just promise you'll sing for us when we bring Mr. Hart back," Harris said with a weak smile. He blamed himself for Danny's disappearance. Crosby had been short with him, and Partha could often be found by his side, concern written in the slant of his eyebrows. Daphne wanted to tell the poor man that there was nothing he could have done, but she knew he wouldn't listen.

She led Colton to the abandoned room, instructing him that he couldn't leave under any circumstances. She would lock the door behind her, and keep the key so that no one could get inside. Colton listened in silence, expressionless as he took in the empty, dusty room.

"I'm sorry to leave you here alone, but I promise I'll come

often. We have to be careful now. Until we find Danny, you're not safe here." *And even if we do find him.*

"But when will that be?" Colton asked. "When will they find him?"

"I don't know, Colton. The major sent out search parties, so maybe we'll learn something by the end of the week."

But by the end of the week, there was still no news. Wires had been sent to every major city, to every senior officer who wasn't currently preparing for the Queen's celebration in Delhi. They would send back word if they learned anything. Strangely, no wires had been sent to London.

"Surely Danny's parents ought to be told," Daphne said to the major.

Dryden coughed into his fist. "You must understand, my dear, that we are responsible for your life, as well as Mr. Hart's. If word were to get out, there would be an inquiry that would slow our progress. I'm sure we'll find him in a jiff."

By the end of the second week, there was still no news.

Daphne begged more cigarettes off Partha. He gave her a disapproving frown even as he handed them over. She slipped him an anna and lit up in her room, needing to settle her nerves somehow.

Two weeks turned into three. Three into four. They were well into December now, and Christmas was around the corner. Daphne asked if the major would finally send a wire to London, but Dryden bumbled through a response that amounted to, "No, not yet."

To make matters worse, another tower had fallen, this one in Edava, a small town to the south. Daphne begged the major to let her go, but he said he couldn't risk it.

Meena and Akash were the only reason Daphne wasn't tearing out her hair. They stayed in their Agra home most days, but often came to the cantonment to see her. The burn on Meena's cheek was healing, but it would scar.

Akash looked worn thin. One day, Daphne sat him down and asked if he was taking care of himself.

"My needs do not come first. Besides, I know this is hard for you."

If it was hard for her, it was impossible for Colton. Every time Daphne went to see him, he was sitting preternaturally still, vacant-eyed and quiet. That worried her more than anything else.

She brought him books from the British soldiers, but he barely touched them. He spent his time wrapped up in his own thoughts, his own nightmares.

But Daphne was used to speaking to someone who had become withdrawn.

"Colton," she tried one day, "please talk to me? It'll be easier if you shared your troubles with someone. I know you're upset, but we're doing all we can. We'll find Danny, or he'll come back on his own. He's strong, remember? He saved you. He saved Enfield."

The spirit looked at her then. Really looked at her. She was stunned at the level of pain within his amber eyes. It was like

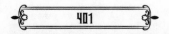

falling through an endless hole, never knowing if you would ever reach the bottom.

"He saved me," Colton agreed, "but I can't save him."

"Don't say that."

He stood, walking toward the small window at the back of the room. "I've been thinking. What if I made myself known? What if the people who took Danny could have me, too?"

"What? No. Absolutely not."

"They wanted me, obviously, or they wouldn't have sent that letter. I could take his place."

"Don't be absurd."

Colton clenched and unclenched his hand. "Why is it absurd?"

"It's more dangerous for you than it is for him!"

Colton turned away in vexation, grabbing the wooden chair beside him and throwing it at the wall. It splintered with a loud crash, and Daphne flinched.

"How can it be more dangerous for me when I'm already—?" He cut himself off, trembling, then sat on the dusty bed and crossed his arms as if he wanted to shrink in on himself and disappear.

Daphne stood there, slightly afraid, wondering what to do. As she took a tentative step toward him, there was a small knock at the door.

"Daphne? Are you all right?"

Meena. Daphne exchanged a look with Colton, but the spirit didn't budge.

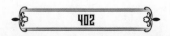

Daphne cleared her throat. "Yes, I'm fine. Is something the matter?"

Silence. Daphne stood still, willing the girl to leave. Then the door slowly creaked open.

"I followed you because Akash wants to see you, but I heard a crash. Are you—?" Meena stopped at the sight of Colton. "Oh. Who's this?"

But when she got a better look, her mouth parted. "You look . . ." Meena glanced between him and Daphne. "Who are you?"

Colton stood before Daphne could answer. "My name's Colton. I came from Enfield."

Meena gasped. "You *are* the one. Danny's spirit."

Colton perked up, barely registering the alarm on Daphne's face. "He's told you about me?"

"A little. But—how?" She glided into the room like a sleepwalker led by a dream. Colton was motionless as she lifted a hand and carefully put it on his arm. She shivered and muttered something in Hindi. "This isn't possible. It can't be. A clock spirit from England, in India?"

"We didn't think time running without the towers was possible," Daphne pointed out.

Meena exhaled shakily. "This is truly a miracle. It must mean something."

"Yes, it means that whoever took Danny wants Colton as well," Daphne snapped. "And we're not going to let that happen."

Meena kept staring at Colton, but eventually she bit her

lower lip and turned to Daphne. "About Danny. Akash wanted to see you."

"Akash? Why?"

"He wishes to tell you something. He's waiting for you outside."

Daphne wavered. She didn't want to leave Colton alone with Meena, but the girl was a clock mechanic, the only other one in the cantonment. The only other one she could trust.

And if Danny had told her about Colton, that must mean he trusted her, too.

"Please tell no one about this," Daphne urged.

"I won't. Go see Akash."

Anxiety sank its talons into her lungs as she left the room. Outside, she was greeted by a cool evening, the sunlight persisting even though the first star had already appeared above.

Akash was waiting down the road. He was dressed in his flight suit, goggles hanging around his neck, a pack slung over his shoulder.

"Akash? What's going on?"

He studied her face with those dark, unreadable eyes. "The soldiers have been keeping me busy delivering messages, and I needed to take care of Meena, otherwise I would have done this sooner. I know you've asked to help in the search for Danny and the major won't allow it, so I've decided to go in your place."

She rocked back on her heels. "What?"

"It's been too long, and no one's had any word. I'm going to Meerut to see if I can find any sign of where he was taken."

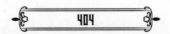

Akash's eyes shone, his usual certainty replaced with something calmer, softer. "Wish me luck?"

She threw her arms around his neck. He stumbled back in surprise, then hugged her just as tightly.

"Thank you," she whispered. "Thank you for doing this. Please, please be safe."

"I will." He pulled back, then showed her his hand. On the back, he'd drawn a diamond.

"Give me some of your invincibility," he said. "Give me some of your strength."

She placed her hand over his, then put them against his chest. "It's yours."

Here, at last, hope began to well within her, like a moth emerging after a storm. A whisper against the cold, a flutter of white amid the gray. It was neither beautiful nor ugly; it was the truth of living things.

He leaned toward her, or maybe she was leaning toward him. She could smell him this close—clean and earthy, like the plains after a monsoon.

Their lips touched, just barely at first. Then he pulled her in. She didn't know what to do with her arms, so she wrapped them around his waist. It felt good to hold him, to keep him together and prevent the pieces of him from drifting apart. As if she were weaving a protective spell over his body, warm and solid against her own.

Two more stars had joined the first by the time they separated. They breathed in the quiet evening air and avoided looking

into each other's eyes. She was afraid that if she did, it would be for the last time.

He turned, and she watched him go, still feeling the phantom pressure of his lips on hers.

"Akash," she called. He looked over his shoulder. "Come back. Come back with him."

He smiled slightly. "Haan, Miss Richards."

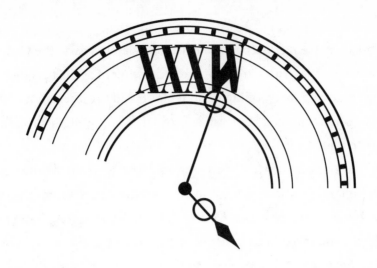

XXXV

Days passed as Danny wasted away in his room. Zavier and the others insisted that he could walk around, that he didn't have to act like a prisoner, but he knew that as long as he remained on the airship, that's exactly what he was. One small step into their territory and he'd be lost.

As if he would agree to help them now. After their demonstration, he had spent the rest of the day in his room thinking about Enfield and Colton and what the *Prometheus* crew intended to do. How their actions would necessitate the death of Colton and everything he loved. Everything that made him Danny Hart.

They fed him three times a day. They let him bathe, and even gave him a razor to shave when the stubble grew too uncomfortable. Jo came every day to speak with him, and left behind books: Ovid, *The Aeneid*, Dante's *Divine Comedy*. Danny liked to pass the time by imagining which circle of Hell was reserved

for each passenger of the *Prometheus*. Zavier was easy: the Outer Ring of the Seventh Circle, where those violent against property were thrown into a boiling river of blood and fire, then shot with arrows by centaurs. At least it provided Danny with pleasant daydreams.

He knew he was losing weight. His skin, which had browned in the sun, was fading back to its usual pallor. The worry ate his bones—worry about Colton, his parents, Meena, Daphne, Harris, and the others. What were they doing in the wake of his disappearance? Were they searching for him? Did they think he was dead?

Loneliness took the shape of a dark skyline, so far-reaching it was difficult to find where it ended. If it even had an end.

The worst of it was when the ship prepared for Christmas. Danny had no idea how much time had passed until then, and it was a shock to his system. Red and gold streamers lined the hallways, bells jangled in all corners of the ship, and someone had even put a wreath on his door. He tore it down the moment he saw it.

Liddy and Prema made cookies and offered him some. Danny refused.

"It'll do you no good to mope," Prema said gently. "Have one. Please?"

"No, thank you."

"Probably thinks we've snuck some sort of drug in 'em," Liddy sneered. She bit off the head of a gingerbread man, making exaggerated chewing noises. "Yum, no drugs!"

Danny still refused their offerings, and they left him alone. That didn't mean the others didn't try to get him into the holiday spirit. Edmund could be heard bellowing carols at odd hours of the day, and Jo had taken to spicing the eggnog and sneaking it onto Danny's food trays. Some idiot had even hung mistletoe over Zavier's office door.

Danny wanted no part of it. He kept to himself in his room, curled up on the bed, thinking about his mother and father alone on Christmas so soon after they'd been reunited as a family. Cassie biting her nails as she fretted. Colton needing him. At least in his room, no one saw him give in to frustrated tears.

After the demonstration, Zavier gave Danny some space, then made not-so-subtle attempts to talk to him. Danny resisted all of his advances; it was clear Zavier didn't possess his aunt's charm.

Jo ended up relaying all conversation between them, but after a few weeks of this back-and-forth, the young man finally summoned Danny to his office.

When the door opened, Danny was nearly bowled over by a disturbing sight: Zavier, *laughing.*

Zavier saw him standing in the doorway and his mirth blew out like a candle. A girl sat on the edge of his desk, younger than him by a few years. Danny had seen her a couple of times around the *Prometheus,* but didn't know her name. When she turned to look at him, he was startled to see she had Zavier's gray eyes.

Zavier made a few motions with his hands at the girl, who nodded and gestured back. Danny recognized it as sign language. One of the mechanics back home was deaf and required an interpreter on assignments.

The girl slipped off the desk and smiled at Danny as she walked by, closing the door behind her. Uncertainly, Danny made his way over to a chair.

"Your sister?" he guessed.

"Yes." Zavier watched Danny carefully, as if he had pointed out a weak spot in his armor. Quickly changing the subject, he said, "I've given it some thought, and I think it's best that I tell you everything concerning Enfield."

Danny sat up straighter. "You will?" Suspicion tempered his eagerness. "Why?"

"It's not fair for me to keep the information from you, especially since you're Enfield's clock mechanic."

That couldn't be the reason, but Danny didn't argue. Whether it was a new tactic or Jo had convinced him to confess, he needed whatever information Zavier was willing to provide.

Zavier drummed his metallic fingers against the desk. "There is another airship called the *Kalki*. That crew has their own goals—chiefly, to drive the British out of India."

Danny sat back. Of all his theories, he hadn't expected this.

"The *Kalki*'s crew is made up of Indian rebels who believe that the rebellion twenty years ago should have succeeded. We respect their mission, and they respect ours. Sometimes we work together, help each other if needed. So I know why they attacked Enfield: to Stop the town and cease the production of firearms."

Danny closed his eyes and thought back to his visit of the weapons factory. He'd known it then, and he knew it now: Enfield should have never been involved in such business. "Well, it sounds like they succeeded," he said flatly.

"Yes, but not quite. The town Stopped before the tower completely fell."

Danny opened his eyes. "And Colton?"

Zavier laced his fingers together on the desk. "I may have lied before about not knowing where Colton was. It's true that we don't know where he is currently, but we do know that Colton went to London."

"He—what? How? Why?" When he'd taken Colton to London last year, the spirit could barely keep his eyes open, let alone walk.

"We're not sure how, but a contact saw him at your house."

"You—" Danny half-rose out of his seat. "You have spies watching my bloody house?"

"Not consistently, but yes. Also, our spiders listen in."

"Have you done anything to my parents? I swear to God, if you've touched them—"

"No one has touched anybody. They're safe, Danny. I promise."

"And Colton?"

Zavier hesitated. "We're not sure."

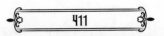

Danny's limbs shook with rage and fear. His head swam with information, with consequences.

"The rebels have told us that the short supply of guns is becoming troublesome for the soldiers," Zavier went on, "but it's not a significant enough move for their cause. They have . . . something else in mind."

Danny thought back to the riots he'd heard about, sparking here and there throughout the country. What else could they possibly do?

And then he remembered the dark looks on the Indian soldiers' faces whenever Delhi was mentioned, the reminder that the Queen was now their Empress, whether they wanted it or not.

"They're going to do something at Delhi," Danny concluded. "Aren't they?"

Zavier studied him, the caution back in his eyes, in the set of his shoulders. Eventually, he nodded.

"They're going to assassinate the viceroy."

The words were a kick in the gut. *"Assassinate?"*

"You must know Viceroy Lytton isn't popular. When we started working with the *Kalki* rebels, we struck a deal. They would cause distractions—the riots—so that we could rig explosives within the Indian towers. In return, we'll give them a distraction when the time comes. Lytton's going to be at the Delhi durbar to stand in for Queen Victoria during the New Year's celebration. It's the perfect opportunity to make sure all eyes are on them, to turn the event into something symbolic."

Zavier shrugged. "We don't have to like their actions, as long as it helps our mission."

"All this so you can attack the Delhi tower?" Zavier said nothing, and Danny kicked the desk in agitation. "You're just going to let them kill a man to be *symbolic*?"

"It's not our decision. The *Kalki* crew has their goals, and we have ours."

"But you can stop them. Can't you imagine the panic this is going to cause? How many deaths will pile up on either side?" He thought of his friends caught up in that chaos—Meena, Akash, Daphne. "India is still reeling after the first rebellion. Don't stand back and let another one happen."

"I thought you were sympathetic to the Indian cause?"

"That doesn't mean I want to watch them *or* my countrymen die!"

"You're straying from the larger picture."

"It looks plenty big to me!"

"*Time,* Danny. Aetas. The towers. Once we've solved the bigger problems, we can turn to the smaller ones."

"This is *small* to you?"

"Compared to the power of gods? Yes, it is."

"You're not being rational."

"Magic, Danny, is not rational. I thought you of all people would know that."

Danny clutched the arms of his chair. "I want to go back to my room now."

"If you wish." Zavier rose to summon an escort, looking disappointed.

Danny's mind raced. He had to warn someone. Major Dryden, or Captain Harris, or another officer who could put a stop to this. If only he could get back to Meerut . . .

An idea struck Danny so suddenly that he nearly wrenched his back turning in his seat.

"Wait!"

Zavier paused, his hand above the doorknob. "What is it?"

"I . . ." Danny forced himself to look innocent, lowering his eyelashes as he stared at the floor. "Maybe I—Maybe I do want to help you."

Zavier turned back completely, waiting for Danny to continue.

"Maybe we really should be focusing on the bigger picture. But I'm still not sure what to believe. I know what I saw, but what if Aetas's power wears off? What if time *does* Stop in these places you've freed?"

"That won't happen."

"But how do you know for certain? I want to see Meerut. I want to see that the city is still running. Then I'll give you my decision."

Zavier eyed him with that familiar caution. "I can show you Meerut," he decided. "But only from the air. We're not landing."

"That sounds fair. Thank you."

A rare smile flitted across Zavier's face before he opened the

door and asked for Edmund to escort Danny back to his room. As Danny made to leave, Zavier stopped him.

"Here." He handed Danny the small cog. "Dae can't make sense of it. I'm sorry for keeping it from you for so long."

Danny's hand trembled as he took it. Touching the cog was almost like touching Colton, and it suddenly gave him all the courage he needed.

"Remember: Meerut," Danny said.

"Yes. Meerut."

He should have known.

The pockets of Indian rebellion just before the clock towers fell. The rumors that something was going to happen to the Delhi tower during the New Year's celebration. Danny had anticipated the terrorists using the celebration as a distraction; he just hadn't anticipated rebels using the terrorists as a distraction in return.

Both sides benefited, and everyone else lost.

Danny had read about the massacres during the uprising. Indians slaughtering British citizens, British irrigating the Indian plains with rebel blood.

He saw the oppression all around him, the indignation in Meena and Akash's eyes. He wanted India's freedom, too.

But not at this cost.

Sacrifice what you want for what is right, Zavier had said. Hypocrite.

The airship had traveled north since the incident at Edava, and now they flew somewhere near Nepal. They could easily hide in the clouds, but they'd had to land twice for fuel. Both times, Danny was kept under tight watch in his room. He hoped that someone would recognize the ship and stop Zavier, but no one ever did.

Christmas came and went. Again, the crew tried to lure Danny into a sense of false security, popping Christmas crackers with colorful crowns, promising cooked goose and rosemary potatoes, but he accepted none of it. His stomach growled in displeasure, but he couldn't stop thinking about the approaching New Year. He couldn't let anything distract him.

The crew had given him other clothes, but he insisted on wearing his own outfit the day after Christmas, when Zavier said he would take him to Meerut. It was wrinkled and the cuffs were frayed, but at least someone had washed it.

Zavier came to his room, handcuffs at the ready. He saw the look of disgust Danny gave them and shrugged. "I have to be sure."

"You don't trust me?"

The young man raised his eyebrows. "You don't even trust *me* yet. You said you would give your answer after you saw Meerut. Until then, you'll have to bear it."

Danny held out his arms and Zavier fettered his wrists

together. At least Colton's cog was safe in his pocket, providing some small measure of comfort.

Zavier led Danny to a hangar built in the belly of the ship. It housed a small aircraft, its engine already warm and running, the same one that had carried the water to Edava. Danny looked around, and Zavier seemed to read his mind. "We have none of Aetas's water left. We could go back for another batch, but that'll take a few days. It would be much simpler if you just told us your secret about Enfield."

Danny bristled, but decided not to respond.

Zavier opened the aircraft doors, one on either side. There was room for two people to sit in the cockpit. Danny clambered into the seat without controls, wriggling his hips awkwardly since he didn't have use of his hands. How the hell was he going to do this?

Zavier slipped in beside him, then shifted so that Danny could see the metal rod at his belt. The threat was clear. Danny still didn't know what it did, but it was bound to be unpleasant.

The hangar opened. Danny held his breath and stared at the expanding sliver of sunshine that grew into a sheet of crystalline blue. How many feet were they above the ground? How steady was this aircraft, anyway?

Zavier took hold of the controls and urged the plane forward, out of the hangar. Danny bit his lip to conceal a startled noise. They were going to drop. They were going to fall right out of the sky. At least Zavier would die alongside him, a minor consolation.

The aircraft did drop, but only a few feet. A small yelp escaped him.

Zavier glanced over. "Don't worry, there are parachutes." He pointed past Danny, to the side of his seat. "I'm a relatively good pilot. My aunt and uncle taught me."

"You don't say." Danny sank down into the seat. The less he could see of the open sky, the better.

"How do you like her? My aunt?"

She's the only sensible one on that ship. "She's all right."

"You know, you should try to get to know the others instead of locking yourself up in your room all the time."

Danny tried not to laugh. He tested the handcuffs; they only had two inches of give between his wrists.

"Do you honestly think that if enough time passes, I'll think of you lot as my friends? Sorry to disappoint, but I already have friends, and they're looking for me as we speak." At least, he hoped so. "I'm not in the market for new mates."

Zavier shook his head. "Never mind."

They flew in painful silence. Danny closed his eyes and listened to the thrum of the aircraft, tensing whenever an air current made it shudder. About forty-five minutes later, Zavier cleared his throat.

"We're here."

Danny sat up and looked out the window, and the bottom of his stomach dropped out. There it was—Meerut. Danny's eyes automatically scanned the city for signs of Aditi's tower, even though he knew it wouldn't be there.

"Get closer," Danny demanded. "I can't see anything." He thought he heard Zavier sigh softly before he brought the plane farther down, making circles over Meerut like a vulture.

People walked through the streets. Wares were bought in bazaars. Devout worshippers visited the temples. Life continued without the tower, just as Zavier had promised. Danny's throat tightened.

"I told you, Danny. We don't need the towers anymore. Meerut is free now. Imagine if everywhere in the world were like this."

Danny didn't respond. He continued to stare out the window, heartsick and defeated, thinking of Colton's broken tower and what would happen to it when time resumed in Enfield. He leaned his forehead against the window as his vision blurred.

"If you're worried about the spirits," Zavier continued, "and if you're worried about Colton . . . I'm sure we can make some sort of deal. Find a way to keep Colton safe. If you help us free Aetas—"

But Danny stopped listening as something below caught his eye. Just outside the city, planes were docked along the tarmac. One of them had familiar red letters scrawled across its side.

The *Silver Hawk*.

"We can't be sure of Aetas's powers. It could be that he—Danny?"

Danny didn't think. If he stopped to think, he wouldn't be able to do it. He tore the parachute from the side of his seat, then shoved the cockpit door open. He was nearly sucked out by the rush of air, stingingly cold against his face.

"Danny, what are you doing? Stop!"

He looked over his shoulder. "Sod off, Zavier."

Then, deciding that he needed at least some say in it this time, he jumped.

His scream was eaten by the roaring air all around him. He was cold and hot all at once, tumbling toward the earth at a speed he'd never imagined his body reaching. He fumbled with the parachute as best he could with his hands still handcuffed, panicking when he couldn't find the string to pull.

He looked down. It was a mistake. Meerut was coming up fast, and if he didn't find this one—damned—string—

His hand clamped around it at last and he pulled for dear life. The tan fabric shot out of the folded canvas sack, and he screamed again as he nearly lost his grip from the force of the updraft. He held onto the ends desperately, no longer plummeting.

"Oh, thank God," he gasped. "Sweet bloody Christ, thank you." His mother would have smacked the back of his head for that remark. The notion only made him laugh giddily.

Danny thought jumping would be the most difficult part. He wasn't prepared for the fact that Meerut was still underneath him, all hard roads and buildings. Trying to direct the parachute didn't work, but at least he could pull himself a couple inches one way or the other.

A rooftop loomed beneath his feet. He tried to reach for the end with his foot, but misjudged the distance and ended up toppling over the side. He landed on an awning and bounced into the road below.

He landed with a hard thud. Groaning, he curled onto his side.

"Up, Danny, up," he grunted to himself. Coughing, he rose to his knees, then staggered to his feet.

He had attracted spectators. They stared at him as if he were a street performer and they were waiting for his next move. Some glanced at his handcuffs. Danny gave them a small bow and took off running down the street.

The area didn't look familiar, but within a minute he spotted a street he and Meena had walked down a few times. He darted toward it.

"Meena! Daphne! Akash! Captain Harris!"

As much as he didn't want to attract attention, a frantic British boy with his hands cuffed together yelling random names at the top of his lungs would draw any eye, and he drew quite a number of them as he darted past.

"Meena! Daphne! Ak—" Someone grabbed his arm and swung him around. "—ash!"

The young Indian man gaped at him, taking in the handcuffs. Then he looked over Danny's shoulder, where he only now noticed the parachute that had been limply trailing behind. Right, well, Danny would never show his face in Meerut again.

"What are you doing here?" Danny demanded.

"What am *I* doing here? I'm looking for clues as to where *you've* gone!" Akash's eyes went back to the parachute. "I think I found a fairly large one."

"All right, look, there's no time for questions. You have to get me to your plane."

"But there's a lieutenant here—"

"I don't care! We need to leave *now*!"

Akash nodded and ripped the parachute strings from Danny's back, and the pair took off running, Akash leading the way out of the city. He hailed a tonga and they jumped into the back. Akash shouted at the groom and they flew down the road, the groom expertly darting around pedestrians.

Near the tarmac, they jumped off and the driver shouted at them to pay. Danny sprinted for the *Silver Hawk*, but saw something that made him trip and nearly fall.

Another plane had landed. Zavier got out of the aircraft, his face pale.

"Danny, stop! You can't trust these people!"

Akash tried to climb into the *Silver Hawk* to start the engine, but Zavier moved with surprising speed and knocked him down. Danny did the only thing he could think of and jumped on Zavier, pinning him to the hot tarmac.

"Danny, listen to me," Zavier choked out. "You say you have friends, but you don't know them any more than you know us. You won't be safe anywhere!"

Danny raised his hands as if to strike, but Zavier grabbed the metal rod at his belt and stabbed it into Danny's midsection.

He fell over with a screech of pain, his body jerking as painful currents of electricity traveled through his limbs. The rod was removed, but not quickly enough to prevent Danny from being momentarily paralyzed.

"I'm sorry—it's for your own good—"

Akash roared and kicked Zavier in the head. Zavier went down, scrambling for the metal rod that had flown out of his hand.

Akash hauled Danny into the plane, grunting and swearing in Hindi.

"Danny!" Zavier yelled, but his voice was cut off when Akash slammed the aircraft's door shut. He jumped into the pilot seat, flipped a few switches, and took off faster than Danny had ever seen a plane go. Danny clutched a seat so he wouldn't slide to the back of the plane, only letting go when they were level.

"Danny, are you all right? Did he hurt you?"

"Give me a minute."

He focused on breathing. In, out, in, out. He winced with every inhalation. The spot Zavier had attacked hurt the most, his abdomen sore and sending pangs through his chest whichever way he moved.

He stood and carefully made his way to the seat next to the pilot's. Akash's eyes were wild, but he examined him for signs of injury.

"I'm fine," Danny murmured.

Akash sighed through his nose. "He's not following us."

"He thinks we're going back to Agra."

"We *are* going back to Agra."

"No, we're not." Danny clenched his hands. "We're going to Delhi."

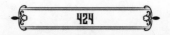

". . . May I ask why?"

"Queen Victoria's celebration is being held there."

"And you want to join the festivities, is that it?"

"Not me. Rebels. They're looking to start another rebellion."

Akash's hands tightened on the controls. He glanced over again, but Danny wouldn't meet his gaze.

"What do you think we can do about that?"

"I don't know, but that bastard is going to find me again one way or another, and it'll be relatively soon if we go back to Agra. For now, let's go to Delhi. We'll send a wire to the others when we get there." Danny realized that his words sounded like an order. "If that's all right with you. If not, you can drop me off and I'll find a way to get there on my own."

Akash shook his head. "I promised Daphne I would come back with you."

The corner of Danny's mouth ticked up. "You're calling her Daphne now?"

A blush spread across Akash's face. "I'm trying it out."

They fell into contemplative silence, and Danny's smile disappeared. His body was stiff with soreness and fatigue, and on the edges of his consciousness he felt the delayed effects of his escape creeping closer.

"It'll be dangerous," Danny whispered.

"I am aware."

There was nothing more to say.

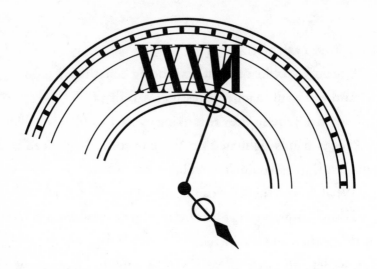

XXXVI

The Imperial Assemblage had collected on a plain four miles northeast of Delhi, beside the infamous ridge where Indian rebels had clashed with British soldiers twenty years before. Danny didn't know whether choosing this spot had been accidental or not, but it cast an ominous tone over the upcoming celebration.

As they flew to Delhi, Danny told Akash about what he had learned.

"We heard of what happened in Edava," Akash said. "Meena and Miss Ri—Daphne were upset, but the major wouldn't send either of them to investigate. You saw it with your own eyes?"

"I wish I hadn't."

"Are you sure about what you heard, though? About the viceroy?"

"Very sure." Danny flexed his right hand. A tremor had been

going through it since Zavier zapped him with that metal rod. "I can't say how they're planning to assassinate him, though."

"Did this man, Zavier, say anything more about the attack? Did you see anything suspicious?"

Danny sighed and tried to think back. He had told Akash about the ship, the people he had met, the pieces here and there that had made up the whole of his imprisonment. It was shocking to look around and find he wasn't still on the *Prometheus*.

"I tried to read some of his papers, but I couldn't understand them. There was even one in French. Think they might be dealing with other foreign contacts?"

"French? What did it say?"

Danny tried to rub his face with his hands, but he was still handcuffed. They would have to do something about that. "I've never been good with French. I think it was foo-duh-jwa?"

"Feu-de-joie? Furious joy?"

"Yes! You speak French?"

"No, Daphne and I saw the same message in Lucknow. She translated it back in Agra. We don't know what it means, though. Do you?"

Danny slumped back in his seat. "No idea."

There was a closed-in hangar for private aircrafts to dock outside the city. Delhi was massive, and the sheer scale made Danny sweat. It was cooler now in December than it had been when they'd first arrived, but the humidity still made him feel as if his skin were shrinking. The air hit him like an arid ocean swell when Akash opened the door.

Danny climbed down the ladder as best he could. Akash eyed the handcuffs with a frown. He climbed back into the plane and reemerged carrying a scarf, which he wrapped around Danny's hands. "It'll have to do. Wait here while I get the *Silver Hawk* registered."

That done, they headed into the city. "What's the plan?" Akash asked.

"The plan is to make a plan."

Delhi was packed with people, and Danny's breaths grew shallower, his senses overwhelmed after his month of near-isolation. The smell of smoke and the press of sweating bodies nearly did him in until Akash pulled him into a shadowed alley.

"I want you to sit here, out of the way, while I find help," he said. "Can you do that?"

"I'm not a child."

"I won't leave unless you agree."

Danny rolled his eyes. "Fine."

Akash walked to the alley's mouth, looked both ways, then slipped back into the throng.

Danny sat at the base of the stone building. It smelled like piss and rotting sewage, but he didn't care. His mind was riffling through scenarios and theories. What did furious joy mean? How would Viceroy Lytton be targeted? How much time did they have? When would Zavier find him again?

He laid his forehead on his knees. He couldn't go back to that airship, to those people. Enfield, Colton, his parents—they needed him. As soon as this was over, he would go back to London and . . .

And what? Let Zavier and his cronies destroy more towers?

"Bollocks," he whispered. "No one can win here, can they?"

A noise made him look up, but it was only Akash coming back. He knelt before Danny, out of breath and wearing a victorious smile.

"Hold out your hands."

Danny shifted and did as he was told. Akash unwrapped the scarf, then picked up a wicked set of shears. Danny recoiled.

"You're going to chop one of my hands off with those! Where did you get them?"

"A blacksmith wasn't looking."

"You've done this sort of thing before, haven't you?"

Akash shrugged. "Meena and I were bored as children. We needed something to pass the time." When Danny's lips thinned, he laughed. "We always gave back what we took. Now show me your hands."

Danny reluctantly extended his arms again. Akash studied the handcuffs, then wedged the shears between the metal cuff and his right hand. Danny closed his eyes tight, felt a pinching sensation by his thumb, and heard metal clatter to the ground.

"Once more," Akash said. Danny peeked as the shears bit into the metal of the remaining cuff, and then he was free.

He rubbed his wrists. "Now what?"

"Now, I return these."

When Akash came back ten minutes later, Danny said, "The only thing I can think to do is find the highest-ranking officer we can and tell him what we know. That way, the soldiers have more information about the terrorists *and* the rebels, and they can put a stop to the assassination before it's too late."

Akash frowned, doubtful. "Do you think they will believe you? Major Dryden is one thing, but he's in Agra." Danny ignored the hint of accusation in his voice. "No one here will know who you are, nor will they trust you. Especially with me at your side."

"We have to at least try. Do you know where the nearest billet is?"

"I've run messages here many times. Follow me."

They waded against the stream of people, toward an eastern section of the city. The smell of roasting lamb and potatoes made Danny's stomach tighten, but he forced himself to stay on course.

The squat, whitewashed building was separated awkwardly from those around it. Akash gestured to Danny to go in first. He was almost immediately stopped by a British private.

"What do you think you're doing?"

Danny floundered, but Akash thought quicker on his feet. "We need to see the senior officer here."

The private raised a self-important eyebrow. "And why is that?"

"We're messengers. We bring word from Major Dryden in Agra."

The private considered this, eyeing them contemptuously. They were rumpled and likely carried the smell of the alley with

them. "Our officers have gone to the durbar already. We're to follow in the morning. I'm afraid you won't find who you're looking
for here."

"There has to be someone," Danny insisted. "Surely they left
behind a few soldiers in charge."

"There's Corporal Fledger, but good luck speaking to him.
He's busy with the preparations."

"May we at least try?"

Shrugging, the private turned and led them down a hallway.
He knocked on a door and a voice barked out, "*What?*"

"Messengers to see you, sir. They're from Agra."

The door opened, and a frazzled man with a cleft chin leaned
out.

"Message, then." He held out his hand.

Danny cleared his throat. "It's a verbal report, Corporal."

The man clenched his jaw and gestured them inside with a
sharp flick of his fingers. Danny caught the private's disappointed
look before the door closed on him. No doubt he was starved for
gossip.

"Spit it out," Corporal Fledger ordered, returning to his desk
where he resumed organizing his scattered notes.

"Sir," Danny began, "we have some troubling news. Viceroy
Lytton is in danger. We think there may be an attack during
tomorrow's ceremonies."

Corporal Fledger put his hands on his desk and leaned forward. "And?"

Danny blinked. "And? What do you mean, *and?*"

"He's the viceroy. If at least ten people don't want him dead, he isn't doing his damn job!"

"But, the Indian rebels—"

"What's this, unhappy Indians? I'll alert the papers." Fledger glowered at Akash. "Listen, boys, tell whoever you work for that I'm far too busy to waste time on conspiracy theories."

"Sir, if you would just listen—!"

"The viceroy is guarded day and night. The rajas are too greedy to off the likes of him. And, by God, if one mutiny was snuffed out, so will another if it comes to that. Now, kindly leave me to my work."

They were shooed out of the room and the door was slammed in their faces.

Akash shrugged. "I told you they wouldn't listen."

"They have to! Doesn't he understand?"

"I'm sure he's heard all manner of threats. It's their job to expect the worst, after all."

Danny bit his knuckle, thinking. "We have to do something if Corporal Arsehole won't. We need to tell the senior officers."

"And how will we do that? Sneak into the camp?" Akash saw the look in Danny's eyes and his own widened. "Really?"

"It's the only option we have left."

"It isn't! We can still go to Agra and—"

"Get caught by Zavier again? Absolutely not."

"If a corporal won't believe us, what makes you think a colonel or a general will?"

"I don't know, I just—I just have to do everything I possibly can." He ran shaking hands through his hair. "First, we need to find a laundry room."

Danny picked through the washed sepoy uniforms drying on a rack. "This one looks like it should fit you."

"We can't just take them."

Danny snorted. "Says the man who stole from a blacksmith."

"I only steal what can be given back." Akash licked his lips, more nervous than Danny had ever seen him. "What if we can't return these? If the British officers catch me . . ."

Understanding made Danny grimace. "I'll take the blame, if it comes to that. Besides, we don't have much choice."

Akash grumbled in Hindi as he pulled on the uniform. The closest fitting British uniform Danny could find for himself was tight in the shoulders, and he could see a bit more boot at the ankle than he would have liked. Now that he thought about it, his normal clothes had felt a little uncomfortable lately. Maybe he had grown again. His mother would have a fit.

Danny pulled a cap down low over his eyes. "There, that shouldn't draw attention." Danny rummaged through his discarded trousers, drawing out Colton's cog. Putting it in his new pocket, he nodded to the door. "Now we need a place to think till morning."

They found an abandoned room that looked to have recently housed a couple of officers. Akash worried that said officers

might still be in the city, but after a glance at the empty drawers, Danny rather doubted it.

Hungry, they sat in the dark and murmured plans, all of which made little to no sense.

"But if we find the viceroy himself—"

"What do you think he would do?" Akash asked. "Sit us down and discuss his assassination over tea?"

"It's what I would do."

"Of course *you* would, but you're not the viceroy. He is very important, and very busy. We'd never be given a private audience, and we have no idea who the rebels in the camp might be. They could be in his personal guard, for all we know."

Danny chewed on his thumbnail. He could hardly see Akash in the darkness, but he heard him tapping his fingers against his thigh. Daphne did the same thing when she was working through a problem.

"We should have just gone back to Agra and warned the major," Akash said.

"Yes, and then have the whole cantonment attacked. Brilliant idea."

Akash sighed. A few minutes of silence crept by, and Danny lay down on the hard bed. He wanted to sleep, but his mind kept whirring, desperately seeking a solution.

"Danny? Maybe . . . Maybe we should just let it happen."

Danny slowly sat back up, staring at the dark shape that was Akash. "What are you saying?"

Akash shifted. "I don't want anyone to die, on either side.

But maybe, if an attack is inevitable, we should just let it happen. Maybe it won't even succeed. Us becoming involved might not change anything."

When Danny stayed silent, Akash stood and joined him on his bed. "Danny, please listen. Do you know what they call Lytton's rule? The Black Raj. He's a man who likes finery—he doesn't care about the Indian people. Even when a British man killed his Indian coachman, Lytton only fined the man thirty rupees. For *killing* a man, just because he was Indian."

"So all the Indians want Lytton dead?"

"No, that . . . that's not what I mean." Akash rubbed his hands against his trouser legs. "All I'm saying is that maybe this is over our heads. We shouldn't risk ourselves and the others on nothing more than a guess."

Danny lay down again, nudging Akash off his bed. "You can stay here in the morning, then. I'll go by myself."

Akash stood there a moment longer, then returned to his own bed. Danny listened to their combined breathing in the small space.

"I'll go with you," Akash finally whispered. "I promised Daphne."

"That's not reason enough."

"*And* because I'm concerned for you."

Danny closed his eyes and turned onto his side. "Thank you."

He hoped he wouldn't come to regret the decision.

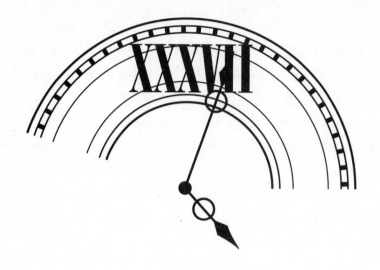

The next morning was chaos. Corporal Fledger barked orders for privates to hurry to the autos, which awaited them outside the city. They would be spending the next two days at the campgrounds. Tomorrow was New Year's Day and Victoria's coronation as Empress of India.

"Smith, are you a bloody woman? You don't need all this for one night! Higgins, fix your damned hair, you look like a fool. You two!"

Danny and Akash, who had tried to sneak past the corporal in the hubbub, froze. The corporal consulted his list, then jerked a thumb over his shoulder.

"Auto four, and be quick about it!"

Danny's "Yes, sir!" was closely followed by Akash's "Haan, sahib." They hurried away from the screaming corporal and into the busy Delhi street, thankful they hadn't been recognized.

Danny hesitated and turned toward the Delhi clock tower, as if tethered to its power. He remembered Zavier's threat all too well. He could stay here in the city. He could try to protect the tower along with the soldiers assigned to guard it.

But if the rebels succeeded, even more towers would fall, and even more innocent lives would be taken.

He had to weigh one soul against thousands.

Hand tight around the small cog in his pocket, Danny turned in the direction of the durbar.

It was easy enough to follow the other privates toward Delhi's perimeter, where a row of battered autos waited. Danny and Akash approached an officer with a clipboard, who glanced at the names on their uniforms.

"Wilson and Chopra, auto four."

The driver took off as soon as they were inside. Danny looked behind him as the city grew smaller, hoping that the real Wilson and Chopra wouldn't look for auto four and already find it gone.

It didn't take long to reach the enormous durbar campgrounds. They'd overheard that it had taken thousands of laborers to prepare all the tents, the parade grounds, and even a replica of the throne of England.

The British driver glanced back at them and grinned at their awe. "The rajas have already come, and what a spectacle they made of it. The viceroy arrived a few days ago. Shoulda seen it, riding in on a big ol' elephant, cavalry and trumpeters trailing along."

Danny did in fact see the elephants on the outskirts of camp. They were clad in chainmail, their faces painted orange and green,

with festive streamers hanging from their tusks. He swallowed. As magnificent as they appeared, it wouldn't take much for one to step on him and crush him into jam. People were meant to *ride* them?

They clambered out of the auto when it parked, finding themselves on an avenue between tents that stretched toward the parade grounds. The sheer number of soldiers and servants milling about, combined with the village-like quality of the tent formations, was overwhelming.

"Chod," Akash said under his breath. "How are we supposed to find the viceroy in this?"

The officer who'd waved them inside approached them. "You two, where are your accommodations?"

"We don't know," Danny admitted. "No one told us."

The soldier looked furiously through his notes. "Chopra—you're in E45. Wilson—N15."

"But we don't know where—"

The officer turned back to his work, arguing with a sepoy in Urdu. Akash tugged on Danny's sleeve and they ducked around a tent.

"We should probably split up to cover more ground," Danny suggested.

"Let's at least try to find out where the viceroy is staying."

Agreeing to meet back at the same spot around noon, they took off.

Danny was sweating under a fierce midmorning sun as he weaved through the other soldiers, trying to get his bearings.

There was plenty to take in. Large, ornate tents had their flaps pinned back to reveal Indian princes reclining within, sipping cool drinks. Other tents weren't quite as grand, and Danny noticed that while a few had special banners embroidered with coats of arms and crests, others did not. The poorer rajas could be seen sulking and glaring at the servants of the richer princes. One loudly complained to a British soldier in the middle of the street, his red turban wobbling with anger.

"I do not see why it is different," he said. "I would like a banner as well!"

The soldier rubbed his temples. "It's only the rajas of the *feudatory* states who get to have banners, not the independent ones."

But the rajas, vain as peacocks, all wanted to outdo one another. The number of servants and the quality of their ornamentation were on full display. Even the entertainment was pitted against each other; many had brought servants who doubled as musicians. One raja had gone so far as to bring a whole corps of Indian bagpipers dressed as Scottish Highlanders, complete with pink leggings so as to look "authentic." Another boasted a piper with the most enormous yellow headdress Danny had ever seen. There was even a musician with gilded armor, whom Danny felt especially sorry for. But his personal favorite was a poor raja's attendant who ground out "God Save the Queen" on a hand organ.

Distracted as he was by his surroundings, Danny tried to look for someone to speak to. Every officer he encountered brushed him aside or barked at him to get back to his duties. Danny got the sinking feeling that Akash had been right after all. No one would listen to a young private with grandiose threats.

He asked a couple of lesser-ranked soldiers what was going to happen at the coronation the next day, and what they were expected to do. He received looks of surprise and contempt, mistaken for a green private who hadn't bothered to listen to his superiors. Still, he was grudgingly given basic information: the layout of the four durbar sectors, where the viceroy's camp was, and that all soldiers were expected to attend Lytton's speech.

"We even get an extra day's pay," a second lieutenant said. "And I heard the ones who were exiled after the Mutiny will be granted amnesty."

"They'll be pardoned?"

"I expect so."

He wondered if Zavier and his rebel friends knew, and if they'd even care.

Before he went back to the meeting spot, he wandered toward the viceroy's camp, which was heavily guarded. Tents were neatly lined in two rows that extended all the way to a huge tent. Nearby, an iron structure had been raised, painted in the colors of Her Majesty's flag.

Patrolling soldiers gave him disapproving looks. Danny nervously smiled and retreated. There was no way to get to Lytton directly, then; he couldn't even convince a low-ranking officer to bring Lytton a message.

Danny stopped in his tracks. *Message.*

"Is there a telegraph here?" he asked a passing soldier, who pointed the way to a command tent near the center of the durbar. Danny eventually found the tent where a few officers were flipping through papers and wiring commands through a clunky metal telegraph.

Danny approached the man handling the telegraph machine and cleared his throat. The man blinked up at him through thick spectacles. Danny didn't think he was a soldier. All the better.

"Message needs to be sent down to Agra," Danny said in his best authoritative voice. "To Major Dryden's cantonment."

The man readied the machine. "And what is the message?"

Danny forced himself not to wipe the sweat from his forehead. The communication had to be something obvious, but not so simple as to avoid notice. The man waited patiently, and Danny took a deep breath.

"D.H. in Delhi," he decided at last. "V.L. requiring his service." But how to tell them he was in the camp, and not the city? "Er . . . God save the Queen."

The man obediently typed out the message. "Anything else?"

Danny hesitated. A bead of sweat rolled down his temple.

"Yes," he said softly. "Can a message be sent to London?"

"Of course. Where to?"

"The office of Clock Mechanics Affairs."

"Let's see." He tampered with the telegraph and nodded. "What's the message?"

Danny curled his hand into a damp fist, then loosened it. "Christopher's son is alive and well."

"Is that all?"

"Yes, thank you."

Danny left the tent in a daze. It was only by luck that he managed to stumble upon Akash.

"Anything?" Akash asked.

"I found out where Lytton's camp is. And I sent a wire to Agra for Dryden."

Akash looked impressed, and also a little scared. "What did you say?"

"That we need assistance here, if they understand the message."

"And if they don't? What do we do then?"

"Then we'll need to figure this out ourselves."

"Oh, good," Akash mumbled. "And here I thought it would be something difficult."

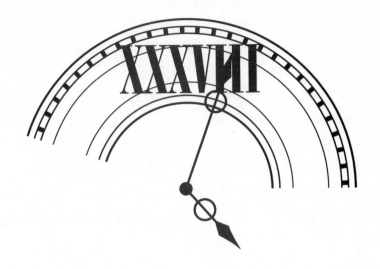

Daphne was thinking about her mother. It had been painful spending Christmas here, in spite of the soldiers' quaint festivities (mostly drunken caroling). She knew her mother would be disappointed that she hadn't come to visit. Or at least, it was her selfish hope that her mother had even noticed her absence.

But a messenger from Dryden drove all thoughts of guilt from her mind.

She hurried to the counsel building. Meena and Crosby were already there. The major paced, scowling at the floor. Daphne skidded to a stop, grabbing the back of a chair.

"What happened?" she asked them.

"There's been a wire from Delhi," Dryden said, pointing to a piece of paper on the table. Daphne snatched it up and read it.

"But what does it mean?" She read it again. "D.H. is Danny Hart."

"That is what we believe, yes," Dryden said gravely.

"And V. L.? Who or what is that?"

"We think it stands for Viceroy Lytton."

Daphne frowned. "Viceroy Lytton? Why would the viceroy require Danny's service?" *Where the hell has he been? Why didn't he come back to Agra? Is Akash with him?*

Crosby plucked the message from her fingers. "That is what we are undecided on. I still say it's a false message. A trap of some sort."

"A trap for who, Lieutenant?"

Daphne looked at Meena, who was tugging on her braid and staring at the letter still in Crosby's hand. As the men argued, she calmly cleared her throat.

"'God save the Queen' could mean that Danny is in the durbar itself, rather than the city," Meena said.

The other three fell silent, considering the possibility.

"It's far more likely he's at the clock tower," Dryden said.

"Then we must go there," Meena said. "Either way, we have to find him."

"Indeed. Crosby, I want you to gather a small search party and head up to Delhi. Join the clock tower guard."

"Sir, tomorrow's New Year. The coronation."

"Yes, and everyone will have their eyes elsewhere," Dryden said, "so we can smuggle Mr. Hart out without fuss."

"But what's he even doing there?" Daphne demanded. "This isn't like him. Major, please let me go. I need to speak with Danny and find out what's going on."

"Miss Richards, I'm sure that once he's back here, he'll be able to tell us exactly what's happened."

"Sir, *please.*"

Crosby gave the major a look that plainly said he was tired of this nonsense, and Dryden sighed.

"I'm sorry, but after what happened in Meerut"—he nodded to Meena—"I will not risk the lives of any more clock mechanics in this camp. Not even for the Delhi tower."

Fuming, Daphne turned and stalked out, Meena on her heels.

"Akash might be there, too," Meena whispered. "Do you think he's with Danny?"

"I hope so. Even if he is, I have to go. Something's not right. The way Danny worded his message, it's as though there's something else he couldn't say."

She didn't realize they were walking toward Colton's room until they were right in front of it. Daphne took a deep breath and unlocked the door.

Colton stood as they entered. In one hand, he held the picture of Danny.

"There's been news," Daphne said. "We think Danny is in Delhi."

"Are we going to find him?"

"The major says I can't go, but I'll find a way. Don't worry, Colton. I'll bring him back."

Colton stuffed the picture into his pack. "You have to take me with you."

Daphne glanced at Meena. "Colton—"

"You have to." He put his hands on her shoulders, the most

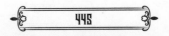

interaction they'd ever had. It felt strange, like the air around them shifted slightly to acknowledge her. "Daphne, please. I know he's in danger. I have to help him."

"You're in danger, too, if you haven't forgotten."

Colton stubbornly set his jaw. "If you leave me here, I'll reveal myself. If people are looking for me, I'll let them find me."

Daphne swore and rubbed her hands over her face. "You're just as bad as he is."

Yet life had been breathed back into Colton. His amber eyes, ominously vacant until now, were suddenly lit with determination like the pop and flare of a bonfire. Hoping she wouldn't regret it, Daphne gestured toward the door.

"Come on, then."

Wearing the cog holder on his back, Colton grabbed his pack and followed Daphne and Meena into the deep evening blues outside. Meena looked nervous walking around with a clock spirit, but no one else could feel the pull coming off of Colton's body. To the soldiers, he was just a boy who may or may not have been lost.

Daphne's plan was to find an auto and drive to Delhi, but when she shared her idea with Meena, the girl stopped her short.

"We can't," she whispered. "The autos are locked and the keys are all hanging in the major's rooms. He'll know we've taken one within minutes."

So much for doing this on her own.

Then a new thought took hold. "The officers have their own keys, don't they?"

"Yes."

There was only one officer she trusted in this cantonment.

They found Captain Harris packing an auto with Partha. Daphne breathed a sigh of relief.

"You've heard, then."

Harris turned around, startled. Partha looked between him and the girls, frowning.

"Heard?" Harris repeated blankly.

"About Danny."

"Oh—yes. Mr. Hart's wire."

Daphne squared her shoulders. "The major is sending you and Crosby to Delhi, but we want to go, too. I'm asking you to take us."

"I . . . what?" Harris frowned at Colton. "And who's this?"

"Captain, Danny might be in trouble. We *have* to go."

Harris rubbed the back of his neck. "I don't think this is a good idea. It's better for you to stay here, where it's safe."

"We're not safe anywhere, apparently!"

"Miss Richards, please—"

"Captain," Meena said softly, uncertainly, "if you do not take us to Delhi, then I will be forced to tell the major your secret."

The blood drained from Harris's face, and Partha's head shot up, eyes wide with horror. Meena winced at their reactions, but didn't lower her gaze. The men looked at each other as though they'd both been sentenced to the gallows.

"Secret?" Daphne repeated. "What secret?"

"That they are lovers," Meena said.

Daphne looked at the two of them again, only now seeing the signs. The soldiers stood stricken. Meena looked miserable.

Colton stepped forward, his expression wondering. "You're like us, then."

Harris looked him up and down again. "What? Who *are* you?"

"I'm ... I'm Danny's ..." Colton looked at Meena, who finally dropped her gaze. "Lover."

Again, the captain and the sepoy were struck speechless. Daphne balled her hand into a fist, feeling her heartbeat struggle against her palm.

"I promise to keep any secrets you may have," Colton said, "but please, help us. Help *him*. What if he were in danger?" Colton pointed to Partha, who looked away.

"You're the one he spoke of," Harris murmured. Shaking his head, the captain took a steadying breath. "If we bring you to Delhi, will you promise not to say anything about Partha and me?"

"I give you my word," Meena said.

Harris exchanged another helpless look with Partha. "We'll leave before daybreak."

"Can't we go now?" Daphne demanded.

"The major will suspect something. The men will be celebrating the New Year at midnight. If we stay until then and make a show of going to bed, we'll be in the clear."

"Don't worry," Colton told her. "I'll make sure they won't

leave without us." He unceremoniously climbed into the back-seat of the auto and locked himself inside, arms crossed.

"Captain, you do promise to take us?" Daphne insisted. "You won't go back on your word?"

He cast his eyes skyward, as if pleading with the heavens. "Lord help me, but yes, I promise."

Daphne bent toward the window. Colton met her gaze.

"You'll be all right here?" He nodded. "We'll be back soon."

She glanced at Harris and Partha, urgently whispering to each other. *Lovers,* she thought with renewed surprise. Before turning away, she looked into the back of the auto, where Harris and Partha had stored their rifles. She supposed it was better to take precautions. There was no telling what they would find in Delhi.

Or who.

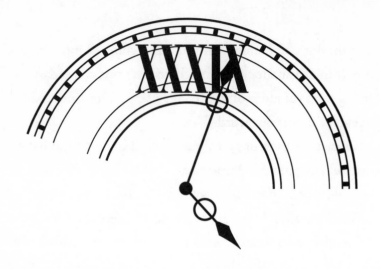

As Danny and Akash prowled through the tents, stars began to speckle the sky. In the cantonment, it wasn't irregular to see soldiers drunk and singing at three in the morning. Since tonight was New Year's, the soldiers were taking full advantage of having no curfew.

"Huh," Danny said. "Tomorrow it'll be 1877."

"And your queen's big day. Do you think Dryden has seen your message?" Akash asked as the gas lamps around them flared to life.

"I hope so. He must have the means to speak with Lytton."

"And if Lytton won't listen?"

Danny threw his hands in the air. "Then the man will just have to be—" He checked himself, swallowing the word. "Let's not dwell on that, all right?"

"Danny," Akash said softly, "why are you doing this, anyway? Whose side are you on?"

"What do you mean?"

"You see how they treat us. You haven't even seen the worst of it. If I told you some of what I've seen and heard . . ." He shook his head. "I thought you knew this occupation was wrong."

"Of course it's wrong," Danny whispered back. "I don't want India to be a prize for the Queen. I don't want our soldiers to humiliate yours. I don't want a *Black Raj.*"

"Then why—?"

"Because you know what a second rebellion would do? People would die. Your people, and mine. And we'd be stuck in the middle of it all. Daphne and I might never be able to go home. I might never . . ."

He might never see Colton again.

"So your answer is to let this oppression continue," Akash said, voice flat.

"No! That's—I don't know. There's no black and white here. You think one side is the villain and one is the hero, but that's not the case. It's more complicated than that." He paused. "Do you think I'm evil?"

"No, of course not."

"Good, I don't think you're evil, either. Or Meena. What about Daphne? Think she's evil?"

Akash's eyes shifted. "No."

"And yet there are cruel people on both sides of this potential rebellion. Violence will only create more violence. It won't ever stop, don't you see that?" Danny rubbed his eyes, exhausted. "Besides, if this plan succeeds, the rebels are going to help Zavier take down more towers. I can't risk that."

It was an argument he knew he shouldn't even take part in, given who he was and where he was from. Akash and his people deserved better than that. In truth, Danny still didn't know where right or wrong stood, or if he was even within sight of their horizons. Maybe it was enough to constantly be in search of the difference.

And hoping, in the end, he chose the lesser evil.

He dropped his hands and lifted his chin in the direction they'd been walking. "Let's keep going."

They studied the tents, looking for a senior officer. But the officers must have all been celebrating elsewhere; Danny and Akash only saw low-ranking soldiers, laughing and popping party crackers. One kept shouting "Happy New Year!" to anyone who passed by.

Danny slowed to a stop when he heard a voice say *Lytton*. Akash stopped beside him, and Danny motioned them to the tent from where he'd heard the voice. Standing in the shadows, they cocked their ears. The majority of words were in Hindi.

"What are they saying?" Danny whispered.

"I think there are a few rajas inside. They're complaining about a party the viceroy held a few days ago. The British officers were making fun of the rajas in English, forgetting the rajas know English quite well."

Danny rolled his eyes. "No one's ever happy here, are they?" A thought struck him, and he let out a groan. "What if the rajas are in on it, too? What if some of them are rebels?"

Akash nodded reluctantly. "It's possible."

"You there!"

They spun around. A British lieutenant was moving in their direction, mustache aquiver.

"What are you two doing, loitering about in the dark?"

"We—We were just—" As Danny hesitated, Akash swayed beside him and leaned against his shoulder. He made a motion like he was doing up his trouser lacings.

"Had to relieve myself, sahib," Akash slurred. "Haaappy New Year!"

The lieutenant looked him over, disgusted. "For Heaven's sake, do that *away* from the rajas' tents! I'll have your head on a spike if I catch you at this again. You, there. Make sure this one gets to his tent tonight."

"Yes, sir." The lieutenant made to leave, but Danny sprang forward. "Sir? I was wondering what the schedule for tomorrow will be."

"Your senior officer hasn't told you?"

"I don't believe so. Not in any detail."

"The viceroy will give his speech in the morning. Each regiment has their own place on the parade grounds, so I would suggest asking your senior officer where that is. You lot will be toward the back, I wager. After the viceroy's speech will be a feu-de-joie, and after the ceremony, you are to go back to your post immediately."

Both Danny and Akash jumped at the now-familiar French phrase. "Feu-de-joie?" Danny repeated. "What does that mean?"

The lieutenant grunted. "The salute, boy, the gun salute."

Gun salute. "Thank you, sir."

The lieutenant gave Akash one last look of disgust before he turned and walked away.

Danny swore. "The assassin might be planning to shoot the viceroy during the salute."

"How do we stop him?"

Danny shook his head. He had no idea.

There was a sudden commotion as the countdown to midnight began. The soldiers called out "Three! Two! One!" before a tumultuous cheer rose above the tents. Danny clapped along with the rest, but the moment's impact was lost on him. He was already living several hours from now, in the light of an uncertain dawn.

They found Akash's tent first. Other sepoys had taken off their shoes outside. Akash did the same, but looked helplessly at Danny.

"What if the real Chopra is inside?"

"Then pretend you're drunk and sleep on the floor."

Akash glanced up and down the street, then leaned in, lowering his voice. "There's nothing we can do if the rebel's plan is already in motion. You must know that."

"We'll see what the morning brings."

Danny found his own tent and slipped inside, hoping no one would talk to him. A few of the cots were empty. Danny took off his boots and the outer jacket of his uniform, then curled up on a cot with his back to everyone else. He wondered where the real Wilson was, and if he had been assigned to another tent. That was, quite honestly, the least of his worries.

He held the small cog as the other soldiers settled down, wishing that he could Stop time, that he could prevent this disaster from happening.

But this wasn't Enfield.

Really, who was the villain here? Zavier? The rebels? The British?

He didn't know.

He was afraid to find out.

Morning came an eternity later, and Danny still had no ideas. The soldiers got up to shave and don their best uniforms, but Danny had to settle for wrinkled trousers.

He found Akash in the mess, where the soldiers shoveled porridge into their mouths like it was a competition. Akash didn't look like he'd slept, either.

"What are we going to do?" Akash asked.

"Just look out for anything suspicious. If we see an officer, we can try to convince him. Otherwise, we'll have to wait for Dryden."

If Dryden was even coming.

And there was still the matter of the clock tower. Danny's power kept straining toward it; he wished he could duplicate himself and guard the tower with the soldiers inside the city. Zavier was nearby, he was sure of it. He could imagine him on the observation deck of the *Prometheus*, waiting for his chance to strike.

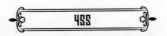

The soldiers filed out of the mess into a clear yet strangely chilly dawn. The men were in high spirits, their hair slicked back and boots shined to perfection. Danny noticed a few disapproving glances at his messy state.

On the parade grounds, ranks of infantry and cavalry marched with banners and standards fluttering in the wind, their drums puncturing the air with deep, reverberating pulses. The rhythm synced with Danny's heartbeat and made his chest ache. He looked at the other regiments already in position, flawless squares of bodies all turned toward the dais where the replica of the Queen's throne sat. Someone had brought a large portrait of Her Majesty and placed it on the throne, a gaudy if necessary reminder of why they were all gathered.

To the right, Danny noticed an assembly of riflemen standing at ease, guns perched on their shoulders. His breath caught.

"That's them," he hissed at Akash as they got into position.

"Should we do something?"

Danny bit his lip. A colonel was walking down the line, hands behind his back, making sure not a hair was out of place. Danny was about to draw his attention when a roar went through the ranks. Viceroy Lytton had taken the stage.

Lytton was a composed-looking man with dark hair and an impressive beard. He was neither portly nor broad, but held himself in a way that made him seem large, as if his reputation had a direct correlation to his stature. He cut an interesting figure in a long blue satin mantle, an insignia of Knight Grand Commander sewn onto his breast.

Lytton held up his hands to quiet the cheer before gesturing to the portrait of Victoria.

"This day belongs to our beloved Queen, now Queen-Empress of India. And what a fitting title it is. Her Majesty . . ."

His voice droned on as Danny looked around, waiting, searching, hoping. Dryden had to come. He had to be here.

"And now, the proclamation." Lytton stepped back and allowed a man dressed in a herald's tabard to come forward. The herald began to read the official proclamation in English, then read it again in Urdu. Danny's eyes kept darting to the riflemen, but not one of them had moved.

Who will it be? When is it coming? Sweat dripped into his eyes and his breathing grew uneven, body humming with the urgent need to *move*.

If Dryden wasn't coming, he would need to take matters into his own hands.

One soul against thousands.

XL

The auto sped furiously from Agra to the camp outside of Delhi. Daphne was staggered by the durbar's size and gaped as they drove past.

Or at least, she thought they would drive past. She rocked forward when Partha slammed on the brakes. Without a word, Harris leapt from the auto.

"Captain, what are you doing?" Daphne demanded, opening the side door.

"Please stay inside, Miss Richards. Partha will take you to the clock tower, where Mr. Hart is." Harris opened and closed the boot, holding his rifle. "I'm required here."

"What? But I don't under—Colton!"

The spirit had thrown open his door and took off running toward the camp, his boots kicking up clouds of dirt. Harris swore and followed. Before Daphne and Meena could get out,

the auto jerked forward and they were thrown back into their seats.

"Partha!" Daphne yelled. "Stop!"

"I can't, Miss Richards." He glanced back at her, eyes tight with regret. "I apologize."

Meena shouted at him in Hindi. Whatever she said made Partha clench his jaw, but the sepoy wouldn't stop. They zoomed into the city, navigating congested streets and earning more than one curse as Partha sped by rickshaws and pedestrians.

Daphne felt the tower before she saw it. It was tall and narrow, trimmed with marble, and topped with a fat bell enclosed by columns.

The street around the tower was teeming with guards. When it became clear they wouldn't move another inch, Partha parked and got out. Daphne scrambled after him.

"What do you think you're doing?" she shouted over the noise in the street. "Why did Captain Harris go into the durbar? Why didn't you stop for Colton?"

He gave her that expression again—that same complicated mix of sadness, frustration, and determination.

"I am very sorry you had to get involved in this, Miss Richards," he said. "Please get as far away from here as possible."

Daphne's prickling doubt turned into dawning horror. Meena gripped her arm as she came to the same realization.

A dull roar filled their ears. Daphne looked up and saw the edge of an army-issued airship flying the British flag, dutifully patrolling the skies. But as she watched, it was shortly joined by another, this one even more massive as it emerged from the clouds like a monster rising from the depths.

The same ship that had attacked the *Notus*.

"Run," Partha said.

"Hey! You lot! What do you think you're doing?" Crosby turned from his station and started toward them. At that moment, the airships began to attack each other with earsplitting cannon fire. "What in the hell—?"

Partha removed the pistol at his hip and shot Crosby in the stomach. Meena screamed as the lieutenant doubled over, coughing up blood. His brown eyes were wide, his teeth stained crimson.

"Indian—bast—"

Partha shot him again in the head, and Crosby went down.

Daphne couldn't move, couldn't react. Her body had become nothing but the pulsing whir of the airships above. Sepoys began to flood the street, tackling and shooting and stabbing the British soldiers.

"Daphne!" Meena screamed. "Move!"

Blood spread. The tower trembled. Bells rang. Time shivered. The world descended into chaos and impulse and the slowing of the second hand—*tick*.

A tremor in the air as time began to unravel.

Tock.

Danny's hands were shaking as the herald finished the proclamation in Urdu, his clothes damp with sweat.

"We can't do anything," Akash whispered. "It's too late."

Danny ignored him. The riflemen were moving into position. Now or never.

Then Danny saw something that gave him a surge of renewed hope. Captain Harris had somehow joined the proceedings, standing toward the back of the riflemen.

Harris! Had they read his message? Had they figured out the rebels' plan? But the start of Danny's relieved smile quickly died when Harris, along with the others, drew his weapon up to fire.

I'll always fight for the promise of an easier tomorrow, Harris had said. *Right or wrong, selfish or not, this is what we want.*

Whatever it takes.

Everything became clear, each detail cut precisely like facets in a diamond: the determination in Harris's eyes, the stance of the sharpshooter he was, the pleats in his trousers, the glint of the rifle—an Enfield rifle. Even from this distance, Danny could see its B3005 serial number.

Danny turned to Akash. He'd seen Harris, too.

"We have to do something," Danny said, sounding strangely calm despite the turmoil inside him.

But Akash only stood there, an unspoken apology in his eyes. Danny took a step back.

"No," he gasped. "God, not you, too!"

"Danny—" Akash tried to grab him, but he was already

turning to the stage. The first cracks of the furious joy began to split the air, drowning out the sound of Akash calling his name.

Colton hadn't known he could run like this, even though fatigue tore through his blistered side and into his chest, tightening his body with pain. He pressed on, determined to find Danny before anyone else.

There were so many people, all their heads turned toward a platform where a man dressed in blue stood before a throne. Colton stopped and searched the crowd, desperately calling Danny's name.

Something pulled at him, a tiny pinprick of his own power. He had felt it in the auto and knew he had to follow. *The cog.* He moved toward it, shoving his way through the crowd, following the pale thread that would lead him to Danny.

"Where are you?" he whispered. "Where are you?"

And then he saw him. Even from the back, Colton knew him. For some reason Danny was dressed as a soldier. He was looking to the right, his body rigid. He turned to an Indian boy standing beside him before he started running—not to Colton, but to the platform. Colton pressed forward again.

"Danny!" he cried out. "Danny!"

Then a loud sound broke the morning air, a fearsome banging that hurt his ears. Large, gray animals—*elephants*, he thought distantly—lifted their trunks and trumpeted. Men with guns were shooting into the air in a strange pattern; as soon as one

fired, the soldier on his left fired, until the effect was a rippling cascade of sound.

Colton's voice was lost in the din. But something made Danny stop and turn. Something compelled him to look over his shoulder, a finger plucking the thread between their bodies.

Danny saw him. Their gazes locked. His eyes widened.

His lips shaped Colton's name.

For a moment, time froze. There were no soldiers. No guns, or elephants, or even India. Just two boys, so close and so distant. Colton reached out a hand for him, still so impossibly far away, but somehow thinking their fingers could touch if he just willed it enough. Danny took a step forward.

And stopped.

A tear ran down his cheek.

He mouthed the words, "I'm sorry."

Then he turned and kept running.

Colton tried to follow, but Danny was too fast. He watched helplessly as Danny launched himself onto the stage and pushed the man in blue out of the way.

A bullet struck Danny in the chest.

Colton screamed, fighting to get past the sudden mayhem of soldiers running in all directions. His eyes were only on the spray of blood that had burst from Danny's chest, the look of shock and pain on his face. Danny stumbled back into the throne and fell, making the Queen's portrait topple over.

Time heaved and groaned. The earth shook. Danny's blood tasted the air and made it writhe, static and sparking and surging.

"Danny!" he yelled. *"Danny!"*

Hands grabbed Colton from behind and ripped the cog holder off his shoulders. The weakness intensified and he grew limp, collapsing into the arms of the person holding him up.

He hadn't noticed a shadow falling over the camp. An airship hovered above them, its engines whirring loud enough to drown out most of the confused yelling below. On the platform, a figure wearing dark goggles had picked up Danny and thrown his unmoving body over his shoulder like a rag doll. Blood poured from Danny's chest, his hands stained with it.

"Danny," Colton whispered again. He couldn't keep his eyes open, but he had to see where they were taking him. He had to follow. He had to . . .

Daphne struggled as she and Meena were pushed into the airship. She could barely make sense of what had happened below, except that someone had grabbed them and forced them into a small plane. And now they were here. A large Indian man with a turban had hold of her, while a tall English boy restrained a squirming Meena.

"Let go of me!" she growled, twisting her arms again without luck.

"We can't do that, Miss Richards."

She froze. The voice belonged to another English boy, who stood at the end of the metallic hallway. His clothes, dust-stained and wind-whipped, were soaked with blood. He was using a small towel to wipe his hands, leaving streaks of crimson on the fabric.

A pair of tinted goggles hung around his neck.

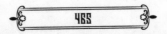

Something raw simmered inside her, equal parts fear and fury. "What have you done?" she whispered.

The boy looked at her, then at Meena, whose teeth were bared. "I haven't done anything. The rebellion has failed, and I made the most of the distraction."

Tremors ran through Daphne's body, becoming stronger when she looked again at the dark splotches on the boy's skin and clothes.

"Where's Danny?"

He regarded her with half-lidded eyes, a sleeper fully in control of his dreams.

"Exactly where he needs to be."

"You were out again."

Colton opened his eyes and smiled up at Castor. His head was resting on his lap. Castor ran his fingers through Colton's hair.

"What do you dream about when you sleep?" Castor asked.

Colton's eyes traveled up to the clouds. An alder tree's branches swayed and whispered above them, telling him secrets he wished he could keep.

"I dream about time," he said. "And music. And the wind. And how old the earth is." He turned his head and kissed Castor's palm. "I dream about freedom."

"But you're already free."

"Maybe." He lined up his fingertips with Castor's, nerve endings to nerve endings. "Or maybe I'm trapped in a dream that will never end."

Castor's lips touched his cool brow. "Then maybe you should wake up."

The smell of oil roused him. Colton opened his eyes slowly. He sat slumped against a metal wall. In fact, he was surrounded by metal walls, only the one on his right was made of bars.

Colton slowly turned his head and saw that someone had leaned his cog holder against the wall of the corridor outside. They had taken off the leather cover, and the bronze metal gleamed dully in the torchlight. With his central cog so far away, his body had become more transparent. He lacked the strength to even stand.

"Where am I?" he mumbled. The last he remembered, he had been in the middle of a crowd of panicked soldiers.

And Danny had been shot.

The reminder was enough to make him sit up, groaning as his side protested.

"Danny," he called. It was barely more than a whisper. "Danny!"

He gripped the metal bars and tried to stand, but it was impossible in his current state. He fell against the bars, shaking and enraged by his own weakness.

At this rate, both he and Danny would be dead.

The thought made him gather his remaining strength to shout, "*Danny!*"

A door opened at the end of the hallway. Colton watched as a figure came into view, but it wasn't Danny. The young man was broad-shouldered and well-groomed. The sleeves of his shirt were rolled up high enough for Colton to see that his right arm was made of metal.

There was a strange, sharp sensation coming off of him—something Colton had felt before. A compelling aura that fascinated and frightened him.

He knelt before Colton, fixing him with penetrating gray eyes. Colton stared back.

"So," the young man said. "You're Colton."

"Who are you?"

"My name is Zavier. You're on an airship called the *Prometheus*. We're very happy to have you with us, Colton. We've heard a lot about you."

Colton wrapped his hands around the metal bars. "Where's Danny?"

"I know you don't understand yet, but you will. You see, our plans have fallen through. There will be no second Mutiny in India. While the rebels lick their wounds, we need a new strategy. You'll teach us a lot about the clock spirits, and where we'll go from here. You're going to be invaluable to us."

"What if I don't want to help you?"

Zavier took a slow, deep breath. "You need to think carefully

about that. You wouldn't want anything happening to Enfield, after all."

Colton gripped the bars tighter. "Bastard." He'd heard Danny use the word before, and it felt strangely good to say it now.

Zavier stood and gestured to the cog holder. "If you want these back, you'll have to be nicer than that, Colton."

It was then he saw a smudge of dark red on Zavier's neck, partially hidden by his collar, where the strange pulling and ebbing sensation was coming from. It was metallic, thorny, seductive.

Blood.

Danny's blood.

Colton threw himself against the bars. "Tell me where he is!"

"Think about it." Zavier turned and walked back to the door. Colton pressed his forehead against the cold metal.

"Please, just tell me! *Please!*" He kept calling until the door closed, leaving him in darkness.

"Please," he whispered, sliding to the floor, curling up against the pain and devastation wracking his body. "Please, please . . ."

He tried to find that small pinprick of power again, to grasp at any sign that Danny was here, that he wasn't alone. Colton listened beyond the airship's engines for a sign.

Far below, he thought he heard the ocean.

The British Raj, the Enfield Rifle, and the Rebellion of 1857

India won its independence on August 15, 1947.

That was only seventy years ago, and ninety years after the First War of Indian Independence (or, as the British called it, the Mutiny) in 1857.

India has a long history of occupation. When the Mughul Empire was on its last legs, the British East India Company—at first only interested in trade—defeated the French East India Company for territory, becoming *the* military and political force in India in the mid-1700s.

The Company was a private army whose numbers only grew as the decades went on. Even as they improved roads and introduced an early railway system, they treated Indian culture and beliefs with disdain, and actively eradicated traditions they considered to be "barbaric." However, many Indian soldiers joined the Company, mostly those of Hindu, Sikh, and Muslim faiths.

The use of Enfield rifles by the Company created a conflict for the Hindu and Muslim soldiers who refused to bite off the cartridges lined with beef and pork fat, as this was in conflict with their religious practices. The British officers refused to listen to their complaints, commanding them to use the rifles anyway. With tensions already high between the British and Indian soldiers, and the Indians believing that the British were forcing Christianity upon them, this was one of the last disputes that led to the infamous rebellion.

(Although the British called it a mutiny, the Indian people tend to refer to it as the First War of Indian Independence. There's been some criticism regarding the term, however, since there were earlier uprisings against the British before the 1857 rebellion, including the Vellore Mutiny in 1806 and the First Anglo-Sikh War in 1845.)

The rebellion of 1857 was filled with atrocities committed on both sides, and caused a devastating setback to India. When the Indian rebels were subdued, the rule of India passed from the Company to the Crown, marking the beginning of the British Raj.

In *Chainbreaker*, I only begin to scratch the surface of the Raj. There are many details and historical examples that I wish I could have included, but had to put aside for the sake of space and context. It was an uneasy time for everyone involved, as the British attitudes toward the Indian people had soured even further. Indian soldiers were given the worst provisions, the worst weapons, and the worst accommodations. It didn't help that those who were officially in control of India—Queen Victoria and Viceroy Lytton—did barely anything to improve the quality of life or society.

Here is where I deviated from history a bit: in *Chainbreaker*, I've built on the likelihood that there were still rebels trying to rouse the country into a second rebellion. In our timeline, this did not happen.

Here's what really happened:

Before World War I, there was a growing nationalist movement in India, and the aftermath of the war only made that movement stronger. The high casualty rates, sickness, and interruption of trade were a harsh blow for India, and different factions unified in their desire for independence. This led to the Government of India Act in 1919, which stated that both Indian *and* British legislators held power over India, requiring them to make important administrative decisions together.

In 1915, Mohandas Gandhi returned to India from South Africa, where he had been perfecting his methods of nonviolent protest to free Indian political prisoners. Although new revolutionary movements began cropping up at the beginning of the twentieth century, Gandhi's nonviolent movement slowly overtook these revolutionary groups. He called upon thousands of Indian people to leave their jobs and take up the protest with him, which, granted Gandhi's immense popularity as he became more known throughout the years, was followed by many.

In 1947, the Indian Independence Act was signed, which not only partitioned Pakistan from India, but made them both self-run, democratic nations. This resulted in even further bloodshed, as the animosities between Hindus, Sikhs, and Muslims escalated to alarming, fatal levels as the British hurried to enact the partition. After a long, difficult, and violent struggle, British rule was finally ended in India.

India has a history that runs deep and rich, and I can only hope I did it justice in this book. Being half-Indian and growing up between cultures, I wanted to explore where exactly that line met, not merely in the characters' interactions with one another, but within the country itself. It's not only a reflection of history, but a reflection on culture, diaspora, and resistance in the face of oppression.

ACKNOWLEDGMENTS

It has been A Year, and I'm amazed that this book still came out at the end of it. I had no idea when I wrote the first draft of *Chainbreaker* in 2014 that I would be publishing it during a time like this.

But here we are, and I'm so grateful that I could continue Danny and Colton's story while exploring more of my own history and converting it into something that I hope readers can relate to.

Of course, I have several people to thank for this, and for guiding me throughout this process:

First, all of the love to my editor Alison Weiss, who understood this story from day one and has been one of my biggest advocates. Thank you for all of your time (har) and attention, for answering the questions I send you late at night, and putting up with my stubborn grammatical habits. Thank you to the Sky Pony team, including Ming Liu, Leslie Davis, Joshua Barnaby, and Sammy Yuen for that *amazing* cover. Thanks also to William McAusland for the fantastic India map.

For her dedication and compassion, many thanks to my agent, Laura Crockett, and the whole Triada team. Thank you guys for all the support as I bumble my way through this whole "being an author" thing.

Thank you to Forever Young Audiobooks/Pamela Lorence for acquiring these silly clock books, and to Gary Furlong for bringing my characters to life.

To my writing family—Traci Chee, Jessica Cluess, Emily Skrutskie—thank you for letting me yell in your DMs and crash on your couches. You're all so amazingly talented, and I'm lucky to consider myself your friend and critique partner. Traci, thank you for making weird faces with me. Jessie, why are we the same person? Emily, keep sending me stupid memes and headcanons. (Another special shout out to Cole Benton for being just A Really Cool Guy.)

I need to give a shout out to the wonderful people in the Kidlit Authors of Color, Fight Me Club, and PW '14 groups. You are all amazing.

Thanks to Akshaya Raman for being my desi/writing/whining buddy, and for baking me a cake *and* reading a draft of this book. I owe you brunch. Thanks also to Shveta Thakrar for reading and providing notes, and for checking in on me now and then. You're a star. Thank you to Preeti Chhibber (and her mom) for double-checking my Hindi/Urdu. All mistakes are mine.

I would be amiss to not thank my two favorite booksellers, Allison Seneca and Nicole Brinkley. You folks keep doing what you're doing. Thank you for screaming with me and sending me books. (Allison, meet me in Vegas.) Also, thank you to the lovely people at Kepler's Books.

Huge thanks to the people who have given me joy this year: Tori Ryan (for all of the amazing *Timekeeper* fan art), Lola

Baldsing (also for the fan art, especially the *corgi fan art*), Grace Fong (for being a stan with me), Wendy Xu (for the hot birbs), Eric Smith (for all the cheerleading), K. Kazul Wolf (FFXV broke me), Victoria Schwab (for being an A+ role model), and E.K. Johnston (for the lovely Canada retreat).

To the book bloggers/vloggers/reviewers: you folks do important work. Thank you for all you do.

To my readers in general: where would I be without you? Thank you, from the bottom of my heart, for supporting me. All the fan art, beautiful edits, quote graphics, Tweets, and emails mean so much. I can only hope to continue writing stories for you all. (Also, sorry about that cliffhanger.) (Not really.)

Thank you to my family for all their support and love. Thank you to Ellen Gavazza, who might as well be family, for always being there.

Most of the thanks, of course, go to my mother Harjit Sim, who patiently lets me do my work ("What, you're not done yet?") and indulges me even when I'm in a bad mood. This book wouldn't have existed if a little girl hadn't emigrated from India to America to begin a new life. Love you, Mama.

And to my father, Steve Sim: this book wouldn't have existed without you either. If you hadn't read to me when I was young, if you hadn't instilled a love of the written word in me, I wouldn't be where I am now. But you always believed I would get here. I'm so thankful for all you did for me, and that I got to see you hold *Timekeeper* in your hands. I'm sorry you won't be able to hold this one. The last time I saw you, I showed you the cover for

Chainbreaker, and you smiled. That's what I think of when I look at this book, and for that, I'm grateful.

I love you. I miss you.